Amy and Emily were holding hands. Their eyes were locked tight in intense concentration. Their tiny shoulders rose and fell in time with their rapid breathing. All of a sudden, dozens, then quickly hundreds, of ladybugs began to fly around the roof opening. More and more followed, until the air and ground were thick with them. Gideon watched the infestation in amazement, wondering where all these beautiful insects had come from. The little red-and-black bugs were everywhere—in the air, on the ground, crawling all over them—but not a single one landed on the girls. It was as if they were attracted to the twins by some ethereal force but at the same time were unable to light upon them.

Dr. Sossoman looked up at Gideon. Hope filled her teary eyes. Charlie was smiling from ear to ear. Reyes could scarcely believe her eyes.

"Be prepared," Sossoman said, her tone ominous. "I don't know what, or when, or how, but be prepared for what is about to happen." She made the sign of the cross across her breast and whispered, "God bless anyone caught up in their wish. They are simply children. They don't know what they are about to cause."

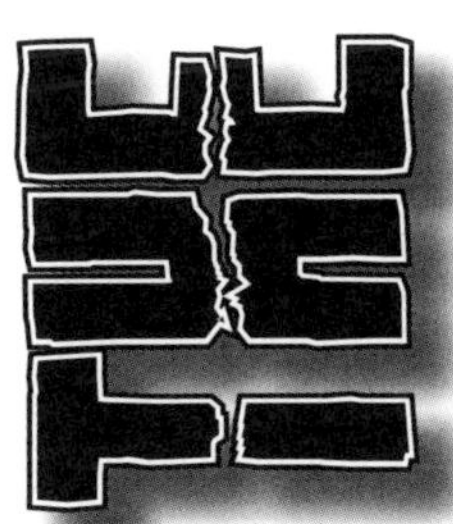

RICHARD FOUNTAIN

An Imprint of The Overmountain Press
JOHNSON CITY, TENNESSEE

To Andrea, whose support, patience, and encouragement made the writing process a journey worth traveling. Thanks for coming along with me.

And to Richie, Amanda, and Julia. This was all done for you.

This book is a work of fiction. All names, characters, places, and events are either the product of the author's imagination or are used fictitiously. Any resemblance to actual events or persons, living or dead, is entirely coincidental and beyond the intent of either the author or the publisher.

ISBN13: 978-1-57072-326-1
ISBN10: 1-57072-326-5

Printed in the United States of America

1 2 3 4 5 6 7 8 9 0

PROLOGUE

1206 A.D.
Nariin, Mongolia

Peals of thunder rolled across the barren plain. In the distance, thick mottled clouds of smoke and dust rose into the air, the columns reaching angrily toward the heavens. The acrid pilasters of ash and debris smoldered from within, fed by billowing flames that fumed with rage. A kaleidoscope of colors clashed and battled for supremacy within the clouds. Fiery yellows and reds signaled devastation and destruction. Shades of black spoke of death and loss.

High above the steppe, strong winds mixed the cloud colors into a gray mask that hung over the land like a weathered tapestry. The filament blocked most of the new dawn's light, casting the bright morning into shadow. Obscured by the pall, the rising sun lay like an open wound, its brilliant rays diffused into an ugly red sore.

The smoke continued to rise unhindered by the morning's dawn. Day slowly turned into an unnatural dusk.

In the small village of Nariin, anxious residents watched in rapt fascination and fear as a small cloud of brown dust separated from the pillars of fire and began working its way toward them. Torturous minutes passed as the cloud drew closer. Underneath them, the ground began to shake, vibrating with a steady rhythm that grew stronger with each passing second.

The villagers waited.

Ringed by low-rising hills, Nariin was a thriving village of commerce and industry. From the barren land, its inhabitants wrested wheat from the fields, spun fine threads from the milk of silkworms, and produced some of the area's most durable textiles. It was a hard but proud living that knit these people together. They relied upon one another as only those who survive in harsh environments can. Harvest to harvest, generation to generation, these poor but simple folk lived and died by the success and failure of the community.

A few short leagues east was their closest neighbor, the village of Bukhaara, the unfortunate origin of the fire and smoke. To the west lay the village of Xi. Unlike Bukhaara, the skies above Xi remained clear. It was an omen, a reminder to the villagers of the decisions they had made.

Closer to Nariin, the thunder changed, becoming more distinct, purposeful. Thudding hooves could now be heard heading north and south, splitting up to encircle the village. The dust followed the noise. Inside the village market, elderly men and women clutched their daughters and grandchildren. Young children held tight to their mothers. Babies wailed, their infant senses tuned in to the fear that saturated the village. The entire community—what was left of it—was in attendance.

The thundering noise ceased. So, too, did the crying. The village was cast in silence. On the nearest hillock, a lone figure appeared on horseback. The man sat high on the saddle of a large black stallion. He was clad in dark leather held together with bronze rivets and heavy thread. A plain bronze helmet adorned his head. A curved dagger was strapped to his chest. The steed's body and flanks shined silver with sweat, its chest and neck ringed with foam.

The man shifted in the saddle to better observe the villagers. His stirrups were close and tight, giving him the preferred position of a warrior experienced in open-field combat. In his left hand was a composite bow; the yak horn, sinew, and birchwood weapon was strung against the curve, giving it great range and accuracy. The bow was the Mongol weapon of choice. It had such great range that his arrows could easily reach the villagers from where he sat.

The warrior stood high in the stirrups and shouted, his voice carrying loud and clear into the valley. "Your men and boys are dead, their spirits lost! Their bodies lie in the field, wasted and bloody!"

The villagers were stunned with horror. Many wept at the loss of their husbands, sons, brothers, fathers, and lovers. Others stood agape at the enormity of their fate, unable to comprehend the cascading events that led to their doom. Most, however, stood proud and defiant, a testament to the brave and hardy life they were forced to live in this dangerous and rugged land.

The warrior raised his bow in triumph and continued. "The village of Bukhaara made its decision. It is now destroyed. You, too, have decided. Let it be known, no mercy shall be shown to any who stand in my path. I am Temüjin," he rallied. "My strength is fortified by Heaven and Earth."

On Temüjin's command, ten thousand Mongol warriors atop ten thousand sturdy horses rose to the hills around Nariin. The ring of men and beasts was darker than the darkest forest, tighter and denser than any thicket, more deadly than any menace ever faced by the villagers. The eight hundred defenseless villagers shrank into a tight circle, preparing for the onslaught to come.

Without another word, the horde charged, thundering down the hillside, spears low, swords wet with blood from the previous battle. These battle-hardened warriors would not need their bows. This was a slaughter, one of countless massacres, a message to anyone who was still willing to defy the Mongol lord.

Evening had long set upon the steppe of Mongolia before the warring armies made it back to camp. Comprised of several neighboring tribes, each clan was quick to disperse and revel in their victory or tend to their wounds before bedding down for the night. Tomorrow was likely to be another bloody day, as returning scouts had reported a large band of Tatars amassing to the south.

Temüjin entered his tent complex in a rush, ignoring the servants who barely avoided his angry path. Despite his victories, the bloodlust was slow to leave him. Those close to Temüjin were keenly aware of his wild mood swings and knew to keep their distance or suffer his wrath.

News of the Tatars angered the Mongol. Years before, a Tatar tribal leader had murdered his father, Yesugei, forcing the young man and his mother to live as outcasts, surviving by fishing and foraging for berries and wild onions. For meat, they snared whatever they could, mostly small rodents. The experience left a lasting impression on Temüjin, who later vowed to rid the world of his father's enemies.

"Where are my shamans?" Temüjin cried, losing patience with those who were avoiding him. "I seek counsel!"

A shuffling old woman emerged from an adjoining tent, the cloth flaps encircling her like a shroud as she floated in. Her eyes downcast, the woman knelt at Temüjin's feet.

"*You?*" Temüjin cried in fury. "I asked for my shamans, not an old *bagsh*."

The teacher cringed at the warlord's rebuke but held her ground. "My lord," she replied nervously, "your shamans are no longer. This morning, a team of horses ran wild and trampled their tent, killing Toghrul and Tolui. Jebe was critically wounded and died just a short time ago."

Temüjin flew into a rage, lifting the old woman clear off the floor until her face was level with his. "It was the *ijil yum,* the twins, wasn't it?" he yelled, spittle flying from his mouth. Eyes narrowing dangerously, Temüjin sneered. "They caused this to happen. They couldn't stand the competition," he cried, throwing the woman across the tent like a rag doll. The teacher landed with a thud, sliding through the doorway and back into the adjoining tent. Temüjin quickly followed after her.

A deft politician and skilled motivator, Temüjin didn't trust shamans, so he was not entirely displeased by the news of their death. Unlike his warriors, the shamans served his mother; he was often annoyed by their petty bickering and misguided premonitions. If it weren't for his superstitious mother, he would be rid of all *bariachs,* or charlatans, whose counsel left him doubtful and uncertain.

Yet, for all their wasted efforts, the shamans had served a purpose. The Mongol people had many superstitions, and the shamans were an effective tool to dissipate fear and uncertainty. Temüjin often used them as puppets, the fear of a slow and painful death keen on their minds as they dispensed advice that supported his brutal objectives. It was an awkward but necessary alliance that worked well for the Mongol lord.

The twins, on the other hand, were entirely different. Given the names Heaven and Earth by his mother, these orphans were completely without fear and looked at death as a matter of course, as an event that was preordained and not to be dwelled upon. Unlike the shamans, they could not be easily controlled and their allegiance was suspect.

Entering the tent, Temüjin looked upon the cause of his anger. The teacher scrambled over to her wards, fearing Temüjin might attack.

"Why are my shamans dead?" he demanded. "Speak for yourself."

The twins did not immediately respond. Alike in every way, the young girls swayed back and forth in unison, their eyes closed tight, mouths slightly agape, arms held straight out in front of them. Saliva dribbled from Heaven's mouth, falling down upon her red tunic. Blood ran down Earth's wrists, evidence of tightly clenched fists and sharp fingernails that bit into her palms. Their brows were etched with intense concentration.

The sight unnerved Temüjin. In this state, the *ijil yum* were extremely dangerous. Power radiated from them. Their abilities were palpable, like feeling a cold breeze on the skin, the presence not seen but felt. The hair on the back of his neck and along his arms rose on end at the sight of the two entranced children. He held his breath, knowing well he could not predict what would happen next.

Temüjin worked hard to control his unease.

The silence was heavy inside the tent, the air thick and musty. Looking around, he caught the sight of a small brass brazier in the corner; a thin wood pipe was off to the side. A soft tendril of smoke drifted into the air. Temüjin took a cautious sniff. He detected the mild aroma of roasting almonds. Intermingled in the smoke flew hundreds of fluorescent red-and-blue dragonflies. The insects were thickest around the girls. They buzzed over, between, and behind them, creating a living halo, a shroud that pulsed to its own rhythm. Not a single dragonfly landed on the girls.

A small smile spread across Temüjin's face. He relaxed slightly. The twins were under control, the spent narcotic working its way through their system.

"What are they wishing for?" he whispered to the teacher.

"News of the Tatars came in before sunset, my Lord" she replied. "I knew you would be angry, so I induced the girls with opium. They have been gone for a while but should return soon with good news."

Temüjin was not so sure. One could not predict with these two.

As if they were reading his mind, the girls slumped into each other. Heaven then fell back, her body convulsing slightly before she succumbed to unconsciousness. The weaker of the two, Heaven was prone to seizures following these "sessions" and would be incapacitated for hours. Just as suddenly, the insects scattered to the far corners of the tent, as if they had been repelled by a strong wind.

Struggling to sit upright, Earth stretched her muscles, yawned, and opened her eyes. The normally chestnut-brown orbs were replaced with an eerily opaque whiteness. The cataracts were a side effect that afflicted Earth whenever she used her gift. Until she regained her strength, the blindness would render her vulnerable to anyone or anything that posed a threat. Temüjin made a mental note to increase the girls' security.

"What news have you to report?" Temüjin demanded, his voice hoarse with excitement and nervousness.

The eight-year-old *sovin,* or oracle, replied, her voice confident and strong: "The Tatars will not last through the morning. A terrible storm approaches from the east. The Onan River will rise. In the dark of night, a great wall of water will overflow its banks. The enemy camp will be reduced to ruins. Many men and horses will be sent to their death. Your army will easily destroy what is left."

"You have seen this? It is true?"

"We have wished it. It is to be, my Khan."

"Khan?" Temüjin replied, confused. "What do you mean?"

The proud voice that answered came from behind. It was the voice of Temüjin's mother. "By the next full moon, my son, you will be crowned Genghis Khan, emperor of emperors, ruler of Mongolia. Temüjin will be no longer. All our efforts are coming to fruition."

The Mongol lord turned back to the child. Growing excitement crept into his rugged voice as he whispered, "Genghis Khan? Is this true?"

"We have wished it," Earth replied. "It is to be."

CHAPTER 1

Present Day
Lisbon, Portugal

Founded by the Phoenicians, conquered by the Romans, and enriched by the spice trade, Lisbon is a city with over twenty centuries of rich and tumultuous history. Early records depict a tempestuous upbringing. Constant battles subjugated the city as the Phoenicians, Greeks, and Carthaginians battled one another for supremacy. Then the Romans came, occupying the city for more than two hundred years. The Moors followed with four hundred years of Islamic law, until finally it was the Christians' turn to rule.

The Age of Discovery had begun.

In 1434, a Portuguese ship sailed beyond the West African coast, past Cape Bojador, breaking a long-held maritime belief that the world ended abruptly. Then in 1497 came Vasco da Gama and the sea route to India. Discovery led to wealth. The expeditions that followed transformed Lisbon into the opulent seat of a vast empire. The best sailors, mapmakers, and shipbuilders swarmed to the capital, bringing with them the foundations for commerce and industry. In just a few decades, Lisbon became the world's most popular trading center and a maritime superpower.

Unfortunately, Lisbon's glory days on the world stage were short-lived. Torn apart by civil unrest, marred by military insurrection, and weakened by political chaos, the city was transformed into an authoritarian police state that lasted well into the twentieth century. While the country languished, Spain and then France surpassed its greatness. The British Empire flourished and then collapsed. Now it was America's turn to rule as the world's lone true superpower.

Despite Lisbon's tumultuous past, or perhaps because of it, the well-dressed Italian loved the sprawling city nestled on the banks of the Tagus River. He relished its simplicity, the calm serenity of being close to the ocean. He saw the hodgepodge of time periods and eclectic cultures as a source of charm, not as an indictment or weakness. A natural explorer, he likened the city's hills, the medieval facades, the wonderful art-nouveau buildings, the black-and-white mosaic sidewalks, and the open-air shops to more modern versions found in Tuscany or along the coastline of Ireland. Lisbon had developed, and lost, an illustrious empire, but the people reflected none of it. They had adapted well, overcoming history's ills, decrying in the process the isolationist paranoia and malaise that many nations of its kind fall into.

He especially liked the people. Studious, hardworking, and religious, the Portuguese had a zest for life and a passion found nowhere else on earth. For that reason alone, he felt at home here, at peace.

Then there was the other reason he favored Lisbon, one that had nothing to do with the people or culture. Lisbon was the perfect place to be a spy. Like in Spain during World War II, the spooks swarmed to Lisbon. It was a breeding ground, an incubator, a place where information and loyalty were sold as cheap commodities. The intelligence community here was a carnivorous, incestuous group, preying on unsuspecting or untrained agents without mercy. While the rest of the world had polite, oftentimes antiquated rules of engagement, Lisbon had none. It was the one place, the last bastion held over from the Cold War, where governments could operate without remorse or reprisal. As such, Lisbon was a dangerous and deadly place for those in his profession. The risks of doing business here were enormous—but so were the rewards.

The Italian looked down at his unfinished meal and sighed. The *bacalhau* was luscious. Fresh caught, the large fish was prepared in traditional Portuguese fashion with small red potatoes and leeks broiled in a savory garlic, olive oil, and lemon sauce. The accompanying muscatel was equally delicious. Made in the sunny Douro Valley, the muscatel grapes grew in schisty soil on terraces built into the landscape. The only way to harvest these succulent grapes was to climb the hillside and pick them by hand. It was a harsh and inefficient way to run a vineyard, but the effort resulted in some of the world's finest wines.

The Italian picked up his glass and sniffed the rich red liquid within. The hint of raspberry and cassis with overtones of rockroses and violets rose to greet him. He took a sip. The flavor was smooth, elegant, and balanced, with a complex softness that held little acidity. It was a marvelous wine, one that could be found only in this region of the world.

The Italian was seated alone at a small, inconspicuous table at the rear of the Casa da Comida, a small bistro on the Rua Rodgrigoda Fonseca. It was still light outside, but that would change quickly as the sun was close to the water. A Verdi opera played softly in the background. Barely above the opus simmered the effervescent murmur of hushed conversation, tasteful laughter, and polite dining sounds of patrons enjoying their meal.

He felt comfortable in this surrounding, situated with his back against the wall in a small booth built for four. He was dining alone and had no plans for visitors. The waitress was not pleased to give up the prime location to a single patron, but he had insisted. The fact that he looked well-off dressed in his fine Italian silk suit, handmade leather shoes, and designer tortoise-shell glasses raised her hopes for a nice gratuity when the meal was done.

In a single glance, he could see every corner and recess inside the small restaurant. The kitchen exit was ten paces to his left, and the street entrance was forty-five degrees to the right, roughly thirty paces away. The narrow entrance door was sandwiched between two large windows overlooking the bay.

It was a beautiful afternoon; summer was in full bloom. Outside, he could see the yachts and sailboats rise and fall with the waves. When he closed his eyes, he could smell and taste the sea salt as it rode the breezes inland. The sidewalks were close to full capacity, and a steady stream of humanity passed both ways in front of the open windows. The restaurant's awnings shielded most of the setting sun, but enough orange light penetrated to add soft ambience to the already fine surroundings.

The Italian casually checked his watch. The luminescent dial showed that it was just shy of eight o'clock.

A few minutes later, he spotted his first target entering the restaurant. *Right on time,* he thought to himself. Give the Americans credit—if nothing else, they are punctual. The new patron was tall, well over six feet. The man scanned the room, swiveling his head on broad, muscular shoulders. His survey was quick, perfunctory, and obvious. The inexpensive blue wool suit he wore was typical of American agents: off the rack, ill-fitted, and wrinkled from too much travel and not enough care. The white shirt underneath was buttoned to the top, and a red-and-gray-striped tie hung just short of his waist. A few weeks on the street would have taught him to blend in better, assimilate to his surroundings. It also would have tempered his enthusiasm. This was a dangerous game, being played by equally dangerous individuals. There was no romance in what the Italian did. He learned that a long time ago. This agent was too green to realize it. As a result, everyone in the restaurant would see him for what he was: American. Every spook in town would have an entirely different assessment: fresh meat.

Foolish, the Italian thought with a slight shake of his head. You didn't have to be an intelligence officer to know that this man worked for some government agency. His dress, demeanor, and posture advertised his occupation to anyone paying attention . . . anyone like the Italian, who missed nothing.

* * *

Special Agent Robert Peterson, nicknamed "Petey" by his FBI classmates at Quantico, was new to Lisbon. That didn't mean he wasn't well traveled. He had been all over the world while in the Army—Saudi Arabia, Somalia, Guatemala, miscellaneous parts of Europe—but never to Portugal. Intelligence work was also new to him. An ex-military man from a strong military family, he was the first male in generations who did not serve his twenty years until retirement. The only other one he knew of was an estranged uncle, someone he met once but didn't quite remember. That uncle died in Vietnam, twenty-five years old and three tours into his service. For Peterson, six years was long enough. A blown knee during routine training at Fort Bragg ended his military career. After that, it was sheer luck—a chance encounter with a desperate recruiter—and glowing references from his Army superiors that got him into the Bureau. It certainly wasn't his grades. He had barely graduated college and didn't even bother enlisting as an officer candidate. Noncommissioned status was good enough for everyone else in the family, and it sufficed for him as well.

Agent Peterson was more than a little nervous. His palms were slick with sweat, and his right eye twitched slightly. This was his first real assignment, and he desperately wanted it to be a success. His peers had whispered that he could make a name for himself in Lisbon. He could prove himself quickly, move up the ladder, and take on more responsibility. He was green enough to believe what they said and naïve enough to think that he alone could make a difference. His role in this mission would be small, he knew that, but he was comforted in the knowledge that none of his classmates were chosen to make the trip. He was handpicked to join this team.

A small bulge at his left shoulder hinted at a concealed weapon, the Beretta M9 handgun. The Berretta 92FS, designated the M9 by the United States military, is one of the most tested and trusted 9mm sidearms in the world. Accurate and powerful with little recoil, the M9 will slow, or downright stop, whatever it hits. It was exactly what he wanted in a weapon, flexibility for use in both offensive and defensive situations.

As he was trained to do, Agent Peterson took in everything, including the lone man sitting in the back. Seemingly enjoying his meal, the finely dressed man was in his mid-fifties, hair graying at the temples, slightly overweight and out of shape. *Too much time behind a desk,* the agent surmised. He wasn't a threat.

The restaurant appeared secure, so he made his way to an empty table along the left-hand wall. The man he was meeting would be along shortly. Peterson ordered a drink from the waitress and settled in to wait.

* * *

A short distance away, the Italian was smiling to himself. So, the information he had *was* correct. The agent appeared exactly like he did on his dossier: young and naïve. Clearly, the FBI's Counterterrorism Unit considered this a low priority to send someone so junior. He should have known better than to doubt his source. Still, he hadn't been given much time to set up this operation, and the information *had* come to him secondhand. There was always the chance for error or misinterpretation. What if the meeting place was wrong or had been changed? What if the time for the meet had been this morning instead of this evening? Too many variables existed. He had been given no time to verify the facts or plan for contingencies. As it was, he had arrived only a few short hours ago, just enough time to get ready and into place. And wait.

None of his worries mattered now, as the second man entered shortly after the first. This one was more circumspect, professional. His head never strayed from his objective, yet his eyes never stopped moving. They absorbed every detail, memorizing faces, planning escape routes, looking for any sign or warning that this was a setup. The smile on his face was for show only, the straight white teeth a distraction to the man's real purpose and nature. His eyes held no warmth, only drive and intent.

The information the Italian had on the Russian was sketchy at best. Still, it took but a few seconds for him to judge the man. It was all there, if you knew where to look. It was in his walk, the way he carried himself on the balls of his feet, the compact, economical sway of his arms. Every movement had a purpose, a function meant to bring him one step closer to his goal. Even the act of blinking his eyes and breathing in and out was done without any wasted effort. The Italian had seen men like this before. He had trained with them, fought alongside them in combat. In a few instances he had been forced to kill men like this. The Russian was a predator, a cold-blooded killer, someone trained by the military and experienced in the field. He was a deadly weapon, not to be trifled with or underestimated.

The Russian agent showed no signs that he was armed. The broad Slavic features included high cheekbones, a wide nose, and bushy black eyebrows that were placed impossibly close together. Peterson guessed that the man was a full head shorter than him, though equally broad at the shoulders. The man rippled with energy. His forearms were thick and sinewy, the muscles and veins twisting and turning, intertwined until they reached his strong hands.

The Russian approached the table and sat opposite him. He set a small brown valise between his feet.

As instructed, Agent Peterson did not offer to shake the man's hand or engage in pleasantries. This meeting was all business. When the waitress arrived a few seconds later, he waved her off. The drink he had ordered sat untouched, a ring of condensation collecting on the wooden table. The agent's pulse quickened. The game had begun in earnest.

"Do you have what I seek?" the Russian asked, coming straight to the point. His voice was baritone deep and heavily accented.

Peterson motioned toward his suit jacket. "The facility plans, grounds layout, personnel briefs, I have everything you asked for. Do you have something for me?"

"One hundred thousand American dollars," the Russian replied, his eyes glancing down at the valise between his feet. "You know," he said in a patronizing way, "it's very dangerous for me to be carrying this around. Someone could get hurt with so much money."

"I don't think you'll have to worry about that anymore," Peterson said, equally condescending in his reply. "You have what you seek, and I'm going to enjoy my vacation." So far, everything was going according to plan. He pulled out the thick envelope and slid it across the table.

The Russian opened the envelope and peered at the contents within. Satisfied, he tucked the envelope into his breast pocket. "To betray your country like this, it must bother you a little, no?" he prompted with false sincerity.

"Not really," Peterson replied a little too quickly. *Stick to the cover,* he told himself. "The Army discarded me. I got injured serving my country, and what did they do? They didn't want me anymore, so why shouldn't I take care of myself? No one else is going to."

"Indeed," the Russian replied. He pulled his briefcase onto the table and laid it in front of him. "Think you can handle this?" he asked.

Peterson smiled broadly, relief flooding through him. The deal was coming to a close. He had succeeded. His feet were set upon a new path, one he knew was destined for greatness.

The Russian smiled in return, his teeth large and white. For the first time since the meeting began, the man's eyes sparkled. But they did not sparkle with warmth. Instead, they displayed immense cruelty and utter lack of compassion.

Peterson blinked hard, not able to comprehend the sharp pain in his chest or his sudden lack of breath. Things were going so smoothly; now was not the time for a panic attack. His eyes drifted down to his chest, but strong, calloused fingers under his chin kept his head from following.

"Don't worry, my friend." He heard the Russian say. "This was meant to be. Nothing personal, you understand."

Agent Peterson's mind raced, but he could not find the words to speak. His eyes rose to meet those of the Russian. The last thoughts to ever cross his mind were how *cold* they looked, how *different* the assassin now looked. Then he slipped away into nothingness.

No one paid any attention to the two men. Patrons were completely absorbed in their meals, their partners, or in the beauty of Lisbon outside. Their ignorance was a blessing for the Italian, as it gave him one less thing to worry about. It allowed him to focus his complete attention on the meeting.

"Is the meal not to your satisfaction?"

The sudden appearance of the waitress startled the spy, forcing him to tear his eyes away from the agents

"Delicious," he replied smoothly, hiding his irritation. He spoke in perfect Portuguese with only the hint of an Italian accent. "The *bacalhau* is excellent. Please give my thanks to the chef. And the wine, every bit as good as I remember it."

The waitress looked down at him with a raised eyebrow. The fish on the plate was cold and the wine was warm. It was clear that the Italian had simply been moving the food around, having taken but a few bites.

"I just arrived this morning," he said with a sheepish grin. He needed to move the waitress along without alerting the two men of his interest. "Forgive me. My body hasn't caught up with the change in time zones yet." Movement at the American's table caught his attention, but he forced himself to ignore it. *Not yet,* he told himself. "Truly, the meal was excellent, as well as the service." He added the last with a flourish.

The waitress smiled broadly and bowed her head. Having caught the compliment she wanted, she sauntered off to the next table, confident that a healthy tip was in hand.

Frustrated by the interruption, the Italian refocused on the two men, only to find the Russian standing. His hand was on the American's shoulder.

What happened? Did the exchange take place? Damn that woman, he thought.

The Russian nodded his head to the passing waitress and turned to the door, briefcase back in hand. His right hand rose and absently patted his breast pocket, confirming to the Italian that a transaction had taken place. He strode quickly to the door, pausing briefly in the bright sunset before joining the throng of pedestrians.

The Italian looked back at the American. The agent was seated upright, his eyes focused on the Russian as he left.

What did I miss? the Italian thought.

The presence of a foreign but familiar odor fought its way into his consciousness. His heart sank. It was only a trace amount, but the burnt, acrid smell was distinctive. It was a smell he knew intimately. *Cordite.* The pungent smell carried the faint but unmistakable odor of cheap gunpowder, the kind made in Eastern Europe for subsonic ammunitions. It was intermingled with the pleasant odor of Portuguese cooking but was recognizable nonetheless.

The American had still not moved. The Italian now knew why. He was dead, a gunshot to the heart. The hint of a red stain appeared on the man's cheap pants. A larger bloom covered his breast, under his rumpled suit. Soon it would be visible for everyone to see.

"Shit," the Italian swore out loud, not caring who heard him.

Ignoring the looks of disturbed patrons, the Italian sprang into action. He threw Euros at the table, not caring whether the amount was right or wrong. He raced to the door and then outside, standing on his toes to see if he could spot the Russian on the crowded sidewalk. His spirits lifted. He saw him fifty yards away, walking at a brisk pace up the Rua Rodgrigoda Fonseca. The Italian took off after him, carefully threading through the crowd, eager to close the distance. After twenty yards of frantic running, he came to an abrupt halt. He was not alone in his pursuit. Ahead of him were two more agents, one a man, the other a woman.

Probably American, the Italian surmised. Both were doing their best to blend in with the afternoon's mass of people.

He frowned deeply. Neither agent was included in the dossier he received yesterday, but here they were, only slightly less obvious than their dead counterpart. *So, the rookie agent had backup waiting outside the restaurant,* he thought. These two didn't know their partner was deceased, or else they would have taken action by now. The Russian would never have walked out of the restaurant alive. Instead, they were conducting surveillance, following whatever script had been agreed to beforehand. The man inside made the transfer and identified the mark. These two were following the Russian to see where he led them.

The information passed to the Russian was worth killing for. That surprised him. The two agents waiting outside the restaurant weren't supposed to be there. That bothered him. Were there more agents involved? What about the Russian? Did he have backup? If so, where? This mission had too many variables, too many holes that needed to be filled. Nothing had gone as expected. He fell in step behind a tall, shapely woman with a wide-brimmed straw hat. His stride matched hers perfectly.

CHAPTER 2

Piotr Vasilevich knew he was being followed. He wasn't worried. He had spotted the support team two blocks before he even reached the restaurant. This was Lisbon after all, a city he knew only too well. To not notice the awkward, rushed placement of American agents outside the restaurant would be to admit that his skills had diminished. They had not. The American cover team was more experienced than the agent inside, he could see that, but they were still not in his league. They were not spies, not trained to act, think, and plan like an intelligence operative. They were from the FBI's Office of Counterintelligence, nothing more than glorified policemen. He had dealt with policemen in his own country—he could deal with these, too.

Killing the young undercover agent was unavoidable. Too much was at stake. His orders were clear. Once he possessed the information, he was to eliminate all witnesses, leave a cold trail for any who chose to follow. He beamed with confidence. The American's death had been a stroke of genius, a testament to his skill and tradecraft. The restaurant was full, as expected. His target was not three feet away, seated against the wall as prearranged. The transaction took place as planned. The envelope placed on the table, the briefcase full of cash ready to be handed over. The timing had to be just right, but he pulled it off. One .22-caliber bullet straight through the heart. The agent never suspected the double cross. To walk out of the establishment minutes later, his opponent dead, information in hand, and no one else aware of it? Sheer brilliance.

The briefcase was one bullet lighter. The weapon inside had been fired from a trigger built into the handle. Special insulation lining the case, coupled with a short but effective silencer, had virtually eliminated the sound of the gunshot. Any sound that did escape had been absorbed by the ambient noise inside the restaurant. All that remained was to make sure the agent was propped upright, turn around as if nothing had happened, and leave.

Once outside, he needed to draw the American team away. He would not take any undue countersurveillance measures to elude them. *Let them follow,* he thought. His pace was quick but unhurried. His destination was sure, though not obvious. After a few blocks, Vasilevich came to the alley he was looking for. He turned sharply into the narrow side street and quickened his pace.

Soon, he thought, *it will all be over.*

The Rua Rodgrigoda Fonseca bustled with late-afternoon shoppers, chic women on holiday, their arms laden with boxes and bags from Lisbon's finest ateliers. Traffic on the narrow, gently curving road flowed sluggishly. Only the couriers on mopeds and motorcycles moved forward with ease.

The Russian led the American team for three long blocks before turning into a side alley. All the while, the assassin appeared unhurried and unconcerned. The Italian was amazed at the level of self-control, at his ability to suppress the instinct to run from the scene of a crime. One would never know by looking at him that he had just murdered an American FBI agent in cold blood. He was a stone-cold professional. The Italian suspected that the man was ex-KGB now working for the Foreign Intelligence Service—commonly referred to as the SVR—though he could be from the GRU, the military defense apparatus that employs Spetsnaz special forces soldiers. Even today, the GRU remains largely untouched from the Soviet era and has greater resources for collecting foreign intelligence than the SVR. It was a stretch, thinking that the Russian military would operate so openly in Lisbon, but until he knew more, he couldn't rule out the possibility.

The final option was the most unpleasant. The Russian mob was known to be expanding, reaching its tentacles into hot spots around the globe. Could they be involved? The fall of the Soviet Union and the subsequent downsizing of the Russian military had left many career intelligence officers in the lurch. In the last decade, the Russian mob had experienced a meteoric rise in its membership, eclipsing many large multinational corporations to become one of the largest employers in the former Soviet Union. Many crime syndicates were even known to offer full health and retirement benefits. If they were involved here, then there was no telling what they had planned. At least the professional military apparatuses operated within the bounds of reason. In that sense they were predictable. The Russian mob, however, was renowned for its systematic and oftentimes dysfunctional use of brutality. And worse, their motives weren't always clear.

Still walking a few paces behind the tall woman with the straw hat, the Italian glanced ahead over her right shoulder to see if the FBI agents were going to follow. The agents had stopped, unsure whether to cross into the alley. Valuable seconds passed as the two agents argued, their heads bent close in discussion. The male pointed aggressively after the Russian, while the woman argued for caution. She was clearly in charge. She spoke a few words into her partner's ear. His hand dropped limply to his side while she decided what to do next. Her decision came quickly. With a sharp nod of her head, she ordered them forward.

The Italian had to make a quick decision himself. Was the alley a common path used by pedestrians, or would it be deserted, used only by those with an intent purpose, like the Russian and the Americans? Absorbed as he was in his own thoughts, he almost ran into the woman in front of him. She had stopped abruptly fifteen feet from the alley to check for something in her purse. The Italian dodged around her into the pedestrian traffic. When he reached the alley, he walked straight past.

Shit, he swore. He should have seen it earlier. While everyone else on the sidewalk was hurrying and jockeying for space, this woman was keeping exact pace with the American agents. While everyone else was trying hard to get someplace, she was unconcerned with her surroundings, focusing entirely on her quarry. Almost running into her had been his good fortune. If he hadn't seen her reach for the small black gun inside her open purse, he never would have made the connection. She was the Russian agent's backup.

Damn it. If he had been paying attention, he might have noticed her sooner. Now he had to change plans, fast. The Americans were walking into an ambush.

Special Agent Natalie Reyes knew she was walking into a trap. The only question was when and how the attack would come. She also knew that Agent Peterson was dead. If he were alive, he would have reported in by now. If his equipment had failed, her cell phone would have rung. If he could not get a signal, he would have caught up to them on foot. He was too green, too new, not to follow her instructions. He hadn't become jaded by the caste system within the FBI, hadn't been around long enough to plan behind the supervisor's back or disregard a direct order.

That left only one option: the Russian had killed him. She didn't know how he had done it. That didn't matter. Peterson was her responsibility. She was the team lead, he was the rookie. She was the mentor, responsible for showing him the ropes. He was the student, out on his first big assignment. If it had been up to her, he never would have entered the restaurant. That was *her* job. Washington, however, disagreed. Specifically, her superior felt differently, thought Peterson deserved the opportunity.

Damn politics, she thought. Peterson had graduated middle of his class at Quantico and was nothing but an average rookie agent. It was his military connections, all-American good looks, and selfless ass-kissing that put him in this position. All he needed was field experience to round out his portfolio. The trail of evidence that led the team to Lisbon pointed to the Russian. The assignment was supposed to be benign, a simple transfer, a sting operation. Surely, her supervisor argued, Special Agent Peterson could handle it. That assessment was proved wrong the minute she saw the Russian. Peterson was no match for this level of player. She instinctively knew then that things would turn out badly.

Reyes didn't have time to mourn Peterson's death. That would come later, along with the endless explaining and paperwork back in Washington. The guilt would hit her like a ton of bricks. She had seen it before in other agents who had lost team members. Fortunately, Peterson had been with her only a few weeks. The bond between them hadn't cemented. Still, it was going to hurt like hell.

Now she had to get the bastard who did it. To hell with the mission. You don't kill a cop, a federal agent, and just walk away, saunter down the street like you were the god Zeus. The Russian must be brought to justice.

Reyes and her partner spread out. She took the left wall. He took the other. The alley was nothing more than a long, winding path, the corridor sloping upward, curving to the right. Debris littered the ground. A shallow drain in the middle trickled with fetid water. Full trash cans lined the walls, piled atop one another next to doorways that led into restaurants, shops, and tenements. Overhead were windows, mostly open and lined with colorful curtains fluttering outward in the early evening breeze. The echoes of babies crying, children playing, mothers laughing, and fathers shouting orders filled the space. Weathered ropes secured to the casements were strung across the alley in a confused jumble of geometry that would give a mathematician nightmares. Freshly washed and drying pants, shirts, and undergarments hung from the lines, obscuring much of the sky from view. The modest light that did penetrate came from the setting sun and the soft glow of open windows and doorways. The promise of streetlamps and porch lights did not exist here. In a few minutes, the entire alley would be cast in shadow.

Reyes could still make out the Russian killer some fifty feet ahead of them. Like a piece of driftwood on the crest of a wave, he appeared and then disappeared. One second he was there, the next he had turned at a bend in the alley. When they reached that bend, there he was, only to disappear around the next one. The man's pace had not faltered. He still showed no sign or acknowledgement of their presence behind him.

Aside from the three operatives, the alley was deserted.

Like her partner, Natalie Reyes pressed on, her weapon drawn. Caution kept her from charging forward. Pride kept her from retreating to the safety of the crowded waterfront. Sweat trickled down the middle of her back. Her armpits were already soaked. Perspiration beaded above her lip and on her brow. Her breathing was forced and shallow. She could feel her heart pounding in her chest, the blood coursing loudly in her ears. Fear and adrenaline always did that to her. She welcomed it. It gave her an advantage, an edge.

Up ahead, the alley straightened abruptly and emptied into a large courtyard. Three more alleyways intersected with the square. The one directly across continued east, the others north and south. Hovering over the center of the small courtyard was a single incandescent lantern. Suspended by wires, the lamp was bright against the darkening sky. Its light reached most of the area but was most effective at the center. Underneath the lamp was a small stone well. Affixed to the well was a rusty, brown water pump. A wide swath of wet pavement and drying footprints indicated recent use.

All of the tracks pointed to the presence of small children and mothers. None of the footprints indicated the passage of the Russian. The square was empty. Without a word, the agents split in two. Reyes checked left around the square, her partner went right. The plaza was eerily quiet. The only sound came from the agents' shuffled footsteps across the weathered stone underfoot. Even the wind seemed to die inside the square, like it was waiting for permission from some unseen force to blow again.

Where did the Russian go? Reyes asked herself. Every door leading into the square was closed shut. Every window had its curtains drawn. It was as if the residents were warned in advance to get inside, to stay out of the way, hidden from sight.

The back of Reyes's neck prickled with energy. She glanced around the square, her eyes absorbing every detail, analyzing the area for an imminent threat.

This was it. The absolute silence gave it away. At this time of night, this would be a common place, somewhere for the entire community to gather and share the day's tidings. He was here, watching, waiting. She could feel it. Her instincts screamed, *Get out. Move. Now.*

The FBI special agent spun on her heels, a shout of warning on her lips. The words never came. She was too late. Reyes watched in horror, helpless, as her partner's head exploded in a spray of blood and bone. A second silenced shot punched through his chest, adding more color to the light brickwork of the tenement building. The agent collapsed to his knees and slid sideways onto the cobblestone. Blood began to pool underneath him.

The entire horrific ballet had occurred without sound.

Agent Reyes snapped to attention. Years of training and field experience took over, propelling her to move. She dove away from the exposed wall, milliseconds ahead of the bullets that punched into it. Running for her life, she briefly considered retreating back to the dark alley but quickly disregarded that option. The Russian would expect it. Instead, she raced to the center of the square, sprinting to the relative safety of the small well.

Bullets buzzed past, a few coming impossibly close to her head and shoulders. Others ricocheted off the stone pavement as the Russian shifted aim, trying instead to take her feet out from under her. Reyes fired blindly in the direction she thought the shots had come from. She wasn't even close. The Russian's rate of fire continued unabated.

Reyes closed in on the well. Meanwhile, the Russian's aim was getting better. Her time was running out. She knew it. If she didn't act fast, the next bullet would find a home inside her. She was too easy a target. Reyes dug deep, summoning every last bit of strength, and dove. Her feet left the ground. Her entire body stretched outward, arching toward safety. She willed herself forward. Bullets flew past, over, under, and through penetrable cloth, but not flesh. When she hit the ground, the air was knocked violently from her lungs. Her knees banged painfully into stone, and her elbows scraped mercilessly against the sandy grit. But she was alive. Bloody, torn, banged up, but alive.

Ignoring the pain, Reyes struggled to an upright position on her damaged hands and knees. Breathing deep, she risked a glance over the stone well—and almost paid for the peek with her life. Sharp stone fragments flew from the top of the well, stinging her forehead and forcing her back down. She grimaced in pain. Blood trickled into her eyes. The Russian was close, positioned in the dark recess of the north alley, just outside the bright light. She couldn't see him, but the muzzle flare gave him away.

Reyes took stock of her situation and was frustrated by what she saw. The well may have saved her life, but now she was trapped. Her assailant had every exit covered. Overhead, the bright light beamed like an unwanted beacon. If she could take it out, she could make a break for one of the three remaining exits. The Russian would be a fool to follow her in the darkness. Or, she could make for his position and try to take him out. Wounded and alone, he would never expect her to take the offensive.

Reyes raised her weapon, sighted through one eye, and pulled the trigger.

The bullet never left the gun. Sharp pain shot through her hand and up her arm. The Beretta was torn from her grasp. The weapon clattered to the ground, well out of reach. Stinging numbness paralyzed her thumb and fingers. Her forearm lacked feeling or sensation. Reyes flexed her hand and grimaced. Someone had shot the gun from her hand. It was an excellent shot, one made by a skilled marksman.

The click of high heels on hard stone reverberated inside the square. Eyes wide in shock, Reyes turned back to the alley, the one she had come from just minutes before. Dread flooded over her. Walking into the light was a tall, beautiful woman. In her hand was a Russian Makarov 9mm pistol, a long, smoking silencer attached to the barrel. The woman's pale face was framed by shiny black hair. Thin red lips smiled broadly, revealing two even rows of bright, white teeth. Dark eyes looked down with satisfaction.

The trap was set and sprung. Agent Reyes sank back against the cold stone well, defeated and disgusted. She couldn't believe her life would end this way. Behind her, she heard the mocking laugh of the Russian assassin. The woman raised her pistol until it was even with Reyes's head.

Reyes turned and looked the woman in the eye. "Bastards," she said out loud.

CHAPTER 3

Piotr Vasilevich emerged from the darkness. He expelled an empty clip from his silenced Makarov and slapped a new one in. His partner, lover, and wife of three years stood over the remaining American agent, the last witness.

The afternoon had gone exactly as planned. The classified information was nestled safely in his breast pocket. One American agent was dead, though surely discovered by now, at the restaurant. Another lay across the courtyard, blood draining from the wounds to his head and chest. The third would join her partners soon.

Three American agents in one day, he thought with pride and growing exhilaration. He hadn't had this much excitement in a long time.

His beautiful wife stood proudly over the woman. Her legs were parted slightly, seductively. This was *her* plan. It had been her idea to eliminate the first agent inside the restaurant, then lure the others into the alley and finish them off in this courtyard. She was a brilliant tactician, capable of planning every detail required to pull off a mission of this magnitude.

Seeing his wife standing over the American woman pleased Vasilevich. He was aroused by her power, her ability to act, to kill without compunction. The mission was almost over, but only now did he start to breathe hard. His heart began to race. His thoughts drifted to the night they would have together once back in their apartment. The night promised to be full of lust and passion. A tantalizing thought entered his mind. Maybe she wouldn't wait until they got back. It was dark now. The moon was low in the sky. The danger would only add to their excitement.

Yes, he decided. He would take her long before they got home.

Vasilevich met his mate's stare, conveying with a look the passion that coursed through his veins. The woman smiled knowingly. *Patience*, she said with her eyes. *It won't be long now.*

Natalie Reyes watched the courtship between the Russians with a mixture of envy and disgust. They had something that she did not—a lover's passion, a shared bond built on common experiences. Fourteen years in the FBI had defined every relationship she had as an adult. Two marriages, both ruined. No kids waiting at home. Boyfriends were few and far between. Her only friends carried a badge. The career had always come first, devouring her social life in the process. When opportunity presented itself, she was the first to volunteer, the first to go wherever the case led her. The Bureau thrived on results, and that's exactly what she provided. She never once considered her work a sacrifice, nor were the sacrifices she made worth crying over. Regrets were for other people, weaker agents.

Now that she was going to die, her entire world came into doubt.

Seeing the knowing glances, the overt sexual tension, and the allure that passed between her attackers roiled her insides. Was it jealousy she felt, or rage? Reyes was hard-pressed to choose one emotion over the other. More than likely, it was both.

She did not think it would go like this. She thought it would be more like her partner across the plaza—quick, painless, without complication or contemplation. She never considered the idea that she would have time to reflect on her life, to second-guess the decisions she had made, to regret the way she had treated the people who cared for her.

Damn it, get a grip, Reyes said to herself. *You don't want to die with the shroud of doubt hanging over your head.* She took a deep, shuddering breath and closed her eyes. She willed herself to calm down, banishing everything but the moment from her mind. Her sharp fingernails dug painfully into her torn and bloody hands. Reyes was used to controlling her emotions, hiding her true inner feelings from the competitive, testosterone-driven environment in which she worked. She repeated the mantra "There's no room for weakness" several times.

The exercise worked. When she opened her eyes again, her expression was completely devoid of emotion. The analytical, dispassionate side was back in charge.

Reyes took stock of her surroundings. Her weapon lay eight feet away on the stone pavement. Even if she could have reached it, the assassin's bullet had rendered it useless. The Beretta may as well have been back in the United States for all the good it did her. Anyway, the fastest person in the world couldn't outrun a marksman at ten paces. She wouldn't get two feet before the woman put a bullet in her. The assassin remained out of reach, too far to sweep the legs out from under her. Not that that was an option. Both of Reyes's knees were scratched and swollen from her dive across the courtyard. It was easy for her to ignore the pain that throbbed in her joints, but she knew any quick motion or action was out of the question. Her hands moved slowly along the ground. Course grit clung to the open wounds in her palms, but nothing else. No fist-sized rocks to disarm or sand to blind.

Finally, Reyes caved in to defeat. Her attackers had chosen their location well. It was the perfect setup.

Behind her, she could hear the Russian agent approach. She didn't bother turning around. Everything she needed to know was conveyed in the eyes of the woman.

This was his kill.

The crack of gunfire shattered the silence. Reyes's entire body convulsed upward at the sound, and her breathing stopped. She landed heavily against the well, her head banging forcefully into blunt stone. When her eyes opened again, she was amazed to realize that her surroundings had not changed. Heaven was not before her. She was still alive. The pain in the back of her head proved it.

Confused, Reyes looked up in time to see the woman's eyes roll back in her head, a split second before she fell to the ground . . . dead. The confident smile that mocked Reyes moments earlier was gone from her face.

Movement in the shadows confirmed the presence of another subject. Then, two more bullets flew over her head. She heard the Russian grunt behind her and then collapse to the ground. The moaning that followed confirmed he was still alive, but barely.

It all happened so fast. Whoever had saved her was skilled enough to kill and disable two experienced operatives in the blink of an eye.

The Italian emerged from the shadows into the bright light. He pointedly ignored the American agent's stares as he checked on the Russian. He was still alive, but not for long. One bullet had punctured his upper torso, likely collapsing his right lung. Pink froth bubbled at the corners of the assassin's mouth. His breathing was ragged and uneven. The other bullet had entered his right shoulder, shattering the collarbone. The Italian checked for exit wounds and found none. The soft-tipped bullets he used were meant to enter the body and stay there. The one that hit the lung had probably caused extensive internal damage.

The Russian opened his eyes and stared at the Italian. Recognition soon followed. He remembered him from the restaurant. "Why?" he asked, his voice coarse and grainy.

The Italian ignored the question. He reached inside the Russian's blazer and pulled out the sealed envelope. Bright red blood smeared across the once pristine surface to resemble a cruel Rorschach test. The Italian wiped the blood off on the Russian's coat, folded the envelope, and tucked it carefully into the pocket of his fine silk suit.

He turned his attention back to the assassin. "Who sent you?" he asked coldly.

The Russian's eyes were baleful in return. The Italian dug a thumb into the man's injured shoulder, penetrating deep into the wound. The man screamed loudly and writhed in pain.

"Once again," the Italian asked in English, his eyes turning hard and cold. "Who do you work for?"

The Russian stared back in return, saying nothing.

The Italian raised his thumb again. "I can make this very uncomfortable for you, or I can make your death swift and painless. Choose quickly. I want answers. Now."

The soft wail of sirens could now be heard in the distance.

The Russian smiled weakly.

Finally, the Italian thought, *the neighbors decided to call the police.* They probably got up the nerve once they saw that the Russian was no longer going to be around. He wondered briefly how much was paid out to set up this ambush. It didn't matter. He refocused on the Russian.

The man was fading rapidly into shock and unconsciousness, though if the Italian had to guess, he would still be alive when the police arrived. He needed to work faster. He dug into the shoulder again, his thumb grinding against bone and nerve. The Russian's scream split the air in a shattering cry. His teeth ground loudly against the pain, and his face turned a deathly pale.

The Russian fought back. "*Poshyol ty.* Screw you," he grunted in halting English. "I will tell you nothing."

The Italian sighed loudly. This was going nowhere. The Russian was too well trained. He didn't have the time for a proper interrogation, and this wasn't the place to conduct one, especially with the American agent hanging on every word. Besides, the authorities would be here soon. Frustrated, he stood up, his shadow from the light above falling over the critically injured man.

"Very well," he said.

The Italian fired one shot through the man's forehead. The Russian's body convulsed once and then lay still.

The Italian bent back down to the still assassin. A quick search of the body revealed no identification or papers of any kind. No instructions. No money. No evidence. He was a professional. That alone told the Italian a great deal. The woman was likely to have nothing on her as well. They were a good team, probably trained by the same people.

But by whom, exactly? he wondered.

Finished with the Russian, the Italian turned to the American agent and found himself staring down the barrel of a Makarov 9mm pistol. The safety was off. Dangerous amounts of pressure were being applied to the trigger.

The Italian smiled. The enterprising agent had taken the pistol from the dead woman's grasp and was now aiming it at his chest.

"Don't move," she said. Shock still registered on her face. "Shit. Why did you have to do that? You killed him. He had information that could have helped my investigation, and you . . . you shot him." Shock turned to anger. "What the hell is wrong with you?" she yelled.

"You're welcome, by the way," the Italian said casually. He moved close to the agent. The weapon's sights were now aimed at his head. He continued rationally. "The Russian was never going to divulge his employer nor what his mission was. He was too well trained for that."

"You don't know that," she replied, her voice laced with frustration. "Given proper medical treatment, he might have spoken to the authorities."

"No," the Italian chided, cocking his head to the side. "He would have taken his own life well before then. Or, more likely, someone would have taken it from him. This is Lisbon. That's how things are done here. Besides, I don't have time to waste on idle conjecture."

The FBI agent was incredulous. She glanced over at the Russian. The gun wavered in her hand. She knew instantly that she had made a mistake. Displaying lightning speed, the Italian lashed out with his right hand and twisted the gun from her grasp.

Mouth agape, Reyes looked at the man, unable to comprehend what had just happened. The Italian was at least fifteen years older than her, closing in on middle age. He had salt-and-pepper hair and a beard that matched. He was slightly overweight with a stomach that fell over his belt. There's no way he could have moved that fast—but he had.

The Italian smiled wide, showing her his bright, even, white teeth. His eyes sparkled with an intense, intelligent blue, which surprised her even more. Despite the detached cruelty she had just witnessed, the eyes that looked back at her were kind and caring, even understanding. It was as if he were a different person, like he had stepped out of one personality and into another. His eyes also showed a hint of mirth, like he was laughing at a joke he could not share. Wrinkles at the corners added to the illusion that this was a game he enjoyed.

Reyes watched, helpless, as he tossed the weapon into the well and then turned around to leave. The hollow splash of water broke Reyes from her shock. She got up to follow.

Sensing her movement, he turned around. "Please," he said forcefully.

"Do not follow me. I can tell that you're well trained at surveillance, and I don't have time to lose your tail. I would hate to have to do something that I would later regret. Stay here. Wait for the *Polícia*. They will have many questions for you."

Damn it, she thought. He was right. She couldn't leave the crime scene, not with her partner dead across the plaza.

"At least tell me your name," she implored.

The Italian smiled again. "That would not be wise," he said. "Take care of yourself. And don't try looking for me. I will not be found."

Reyes watched as the stranger turned his back and disappeared into the shadows. Physically and emotionally spent, she collapsed against the well, resigned to the long night that awaited her. The authorities were closing in. She had a lot of explaining to do. Two FBI agents killed on foreign soil. Two assassins, equally dead. What a screwup. She needed to compose her thoughts. Should she tell the truth, or some fraction of it? What was the truth? Damned if she knew. Try as she might, she couldn't take her mind off the man who had saved her life. Somehow, she knew, they would meet again. They were connected. She didn't know how, but she felt it. Their paths would cross again. And when they did, she vowed to be ready.

The Italian entered his hotel room two hours later and slumped into a comfortable leather chair. He was exhausted. The day didn't go exactly as planned, not that they ever do. Still, this was supposed to have been a simple exchange of information and currency, followed by an equally simple arrest. The Russian was buying classified information from someone he thought was a disgruntled government employee. Judging from the night's events, the Russian knew all along it was a setup, which puzzled the Italian.

In most cases, the prospective buyer would have walked away from the deal. If the authorities were involved, it was unlikely that the information would be surrendered willingly. Why put yourself in jeopardy? Most professionals wouldn't. They would try to find another source. This case, however, wasn't like most others. The information the Russian sought was important enough, at least to him, that he went through with the deal even though he knew it was a setup.

Why would he do that? The answer was simple—time was critical. Whoever needed the classified information required it quickly, which meant a small window of opportunity. Whatever was going to happen was meant to happen soon. Otherwise, the Russian wouldn't have gone to the trouble and risk of staging such a deadly and public cover-up. Time, or the lack thereof, had forced him to act irrationally, outside the scope of normal operations. A much larger operation must be in play. The facts as he knew them just didn't add up. Too many questions remained unanswered.

The Italian reached into his breast pocket, pulled out a cell phone, and dialed a secure number from memory. The line rang once.

"It's me," he said.

"It's about time." The male voice on the other end sounded tired, worried. "What took you so long? It's been hours since the exchange was to take place. Did everything go as planned?"

The Italian sighed heavily before replying. "I had to be sure I wasn't followed. It took me a while, and I came into the hotel through a side entrance. By the time I leave tomorrow, if there's any surveillance in place, I should be able to slip past unnoticed. As for the mission. . . ." The Italian paused, giving the man on the other end a silent warning of what was to come. "Keep your ears open. You're going to hear a lot of screaming after tonight."

"That bad, huh?" The man sounded concerned.

"It's not good." He filled him in on the night's events.

"I take it you're all right?"

"Yes, I'm fine," the Italian replied. "But we're still no closer to figuring out what's going on." Frustration crept into the agent's voice. "I have the blueprints, but the Russian felt it was more important to die than tell me who he and his partner worked for, or who he was for that matter."

The Italian paused, thinking. The man on the other end of the connection was silent. "They went to all this trouble," he continued. "The FBI, the Russians, and for what? It doesn't make sense. There is a larger operation in play here, one that our intelligence hasn't picked up on. It's got to be flying way under the radar."

"The Russian agent—you searched him?"

"Yes," the Italian replied. "He was clean. Real professional."

"No identifying marks, tattoos, anything like that?"

"Nothing that I could see. Besides, I didn't have time for a thorough search."

"What about the woman, the FBI agent?" the man asked. "Does she know what's going on?"

"I don't think so," the Italian replied. "She wanted information from the Russian, too. She was very angry that I killed him. No, I think we're back at square one. This was a dead end."

"It may not be all that bad," the man said. "I'll bet the FBI has a dossier on the Russian. Standard procedure on their part. I'll place a couple of calls and get a copy." The man on the line changed the subject. "Can the woman identify you?"

"My cover will hold," he replied, confident. "There's nothing to worry about."

A long silence interrupted the conversation. The man on the other end was thinking. "All right," he said after a minute. "Get some sleep. I expect to see you back here tomorrow. I'll have more information by then."

The line went dead.

The Italian threw his phone on the bed, stood up, and walked into the adjoining bathroom. He turned the shower on full, undressing in front of the mirror as the water heated to a healthy steam.

He smiled at his reflection, admiring the foreign image that stared back. Padded shoulders inside his suit coat gave him a broad, brooding appearance. He shrugged off the coat and shirt. Hidden underneath the costume were powerfully built shoulders, chest, and arms. From his waist he pulled a soft, gel-filled prosthetic that added six inches to his midsection. Beneath the false belly was a flat, rock-hard abdomen taut with muscles, the kind you get after doing five hundred sit-ups every day. Next to change was his face. The mustache and beard pulled at his skin, but both came off in one piece. The glue that remained would come off with soap and water.

Inside the shower, mild shampoo dissolved the salt-and-pepper hair into a soft chestnut brown as the artificial coloring ran down the drain. A few minutes later, body soap did the rest, washing fifteen years of lines and wrinkles off his handsome face. In seconds, gone were the crow's-feet, folds, and creases that came with middle age.

When John Gideon emerged from the shower, the Italian was gone. He was now a different man in body and spirit. He was no longer playing the role of Italian businessman. It felt good to be himself once more. Thirty-five years old, in superb physical condition, a deep-cover agent for the Central Intelligence Agency, he reported to the director himself. The only connection to remain between him and the Italian were the blue-lagoon eyes that stared back at him in the mirror.

They were the kind of eyes that could display intelligence, warmth, and passion one minute and cold detachment the next. Now they were tired, rimmed red by lack of sleep, constant tension, and the aftermath of killing.

The director wanted him back tomorrow. Too bad—he would like to stay in Lisbon to see the sights and maybe visit a few friends. He hadn't been to the Castelo de São Jorge in a long time. One of his favorite spots in the city, it was constructed by the Moors on the site of a fifth-century Visigoth fort. In 1147 A.D., Dom Afonso Henriques besieged the castle, ultimately driving the Moors from Lisbon. Within the walls are ramparts, towers, and remnants of a grand palace that was once the residency for the kings of Portugal.

Gideon enjoyed the historic site for both its visceral beauty and tactical perch above the seaport. The castle grounds were well kept, with swans, turkeys, ducks, and ravens roaming freely. The outer walls encompassed the medieval church of Santa Cruz, and from the Câmara Escura in the Torre de São Lourenço, he could see a panoramic view of the city below.

He sighed. Not this time. Work beckoned. Lisbon would have to wait. This case troubled him enough, even without the events that had transpired this evening. The director was upset, he could tell. Hopefully, tomorrow would prove to be more enlightening than today. The only way to know for certain was to get back to Washington and see what the director was able to dig up.

Gideon yawned loudly, smiling at the image in the mirror. His mission here was complete. As a general rule, he didn't sweat over things he couldn't control. He adapted, yes, but to worry about these things was pointless. The only thing he could do now was be patient, see what turned up. *Something* was bound to happen, and when it did, he would be ready.

CHAPTER 4

Over the Taedong River, North Korea

Yun Byung Ki fought to keep the aircraft trim. His knuckles were white on the yoke, his grip tight, trying desperately to compensate for the slick wet palms that threatened his hold on the wildly dancing steering column.

Outside, the violent storm bore down on the small plane. Winds buffeted the craft, tossing it from side to side like a child's toy. Time and again, the sudden downdrafts pushed the aircraft into a dangerous nose dive before competing air currents sent it back upwards, hundreds of meters higher than before. Crosswinds continually tested the plane's two vertical stabilizers.

Yun had no time to compensate for the violent and unpredictable winds pushing him around. It was all he could do to keep the plane in the air, fighting each change in altitude and position as it came upon him. If not for the steady tailwind pushing him forward through the storm, he would have lost control of the aircraft by now.

The heavy rain did not help matters. Driven by the wind, the rain limited his vision to less than a hundred meters. Under normal circumstances, limited vision would not be a problem. Today, however, he was flying an old Antonov An-28, one of the few remaining light passenger and utility transports in the province. It was the wrong plane to fly under these treacherous conditions. The fact that he was flying under visual flight rules made things even worse.

Made in Russia in 1986, the Antonov featured two Glushenkov TVD-10B turbine engines, each capable of producing over 900 horsepower. Both props were pushed to their manufacturer's limits, each engine straining to keep the craft aloft. The Antonov also contained Cold War-era avionics, but most of the instrumentation was either broken or had been stripped for use in other aircraft.

Damn the Party, cursed Yun, *for not providing the funding needed to maintain these planes.* He knew, even though it was never spoken out loud, that the Democratic People's Republic of Korea had little resources to afford anything new or modern. North Korea was a paranoid military state, and most often the nation's resources went to fund the war machine.

Millions of republic comrades, mostly peasant and rural families, were hungry from a long season of blight and starvation. Countless thousands had died the past winter, the victims succumbing to the cold, to hunger and malnutrition, or to the poor nation's inability to provide consistent or timely medical care. Crops promised to feed millions were spread thin and still weeks from harvest. Food supplies remained dangerously low, and the Communist infrastructure was slow to respond to the escalating domestic crisis. Generous food aid from wealthy nations was either tied up in bureaucratic red tape or had been siphoned off to feed the already rich and fat.

North Korea truly belonged to the elite few. The government fed the politicians and the military first. Everyone else fell into a caste system, the poorest getting whatever scraps were left over.

Yun's family survived, barely, only because he had a valuable skill—he could fly. That's why he was flying today. If he did not, someone else would step forward to take his place. And then what would he do? There was nothing else. Many were like him, men who had served in the military and were now forced to look for ways to supplement the meager government rations that slowly made their way to the outskirts of Kaesong. He had mouths to feed, a loving wife to support. It was his *duty* to work whenever the opportunity presented itself.

That was also the reason he was willing to fly under visual flight rules. The Antonov was missing its navigational instruments, many of its primary flight instruments, and most importantly, its radio. This equipment had been cannibalized to keep another aircraft, the one belonging to the provincial senator, running for his frequent trips to Pyongyang, North Korea's capital city.

Luckily, Yun still had his airspeed indicator and altimeter, though he knew one day they, too, would be missing. Everything else would have been nice to have, but they were not necessary to fly the aircraft.

Yun had years of experience with visual flight rules. Under VFR, the pilot forgoes most of the instrumentation, relying primarily on what he can see out the window. The pilot is responsible for seeing and avoiding other aircraft, terrain, and obstructions such as buildings and towers, which is why it is considered suicide to fly at night—or in inclement weather.

But today, Yun had no choice. A prominent family had chartered the plane for a short flight to Pyongyang. Yun had flown for them many times before, and he was always considered first when they traveled. He had yet to refuse them.

In preparing for this flight, Yun was told of the high-altitude, low-pressure system building off the Korea Bay, but it was not due to hit land until later in the day. As the flight was only ninety minutes each way, he was confident he could get there and back before the storm hit. Still, these things were unpredictable. Inexplicably, the storm had raced inward much faster than the meteorologists had predicted, and it engulfed the Antonov midway through the flight.

At first, Yun was merely upset at the inconvenience. Because of the storm, he would have to spend the night in Pyongyang at a friend's apartment. He would fly back tomorrow morning when the storm had passed. Now that it had intensified well beyond what was forecast, he was not so sure.

Yun said a silent prayer. The isolated Stalinist state of North Korea had banned religion a long time ago. Labeled as superstitious and fortune-telling, any form of religious belief was monitored by the cultural zealots within the Party. Anyone caught practicing faith-based religion was sent to prison without exception.

At the moment, however, Yun was not concerned with the state's oppressive strictures. His parents had raised him, secretly, on Catholicism, and at a time like this he found the belief in a superior being comforting. Yun made the sign of the cross over his breast and sighed heavily. Whatever help the Lord could provide was much appreciated.

The Antonov was built to carry seventeen passengers plus the pilot and copilot. Yun normally flew alone, as a copilot meant competition he did not want. Now, he wished he had someone experienced sitting beside him. Tonight's flight was heavier than normal, as twenty-one passengers and the pilot bounced around in the storm. Because of the additional weight, the craft responded slowly, struggling to keep up with the corrections he made every few seconds.

To make matters worse, earlier in the flight he had been forced to lock the cabin door shut. He was tired of the constant instructions provided by his employer and distracted by the yelling and commotion of constantly shifting bodies. His employer would not be happy at the loss of face, but at the moment, Yun had bigger problems to deal with. If he made it out of this alive, he would apologize profusely and ask for forgiveness. Until then, he could do without the interruptions.

Yun glanced at his altimeter. He was flying at twelve hundred meters. He looked out the window, not able to see the ground below. In this storm, tossed about as he was, he could be kilometers off course and never know it.

He had to reduce his altitude. It was a risk, but Yun felt sure he was close to Pyongyang. Where, exactly, he didn't know. He needed visual references to guide his way. Without the radio, he could not communicate with Air Koryo, Korea's national airline that operated out of Pyongyang Airport. Besides, at this altitude the storm pummeled the aircraft. Closer to the ground, Yun hoped the wind would let up, or at least become manageable.

Anything is better than this, he thought.

Yun picked up the in-plane microphone, took a deep breath, and spoke as calmly as he could. "This is the captain speaking. I am bringing the aircraft down to five hundred meters. The winds should reduce in intensity, and the flight should become less turbulent. I will provide an update in the next few minutes."

He then got back to the task at hand and pushed the yoke forward. The plane descended rapidly.

A few minutes passed, but the storm did not let up. If anything, it intensified and became more unpredictable. At seven hundred meters, Yun still couldn't see the ground below. Dark clouds and heavy rain continued to envelop the aircraft.

Yun was worried. Surely he was low enough to see something.

A violent crash against the windshield brought his attention back to the horizon. A large bird, disoriented in the storm, had crashed into the plane, fracturing but not breaking the thick windshield. This was not the first time he had driven into a bird, but the timing surprised him. It was a bad omen.

Yun shook his head and sighed. Again, he looked out the window to see what was below. This time, his heart leapt to his throat. The ground was now visible and terribly close. A quick glance at his altimeter indicated his altitude at just over five hundred meters. But his eyes weren't lying. Yun was actually flying no more than fifty meters above the ground, and he was descending rapidly. He was seconds away from crashing.

His instincts took over. Pulling back on the yoke, he pushed the throttles forward, urging the engines beyond maximum output. The propellers whined, struggling to bring the plane back to a safe altitude. His eyes strayed to the altimeter, seeing for the first time that it was stuck and not responding to his rapid ascent.

Damn the Communist Party, he cursed again. *If they weren't so paranoid, they might actually spend money on things people really needed—like working parts on aircraft like this.*

Yun was too preoccupied with the airplane to see what his low flight had caused. Flying close over the Taedong River, the pilot had unwittingly initiated a cascading series of events that he would never come to appreciate. Faster than the blink of an eye, thousands of red-crowned cranes, baikal teals, spoon-billed sandpipers, and a dozen other species of bird set to the air. Confused by the storm and frightened by the Antonov's loud and struggling engines, the birds flew in thick, mingled flocks. Each bird followed the other's lead, creating a chaotic, directionless mass in flight.

Focused on his aircraft, Yun failed to see the large flock fly directly into his path.

All at once, dozens of birds collided against the struggling Antonov, shocking Yun upright in his seat. Helpless to maneuver out of the large flock, he sat unusually still as the plane shuddered from impact after impact. Suddenly, the right engine, pummeled by the rain of fowl, caught fire and quivered to a stop. The left engine also tore into the flock but continued to run with a sickening whine. The cockpit windshield held, but it was now cracked and splintered, the gore of blood, bone, and feathers obscuring the outside.

Yun was flying blind.

Pyongyang Airport

Kim Sung Jun had just been given clearance for takeoff. The weather was unusually foul, but he was flying a modern Russian aircraft, the Ilyushin Il-76. Fully instrumented, the Ilyushin was a large cargo plane loaded with forty-five tons of military equipment headed for the seaport city of Sinuiju. Located on the border of China, Sinuiju was the northernmost coastal city on the edge of the Korea Bay. The city had long been promised an upgrade for the Third Armored Division stationed outside the city, and this flight would help replenish much-needed equipment, parts, ammunition, and ordnance.

Kim brought the four turbofan engines to maximum takeoff power and sighted down the three-thousand-meter runway. To his left was the Taedong River, its waters running smoothly in a winding path through Pyongyang City to the bay.

The control tower gave the all clear. Kim released the brake and accelerated smoothly down the airstrip. Crosswinds hit the fast-moving aircraft and rain slicked the tarmac, but the plane was a solidly built workhorse. Designed with Russian practicality, the Ilyushin was made to slog through this kind of weather with barely a ripple of disturbance.

The front wheel lifted off the ground with plenty of runway to spare. The rear wheels followed seconds later. It was a smooth and effortless takeoff, one of thousands performed by Kim and his crew of three.

Kim retracted his wheels and settled in for the short ride to Sinuiju. He could make this trip with his eyes closed.

* * *

Yun Byung Ki had spent the last several minutes desperately trying to control his aircraft. The rain outside was slowly dissolving the gore that coated his windows, but not fast enough. Until he could see the terrain below, he knew not where his plane was heading.

Every instrument was now out of commission. Worse, he was having difficulty controlling the plane's yaw. The birds must have damaged one of his vertical stabilizers, or his rudder—or both. He was also having trouble maintaining the aircraft's pitch. The plane wanted to go down, but he knew that to survive it had to go up.

Yun feared that the aircraft was completely beyond his control. It took all of his patience and experience, but ever so slowly, he was able to coax the plane higher. For the first time on this trip, he urged the rain to come down harder.

Slowly, the cracked windows cleared until Yun was finally able to get his bearings from the ground below. There was the Taedong River. The swirling brown water was spotted with wind-driven whitecaps. All along the river, small freighters, junks, and tiny sampans jostled for position. Shore-to-shore traffic made the Taedong look more like a busy city thoroughfare than a waterway.

This close to the ground, Yun could almost see the faces of angry captains and passengers. Some hurried for whatever cover they could find. Others stood transfixed, unable to move. Many raised a fist and shouted. Though he couldn't hear their epithets, Yun knew they were all directed at him.

Seeing the well-known waterway brought relief. He was very close to Pyongyang. If he could follow the river's winding path, he would soon reach the airport. *One problem at a time,* he chastised himself.

Yun was so focused on his immediate problem that he failed to see the large cargo plane until it was too late. Looking up at the last second, he recognized the Ilyushin in the midst of takeoff. Yun hadn't realized he was so close to Pyongyang Airport. The tailwind had pushed him farther along than he thought possible.

The large cargo plane was angled sharply upward, its belly exposed, the wings banking slightly to the right as it climbed over the capital city.

Yun was not a man quick to anger or spite, but in this final moment, he openly cursed the Communist Party for all its failures. His face was a mask of anger and pain. He muttered a final prayer, watching calmly as the cockpit plowed into one of the large turbofan engines on the right wing of the jet.

Death came swiftly as Yun was smashed and wrecked on impact. His body would never be recovered. His passengers were not so lucky.

* * *

The violent collision that overtook the Ilyushin bolted Kim upright in his seat. Throughout the cockpit, sirens screamed in warning and lights flashed danger. The large airplane was banking dangerously to the right. Kim looked out his window, surprised to see that one of his engines was completely missing from its struts. Past the wing, he was further shocked to see a small commuter plane plummeting to the ground.

Where the hell did that come from? Kim swore to himself. They must have been flying low, under the airport's radar.

Appalled at the sight, Kim noticed the round face of a young child peering through one of the plane's small windows. She was wide-eyed in fright and watching him as the plane fell. He followed the plane's trajectory, flinching as it crashed into the river below.

Kim's immediate problem brought him quickly back to the chaos inside the cockpit. The plane was losing altitude. He ordered the right wing emptied immediately. The first officer responded smoothly, and twenty thousand liters of jet fuel spilled from the broken wing. Next he ordered more power to the remaining engines to help compensate for the loss. Kim then leveled the plane off and took stock of the damage.

The aircraft was unresponsive. When the plane continued to pitch right, he knew he had more trouble than he originally thought. He looked outside again to review the damaged wing. What he saw almost stopped his heart.

A piece of fin from one of the small plane's vertical stabilizers had broken off on impact and was now wedged in the jet's right aileron. The aileron was lodged open, forcing the wing down at an unnatural angle. Further inspection revealed a bent and broken spoiler.

The situation was dire. The plane was thrown off-balance and sheering right. If Kim could not remove the obstruction, nothing he did would keep the plane aloft. It would continue in a downward spiral until it crashed.

If this accident had occurred at ten thousand meters, the crew would have time to work through a number of emergency countermeasures. As a qualified pilot with thousands of hours in the air, Kim had trained for every imaginable scenario, including ones similar to this. But at less than five hundred meters, time was against him.

He quickly ran through the options, calculating the odds of success for each one. The process of deduction was instinctual, occurring in milliseconds as the experienced pilot ran through procedures. Nothing he thought of would work. The damage was too severe, too precise, and too close to the ground.

Kim sank back into his chair and watched as the large jet made one more bank to the right. He was defeated. There was nothing he could do. The laws of physics now had control of the aircraft. The plane was going down. No radical maneuver would save him, not with the aircraft weighted down with forty-five tons of cargo.

Kim removed his headset and sighed. His officers recognized the outcome as well. No one said a word. They watched in silence.

Kim looked out the window to see where the plane was headed. A wry, sardonic smile spread across his face. He was going to deliver the military equipment that the government had ordered. It just wasn't going to be delivered in the manner they wanted or in the place they expected. Still, Kim could not help but feel that the government was going to get just what it deserved. His only regret was that those in his flight path would never know what hit them.

Korean Workers' Party Headquarters

The wind-driven rain beat against the windows, casting the already colorless city into shades of somber gray.

Although Pyongyang, with roughly two million inhabitants, was a big city, there were not many people on the streets. There were no vendors, except for a few food stalls. Automobile traffic was light. Most people elected to walk, take public transportation, or ride bicycles. Cars were a luxury few could afford. As such, the streets and sidewalks were clean. Missing was the pollution, trash, or debris found in most large Western cities. The wind and rain had little to wash away.

Pak Te Hwan stared out at the city—his city—waiting anxiously for a sign that it was over, that the president of North Korea was dead.

He was not a patient man.

Across the People's Liberation Plaza, and bordering the Taedong River, sat the enormous Juche Tower, a 150-meter symbol of respect and love for the late North Korean leader Kim Il-sung. In front of the tower, a trio of sculpted figures—the peasant, the worker, and the intellectual—represented the Party's class structure.

The statue was a constant reminder, a painful one, of his station in life. He despised the monument, wanted nothing better than to render it into dust, to eliminate its existence from memory. It was an insult that his office had to face the monstrosity. *Someday*, he mused, *I will erect a new monument. The structure will be magnificent, a testament to the power and influence I exert over the world.*

Pak smiled. He kept such thoughts to himself. A loyal Communist bureaucrat, he knew how the system worked, how to circumvent it to his advantage. He realized that while his office was one of only a few prohibited from being bugged by the intelligence apparatus, there was no guarantee that a rival in the parliament wouldn't do it to gain damaging information. That's why his office was scanned every day by his security staff, to ensure that he had the privacy required to conduct business. Pak was not naïve enough to think his position would save him should he slip and make a mistake. He might now have a position of some power and influence, reporting directly to the head of state, but that would not last long if he displayed anything short of absolute loyalty and devotion to the Party.

One day, Pak thought, *I will not have to hide my true feelings.*

A knock on the door brought him back to the moment. He turned to address his secretary, the intruder on his reverie. "Ko Mi Byun," he said testily. "I wish not to be disturbed."

"My apologies, comrade Vice President," she replied, bowing slightly, "but security at the front gate reports the president's car approaching."

Pak's face blanched ashen white. He spun around and looked past the monument to the parliament building that housed the Supreme People's Assembly, where President Yi Sang Gojong was addressing the 687 parliament members.

What is he doing here? Pak looked at his watch. In his anxious state, he had lost track of time. The president's speech had ended ten minutes ago. The assembly was leaving for the evening.

"Leave me," he ordered. The door closed behind him. *No,* he thought, *this can't be happening. The fool is putting my life in danger by coming here.*

Pak glanced again at his watch. The political assembly was scheduled to wrap up at four-thirty. It was now almost a quarter till five. What was going on? Pak had excused himself from the assembly over an hour ago after his aid reported an urgent message waiting at his office. It was a call he had been looking forward to for the past few weeks.

The president's unexpected arrival was worrisome. As was his practice, he usually mingled with the parliament, shook hands, and entertained family members and friends for at least an hour before retiring for the evening. Why had he left so early?

Pak turned back around at the polite knock. The door opened and in walked President Yi Sang Gojong, alone, without his bodyguards. They were outside the office, to be sure, and would escort him upstairs to his own large, plush suite of offices after he was done here.

The president looked terrible. The driving wind and rain had gotten past the umbrellas his staff usually held aloft. His hair was plastered to his balding scalp, and water dripped from his long black raincoat. More water beaded on his wire-rim glasses. Still, the man smiled broadly when he saw Pak, his face flushed from the unseasonable weather.

"Mr. President—" Pak began, preparing to apologize for his absence during the speech.

He never got to finish. A loud roar thundered over the top of the executive building. Seconds later, a deafening explosion shattered the windows, showering Pak with glass and debris. The concussion that followed threw him across the room and into the president. Together, they landed in a crumpled mass on the carpeted floor.

Stunned, the two men stared into each other's eyes before Pak helped the older man to his feet. Other than a few scratches, they were both unharmed.

Outside, the gray city was awash in yellow-and-orange flames. More specifically, Pak noted, the Supreme People's Assembly building had been reduced to a glowing inferno. The entire structure was carved in two while the middle burned from the inside out.

The president moved to stand beside Pak at the shattered window frame. The sound of bursting flames and billowing explosions reached across the courtyard. Even at this distance, both men could feel the intense heat. The wind drove the acrid smell of burning wood, gasoline, and charred flesh to their nostrils.

Pak looked into the president's eyes and saw bewilderment and awe. Just beneath the surface, almost hidden from view, Pak also saw suspicion.

He knows, Pak suspected, shrinking from the man's hard glare. *Why else would he be here? He must know.*

CHAPTER 5

Twenty-four Hours Later
Mackinaw, Virginia

The alarm sounded like an unwelcome claxon in the night.

John Gideon rolled over and swatted the clock, sending it off the nightstand in a crash of plastic against wood. The noise continued. Forced to wake from his deep sleep, he realized the clamor was not from the alarm clock but from his cell phone perched safely in its charger. Groaning loudly, he reached over and picked up the small device.

"Hello," he answered testily, his voice hoarse from sleep.

"I need you awake, captain."

Though Gideon no longer held the rank, the director liked to use it on occasion. He especially liked to reference it as a reminder to Gideon that although he was no longer in the military, he still had to obey direct orders from his superiors. "Yes, sir," he answered sharply.

Harrison Gorrell was not a capricious man, nor was he prone to acts of whimsy. He was a man with a singular vision of the future. As the newly appointed director of the Central Intelligence Agency, his charter was to clean house, plug the leaks brought on by years of idle neglect, and bring the Agency back to the stature it had achieved during the Cold War.

The director had a tough job ahead of him. He had inherited an agency in turmoil. The American public was seething over recent lapses in intelligence and harbored serious doubts about the Agency's ability to protect the nation it served. Recent polls suggested that two-thirds of taxpayers approved of the Justice Department's recommendation of a complete overhaul. The arrest of CIA agent Robert P. Johannson as an alleged Russian spy didn't help. The mishandled investigation of British nuclear scientist David Lynch, suspected of selling secrets to China, added fuel to an already growing fire. And lately, the highly publicized leaks by CIA operatives abroad all pointed to significant flaws in an organization that worked hard to build an image of trust.

Director Gorrell was not the typical choice for the job, either. He was not a politician. His background was not in law enforcement. In fact, he was not part of the Washington Beltway at all. He was a successful businessman and the former governor of Arizona, a no-nonsense, take-no-prisoners hard-ass who gave up a very lucrative life in the private sector to serve his country.

The best qualities that made him a successful businessman served him well as governor, and then as a special aide to the President. His recent appointment to the CIA, however, took the world by surprise.

Gideon took to him instantly. Like him, the director didn't take shit from anyone. You either towed the line or got out of the way. Progress was not for the faint of heart.

That's where Gideon came in. He was a man who specialized in fixing problems, all kinds of them. Big ones, small ones, you name it—he had a track record of success that was unequalled at Langley. It wasn't long before his unique talents came to the director's attention. One meeting was all it took for Gideon to be reassigned to the director's staff, reporting directly to the man himself.

Of course, it helped that no one on the director's staff knew of Gideon's appointment. For that matter, no one at Langley knew either. Harrison Gorrell needed a specialist, a troubleshooter, someone he could trust. More importantly, he needed someone who was comfortable working outside the Beltway norm and didn't mind political anonymity.

John Gideon was the perfect man for the job.

Still, Gideon was not yet accustomed to the director's unusual work habits. At fifty-four years of age, the man was tireless, working at all hours of the day and night. If he was awake, he was working. He had a staff that overlapped each other, toiling in shifts to keep up with his demanding and erratic schedule. He often called Gideon in the dead of night, waking him from sleep to discuss one matter or another. Most of the time, these discussions were brief, focusing on critical information, the facts and figures he needed to keep abreast of the latest intelligence. Not everyone could get along with only two or three hours' sleep per night, but the director didn't care. When he needed something, you were expected to respond with equal vigor, regardless of the hour or inconvenience. If the director had a home life, Gideon was not aware of it.

Gideon reached over to the bedside lamp, turned on the light, and looked down at the overturned alarm clock. The digital display was rocking from side to side as it dangled upside down from the electrical cord. The time read 4:38 in the morning.

Shit. He had to get up in less than an hour anyway.

"We've got more bodies," the director said.

Gideon was instantly alert. Without knowing it, he sat straighter in bed and drew his shoulders back.

"Where?" he asked.

"Floaters, off the coast of New Jersey." The director sounded concerned. "Four of them. All male."

Gideon rubbed his face and ran a hand through his hair. "Where, exactly?" he asked.

"Two miles off the coast, just past Cape May. They'd just about made the Gulf Stream. Another mile and we'd have never found them."

"Cape May? But that's right across from. . . ." Gideon did a quick calculation, figuring currents, tides, and location. "That means—"

"Kulbeda Station," the director finished.

"How did they die?" Gideon asked, excited by the news. The location was too close for coincidence.

It had been three weeks since his adventure in Lisbon, and the case had grown cold. Every lead had turned into dead ends. Langley was unable to identify the Russian agents. He still had no idea who contracted them and why they wanted the information so badly. It was as if the entire operation had been rolled up in a rug and stored away out of sight.

This latest development was good news, if you discounted the fact that four men were dead. Gideon tuned back in to the director.

"The Coast Guard found the bodies less than an hour ago. Their initial report indicates multiple gunshot wounds."

"Any identification? Weapons?" Gideon asked.

"None."

"What about fingerprints or facial recognition?"

"We're working on that as we speak."

Gideon was wide awake now, his interrupted sleep forgotten. "Where are they taking the bodies? I need to see them."

"I thought you might," the director replied. "They'll be at the Cape May Coast Guard morgue within the hour. The initial report came in through open channels, so local law enforcement and port authorities have already been advised. This is not a federal matter yet, so I think I can get you access without raising a fuss. Still, keep a low profile while you're there. Transportation is on its way to pick you up. Be ready in fifteen minutes."

The director ended the call.

Gideon paused briefly to consider the news. *Four more dead, found less than three miles from Kulbeda Station. Yes, it is definitely too close for coincidence.*

The fifteen minutes passed quickly while Gideon showered, shaved, and dressed. His ride would be there any minute. Sadly, there was no one for him to say good-bye to. The house was empty, quiet. No one would miss his hasty departure.

Truth be told, his job was hell on relationships. Up until three months ago he had been happily married. Then he went on a security-consulting mission in Saudi Arabia. When his assignment ended, Gideon walked into his house, happy to be home, only to find the place empty, devoid of everything he had accumulated over the past three years. Missing was the furniture, television, stereo, kitchen dishes and silverware, all personal effects of any value—all gone. She even took the dog.

The sad part about it was that Gideon knew immediately what had happened. His wife, or soon to be ex-wife, didn't have the stomach to confront him directly. He found the note taped to the fireplace mantel. It was the ultimate Dear John letter. Inside, scrawled with her messy handwriting, were four cold words he would never forget: "I want a divorce."

They had been together for close to five years, married for three of them. Sure, there had been problems, big ones, but they were working through them. He even went to see a counselor. There had been real progress, too. But Sarah wanted a stable life, something his government work could never provide. They often talked about life in the private sector and had even started planning for the future. He had enough experience in security to command a good job with a salary in the six figures. At his wife's insistence, headhunters were actively recruiting him. A nice, comfortable position was waiting for him after he signed his retirement papers. Sarah was happy for the first time in a long while. It was time to cash in, settle down in the big house he promised her, start working on the family she always wanted.

Then he made a mistake. He misjudged her anger at him and his profession. The assignment to the Middle East was unexpected. His last one, he promised. At first, he neglected to tell her the assignment was voluntary. Why create more trouble than necessary? Big mistake. When Sarah found out, she went ballistic. *She just doesn't understand,* he thought at the time. It was a great opportunity. It was also the last straw for his marriage. The woman he loved, who he thought had loved him in return, was gone. She could wait no longer.

Looking back on things, maybe he hadn't misjudged her. Maybe he was looking in all the wrong places for a reason. Perhaps he didn't want to see things the way they really were. Still, it hurt. Really hurt. These things were supposed to last forever, but Sarah's patience had run its course. Who could blame her?

Then, in the midst of his troubles, he got this new assignment. This one wasn't voluntary, but it was welcome nonetheless. The timing was perfect.

After that, things became blurry. He poured himself into his work, burying his problems deep. His personal life could wait. It had been on hold for a while now anyway. What was another few weeks or months?

Headlights splashed across the living room window, alerting Gideon that his ride was outside. Heading toward the back door, he passed by the small kitchen table. On its surface was a thin stack of legal documents, divorce papers courtesy of his wife's attorney. Things were moving fast; clearly she had been planning this for some time. He picked up the documents, prepared to tear them up in defiance. This latest operation might take a while. He might not be available or easy to locate. *Let her go through channels to find me,* he thought bitterly.

Instead, Gideon took a couple of deep breaths. His resentment subsided with each intake of oxygen. The anger was unjustified, but it felt good all the same. Deep down, he knew that the failed marriage was mostly his fault. He made promises he couldn't keep—wasn't ready to keep. Coming to a quick decision, he pulled out a pen and signed the papers. Then he sealed the lawyer's copy in the stamped envelope that came with the documents. Sarah would get the divorce she wanted. No questions asked. It was the least he could do.

On the way out the door, he stuck the envelope in the mailbox.

Coast Guard Morgue
Cape May, New Jersey

John Gideon could smell the morgue long before he reached it. The pungent chemical odor of Formalin, used primarily to fix and preserve body parts, competed heavily with the sickeningly sweet smell of citrus disinfectant. Even worse, he could taste the cold, musky aroma that hung in the air, like he was walking into a butcher shop whose walls were lined with fresh meat hanging on shiny chrome hooks. The combination of smells curled Gideon's lips into a snarl.

Lately, visiting morgues had become a bad habit.

Six weeks ago, he had been forced to visit the medical examiner's office in Philadelphia. A body had turned up at a mall parking lot just outside the city. The victim had been stuffed inside the trunk of a car, sans head and hands. The day the corpse was discovered was particularly hot, well over ninety degrees. This was on top of a week that was much of the same. The heat and humidity had cooked the flesh until the body was shriveled, the skin tough as old leather. The smell of death surrounding the car extended almost one hundred feet in all directions. The police on the scene knew immediately what they were dealing with and didn't bother looking in the trunk until the forensic investigators arrived.

Gideon saw the body a few days later, after the autopsy had been performed. The medical examiner called it a dry floater—as opposed to a wet floater—because the severely decayed corpse was found on land instead of water. Someone had gone to great lengths to keep the man's identity a secret, even going the extra mile to grind off his tattoos. According to the coroner's report, that little feat had been performed while the victim was still alive. The likely instrument was a belt sander.

John Doe, as Gideon referred to him, was the smoking gun that kicked off his involvement in this operation.

Prior to the discovery of the body in the trunk, Signals Intelligence at Langley had been alerted to what the National Security Agency deemed "significant" overseas communications traffic referencing Kulbeda Station, a small military base on the coast of Delaware. The analysts saw a pattern in the data stream but could not connect the traffic to any known party.

Based on this early activity, the director covertly ordered the secretive NSA to reprogram their ECHELON system to look more closely at those individuals interested in Kulbeda. He wanted to connect the dots and see where the evidence led him.

The ECHELON system links the NSA to its counterparts in the UK, Canada, Australia, and New Zealand, creating what amounts to a network of global listening posts. Combined, over three billion communications are tracked every day. Telephone, cell phone, e-mail, Web downloads, satellite transmissions—each is gathered indiscriminately and recorded. ECHELON listens in on these conversations, searching for specific keywords that might affect national security. Hundreds of words like *bomb, gun, assassin, military, explosives,* and *weapons* are fed into the system, and ECHELON looks for matches. When one is found, ECHELON transcribes and ranks the communication based on the perceived threat and forwards the information to an NSA linguist for review. When certain individuals or organizations are recognized as a potential threat, ECHELON is used to track specific communications and patterns. This tool was used extensively during both wars in Iraq and in Afghanistan to track known terrorists and arms smugglers and was instrumental in helping to prevent attacks against the United States and its allies.

As for Kulbeda Station, weeks of intensive scrutiny went into the investigation, but in the end, the effort resulted in mixed reviews. The results were inconclusive. Human interpretation and inexperience once again foiled any significant analysis. *Yes,* the linguists reported, *there is evidence that someone is interested in Kulbeda. However, there are too many random data points. It just doesn't add up to anything.*

Director Gorrell took the analysis differently. To him, it wasn't that the information didn't add up; it meant, instead, that whoever was interested in Kulbeda Station was doing a terrific job covering their tracks.

Now convinced that something was amiss, the director passed what he had on to his star troubleshooter. Unlike the analysts, who sat behind desks in nice, comfortable, air-conditioned offices, John Gideon had extensive experience in the field. He was used to solving complex problems by looking at data from a nonlinear standpoint. And when he factored in the human condition, a new picture emerged. He saw something in the data that the others missed, quickly piecing together a scenario that indicated an escalating pattern of activity clearly leading toward some unknown event. *But what was it?* The question left everyone's head shaking. It was also the one Director Gorrell wanted answered most.

The decapitated body stuffed in the trunk of the car simply confirmed his suspicions. The death, in and of itself, was not the clue, even if you factored in the missing head and hands to thwart identification of the body. Instead, what interested Gideon was the partially digested scrap of paper found in the man's stomach. Barely legible in blue ballpoint ink was written one word: *Kulbeda*.

That single clue drove the director crazy. *Who is this man? What is his connection to the facility?*

Kulbeda Station has no strategic military value, though it does serve an important function. The small base is attached to the Defense Meteorological Satellite Program. Run by the Air Force, the DMSP designs, builds, launches, and maintains satellites that monitor atmospheric, oceanographic, and solar-terrestrial environments. Kulbeda is one of a dozen stations throughout the United States that collect images of the entire globe twice each day. This data is then used in military theaters around the world to assist the United States' armed forces in operational and mission planning.

Was Kulbeda vital to the United States' interests? In the grand scheme of things, yes . . . well, maybe, depending on how you looked at it. Was it worth killing for? Not that he could see, and that was the problem. People had been killed for this station.

So when word came to Gideon that the FBI was investigating an unknown Russian intelligence agent looking to purchase classified plans of the station, he knew he was on the right path.

His instincts never lied. This base was hiding something.

The director had been right from the start—Kulbeda was a problem.

The pungent smell of decay brought Gideon back to the present. Though death was not a stranger to him, the sight of the naked woman, her chest splayed open from sternum to gut on the autopsy table, caused him to blanch white. In this sterile environment, death was academic and detached, the subjects studied with deliberate premeditation. In his experience, death in the field, while brutal and gruesome, was an act of necessity. It happened. Usually, it was unplanned, an aggressive reaction based on life-and-death situations. Sometimes, it was preordained, precise and surgical, planned all the way down to the last detail. Most of the time field operations resulted in no loss of life. The best missions were those where you got in and out undetected.

Working in a morgue was an entirely foreign concept to Gideon. To consciously cut open, dissect, and analyze death went against his nature. He could not fathom working with the dead for a living. In his line of work, if he needed to take a life, he did. Then he tried his best to forget about it. Sometimes it took a while, but he was always comforted in the fact that the people he killed deserved it. The world was a better place as a result.

Inside, the morgue was eerily quiet. Three walls were lined from floor to ceiling with rows of small white ceramic tiles. On the fourth were six refrigerator doors encased in steel, just like those found in an ice cream truck. In the middle of the room was a single stainless steel autopsy table, occupied at that moment by the deceased woman.

Gideon could hear the soft hum of a ventilation system and the gurgle of running water emanating from the table. He wrinkled his nose as the pungent smell once again assailed his senses.

"It's the Formalin."

Gideon started at the sudden appearance of a short, slender man beside him. "What?" he asked, turning around.

"You wrinkled your nose," the man replied, mimicking with his face and hands the gesture Gideon had made. "It's the odor you smell in the morgue. I admit it's hard to get used to. Took months before I could even breathe without noticing it." The man stepped close to Gideon. He spoke in a low tone. "It's even harder to get rid of, believe me. Gets in your clothes, soaks into anything that's organic, particularly leather. Hell, sometimes I can even taste it." The man appraised Gideon, his eyes searching. "You'll be okay. The synthetic stuff you're wearing won't hold the smell. Couple of minutes in fresh air is all you'll need to get rid of it."

Gideon didn't know whether to be angry at the remark about his choice of dress or happy with the observation. Fact is, he wore what he did precisely because he was visiting the morgue.

"You Michael Hayes, from the DEA?" the man asked.

"Yes," Gideon replied, handing over identification supporting his false identity. He shook the man's extended hand.

"David Tharp. I'm the medical examiner here." Tharp walked past Gideon and waved his hand at the corpse on the table. "Pay no attention to the ensign here. Routine heart attack. Plaque buildup ruptured one of her coronary arteries. She was found this morning in the women's barracks. Died in the shower."

Gideon was amazed at the man's casual, almost callous attitude. He could scarcely take his eyes off the gruesome sight, yet the coroner paid little attention to the body and did nothing to preserve the woman's dignity. Instead, he walked over to the refrigerator doors.

"I assume you want to see all four?" he asked.

Gideon nodded.

The medical examiner unlatched the first door and pulled out a gray corpse. Two more followed in quick succession. The fourth man was left inside the cooler.

"What's the DEA want with these men?" the man asked. "They part of a smuggling operation gone bad?"

Gideon's reply was noncommittal. "Just routine investigation of activity in the area," he answered.

The medical examiner was not convinced, but he remained silent while Gideon examined the bodies. This kind of death he was used to—casualties of battle—and he inspected the men with professional ease. Two of them were riddled with bullet holes, the gaping wounds cleansed by the salt water. The third had a single gunshot wound to the back of the head. Death was inflicted close up and was instantaneous. Even though the body had been floating in the ocean, Gideon could still make out the burn marks caused by the muzzle flare of a handgun pressed close to the skin.

"Semiautomatic handgun, probably a 9mm," Gideon estimated. "Anything larger would have blown his head clear off. There would be no evidence left to examine."

"That would be my assessment. We'll find out when I perform the autopsy."

Gideon reached into his pocket and pulled out a pair of latex gloves. Pulling the gloves high onto his forearms, he said, "These other two . . . looks like severe contusions all over their bodies. The bones underneath seem to be crushed in multiple locations. Several skin punctures show evidence of clean breaks." Gideon lifted each arm and leg, probing with his fingers. He turned the bodies over, assessing the damage done to each man. "I can't tell if the bullets killed them or the fall. The ocean seems to have erased any signs of bleeding from these injuries."

The medical examiner looked upon Gideon with respect. "Yes, very good," Tharp said. "The presence of bleeding usually distinguishes antemortem from postmortem injuries. The bodies weren't submersed for long. Still, they were in long enough for the cold water to delay normal changes of decomposition. The water's bitter cold in the bay."

Gideon looked up. He asked, hopeful, "Can you tell where they were killed?"

"Not with any specificity," he replied.

Gideon frowned.

"However, there are clues that can lead us in a general direction." Gideon grew more interested as the coroner continued. "If they were found in or near the Gulf Stream, their core body temperature would have been at least eight degrees warmer. When they were pulled out of the water, I estimate their temperature at sixty-three degrees Fahrenheit. That's consistent with the water of Delaware Bay this time of year."

The coroner took on a professorial tone of voice. He was all business now. "When a body is recovered from water, two critical questions require resolution: was the victim alive or dead when he entered the water? If alive, what is the cause of death?" He turned to Gideon. "Submersion while alive is typically followed by an intense struggle that subsides with exhaustion. Drowning then begins. When the breath can be held no longer, water is inhaled, which is associated with coughing and vomiting. This is rapidly followed by loss of consciousness and death some minutes later. We have no signs of that here. Also, with drowning, a fine white froth or foam can be found in the airways and around the mouth and nostrils. Again, we don't have that. Finally, drowning victims are characteristically over-inflated and heavy with fluid." Tharp randomly chose a corpse and pushed down hard on the chest. A thin stream of clear seawater came out. "These three men were dead before they hit the water," he concluded.

"What about the fourth man?" Gideon asked, somewhat frustrated. There was no real secret to how these men died. It was a hard fact of life, but bullets tended to kill the people they hit. He didn't need a medical lesson to learn that.

"Ah, yes," Tharp said, pleased to have an attentive audience. He pushed the three men back into the freezer. The doors clanged shut with a loud echoing boom that could have woken the dead. He pulled the fourth man out with a flourish.

Right away, Gideon could tell this man was different. Gone were the contusions, lacerations, and bullet holes found in the others. His skin was redder, less gray than his companions. Aside from his waterlogged appearance, he looked almost normal.

"Notice any differences?" Tharp asked.

Gideon studied the corpse carefully. After a minute, he responded.

"Small puncture wound in the back of the right leg with a larger exit in front." He reached a finger inside the smaller wound. "High-caliber bullet—most likely from a rifle." He felt along a soft, sinewy tube. "Looks like it might have clipped an artery." Gideon put down the man's leg and moved to stand before his head. Reaching over the corpse, he opened the man's mouth and ran two fingers inside. When he pulled them out, a white, soapy substance coated his already red fingers. He rubbed the substance between his thumb and index finger, turning the foam pink.

The medical examiner was smiling. Gideon didn't need to depress the chest cavity to know it contained more seawater than the other three.

"This man wasn't killed like the others. He drowned," Gideon said, surprised.

"Yes, though that was likely exacerbated by arterial bleeding. He died much later than his partners. In any event, he was still unlucky." Tharp turned serious. "Can you explain why these men are full of bullet holes?"

Gideon ignored the question. "Given the leg injury," he asked, "how long would he have survived in the water?"

The examiner thought for a minute before responding. "Hypothermia will onset in less than sixty-eight-degree water. At fifty degrees Fahrenheit, a healthy person with a life jacket can survive for three-quarters of an hour. I'd estimate, with his excellent physical condition, including the severe injury to his leg, no medical intervention, in the waters he likely came from. . . ." Tharp closed his eyes and calculated. "No more than an hour."

Gideon was silent for a moment, gauging how much more information he needed.

"Are you familiar with these waters?" he finally asked.

"Why, yes," Tharp answered. "Quite familiar."

Gideon took the question one step further. "Do you have a map available?"

Tharp immediately caught on. He smiled wide. "Yes. Follow me."

The two men stripped off their latex gloves and threw them into the trash.

Gideon was then led from the white-tiled room to a small office. Inside were a desk, coaster chair, and a large gray filing cabinet. There wasn't much room for anything else. The desk was littered with paper, and the chair was well worn. The file cabinet looked like it was used to take up space, but it probably contained important information to both open and closed investigations. Over the desk, a corkboard rectangle was covered haphazardly with yellow, pink, and blue sheets of paper pinned up with equally colorful thumbtacks. A large square map of the New Jersey-Delaware coastline covered the opposite wall.

Tharp moved quickly to the map. He didn't stop to apologize for the state of his office. "Here," he said, sticking a pin in a position just southeast of Cape May, "is approximately where the bodies were recovered. The tide was high just after ten o'clock last night. That would put—"

Gideon put his hand over the map, interrupting the coroner. "No," he said. "That's too early. It would have been closer to low tide . . . much later in the evening."

Tharp turned to face Gideon, his gaze quizzical. He studied the taller man for a moment, wondering how much he knew, and more importantly, why. Gideon stared back with equal measure. His intense blue eyes warned, *Don't ask. It's not your business to know.*

Tharp withered under the pressure. He fumbled awkwardly back to the topic of discussion.

"Er, yes, where were we?" He refocused his attention back on the map. "Much later. Right. Let's see. Low tide started coming in around two this morning. Give or take an hour, factor in a lesser tide, a mild wind . . . I'd place the men's deaths within this radius." He pulled out a yellow pencil and drew a ragged circle on the map. "It's still a large area to cover, but that should narrow down the search."

Pleased with himself, Tharp turned to his guest, but Gideon was no longer paying attention. Seeing the results, he had already turned his back on the medical examiner and was heading quickly toward the exit.

Just before he reached the door, Gideon stopped suddenly and spun around. "One last question," he said. "These men. They were harnessed together, correct?"

Tharp nodded sharply.

"I don't suppose they were tied together with climbing rope and carabiners?"

The coroner's surprised look confirmed what Gideon already knew. He didn't wait for a reply. He was already through the door, a broad smile on his face. Now he had something concrete to report.

CHAPTER 6

Korean Workers' Party Headquarters
Pyongyang, North Korea

Pak Te Hwan ran his fingers through his thinning hair. His hand came away moist, slick from the sweat that beaded on his small forehead.

The KWP vice president was not usually a nervous man, but the past twenty-four hours had tested his resolve. First was the plane crash that left so much of the country's parliament dead. Then, President Yi's surprise appearance, seconds before the explosion. Worst of all was the silent accusation that the tragedy was no accident but had been planned by insurgents, and that he might be the primary suspect, a traitor.

The pressure was almost unbearable.

The fact that the president's suspicions were accurate did not bother the vice president. In fact, Pak Te Hwan *was* a conspirator in the plot to assassinate the North Korean president. He *had* leaked the president's itinerary and was anxiously awaiting the call that would warn him of the impending strike.

What he had not anticipated was the outright brutality of the assassination attempt. He did not plan for the indiscriminate death and destruction, the needless loss of life. Such sacrifice, all to further one man's ruthless ambitions—his own.

Worst of all, he had never considered the possibility that the president might survive the attack. Now he feared that his duplicity might be proven in the subsequent investigation. All his efforts, the back-channel discussions, secret meetings, alliances with powerful Party members and prominent families, might have been for naught. His pursuit of power might come crashing down around him.

If he were charged with treason against the state, death would not come swiftly. President Yi was a vengeful man. He would make Pak—and his entire family—suffer terribly for his crimes.

The telephone on his desk rang loudly, startling the already jumpy Pak. He picked up the phone and answered curtly. A woman's voice announced that President Yi wished to speak with him. Pak was asked to hold the line.

This could be the end. Pak turned pale, anticipation driving the air from his lungs. A full minute passed. Then another.

Despite the cool temperature inside the office, sweat had begun to form on his upper lip. He wiped it away and rubbed his fingers against the flesh of his cheeks and jaw. The silence washed over him, threatening to swallow him into a void of nothingness. Pak was trembling now, fully expecting his door to fling wide on its hinges. His imagination running wild, he could sense the uniformed police officers in the lobby right outside. He could hear them preparing to surge into his office and grab hold of him.

His fingers lingered on the top drawer of his desk. Inside was a small revolver. It was cocked and loaded. He was ready.

Suicide by gunshot would be messy and shameful, but he would not be taken alive. The secret police relished opportunities like this, to detain a man in a position of power and influence. They especially looked forward to arresting dissidents and traitors.

If he were arrested, he would not stand trial. No notice of his disappearance or shame would be given. Storm troopers, as he called them, would place him in a small, sterile room, one with no window, bed, or toilet. The bright light overhead would be too far to reach and would remain lit throughout his interrogation. The small round hole in the floor would be his only escape, but it was designed specifically for the blood and waste to drain away after he was tortured.

These kinds of rooms were used for political prisoners, enemies of the state. Pak had visited the prison many times over the years. His political maneuvers had placed dozens of men and women into the care of its wardens. Sometimes whole families were sent there, never to return. He knew the place all too well.

Lost in his own thoughts, Pak was unprepared when the president's tired voice finally came on the line. He listened attentively, his back stiff, shoulders at attention. His door remained closed. Not a sound came from the adjoining room.

"Mr. Vice President," President Yi began. He came straight to the point. "Preliminary reports from investigators indicate that yesterday's plane crash was not intentional. The storm triggered a midair collision over Pyongyang Airport that sent a large transport plane into a spiral descent, and it ultimately crashed into the assembly hall. The smaller plane was carrying the Myung family from Kaesong to the capital. No one survived the crash, and we mourn the loss of such a prominent family. Based on the evidence, there is little to suggest an act of treason, or that this was the cause of international espionage. My security staff believes this was not an attack against North Korea, or me personally, but an unfortunate series of accidents." The president sighed. The pause lengthened. Finally, he said, "Pak Te Hwan, I must apologize for my behavior yesterday. I was distraught. I know we did not speak, but you saw what was in my eyes, and, I must confess, in my heart as well."

Pak could not believe his ears. The president was absolving him of any wrongdoings. He was being cleared of any participation in what the president had termed an "accident."

Pak's spirits lifted considerably. His fingers closed the drawer, all thoughts of using the pistol forgotten.

"You are a loyal servant to the Party," the president continued, "a trusted advisor. None could ask for a better partner, especially in this trying time as we look to rebuild the parliament. I simply wanted you to know that there is much work to be done and that I am counting on you to help shape the future of the Party."

"Mr. President," Pak stammered into the phone. The lies flowed smoothly from his lips. "I am honored by your support and once again swear my allegiance to you and to the Party. Whatever you need of me, I am yours to command."

"Thank you, Pak Te Hwan. I have been distracted of late. The arrogant, imperialist Americans are once again demanding that we halt our nuclear weapons research and testing. They brought September 11 upon themselves, and now they are bombing any nation they deem remotely responsible, punishing them for existing in a world that is different from their own. I believe Iraq and Afghanistan are just the beginning of their annexation of the Middle East. Their recent successes have emboldened them. Israel is already theirs. Pakistan and India will be next, I am sure of it. Tomorrow, it will be all of Asia. Many of our neighbors are already too comfortable with Western materialism. China can no longer be relied upon to provide aid. They rely too heavily on Western money and influence. The Americans see us as aggressors, and their president still refers to us as the Axis of evil." The president paused briefly before continuing. Pak could hear him sigh heavily over the phone. "It's been a long day. Rest assured, Pak Te Hwan, you will be called upon. For now, go home. Comfort your wife and family. It is late, and tomorrow will be more arduous than today. Good evening."

Pak hung up the phone, his hand visibly shaking. The release of pent-up emotion and stress escaped in a rush. He felt pounds lighter.

He had done it. He had survived this test. Whatever reason President Yi had for leaving the assembly chamber minutes before the crash was no longer a concern. The president's call breathed new life into his pursuit of power. With this open display of confidence, he could operate more freely. The time was ripe to forge ahead, to take his plan one step further. The next time, he would not fail.

I will be North Korea's next leader, he thought. *Then we'll see who commands the world stage.*

President Yi was a small, narrow thinker. North Korea could not survive in isolation. That didn't mean it had to succumb to the power of the United States. If Pak had his way, America would come begging to him.

CHAPTER 7

Kulbeda Station
Curtis Cove, Delaware

The stench of fear was suffocating. It filled DeKay's nostrils and permeated his senses. It was a smell he had come to despise, one he associated with cowardice and weakness. The taste of fear was even worse. It left a lingering impression on the tongue, the aftertaste harsh and choking.

"You mean to tell me, Lieutenant, that you let the intruders escape?" Cross DeKay was not pleased. This was the second incident to occur at Kulbeda Station in the past few months. The first had been dealt with cleanly. He knew that because he took care of it personally. He needed to show his people how he dealt with disloyalty. They needed to know that he watched over his investments with great zeal and that his solution to problems, while sometimes extreme, would be carried out with great precision and brutality. No one was immune to his wrath. It remained to be seen whether last night's intrusion caused any lingering damage. He had no prisoners to interrogate—the incompetent lieutenant had seen to that. DeKay had no dead bodies to run identity checks against. The tide pulled the evidence out to sea, and the Coast Guard retrieved the bodies before his men could get there.

"I asked you a question, Lieutenant," DeKay continued, running his fingers through his hair. "How should I handle this lapse in security? I was under the impression that you had things under control. No more mistakes. What happened?"

"There was nothing we could do," the lieutenant pleaded, his forehead beaded with sweat. "The intruders were tied together. When the lead man went over the cliff, the others fell with him."

The cold look in DeKay's eyes confirmed what the frightened lieutenant already suspected. His life was over. DeKay was prone to fits of rage and erratic behavior. When he was calm, the man was reasonable and could be dealt with rationally. When he got like this, the slightest provocation or prevarication would set him off. The lieutenant scanned the room, looking for support from the others. No one was brave enough to meet his gaze.

The pressure was getting to him. When he continued, he spoke with a slight stutter. "It was the Russians again," the lieutenant volunteered unnecessarily. "We intercepted radio chatter from their comms. I thought that if we—"

DeKay silenced the man with a withering glare. "What happened to secure and contain?" he said. "You gave up the element of surprise. Instead of waiting until they were all together, when they were all in your sights, you decided to go with your own plan." He got up close to the now quivering man. His words spat like venom against the man's face. "The fact is, Lieutenant, you didn't think. You made the wrong decision." He pulled a pistol from his belt. "I don't pay you people to think," he said. "I pay you to follow my orders, to do what you're told."

DeKay circled behind the man and raised his pistol.

"You thought it was a brazen act to sneak up on the intruder." DeKay ground the pistol hard into his neck, forcing the man down onto his hands. "Bring the pistol close, just like this. Could you smell his fear? Did he cower like you're doing now? This man's life was in your hands. For just a split second, a moment in time, you felt like God, didn't you?"

Not knowing how to respond, the lieutenant nodded his head, sending sweat in large drops to the floor.

DeKay bent down and whispered coarsely into the man's ear but loud enough for the others to hear. "I know that feeling. Son, I can tell you with certainty I am a supreme deity. You worship *me*. Any other god pales in comparison to the might I wield. I create the commandments. It is my will that parts these waters."

He paused for effect before continuing in a normal tone of voice. "Just so there's no further misunderstanding," he said, no longer speaking to the lieutenant. Everyone in the room cringed as the words came forth. "When I give an order, I expect it to be followed without question or hesitation. Do I make myself clear?"

"Yes, sir!" the men shouted.

"Excellent." DeKay smiled for the first time.

No one dared move or speak. Not a single eye met DeKay's roving gaze. Not a breath was taken. Silence fell upon the men in the room like a smothering blanket.

Louder than a firecracker, the piercing sound of gunfire shattered the silence. The bullet passed through the lieutenant's skull and ricocheted off the tiled floor, narrowly missing one of his men before lodging in the wall. The body slumped to the floor in the middle of the room.

"Jesus," the man behind DeKay declared in shock. "That man wasn't one of your mercenaries. He was an officer in the United States Air Force.

What happened to just frightening him? You know, send a message. How the hell am I going to explain this? For Christ's sake, DeKay, who's going off on their own plan now?"

DeKay whirled on the man. "Explain it as you deem fit, Colonel Allbright. Just make sure it has no impact on the operation of this station. Am I clear?"

A dangerous look passed between the two men.

The colonel swallowed hard and nodded sharply. It wasn't the first time he'd had to eat his pride. He might be the ranking officer on the base, but his authority was no match against DeKay's viciousness. Too much was at stake with this operation. Another couple of weeks, that's all he needed. Then he would be rid of DeKay forever. He could get on with his life, far away from this place and the madness it created. Besides, this wasn't the first time a man was lost at Kulbeda, and it wouldn't be the last. He would find some way to explain the man's death. Maybe if he postponed the report he would never have to.

The colonel ordered his men to remove the body and then left the office, refusing to meet DeKay's challenging stare. The door closed with an audible click. A long minute passed in silence.

"Was that truly necessary, or was that for my benefit?"

DeKay turned to the lone individual remaining in the room.

"Not just necessary," he replied, "but essential. I handpicked every man on this post. They know that what goes on here falls outside of the chain of command. Now they realize that they're not part of the military establishment anymore, that they're part of something larger, something more important than themselves."

"Yet," the man responded evenly, "except for Colonel Allbright, they have no idea what this base is truly used for."

"They don't have to," DeKay shot back. "Not exactly. They simply have to continue taking orders from me."

"You're playing a dangerous game, DeKay," the man warned. "You're exposing us to the consciences of men who take their responsibilities and oaths very seriously. How can you trust them? How long do you think they will remain loyal, or silent?"

"I don't have to trust them. The minute they become a liability, I'll replace them. My own men can handle perimeter security if necessary. And they won't hesitate to follow orders."

The man appraised DeKay for a long moment before responding. "This project is in your hands now. You know how important this is to the future of the United States. It must not be compromised. We must not be deterred. I've invested too much time and money, over five decades of my life, to have this project derailed. Not now. We're too close to accomplishing everything we set out to achieve."

DeKay's demeanor softened as he looked upon the old man. Arthur Frist was a billionaire industrialist, a philanthropist to the arts, political insider, and consultant to the past six presidents. He was also the reason Kulbeda continued to exist. Without his money and influence, the base would have been shut down long ago.

DeKay knew Frist's history better than anyone else. At seventy-four, he was healthier, more vibrant, than men half his age. The old man boasted a full head of frost-white hair, broad shoulders, and a ramrod-straight posture. His strong handshake made grown men wince. At just over five feet tall, Frist was usually the shortest person in the room, yet his absolute certainty, confidence, and clarity of vision made him tower over most. Many had come to rue their first—and many times last—meeting with Arthur Frist, failing to look past his years and aged appearance to take in the measure of his bright green eyes and the sharpness by which they absorbed the world. Coupled with a quick intellect and a decisive mind, Frist made short order of fools and buffoons and often likened these individuals to chattel or roustabout serfs—people meant to be abused and discarded.

Frist Industries was the largest privately owned defense contractor in the world, rivaling giants like Raytheon, General Electric, and Lockheed Martin. The owner's unflagging energy and unorthodox tactics kept the business large and growing. Moreover, Frist was a shrewd political operator. Lavishly supporting both Democrats and Republicans alike, he was known to prowl the halls of Congress or show up unannounced at the White House. When Frist came calling, the doors were flung wide open only to be closed softly behind as he whispered into politicians' ears.

The product of a strict Midwestern upbringing, Frist was a man of unique passions and haunting ambitions. He was influenced early on by the heritage left by the Scandinavians who settled the region. His father was a prominent lawyer and Presbyterian preacher based outside Indianapolis, while his mother was a talented concert pianist and mathematician. Together, they raised a child who delighted in logical clarity and realism, someone who would grow into a man with the straightforwardness found in philosophers and theologians like Plato and Aristotle.

A man of science, Frist had an innate confidence in individuals but a pathological distrust in organizations. He believed strongly in parsed information and a compartmentalized organizational structure. He harbored a natural mistrust in anything he could not control or understand, with one exception. There were no spiritual upheavals, no disillusionments, and no fundamental doubts or fears when it came to his absolute trust in

God. In this respect, he was righteous, intolerant of doubters, and confident beyond hesitation that a higher being sanctioned every decision and move he made.

"Any word from our contacts in North Korea?" Frist asked.

"Nothing more than what we've heard in the news," DeKay reported, frustration in his voice. "Last count I heard, 492 parliament members were killed in the assembly. Dozens more will likely die over the next few days. The plane crash could have been worse, but President Yi Sang Gojong retired earlier than planned. In his absence, many Party members left the hall. The president was very lucky to have survived."

"Yes," Frist said sarcastically. "He was very lucky, indeed."

"Still," DeKay continued, ignoring the skepticism that laced Frist's reply, "with over half of the parliament gone, North Korea will have to postpone its aggression in the region. Surely, President Yi will prioritize and focus inward and rebuild the Party."

Frist was not so sure. "That's not how the Koreans operate," he said. "All the power is concentrated in the presidency. He's their supreme leader, the embodiment of the Communist system. The assembly enacts his law, his will. There are no checks and balances. Within a month he'll replace the lost assemblymen with an interim parliament made up of his people, many of them direct relatives from Kaesong and Chongjin. In a year, he'll be more powerful than ever. Remember, he already controls the military and intelligence apparatus."

"Then we've actually done him a favor."

"Start planning another attempt," Frist ordered. "Talk to your contact in the DPRK, see if there's an opportunity for us to interject."

A polite knock on the door interrupted the conversation.

"What is it?" DeKay answered testily.

A nervous Colonel Allbright stepped inside the office. His eyes darted to Frist and then back to DeKay.

"Sir, I just received word that the girls are unconscious. It looks like they've been active again."

DeKay's anger was immediate. His fist slammed onto the top of his desk. "I want them separated," he sneered. "Lock them up, bind them, drug them if you have to, but keep them dormant. I will not tolerate their disobedience."

Allbright turned to leave, when Frist suddenly stopped him. "No, Colonel, wait." Frist was silent for a moment, and then he said, "We need to find out what they were up to. Separate them as DeKay instructed. Then interrogate them, individually, and see what they have to say for themselves."

The colonel's face blanched white. "You want me to interrogate *them*?" he asked.

"Heavens, no," Frist replied. "Have the doctor talk to the girls. She seems to have gained their trust of late. See if she can find out, and then have her report back immediately. Tell her, if she can't get what we need, stronger actions will have to be taken."

Colonel Allbright smiled thinly, relieved that the matter was now the doctor's responsibility. Color flowed back into his cheeks. He turned on his heels and left.

Frist shut the door behind him. "We need to move quickly."

"My analysts should be able to come up with something in the next few days," DeKay replied. "We're just starting to get a handle on the Middle East. The last thing we need is for North Korea to start up again."

"Thank you, Mr. DeKay," Frist responded formally, ending the conversation. "Stay on top of the situation. Find out what those girls were up to."

"Yes, sir," DeKay responded.

Frist exited the office, shutting the door softly behind him.

DeKay slumped into his chair and leaned back. He was so close. Another few weeks were all he needed. These distractions were consuming precious time and energy, and they were mounting, getting more difficult to contain. The FBI woman was nosing around again, the blatant assault on the premises last night, and now the girls were acting up.

The colonel handled the FBI agent quite well during her visit last week, but DeKay could tell that she wasn't convinced. Agent Natalie Reyes was likely to be back again. She had probably already heard about the four dead men. It wouldn't take her long to link them to Kulbeda. She was getting too close. He would have to take care of her, before she found what she was looking for.

In the meantime, he had a tough decision to make. These recent complications were forcing him to move up his timetable. He could no longer wait for the appointed hour. If that meant causing some inconveniences, so be it. The risks were worth it. So were the rewards.

DeKay swiveled in his chair to face the door. The lieutenant's blood covered the floor and wall of his office. He grinned at the sight.

Fools, he thought. *They have no idea what I have in store for them. Soon, they'll find out. By then it will be too late—for them, and for Kulbeda.*

CHAPTER 8

Cape May, New Jersey

What are the chances? Gideon asked himself for the hundredth time in the last hour. *A million to one? Two million?* He flipped open his cell phone and dialed Director Gorrell. As usual, the man answered on the first ring.

"What is it?"

The brusque tone of voice meant the director was busy and didn't want to be interrupted. *When wasn't he busy?* Gideon thought with a smirk. The director was in perpetual motion, like a pendulum that never stopped, but he moved at a much faster rate of speed.

"I've seen the bodies," Gideon said without introducing himself.

Even with a secure satellite link, both men knew that technology was too easily corrupted to be trusted. In the last decade, breaking encrypted communications had become an expensive game of cat and mouse. It was the new arms race, to see who could come up with the latest, fastest, most secure communications system the world had ever seen. After that, it was a simple matter of "wait and see" until some nation, group, or brilliant individual cracked the code. Then the process unraveled and started all over again.

It was a game that no one in the intelligence community could win. In fact, Gideon often wondered if the United States wanted to win at all. No doubt, it was a strategy of attrition. Keep our enemy's brightest and smartest assets tied up in a war of mathematics, each consumed with the notion that the United States *could* be beaten. The weapons of tomorrow would not use precisely aimed bullets or intelligent, satellite-guided missiles. They employed mathematical formulas and theorems so complex that only the world's most powerful supercomputers could keep track of the data. It was the United States government's crazy equivalent of the Boys and Girls Clubs. If the world's geniuses were kept off the street, they couldn't be doing other bad things, like developing weapons of mass destruction.

There was yet another more important reason the director never spoke his name out loud. John Gideon didn't exist. He was a ghost in the machine, a figment of the the director's feral imagination. Gorrell didn't even use a code name or phrase to refer to his invisible asset. When they met in person, it was always outside of Langley at a discreet location. If they bumped into each other in the halls of the CIA, neither acknowledged the other's presence.

Gideon's entire existence was a complex shell game. Officially, he was employed as a senior analyst with mid-level security clearance. On the surface, his service jacket was far from spectacular, showing just a hint of field experience in places known to be hotbeds of activity. If someone looked close enough, they would find that he reported into the Counterterrorism group, a complex matrix organization involving a number of federal agencies all collaborating under the spirit of free exchange and unfettered cooperation. His career, while serviceable, would largely go unnoticed by the bureaucrats and the lifers who truly ran the CIA. And if someone did get close enough to start asking questions, a few well-placed shots from above squashed further curiosity. It was just the way Gideon wanted it. He had the best of both worlds: the backing of the Central Intelligence Agency—and the security clearance that went with it—coupled with the ability to move silently among the men and women of the intelligence community.

"Did you learn anything?" the director asked, hopeful.

"Yes," Gideon replied. He updated the director on what he had learned at the morgue, leaving out none of the details from his discussion with the medical examiner. Included in his report was his belief that the men were trying to infiltrate Kulbeda Station but had failed in the process. Gideon finished his account with a statement of fact that surprised the director. "All four were Russian Spetsnaz soldiers," he said with confidence.

Gorrell was silent for a moment. As much as he trusted Gideon's uncanny instincts and his ability to analyze a situation with the barest of facts, this was too important to leave to conjecture or theory.

"How much of this is speculation?" the director probed.

"None of it," Gideon asserted. "I checked out their teeth. The metals used in their dental work were cheap and ill-formed, the bridgework was rudimentary, and the caps were from standard molds. It was shoddy all the way around." Gideon ignored the silence on the other end of the phone. He continued. "I saw enough of that when I was attached to the consulate in Moscow. The elite get the best dentists, but the middle class and the poor are stuck with whatever they can get. We used that to our advantage though—one of the best ways to turn a foreign asset is to offer the services of an American doctor. The dental work on these guys didn't come from a competent dentist. Most Russian soldiers have to use state-owned dental offices, which are usually the worst you'll find."

"That's your evidence?" the director interjected. "Poor dental work? Hell, half the population in the southwest United States doesn't take care of their teeth properly. I can't authorize further action based on that."

"There's more," Gideon continued, unfazed. "These men were in top physical condition. There wasn't more than an ounce of body fat between them. It's the kind of extreme conditioning you get from continuous training, say, for a marathon or triathlon. These men, Director, were not out in the Delaware Bay preparing to swim the English Channel. They were special forces."

"What makes you think they're Spetsnaz?" the director asked. He was more convinced now than he was a minute ago.

"Even more telling than their physiques," Gideon replied, "were their hands. Each man's hands and fingers were hard with calluses."

The director sighed on the other end. "Calluses?" he asked.

"Yeah, calluses," Gideon answered. He rubbed his hands together, feeling the rough surfaces on his skin. "These men, though, didn't have them on their palms, like you would get from a shovel or a hammer. They had calluses on the tips of their fingers, along the outside of their hands, and all across the knuckles. You get calluses like that from extensive, focused training in specialized hand-to-hand combat. Spetsnaz units are famous for it."

"Okay, okay, you've convinced me," the director said when Gideon paused. "So we had an infiltration by a Spetsnaz unit. Now the men are dead. What do you suggest we do about it?"

"It's not that simple," Gideon replied. "A Spetsnaz unit is a highly integrated, eight-man team. Four bodies were found floating in the water. That was likely a reconnaissance team sent to scout a landing area for the rest of the unit."

"That means there are four more men still in the area?"

"Unless they were acting on their own as mercenaries."

The director didn't like where this was heading. "Having a foreign special forces unit operating on United States soil is an act of war," he said coldly. "What could possibly be so important that the Russian government would risk such an act?"

"Like I said," Gideon replied, "the other option is equally viable. They could be working for a third party, someone we haven't thought of yet. The Russian mob, in particular, has deep roots in the Northeast. It's possible that they're involved. Either way, it's unlikely whoever it is will quit just because of last night. They've invested too much already in this operation. And if it is Spetsnaz, they're too highly trained and motivated to just turn away from a fight."

Gideon paused to let the words sink in. The director was silent on the other end.

"There's one other thing," Gideon said at last. "It's more a complication than a problem, and I don't think it will have any impact on my investigation, but you ought to know. I ran into an old friend on the way out of the hospital." Gideon could almost hear the director's teeth grind over the phone. This situation was fraught with problems as it was, and he didn't want to hear about another one. "The FBI agent I saved in Lisbon, Natalie Reyes, is in the morgue as we speak. She's interviewing the medical examiner about the four dead men."

"Damn it," the director spat. "Did she recognize you?"

"No," Gideon replied.

The director's reply was final. He had heard enough. "Take care of it. She can't be part of this investigation. I think you realize that this is bigger than the FBI, bigger than either of us thought going into it. I want this to stay within the Agency, you hear me? Keep this contained . . . and keep her out of it."

The line went dead.

The director's response did not come as a surprise. Gideon flipped the phone closed and threw it on the empty seat next to him. He had already cancelled the helicopter ride back to Washington, D.C., electing to stay in Cape May to see what Agent Reyes had in mind. She had responded quickly to the news of the four dead men. Gideon was lucky he passed her outside the building and not in the morgue itself. It would have been awkward if he had still been talking to the coroner when she arrived. Still, it wouldn't take her long to put the pieces together. And whatever she didn't figure out on her own, the medical examiner was sure to take care of the rest.

Gideon settled back in his seat, his eyes on the door that led into the morgue. *The odds were a million to one. Of all the places she could be today.* Reyes was a distraction he didn't need right now.

He was so focused on the squat brick building that housed the morgue that he failed to notice that others had also taken an interest in the FBI agent. These individuals were not merely here to watch and observe. They had an altogether different motive, one that would soon force Gideon to make a very tough decision.

Natalie Reyes walked out of the small Coast Guard hospital with a skip in her step and a smile on her face. It was turning out to be a beautiful day after all, the first in almost a month. Three weeks without a lead. Twenty-one days of misery and pain. First there was the burial for the two agents killed in Lisbon. That was bad enough, dealing face-to-face with the families and loved ones. She was the agent in charge, the one responsible. They wanted answers. She had none to give.

Back at the Bureau, she was forced to patiently ignore the looks of doubt, disapproval, and contempt from her peers. They were angry at her, letting two of their own get killed like that. Hell, she was angry with herself. The worst, however, were the polite smiles and gentle pats on the back. "A mission gone bad," they would say. "Don't let it get you down."

Her supervisor counseled against responding to any of it. "Let it go," he said. "Focus instead on getting the bastards that set you up."

And yet, the Bureau brass was already screaming for someone's head. Her days there were numbered. Even if she discovered who was behind the killings, she still might not be able to save her job. She wasn't sure she even wanted it anymore. But if she could close the case, she could then walk away with some closure, for herself and for the families who had lost so much. She owed herself, and her partners, that much. Any other outcome was a compromise that she couldn't live with.

Thank God her father wasn't still alive to see this disgrace. He was a twenty-four year veteran of the Bureau, a legendary, no-nonsense, by-the-books criminal investigator who had earned the respect of everyone who carried a badge. Everywhere she went she lived under the shadow of her father and his crime-solving and profiling abilities.

Seeing his daughter struggle and fail like this would have broken his heart. His death the year before had been hard on her, more so than she thought it would be. Even though he had been retired for almost five years, hundreds attended his funeral, including the director of the FBI himself, who gave a stirring eulogy. Now, for the first time in her life, she was truly alone. Her mother had died when she was young. She had no siblings. Her extended family was scattered throughout the country, and she rarely kept in touch with any of her relatives.

Reyes was convinced the Bureau was being lenient on her out of respect for her father. But the deference would last only so long. Anyone else would have been tied to the stake and laid out over an open fire. She knew her luck was running out. It was only a matter of time before Bureau politics and the Hoover bureaucracy reared its ugly head.

So Reyes focused on what she knew. The death of the four men the night before confirmed her growing suspicions about Kulbeda Station. The medical examiner was very helpful. He had already pinpointed the area where he believed the men had been killed. Kulbeda Station was well within the radius he had drawn on the map in his office. He had also made preliminary conclusions as to the time of death. Early morning was his estimate.

Now she had enough evidence to go back and talk with Colonel Allbright, the smug, self-righteous commander of the station. Her previous visits had gotten her nowhere. The man was infuriatingly obsequious, yet he provided little by way of information. He listened attentively, nodded his head, smiled, and provided patently rehearsed answers to all her questions. She was a skilled interrogator with a dozen years on the force and could tell instantly that he was lying. Nevertheless, Kulbeda was a military installation on government land. No crimes that she could prove had been committed there, and she had little evidence to warrant going before a judge.

Now, however, she had strong evidence to support her suspicions. Allbright could not ignore her this time.

Reyes checked her watch and took a deep breath. It was still early, not quite ten o'clock. The sun was bright and warm on her face. A slight breeze blew inward off the water, carrying with it the scent of sea and salt. She still had a few minutes to catch the ferry over to Curtis Cove, the home of Kulbeda Station. It was just a few blocks away. If she hurried, she could get there early enough to guarantee a good seat on the upper deck.

Gideon watched as Reyes crossed the street in front of him and began walking toward the center of town. She looked exactly as he remembered—almost six feet tall, with the trim athletic build of a long-distance runner. She wore an ivory Donna Karan blouse that did nothing to hide her figure underneath. Her posture was straight, chin raised ever so slightly, displaying an air of confidence with just a touch of arrogance. Wavy blonde hair cascaded down in soft curls to the top of her narrow shoulders, long enough to be sexy, short enough to hint at the tomboy underneath. The front locks were tucked neatly behind her ears, giving her a stern appearance that, whether she meant it or not, would keep people at a distance. Still, her face had a graceful eminence to it. Perfect skin, small, straight nose flanked by high cheekbones, green eyes that shined with a sad intensity. She had the kind of family characteristics that were likely passed down from one generation to another, a patrician quality that hinted at aristocracy or fine breeding. Despite her narrow features, her lips were full and red, shining in the morning sunlight without the hint of lipstick. Men on the street went out of their way to glance at her as she walked by. She was attractive, beautiful even.

Gideon felt an unexpected tingle in the pit of his stomach. He wondered what it would be like to kiss her. Go to bed with her. Reyes was beautiful by any modern standard, and he had felt the physical attraction the first moment he saw her in Lisbon. Three weeks later, he hadn't changed his mind. She was the exact opposite of his soon-to-be ex-wife. Maybe that's what attracted him.

Gideon got out of the car and crossed the street. Reyes was now almost a block ahead, walking parallel to him on the opposite sidewalk. He quickened his pace to get closer, using the storefront windows as mirrors so he could watch her discreetly.

It was a trick he learned a long time ago, but it had nothing to do with technique. Gideon believed that most people had a sixth sense, an ability to just *know* when they were being watched. He knew this feeling firsthand. It was an instinct, a gnawing at the back of the neck, that had saved his life on more than one occasion. Over the years he had come to trust and rely on that feeling, just like he did his other senses. To avoid "alerting" her, Gideon kept Reyes in his peripheral vision, looking directly at her only when necessary.

Minutes passed without incident when he spotted Reyes check behind her. *Does she know I'm following her?* he wondered. A few steps later, she did it again, though this time she appeared hesitant, unsure of herself. Gideon scanned the sidewalk and quickly discovered what her sixth sense was trying to tell her. Twenty feet behind her was a tall man walking with a cell phone to his right ear. In his left hand he carried a large, colorful bag from one of the local merchants. His stride was casual, unhurried. He was trying very hard to blend in with the few tourists in the area.

To a casual observer, nothing about the man was ominous, but Gideon knew better. Despite the act, the man's shoes gave him away instantly. They were large black boots, tied high on the calf, with thick, heavy soles designed to travel over and through anything. Standard military gear you could find in any surplus store, but not something you wore on a beautiful day like this. Further heightening Gideon's suspicion was the bulky windbreaker that hung loose on the man's body. It was the perfect jacket to conceal a weapon. Silver-mirrored sunglasses shaded his eyes. He was no tourist.

Gideon was so intent in his concentration on Reyes that this man would have gone unnoticed had it not been for her subconscious warning. Gideon wondered what else he had missed. Casually checking behind him, he discovered who the man on foot was talking to. Trailing a block behind was a slow-moving gray sedan. Moving at a crawl, the car was drawing the ire of passing drivers, but the man inside paid no heed. Instead, he was talking on his cell phone and gesturing animatedly.

Familiar warning bells rang inside Gideon's head. He knew instinctively that these men weren't there for the agent's protection, nor were they admiring her beauty. *Damn it,* he thought. He should have seen this sooner. He cursed himself for not paying closer attention to his surroundings. After the thwarted sting in Lisbon, it was only natural that someone might want the FBI agent out of the way.

"What the hell?" he cursed out loud. First, he almost bumps into Reyes, now this. This day was quickly going from bad to worse.

Gideon absently patted the Sig Sauer nestled snugly in his shoulder holster. He casually reached his hand inside his blazer and turned the safety off. Then he stopped to admire a hip pair of sneakers at the local Foot Locker. In the window's reflection, he watched as the sedan approached. The man in the car continued his animated exchange, ignoring Gideon and everyone else around him. Like his partner, he was too preoccupied with his quarry. Well, that was one problem he could solve right away.

Improvise . . . adapt . . . overcome. He lived by those maxims. Friend or foe, that was a question he could ask later. Right now, he needed to even the odds. The car drew parallel to Gideon, and then slightly past.

Avoiding oncoming cars, Gideon walked into the middle of the street and approached the sedan from behind. The car had a government license plate. A faded Kulbeda Station parking sticker adorned the rear window.

Very interesting, Gideon thought. When he reached the car, he knocked loudly on the trunk. That got the man's attention. The driver eyed him warily through the driver-side mirror but made no attempt to exit the vehicle. Gideon approached the window, flashing his false badge and identification. "Open up," he commanded.

The man inside put the cell phone on the passenger seat and rolled down the window. "What the hell do you want?" he asked angrily.

Yeah, definitely a bad guy, Gideon thought. "Pull over to the curb," he said. "And don't give me any more shit."

The man complied, but not before shooting him a contemptuous glare. Then he pulled into the next space and put the car in park.

Gideon stepped up to the car, a guilty smile on his face. "I'm awful sorry about this," he said.

Caught completely off guard, the driver didn't know how to respond.

But Gideon did. Without warning, he struck out with two rapid punches. His tight fist smashed squarely into the man's cheek and temple, each blow landing solidly on the unsuspecting driver. The man's head snapped violently around. His eyes rolled back and then fluttered shut. He fell forward, landing heavily against the steering wheel. Gideon reached in and felt the man's pulse; it was slow but steady. He would be all right, though he would have to deal with quite a bit of pain when he awoke.

Gideon ran around the front of the car to the sidewalk. Pedestrians who had witnessed the attack parted to let him pass. He ignored the looks of astonishment and shock, focusing beyond the angry murmurs to the second man up ahead. Someone was bound to call the police. At least half a dozen witnesses would provide accurate descriptions of his face. The director wouldn't be happy, but Gideon would take care of it. Right now, he needed to alert Reyes and get away before the local authorities arrived. The last thing he needed was police involvement. This was a small town. They weren't trained for this type of incident or these types of people. Someone innocent was likely to get hurt, or worse.

He wove along the sidewalk like a snake through tall grass. Farther ahead, the second man had moved closer to Reyes and was now less than ten feet behind her. Gideon was too far away—there was nothing he could do to reach her in time.

Sirens in the distance caused Gideon to glance behind him. The police were still a few minutes away, and any attention he had created was left behind at the accident. After the brutality he showed the driver, no one dared to follow him. Gideon turned back to the problem at hand. What he saw, or didn't see, brought him up short. His heart raced in panic. Agent Reyes and the assassin were no longer in sight. The attack had begun.

CHAPTER 9

This second guy was good. Real good. Gideon had looked away for only a few seconds. All it took was a fraction of that time for the unidentified subject to take Reyes off the sidewalk. Gideon scanned the crowd, looking at the faces of those coming toward him. No one appeared concerned with anything that had happened. No one was alarmed by the man's maneuver. It was done so cleanly and efficiently that bystanders thought nothing of the woman's sudden disappearance.

Gideon felt a pang of professional pride for the skill and experience it took to accomplish that feat. There were only a handful of operatives he knew of who could do it with such elegance. Almost all of them were trained by the CIA or Britain's Secret Intelligence Service, commonly known as MI6. At the same time, however, he worried that he might be too late. A man of this caliber wouldn't waste time. He would eliminate his target quickly and quietly before slipping back among the unsuspecting public.

More than ever, Gideon knew he had to act. Throwing caution aside, he sprinted ahead. His strong legs propelled him forward. His hands pushed roughly past pedestrians too slow to get out of the way. After a dozen long strides he came upon a narrow alley. It was the only place the two could have gone.

Gideon removed the Sig from its holster and without slowing ran into the alley. He had the gun raised and sighted before he even cleared the corner. Twenty feet away he saw the assailant. The man had Agent Reyes's arm twisted against her back. His right knee was planted between her thighs. A long, wicked knife was at her throat. Gone were the man's silver-mirrored sunglasses. In their place Gideon saw fresh scratches scored into the man's cheek. At least Reyes had put up a fight, but it wasn't enough.

Gideon didn't hesitate. The loud gunshot echoed in the narrow space. The first bullet sliced across the man's shoulder blades, burrowing an ugly red channel across the width of his back. The second and third shots followed in quick succession. One entered the base of his skull, severing his spinal cord; the other exploded into his right ear.

The assassin fell to the ground in a crumpled heap. The long stiletto dropped from his hand and skittered across the pavement. No longer constrained, Agent Reyes stumbled backward, tripping over her assailant's lifeless feet. Gideon reached her just in time, catching her in his arms.

Bewildered by the fast-moving series of events, Reyes struggled against him. "What's going on?" she stuttered, trying to make sense of it all. "Who was that man?" Looking over her shoulder, she peered into the deepest blue eyes she had ever seen. The eyes were warm and compassionate. They showed great concern with equal measures of relief. Reyes let out a heavy sigh. "Who are you?"

"I don't know who he is, but he was sent to kill you," Gideon replied. "There's another assailant back on the street, but he's been dealt with." Gideon then did something he never thought he would. He answered the last question truthfully, without any thought or care for his official cover. "My name is John Gideon."

Gideon focused his attention on the agent's physical well-being. Outwardly, she appeared all right. Nothing was broken. There were no signs of bruising. On closer inspection, however, he found out just how close she had come to losing her life. A thin red stripe ran horizontally across the hollow of her neck. In places, small beads of blood were beginning to collect, signs of where the blade had actually cut the skin. If he had arrived a second later, she would have been dead.

Gideon pulled a handkerchief from his pocket and held it up to the wound. It was nothing serious, but for a while she would have a physical reminder of how close she had come to death.

Reyes put her hand to her throat and pulled the handkerchief away. She looked at the spotted blood streaked across the white cloth and then down at the dead man at her feet. She swallowed hard and took a deep breath.

"I'll be all right," she said with confidence, though her face was still ashen. "I don't know what to say, except thank you. If it weren't for you, I'd be dead." Pushing off of her savior, Reyes stood up on her own wobbly feet. The FBI agent in her slowly took over. Pulling her badge from her coat pocket, she said, "My name is Natalie Reyes. I'm a federal agent. I want to know who this bastard is and who sent him after me." She looked hard at the dead assassin.

Gideon put the pistol back in its holster and started down the alley, back toward the street. Reyes turned to face him, a puzzled look on her face.

"Where are you going?" she asked, hands on her hips. Gideon kept on walking. Reyes took after him. "You can't just leave! You have to tell the police what happened. I need answers, damn it."

"Sorry," Gideon replied. "That might work in the real world, but not the one I live in. I don't want my name attached to this incident, officially or unofficially."

Reyes stared hard at Gideon, a suspicious look crossing her face. He didn't like the look one bit. She was asking herself the questions he ultimately knew she would. Who was John Gideon? How did he happen to be at the right place at the right time to save her life? Why was he suddenly acting shy about his involvement? Hell, he wasn't shy about killing her attacker. The questions were mounting, and he wanted no part in answering them.

Gideon had to get out. Turning on his heels, he walked briskly back to the street. The police sirens were louder now. In a minute, they would be on the scene. He needed to be far gone by then.

Agent Reyes caught up with him at the sidewalk. She was battling multiple emotions at once—shock at the near-death experience, gratitude for the man who had just saved her life, duty that over a decade of law enforcement had instilled in her, anger that she had let herself fall into this situation. Reyes funneled all these emotions into action. She grabbed Gideon by the shoulder and spun him around.

Gideon turned to face the agent as a sharp sting penetrated his left shoulder. He knew immediately that he had been hit and that the shot was meant for his heart. There was no sound to pinpoint the shooter's location. That meant the assailant had used a silenced weapon, something police officers don't carry on patrol. On instinct, Gideon dove into Reyes, half carrying, half dragging her back into the alley. After twenty yards, he stopped and crouched low. He quickly assessed the situation. There was no place to hide. The dead end looked impossibly close. All the doors were closed. Gideon could but wonder if any of them were unlocked.

"What are you doing?" Reyes yelled.

"There are more out there," he replied calmly. "I thought there were only two, but there must be a larger team in place."

Gideon frowned deeply and chastised himself. He had made another mistake. He should have scanned the area for further backup. He shouldn't have been so narrow-minded. Things happened so quickly that he didn't have time to plan ahead. He simply reacted to what he saw. It was shortsighted. So far he had been lucky.

"What do you mean there's more of them out there? How do you know this?" Agent Reyes was incredulous.

Then she saw the tear in the shoulder of his jacket. Blood had begun to seep through the heavy fabric. *Shit,* she thought. *Maybe he was right.* The next clue erased any doubt from her mind that more attackers were out there. Mere inches from her head, the wall exploded in a shower of concrete and plaster. Another bullet whipped by, so close that she could feel its force as it flew past. Suddenly, the man who had saved her life lunged to his feet, his strong arms lifting her with him. At first, she offered no resistance, letting him carry her along. Then recollection gained control of her senses.

"Hold on!" she pleaded. "Wait a second." She pulled away from his grasp. "I need to find something."

Gideon watched helplessly, exposed in the open as the agent rummaged around in the debris littering the alley. Another bullet entered the narrow stretch and ricocheted off the wall. Gideon pulled his own gun back out and aimed outside the alley's entrance. His earlier gunfire had all but cleared innocent bystanders from the opening, but the vehicular traffic continued to move along the street unabated. He could not see the shooter and dared not fire without a clean shot.

Finally, Reyes found what she was looking for. She lifted a large black object, her service pistol, from under a crumpled newspaper.

Running down the alley, she offered an explanation. "The man that attacked me threw my gun away. I couldn't leave without it."

"Let's hope the delay doesn't get us killed," Gideon yelled angrily. "You can always find a new weapon. Your life is irreplaceable. Next time, I won't wait."

Reyes knew he was right. Her mounting troubles at the FBI, and the pressure she was under, had momentarily clouded her judgment. The higher-ups were watching her closely, looking for any reason, and waiting for even the slightest infraction to discharge her from the service. The margin for error at the Bureau was already infinitesimally small to begin with. Now it had all but disappeared. Losing her weapon would have been a big mistake, but losing her life over it would have been a bigger one. Her reaction was needless and stupid. She also suspected that John Gideon was telling the truth, and that if there was a next time, he wouldn't wait for her foolishness.

Gideon took the lead and ran deeper into the alley. The rain of bullets abated. "He must be trying to get into a better position," he said. "Or else we've forced him to cross the street and come after us. We need to get out of here."

The sound of blaring horns and screeching tires confirmed his second opinion. The shooter was coming after them. Gideon knew that these guys were professionals. If they had a clean shot, they wouldn't miss again. In this narrow alley, it would be like shooting fish in a barrel.

Gideon ran ahead. The first door he came to was locked. He ran to another one while Reyes covered the entrance to the alley with her pistol.

This door was unlocked. Gideon threw the door open and stepped inside. Next to him, Reyes's gun roared to life. He looked back in time to see a man dive to safety behind the corner of the building. Her shot missed the operative by scant inches and punctured the tire of a large SUV. The SUV swerved to the left and crashed into another vehicle. The wreck would tie up traffic even more and virtually eliminate anyone following by car, including the police.

"Not bad," he said.

"First in my class at Quantico," Reyes replied proudly.

"Yeah, well, I wouldn't have missed," Gideon taunted with a smirk.

Together, they ran through the door into the kitchen of a restaurant. When the kitchen staff saw the armed agents, they parted to let the intruders pass. The dining room was empty save for shocked busboys and waitresses preparing for the lunch crowd. Rushing past tables and chairs, Gideon and Reyes reached the front door. It was unlocked.

Back outside, Gideon scanned the street, seeing and sensing no signs of danger. He holstered his weapon and moved to blend in with the tourists who dominated the crowd. Reyes followed suit, walking quickly to stand beside him.

In the distance, a horn sounded the arrival of a ferry. Gideon crossed the street and entered an adjacent park. His pace quickened. If they hurried, they could make the ferry before the assailants knew what happened.

As they walked in silence, Gideon struggled with what he was going to tell the director. He had broken every protocol his undercover life demanded. He didn't regret the actions he had taken, but he would have some explaining to do nonetheless. Even more immediate, however, he needed to figure out how he was going to get away from Reyes. She had a determined look in her eyes and more questions than he could answer. Gideon couldn't help but feel trapped by the circumstances that had brought them together for the second time. He didn't believe in fate, but the coincidence was unnerving.

"Come over here. Let me take a look at your shoulder." Reyes's tone of voice was neutral, all business, yet her eyes displayed compassion and concern.

Gideon walked over to the sink and with Reyes's help was able to shrug off the jacket. The shirt had been torn by the bullet and was soaked in blood. Reyes ripped the shirt open to expose the wound.

The bathroom they occupied was located on the lower deck of the large passenger ferry, near the aft staircase. Underneath his feet, Gideon could feel the powerful drum of the engine as it pushed the ferry across the waters of the Delaware Bay. The rhythmic hum of the propeller shaft was loud inside the enclosed, dingy space. The bathroom offered no windows or access to fresh air from outdoors. The small ventilation fan was working hard to clear the space but was overmatched. The stench of human waste, mold, and mildew was so sweet that it aroused disgust. And the odor of recently applied sanitation products did little to dissipate the strong and cloying smell. Add to that the gentle swaying back and forth, and Gideon knew with sickening certainty that he didn't want to spend more time than necessary down here.

"It's not too bad," Reyes said, applying water to a paper towel. She then began cleaning the area around the wound. "The bleeding has already stopped. It's just a graze, not a deep laceration. A few stitches are all you'll need." She removed the sleeve entirely and then tore it into strips. In minutes, she had applied an adequate field dressing.

Gideon turned to face the mirror and check the woman's handiwork. "Nicely done," he said to her reflection.

Reyes looked back with a questioning look. "Michael Hayes, DEA?" she asked.

Gideon looked down to see her holding his false identification. Her dressing of the wound proved to be a useful distraction while she rifled through his coat.

"Which one is it?" she demanded.

Caught off guard by the discovery, he didn't know how to react. Caught in a lie, he decided to stick with the truth. "If you let me explain," he began, "I can clear this whole thing up." He reached his hand behind him to retrieve his true identification. Before he could act, she had her pistol out of her holster and aimed at the middle of his forehead. For the second time, Gideon found himself looking down the barrel of her gun.

"Don't move," she snarled. "I've had enough of this. I want to know who you are."

"So do I."

The sudden presence of a third person in the restroom startled both Gideon and Reyes. They turned to look at the stranger, shocked to find that he was pointing a silenced Glock 19 at them.

Gideon frowned at the sight of the weapon and the professional ease by which its owner carried it. Used by military and law enforcement agencies the world over, Glocks were highly praised for their reliability, accuracy, and light weight. Designed with a four-inch barrel and shorter, high-impact polymer frame, the compact weapon's firepower was equivalent to most full-size pistols on the market. And since the Austrian-designed weapon had half the components and moving parts of conventional handguns, it was able to withstand the most punishing and unforgiving conditions. All in all, it was a deadly weapon, made even deadlier by someone who knew how to use it.

"Don't move, Agent Reyes," the intruder demanded. "Slowly drop your weapon to the floor and kick it over to me."

She did as instructed. The gun skittered across the floor to the man's feet.

He then kicked the gun farther behind him. "Now, I'll take the jacket."

Frowning, Reyes threw him Gideon's jacket. The man caught it easily and dropped it to the floor. This, too, he kicked behind him.

"Careful of that," Gideon complained.

"Silence," the man ordered. He pointed the gun at Reyes. "I know who you are." The barrel shifted to Gideon. "But who are you? What were you doing following her around?"

Reyes turned to Gideon. "You were following me?" she asked, surprised.

Gideon said nothing. Instead, his eyes focused on the threat in front of him. His expression hardened to that of chiseled stone.

Reyes witnessed the transformation and shuddered. The shift was subtle, but she was an astute observer of the human condition. She could tell that he was balanced, like a cat on the balls of its feet. His posture went from loose and relaxed to a poised, almost hovering stance. In the blink of an eye, his demeanor had changed from polite to deadly serious. His piercing blue eyes—once cool and deep—were now hard and calculating.

Gideon slowly reached out his arm and pushed Reyes behind him. "What do you want with her?" he asked. "Is she getting too close to the real reason for Kulbeda's existence?"

He heard Reyes's slight intake of breath. The man smiled and took a step closer.

"The brass decided that she's been enough of a nuisance," the man responded with confidence. "It's time for her to go away."

Gideon calculated his next reply. "Your team couldn't get the job done in Lisbon," he said, "so now they send in round two? Don't you guys ever give up?"

A look of confusion clouded the man's face. It was brief, but it provided answers to the many questions Gideon had been asking himself the last few weeks. It also created more problems. The man edged closer. He was now no more than a foot from Gideon. "Make no mistake," he snarled in reply. "We hit what we aim for."

The stranger jabbed the gun into Gideon's chest. The barrel pushed painfully against his sternum. The man slowly squeezed the trigger. Any false moves on his part and Gideon knew the man would blow a hole in his breast.

The stranger continued. "One man is dead. Another is unconscious and on the way to the hospital. You're in deep shit. You have no idea what you're up against." Each statement was punctuated by another stab of the gun. "Just who the hell are you?"

Despite the racing heart pounding inside his chest, Gideon forced himself to display an air of calm indifference. He cocked his head to the side. "Sorry," he replied. "But that question is going to follow you to the grave. When I'm finished with you, I'm going to leave your body in that bathroom stall over there and let the janitors find you and throw you out with the trash."

It would have taken an act of absolute self-control and willpower for any human being to ignore the impulse gnawing at the back of the skull and not glance over at the bathroom stall. In times of extreme stress, the instinct to confirm or deny suspicions, to satisfy curiosities that help ensure our safety, can be overwhelming. It's a natural reflex that only those with extensive training and iron-willed discipline can ignore. This guy had very little of either. His eyes flickered toward the corner of the bathroom. His head swiveled slightly on his neck.

It was the reaction that Gideon had hoped for. In that moment of distraction, he leaned back and angled his body sideways, his left arm shielding Reyes. In the same fluid motion he struck out with his right hand.

Realizing his mistake, the killer's instincts took over. Out of reflex, his finger squeezed off a desperate shot. The bullet narrowly missed Gideon, shattering the mirror instead and burrowing deep into the wall.

Before the man could reposition and fire, Gideon's calloused hand connected hard with the assailant, knocking the pistol from his grasp. Gideon then reversed direction, spinning lightly on his right foot. Using momentum to his advantage, his left hand sliced through the air with blinding speed, the hard edge connecting with the soft flesh of his adversary's neck. The would-be killer's windpipe cracked loudly as it collapsed; his eyes sprang open in shock. He gasped uselessly for breath. Still spinning, Gideon snatched the discarded pistol in midair, turned to face the suffocating man, and fired a single shot into the center of his chest. The attacker buckled and fell backward. Blood oozed from a hole in his chest. Ragged, frothy breath came from his mouth.

The whole episode lasted no more than a few seconds.

Moving quickly, Gideon dragged the dying man into the bathroom stall, as promised, and propped him up against the toilet. Next, he performed a thorough search, ignoring the garbled and bloody pleas for help as the man both suffocated and bled to death.

His search came up empty. There was nothing of any consequence. No wallet, identification, money, or keys. Finally, the operative stopped his thrashing. In the last moments of life his eyes turned baleful, glaring at Gideon for vengeance before finally clouding over for good. Gideon then spotted a small tattoo on the man's forearm. His lips turned up in a feral sneer. His reaction was purely instinctual. The tattoo depicted an image of the mythical serpent goddess Medusa, her deadly snakes writhing in anguish, her head impaled by a long, jewel-encrusted dagger, mouth open in a never-ending scream.

"Shit," Gideon said.

"What's wrong?" Reyes asked. "Do you recognize him?"

Gideon reached down, grabbed the man's lifeless wrist, and pushed his jacket sleeve further up his arm. "Do you recognize this tattoo?" he asked. "Ever seen it before?"

"No," Reyes replied. "Is it significant?"

"It's significant." Gideon took a deep breath before replying. "This man is a member of a little-known but sinister network of ex-military officers and noncommissioned soldiers. The tattoo, the Gorgon Medusa, is their brand. They don't usually operate inside the United States, but they go wherever the money is. So that means there's a lot of it involved. And they're formidable. The ranks of the Gorgon Medusa are full of soldiers with elite special forces training and proven combat experience, and it's not uncommon to find former American Army Ranger, British SAS, and Russian Spetsnaz soldiers working side by side. These men hold no allegiances and bow to no nation or cause. As individuals, they are highly motivated and are recruited for their ability to achieve results at any cost."

Reyes blew the air out of her lungs in a rush. "So, they're bad news."

"The worst kind," Gideon answered. "My orginization has been monitoring the Gorgon Medusa for years. Actually, that's a bit of an understatement. We've been tracking the devastation and destruction they leave in their wake."

"What's he doing here, then?" Reyes asked. "How can he possibly be connected to Kulbeda?"

Gideon continued. "This man was a killer. Whoever he worked for, he was not part of any legal military chain of command. He's also what's worst about this organization. Very often, they bring in men that have been mustered out of the service for having serious character flaws. These men end up as convicted felons or spend time in the psych ward. They're just bad men. Period."

"What you're saying," Reyes said, "is that Kulbeda Station, a United States military base, is manned or infiltrated by mercenaries."

He didn't answer.

Though Gideon had more to say, he didn't dare go any further. He needed time to piece together what he knew and what he suspected. The confused look the dead man gave him when he mentioned Lisbon confirmed that someone else had contracted the hit that left Reyes's partners dead. That meant there were at least two separate factions involved in this case, one inside Kulbeda, and one outside. Judging by the four men floating in the Delaware Bay, he had to conclude that the two groups were operating against each other. Now he had evidence that the Gorgon Medusa was involved. The news couldn't have been worse. He had seen hired men like this before, had worked alongside them on a handful of missions inside the jungles of Nicaragua, on the deserts of Afghanistan, in the back streets of Hong Kong. He had seen firsthand the results of their handiwork. The memories were not pleasant.

CHAPTER 10

"Would you mind telling me what's going on here?" Reyes asked once they had reached the top deck of the ferry. "Mercenaries are running Kulbeda. How is that possible?"

"I can't answer that," Gideon shot back.

Reyes turned silent, reflective, and asked the one question he hoped she wouldn't. "What were you doing in Lisbon?"

Gideon stiffened slightly and shook his head.

Undeterred, Reyes continued, "I know it was you that saved my life that night. I've had my gun taken from me before, but never with the kind of skill, precision, and absolute confidence that you just showed. And now I've seen that move done twice in a matter of weeks. There can't be many people who can pull that off. And before you deny it, nobody has the kind of eyes you have when you're ready to do something violent." Reyes shuddered at the memory of the look that overcame Gideon just before he acted. "I saw it once in Lisbon, when you killed that Russian agent. I saw it again just a few minutes ago."

Gideon turned to face Reyes. She looked hopeful, like she needed the answer more than anything else on earth. Gideon sighed. No matter what the rules stated, no matter what the director might say, and for reasons he didn't yet understand, he did not want to lie to this woman. On a personal level, for the first time in years, he found the thought of telling the truth refreshing. It was a foreign concept that he would have to work out later.

"It was you, wasn't it?" she pressed.

"Yes," he finally answered.

Reyes let out a sigh of relief. "Thank you for saving my life . . . and for the truth."

Gideon simply nodded in reply. The fact was he didn't know how to respond, so saying nothing seemed the most appropriate thing to do.

"How can you do things like that? I've never seen someone move that fast, kill so easily, without any compunction. You make it look so natural."

"There's nothing natural about it," he replied, his voice on edge. "Killing is the most unnatural thing in the world."

The fact that he could do it so easily is what caught the attention of his superiors in the Army. It's what helped him excel in Special Forces and what made him a prime candidate for his current employer. He couldn't explain it, but in extreme situations he had always been able to go to another place, become a different person. It could happen in the blink of an eye, like an instant trigger that responds to aggression with even more violence. It was another person, someone he didn't really know, or want to know, who acted with such impunity, killing without thought. Afterward that person went away, yet he was the one who had to live with the consequences, the downside of adrenaline, the bloodshed, and the faces that come in the middle of the night.

"It must be hard."

"It should be," he acknowledged with a sigh.

Reyes sat quietly next to Gideon, letting the moment pass. After a minute, she asked, "So, what's next? You're not from the DEA. My guess would be CIA. You're certainly not with the FBI. We don't operate the way you do."

Gideon closed his eyes and took a deep, cleansing breath. The salt air and the sound of the ocean reminded him of Lisbon. How he wished he could be there right now, sailing off the coastline in a rented sailboat. Just him and the waves, nothing of the real world to remind him what a mess this was turning into.

"You guessed right," he finally said. "But please don't ask anything more about my role there. Talking to you like I am, without permission, I'm already breaking enough laws to spend the rest of my life in prison. I don't want to add the death penalty to my list of punishments."

He meant the remark as a lighthearted joke, and Reyes took it as such. Her laugh was light and airy, her smile infectious. Despite the morning's troubles, Gideon couldn't keep the grin off his face.

"Seriously," Reyes prompted, looking deep into his eyes. "Where do we go from here? We're both working on the same case, but from different angles. Maybe we could share information, help each other out."

"You don't know as much as I do," Gideon confessed. "I've seen your reports to the assistant director of the FBI, and you don't know the half of it."

If Reyes was upset that Gideon had accessed her files, she didn't let on. Throwing aside every rule that he had not yet broken, Gideon used the remainder of the ferry ride to bring Reyes up to date. He told her of the decapitated man discovered outside of Philadelphia and the partially digested scrap of paper that pointed to Kulbeda. He confessed his growing suspicions and how the computer system at Fort Meade matched the mysterious death with her report that someone wanted to purchase plans for the station. The CIA then began to closely follow her investigation, alerting him to the clandestine operation in Lisbon mere hours before it was to take place. He felt fortunate to be in the right place to save her life, but he regretted that he could not do the same for her partners, for which he was sorry. She was surprised to hear of his conclusions, that the men found floating in the bay were Russian Spetsnaz soldiers and that their mission was most likely to infiltrate Kulbeda Station.

All the while, Reyes listened and watched intently. She focused on his calm exterior. She saw him wrestle with what to say and what to keep hidden, and was surprised by his decision to be forthright about events leading up to today. Truth be told, it was more than the story that captivated her. She was drawn in by his rugged good looks, by the deep caring and worry conveyed in his blue-lagoon eyes, and by the confidence he had in himself and his abilities. He was a handsome man with chiseled features that included prominent cheekbones, a fine nose, and a strong jawline that ended in a narrow chin. His brown hair was cropped tight, not quite military short, but not long either. The soft curls were unkempt, making him look like he had just rolled out of bed. His voice was soft, gentle, and respectful with just the hint of a Midwestern accent. But what affected her most was his smile. It was so reassuring—she could but imagine what it would be like for him to wrap his arms around her and tell her everything was going to be all right.

Gideon's story ended without fanfare, without conclusions. There simply were no more facts, and that was the problem. Where was this case going to lead next? Armed with the knowledge that a ruthless mercenary organization was involved and that she was a target of extreme interest, Reyes struggled to grasp the enormity of the situation. She was involved in something way over her head, with players and motives she knew nothing about. This case, her world, had just expanded exponentially. Even after the death of her partners, she was confident the parameters had not changed, that she could still bring those responsible to justice. Now, she was not so sure. Doubt and fear began to creep into her consciousness.

Reyes looked hard at Gideon. Even after all they had been through this morning, he appeared completely unflappable and unconcerned. At this moment, his attention to her was unwavering, like she was the only person who mattered. And what she saw in his eyes was nothing more than mild curiosity and patience as he waited for the next question.

Reyes closed her eyes and took a deep breath. She asked, "So, partner, where do we go from here?"

Gideon smiled broadly. Reyes was making it perfectly clear that the two of them were now on the case. They were a team. That was fine with him. A little interagency cooperation couldn't hurt. And, besides, she was as deeply invested in this as he was. From everything he had seen and read, he had come to know this woman. He knew how she worked, and understood what drove her. She was ambitious, but not to the point of recklessness. She was prone to action but still took time to gather crucial intelligence before making decisions. She was proud and headstrong but still able to recognize that she needed help.

Like Reyes, he realized the situation was close to spiraling out of control. Calling in support from Washington was to admit defeat. It was a last resort he hoped to avoid. The longer he could maintain control, the better chance he had to discover what was going on. He wanted to see this thing to the very end. Besides, he was supposed to be the troubleshooter. He took pride in his abilities, knowing that, in the end, it was going to be his wits, his experience, his daring and cunning, that would make the difference. Having Reyes along wouldn't do anything to alter that. In fact, if he played his cards right, it might even help.

Overhead, the ferry horn blew, signaling the end of their ride across the bay. It was time to take this investigation to the next level. There was a lot of work to be done and a number of leads to follow. It was time to push hard, crash through some doors. He was done waiting to see what would happen next. He was ready to go on the offensive, to tear open the envelope and see what fell out.

CHAPTER 11

Kulbeda Station was quiet. More specifically, the forest that ringed the station was quiet.

John Gideon slowly opened his eyes and peered into the murky darkness. His pupils were large and round, dilated naturally in response to the inky blackness surrounding him. His senses were on high alert, heightened by the adrenaline coursing through his body.

Three long days and nights of planning led up to this infiltration of the base. Now he was here, on enemy territory, slightly ahead of schedule. On a night like this, with the moon full and the sky empty of clouds, the usually forbidding forest became a welcome ally. All around him there was nothing to see except the dark trees silhouetted against an even darker background.

Gideon used the cover to his advantage, tuning his senses to the natural ebb and flow of his surroundings. He closed his eyes again and listened for any sounds of movement in the brush or in the trees overhead. He knew from experience that the eyes betrayed at night. Shadows moved. Colors bled into hues of mottled gray, making it difficult to see the shapes of men and machine. In the darkness, even depth and distance sought to deceive. Visual references could no longer be trusted. Objects thought to be near were often farther away than perceived. Simple calculations, things taken for granted in the daylight, worked against you at night.

The nighttime played tricks on the other senses as well. Sounds appeared closer, more ominous. The winds carried faint but familiar odors, remnants of some lost fragrance left over from the day. Even the sense of feel changed as the night's moisture collected as dew, the condensation sticking to every surface exposed to the night air.

Gideon compensated for these deficiencies. He relied on his ears to help him distinguish illusion from reality. His sense of smell alerted him of predators. Every move he made was practiced, purposeful. His muscles were loose and relaxed yet ready to react to the slightest change in his surroundings. He could feel each layer of clothing move against his damp skin.

Dressed entirely in black, Gideon blended into his surroundings. Like a wraith on the prowl, his passage through the dense woods caused barely a ripple. The wildlife was oblivious to his presence, a tribute to his skill. Crickets chirped in tune. Birds sang and whooped overhead. The occasional bat swooped close as it located and devoured wayward insects. The absence of natural sound would have caused him alarm, alerting him to the presence of predators. In these woods, the only threats to him were the kind that walked on two legs. So far, he had not been detected.

Gideon smiled broadly. He loved the night, operating in stealth under the cloak of darkness. The exercise was more than physical—it was cathartic. He could forget his past, embrace the power, the control he felt over the environment. He was alive like no other time during the day.

Overhead, large maples and oaks created a leafy canopy that blocked out most of the bright moonlight. Only occasionally did the slim rays of gossamer penetrate the dense foliage to provide light for him to see by.

Gideon swung his MP5 left to right one more time, sighting into the cool darkness. The submachine gun was standard issue in special operations warfare. Revered by military and law enforcement in more than fifty nations, the weapon had over one hundred variants and was easily customized for the person or the unit, depending on their tactical objective.

The MP5 Gideon carried had a trigger group that allowed him to choose from safe, semiautomatic, or fully automatic fire. He especially liked the MP5 because it fired from the closed-bolt position during all modes and was extremely accurate and controllable when deployed. The weapon was currently set on single-fire mode. Like the pistol at his waist, the submachine gun fired 9mm rounds and was fitted with a deadly looking sound suppressor.

He breathed a heavy sigh. The area was secure.

He pulled the GPS—global positioning system—unit from his backpack. Using the small handheld device like a compass, he checked his position in relation to that of his objective. The dense terrain and man-made footpaths had forced him a few hundred yards southeast of the target. The setback was not critical or unexpected. He had allowed for this specific contingency.

Gideon knew from experience that the kind of geometric shapes that came with mission planning looked great on maps but were essentially useless in the field. Mother Nature abhorred straight lines and right angles. The old lady casually threw clumps of trees, large boulders, noisy bushes, and dense outcroppings in the way. Shaped by millions of years of growth, destruction, and constant adaptation, there was no rhyme or reason to the woodland layout. No, geometry had its place in the world of man, but not here in the chaotic forest. Each woodland had its own unique layout, a terrain that pulsed to its own beat, a personality that he needed to respect, understand, and work with, not against.

The soft blue glow of the liquid-crystal display spread over Gideon's fingers. The GPS unit provided just enough light for the user and was virtually undetectable to anyone more than a few feet away. He was still over two hundred yards from his objective and another five hundred from the squat buildings that housed the men, technology, and machines that ran the base. His destination lay southeast, into the thickest part of the forest. Gideon adjusted his approach, peering into the darkness, marking his next step with his eyes but burning the path he would take into his subconscious. He would not proceed until he could move with his eyes closed if need be.

So far, the evening had passed without incident. Bypassing the first level of security had been easy. The razor-wire-topped fence was not monitored for sound or vibration. It was a physical deterrent only, meant to keep local residents, curious tourists, and wandering herds of deer off the base. Cutting his way through had been a simple exercise of time and patience.

The twelve-foot section just inside the fence was another matter entirely. It also provided further evidence that he was on the right track. This was the place he needed to be.

Most low-level military installations would not have pressure-sensitive security pads hidden under a thin veneer of topsoil. They would not have camouflaged video surveillance ringing the base. Absent would be the infrared motion sensors capable of detecting the slightest movement or trace of body heat. Yet this facility had all three.

Again, he asked himself, *Why here?*

It had taken him some time to bypass the security, but it wasn't impossible, if you knew what you were doing. And he did.

Once inside the fence, a well-placed shot into a distant oak, the barbed dart carrying a thin line of rope, enabled him to bypass the sensors. He hung upside down, suspended a few feet over the pressure-sensitive pads. There was only one way to avoid the motion sensors. One inch at a time up the rope line, slow as molasses on a cold winter day. The equipment's sensitivity couldn't be set too high, as every time the wind blew, the sensors would be set off. Still, it was time-consuming, and he hated being so exposed. He didn't relax until his strong arms had pulled him safely across.

Next, he had to deceive the infrared sensors. That's where access to technology came in handy. A lightweight, carbon-ceramic alloy developed by NASA and used on the space shuttle lined the middle layer of Gideon's clothing. Both materials were superb heat conductors. Woven into the threads of his jumpsuit, the space-age material conducted body warmth, just like an electric current, into two heat stores located inside the rubber soles of his boots. Troops assigned to the extreme polar regions used this application extensively, and with it Gideon reduced his heat signature to that of a small rodent.

Video surveillance was the final hurdle he had to overcome. He had to commend base security on their selection of technology. The model they employed was highly sensitive, capable of quickly following and zooming in on even the smallest target. Even worse, no matter where he chose to go, he would be within their lines of sight. There was no way to know whether the cameras were equipped with night vision, so Gideon assumed that they were. There was no easy countermeasure for this technology, so he needed to rely on detailed planning to minimize his exposure. It took a couple of nights of surveillance for him to choose a remote location, one where the equipment was set the farthest apart. This was the biggest risk, one Gideon was grudgingly forced to take. Infiltrating at the apex of the cameras' range, during the dead of night, he hoped to be at the point where they were least effective. If he chose wrong or miscalculated, security would be on him before he knew it.

The gamble paid off. Climbing down from the tree, he remained motionless for almost an hour, detecting nothing extraordinary, before deciding it was safe to continue on with the mission.

Security was not due to patrol this area for another hour. Over the past few nights he had watched patiently from outside the fence line. He studied the behavior of the teams, their routines, the way they reacted to the environment. Sometimes he was high up in the trees. Other times, he was just a few feet away, buried under the moss or tight up against a fallen log. There were three different units that patrolled the base each night. Each team was assigned four men—one on point, two flankers, the last taking up the rear. The diamond shape was a classic military design used in patrols and searches. The Secret Service even used a modified version of it to protect the President of the United States.

Gideon spent the nights mapping their patrol routes and learning their routine. Unfortunately, other than their schedules, nothing about their patrols was routine. In an effort to stay unpredictable, they randomly rotated their search patterns. The soldiers even changed places and shared patrol responsibilities. The weapons they used from one patrol to the next varied as well. Sometimes they brought along heavy firepower, other times they packed light and were more mobile. Most important, these men were highly trained and motivated. Whoever led them deserved a lot of respect. There was no urgency to the patrols. They were methodical in their searches. They seldom spoke, using hand signals and the knowledge of each other to communicate. No cigarettes were smoked. No waste was discarded. They were quiet and disciplined. The heavy technology ringing the base was only the first line of defense. These men were the real threat to Gideon.

His senses were primed as he wove his way from tree to shrub to rocky outcropping. The forest moved, swayed, and crept in around him as he moved. Calculating his movements by memory, he knew that he was near his destination. The sudden flush of warmth on his neck brought him up short, his senses instantly alert. He turned sharply around, looking for the source. His weapon aimed into the trees, searching.

He was closer than he thought.

Again, warmth enveloped the back of his exposed neck. He spun around, the hair on his neck and arms rising on end. He swept the area in a complete circle . . . nothing, just the forest. He dropped to one knee, his weapon raised, sighted. His finger was on the trigger, applying dangerous pounds of pressure as he aimed in the direction the "breath" had come from. His heartbeat raced. Perspiration ran down the back of his neck. His armpits were already drenched in sweat.

He waited.

There it was again, this time on his forehead. Warm, moist air, heavily laden with the musty smell of old earth, reached out to caress his skin. He stared into the darkness, seeing nothing. The dense canopy overhead acted like a thick blanket, effectively blocking the moonlight. He could not even see his own hands in front of his face.

Gideon lowered his weapon to the ground and pulled a pair of night-vision goggles from his pack. He placed the goggles over his eyes and swiveled his head from left to right. Bright shades of green popped to life as the night-vision lenses amplified the little available ambient light.

Nothing. Ample vegetation, thick tree trunks, low hanging branches reaching in every direction, but no indication where the air was coming from. He reached to a small toggle on the side of his glasses and switched to infrared. Instantly, the light source went away. In its place he found himself looking at a large orange square radiating heat from the middle of a tree stump. The heat signature shined like a beacon in the darkness.

Gideon reached out his hand. Suddenly, the square began to glow a deeper red. The screen pulsed and beat like a human heart. Milliseconds later, he felt a warm draft flow past his outstretched fingers to envelop his face before moving gracefully past.

I'll be damned, he thought.

Kulbeda Weather Station is located on the southeastern edge of Cape Henlopen State Park, at the confluence of the Atlantic Ocean and the Delaware Bay. Facing the Atlantic, the station is a few short miles from popular Delaware beaches and tourist attractions surrounding the small community of Curtis Cove. The United States Army had established Kulbeda as a military base during World War II as a protection against Germany's infamous U-boats. The station was built atop solid bedrock, and the Army installed camouflaged bunkers and gun emplacements in the dunes and on the rocky outcrops that rise over eighty feet above sea level. No shots, however, were ever fired during the war. In the late 1940s, the base was turned into a weather station run by the Air Force.

Now, post-September 11, those WW II installations were nothing more than empty shells, relics to remind Americans that their borders have never been truly safe. Officially, the base's mission had not changed, though technology had increased its capabilities and scope.

Unofficially, however, Gideon suspected it had changed quite a bit. In planning his infiltration, he reviewed every blueprint and map available of the surrounding area, including the classified ones. Nothing indicated the existence of a secret facility. Moreover, Director Gorrell's covert investigation had also come up empty. His boss had turned over every rock within his grasp, yet he had discovered nothing that pointed to Kulbeda.

Still, the evidence was incontrovertible. Something *was* under the base.

The structure that held the vent was nothing more than a molded concrete pillar made to look like a tree stump. It was clever deception, painted to resemble the surrounding trees and camouflaged by dense shrubs and thicket. Gideon never would have discovered it without the aid of infrared imagery.

One of the perks of working for the Central Intelligence Agency that he liked most was the access it afforded him. Access to the information that led him to suspect the Kulbeda Weather Station, to the infrared satellite imagery he used to pinpoint four different heat signatures, this one the largest, to the technology that enabled him to penetrate its defenses. There were many things about his job he disliked, but the access it granted him wasn't one of them.

Gideon carefully inspected the vent surface and the surrounding area, looking for video surveillance, motion detectors, intrusion sensors, or other devices that would alert base security of his intentions. The area was clear, and nothing was attached to the metal grate. Camouflage was the only deterrent.

Gideon pulled a small toolset from his backpack. Using a screwdriver, he carefully removed the vent and lowered it to the ground. Next, he pulled a large bundle of nylon climbing rope from his pack. He tied one end around the concrete stump and lowered the rest into the opening. He then pulled the black balaclava off his head and leaned into the shaft. There was nothing to see. He ran a calloused hand through his short hair and put the night-vision goggles back on. Even with the goggles, he could not see more than a few feet into the darkness. Using the flashlight was out of the question.

Gideon took off the goggles and stowed them away in his pack. He then removed his field jacket, stripping down to a black, long-sleeve shirt. Next, he found a secure area nearby to hide and camouflage his gear. It was going to be a snug fit, too tight to bring everything with him.

At just under six feet tall, he was in top physical condition. His lean, muscular body, honed and sharpened by years of rigorous training and exercise, was just slim enough to fit into the narrow shaft. The space was only twenty-four inches wide and just deep enough for him to work his arms freely.

"The things I do for my country," he muttered aloud.

Gideon lowered himself into the shaft, holding tight to the nylon rope. The muscles in his arms rippled as he dropped deeper into the black hole. Darkness enveloped him, and the opening above became nothing more than a receding image of sanity. The flashlight attached to his waist was useless in the confined space.

Down he went, hand over hand, deeper into the darkness without any sign of the bottom. The silence weighed heavily upon him, a constant reminder of how truly alone he was. The only noise came from his labored breathing and from the pounding heart that roared in his ears. Sweat gushed from every pore on his body.

Gideon quickly learned that the vent served two purposes, first to exhale the warm fumes of whatever lay below and then to inhale fresh air from above.

Despite the physical exertion, the cool air chilled Gideon's skin and threatened to tighten and cramp his worn and tired muscles. Meanwhile, the rush of warm air made the nylon rope slick with moisture. The combination sapped him of valuable strength, forcing him to fight past the discomfort, fatigue, and tight quarters. It was harder going than he thought it would be, and he quickly found himself struggling against gravity.

He hastened his descent. Fifteen feet turned into thirty. Before he knew it, he was passing the fifty-foot mark. After eighty feet he began to worry. How far down did this shaft go? Was the rope long enough? Would he have the strength to pull himself up afterward?

The desire to move faster grew stronger every minute. Time was running out. He had been descending for almost fifteen minutes. By his calculations, less than twenty feet of rope remained. If he was wrong, if he had miscalculated, he might end up falling to his death. Who would find him then? More importantly, would he ever be found?

The mental strain took its toll on Gideon. Unwelcome thoughts of doubt and failure intruded on his concentration. He was not prone to claustrophobia, but he suddenly felt entombed in metal. The sides of the shaft seemed to squeeze closer together. The crush of gravity pulled harder on his tired hands. The realization that the shaft might become his coffin began to take hold.

Sensing he was dangerously close to a panic attack, Gideon recalled his early days in the Army. Nobody back then was harder on him than his tough-as-nails drill instructors. During officer-candidate training they relentlessly pushed him to excel, to succeed, to become a strong leader. More than once, that rigorous, oftentimes brutal, training pushed him beyond his physical and mental limits, forcing him to fully understand the capabilities of his body and mind. That knowledge would now save his life. After a quick internal assessment, he realized he was nowhere close to the limits he had once been pushed to. He took a deep breath and let it out slowly. He closed his eyes and repeated the exercise. His mind and body relaxed as the panic receded.

Gideon resumed his descent. Through sheer force of will he maintained a steady pace. His hope rose as he passed a small duct. Two more quickly followed. He finally came to an opening large enough to accommodate his size. He crawled into the cavity on his hands and knees. Exhausted, he sat with his legs dangling over the edge. His hands and arms were numb and shaking, and his breathing was quick and shallow. He was close to hyperventilating. Clearing his mind, he sought to calm his tired muscles and bring his body back to normal. This wasn't the first time he had been pushed to his limits. Following combat situations, it was not unusual to experience the downside of adrenaline. He knew how to deal with this kind of physical exhaustion and pent-up stress, and soon enough he had his body back under control.

Breathing better, Gideon coiled the rope. There was not much left. A few feet of the black nylon was all that remained between him and the bottom of this seemingly endless shaft. He was now approximately one hundred feet under Kulbeda Station.

Gideon removed his leather gloves and let the cool metal soothe his sore hands. After a few minutes of rest, he turned back around and began to blindly feel his way into the shaft. Almost immediately the echo of a soft whistle caused him to pause. The hollow sound grew louder, but not by much, until he was suddenly enveloped in a current of warm moistness. The breath of humid air flowed past him and on toward the surface. A short time later it stopped.

This was some kind of main exhaust trunk, he surmised. The mysterious airflow he discovered while back on the surface emanated from this shaft.

At this depth he was much closer to the flow's source. Gideon took a deep breath and let his olfactory senses go to work. At first he detected only the scent of aged wood, machine oil, mildew, and rust. But like tasting a fine wine, his nose began to pick up on other, more confusing scents. Strangely, the exhaust reminded him of home—the neighborhood he used to play in as a child, afternoon baseball with friends at a local park. What he sensed was oddly familiar yet completely out of place. Not knowing what to make of it, he chose to ignore it and move on.

Gideon reached down and pulled a small pebble from the sole of his boot. Peering into the darkness, he tossed the nugget away from him. The sound was small and tinny, but he heard the rock bounce and skitter until it came to rest some distance away.

The shaft was longer than he imagined it might be. He began to shuffle forward on his hands and knees, always mindful of the noise he made. The darkness was absolute, and his night-vision goggles were back on the surface, hidden with his backpack. For over one hundred yards he crawled, completely blind in his confined surroundings. Finally, he came to a ninety-degree turn in the shaft. With no other options available to him, he turned right and followed the duct.

Long minutes passed without change before he saw the first signs of light. A soft glow emanated from a small vent cut into the bottom of the shaft. Gideon reached it quickly, but there was nothing outside to tell him where he was. He continued forward, growing increasingly nervous about his decision to come alone.

Again, doubt plagued him. Agent Reyes was the only one who knew he was here. His boss would never have sanctioned this kind of reconnaissance. It was too risky. Gideon's unease was magnified when he came upon a curved section in the duct. This time, it dropped down at a fairly sharp angle. He had no idea how steep the shaft was or how far it descended. What happened if it suddenly dropped into nothingness?

Gideon was tired of wrestling with his fears. He was a professional. He was not about to go back simply because of adversity. He never would have qualified as an Army Ranger if he had given up after a little pain. Special Forces would never have accepted him if he was a quitter. And the CIA would not have recruited him if not for his ability to think outside the box.

Gideon made up his mind, swiveled on his rear, and pushed off.

Sheet metal and side vents flew past in a rush as he slid down. The occasional cobweb clung to his face. His soft clothing did little to slow his descent. In fact, he gained speed with each passing foot. The free fall continued for another fifteen seconds before he came to a sudden stop as the shaft leveled out. He must have slid downward another seventy feet, maybe closer to a hundred. Now he was truly trapped, as there was no way he could climb back up that shaft without his tools. The incline was far too steep.

Gideon took a ragged breath, not realizing that he had been holding it all along. The end of the duct was only a few feet away. He moved to the large screen covering the shaft. The area outside the vent was dark, but he could make out the rudimentary structure of walls, a window, and electrical wiring. Pulling the combat knife from the sheath attached to his right calf, he pried open the bottom of the screen and shimmied out of the shaft.

The room was small, six feet square at the most. A round, stained-glass window provided some illumination, though the decoration obstructed the view outside the room. Still, Gideon could tell from the dim light that it was mostly dark.

Gideon stood up and bumped into the ceiling. He cursed silently to himself and reached above his head to feel the thin timber planking that made up the roof joists. He pulled out his flashlight and turned it on, letting only the slightest sliver of light shine on the floor as he searched for an exit. A small trapdoor was located in the back corner of the room.

He extinguished the light and pulled his Sig Sauer from its holster. He thumbed the safety off and slowly lifted the hatch. He wished he had the MP5, but he had left it behind on the surface along with the rest of his gear.

The room below was quiet and empty. A small, narrow ladder led down. He carefully descended the ladder, making sure to close the hatch behind him. Now inside a larger room, he could make out the faint lines of long wooden benches running in rows all the way to the front of the building. The windows were also at the front, flanking a small wooden door.

Skirting the benches, Gideon made his way to the windows. The panes of leaded glass were glazed over and emitted a soft glow. He could not see the outside, so he listened for several minutes, trying hard to discern even the slightest noise. Hearing none, he next inspected the door. It was small as well, slightly shorter than he was, and narrow. Made of wood, there was nothing extraordinary about it. The lock was old but of a standard design, and there appeared to be no electronic devices or alarms attached to it.

What the hell, he thought in silence. He gripped the rust-pitted, metal handle and turned it slowly. A soft click signaled that the door had opened. Breathing heavily, he slowly opened the door and peeked through the crack. What he saw took his breath away.

"Oh, my God," he said out loud, not caring who heard him.

CHAPTER 12

Beneath Kulbeda Station

Gideon exited the small room and walked right into a Norman Rockwell painting.

The nighttime image before him was surreal, yet substantially real. His mind rallied to absorb the awesome and bewildering sight, though he was not sure how to process the information his brain was receiving.

This is not possible, he thought, mouth open wide in shock. *I must be dreaming.*

Gideon walked carefully down three wooden steps to stand on the concrete sidewalk of a long, narrow street. Across from him, a small neon sign flashed ICE CREAM in the window of Andy's Pharmacy. To the right was a Wells Fargo Bank, the black-rimmed gold letters inscribed on the large double doors. To the left was Nick's Barber Shop, the red, white, and blue barber pole turning lazily by the front door. Farther down the street, Gideon could see a fire station, a library, and a fresh-meat market.

In the other direction, he saw the shape of a large town hall flanked by a post office and a police station. Interspersed throughout were small houses—Capes, Colonials, and ranches, many with white picket fences and green lawns.

Gideon crossed the street, stealth and security fresh on his mind. Turning around, he stared at the building he had just exited. It was a small white chapel with a plain red door. The stained-glass window on the second floor sat underneath a tall white steeple. Even in the darkness, he could make out the miniature cross affixed to the top.

The lane before him was lined with antique cast-iron streetlights, their soft glow providing light to this strange world. Cherry-red fire hydrants were placed at regular intervals on both sides of the street. A police call box stood out in the distance, the blue orb on top glowing brightly.

This place looks straight out of the fifties, Gideon thought.

Equally amazing were the trees. Decorative maple, oak, and pine trees rose from the ground on lawns, next to houses, beside the dozen shops that made up what Gideon believed to be the downtown area of this . . . place. He walked over to a maple tree and pulled off a leaf. He rolled it around in his hand and brought it up to his nose. It was real!

But this is not real!

Gideon snapped back to the moment and raised his weapon. He checked his surroundings. In the houses, most windows were closed and the lights were off. In those with lights on, the occasional flutter of movement indicated occupancy. The soft sound of music reached his ears, as did occasional voices and laughter.

This place is inhabited, but by whom? he thought.

Gideon raised his eyes to witness another amazing sight. Above him was the night sky—the same one he had just left. But that could not be. He was close to two hundred feet below the surface. Yet he saw stars, millions of them, filling the night sky.

His gaze rested on the constellation Orion. On Orion's belt, the stars Mintaka, Alnilam, and Alnitak shined brightly. So, too, did the reddish star Betelgeuse. Orion's head—marked by three stars, the brightest of which is Meissa—could be easily discerned. The red glow in the middle of Orion's sword was the Orion Nebula. The constellation was right where it should be this time of year, northeast of the full moon, which also shined brightly.

He had always loved the stars, especially when he was in the field and away from the bright lights of cities. They soothed his soul, calmed him, allowed him to exist at a cosmic level where he could forget his worries and forgive his actions. Now he was looking at the impossible.

A bright streak of light crashed into Gideon's fragile sense of reality. A shooting star raced across the sky, its tail long and beautiful before burning itself out as it entered Earth's atmosphere. The display lasted but a moment before fading into nothing more than cosmic debris.

He could not explain what his eyes saw, so he did not try. Instead, he forced himself to view his surroundings with tactical objectivity. For all intents and purposes he was in enemy territory, and he needed to behave as such.

The sign before him read NORTH MAIN STREET. He crouched low and followed the road. He stayed in the shadows, racing from the corner of one building to another. The sudden flurry of birds startled him. Amazingly, chickadees and nuthatches flew from one tree to another and into nearby bushes. Sparrows flitted along the rooftops. Gideon ran a hand through his hair and across the back of his neck. What next? Were Ozzie and Harriet going to invite him in for milk and cookies?

When he reached the first intersection, he crouched behind a mailbox. That's when he realized what his eyes and mind had missed before. Too busy absorbing the fantasy, he did not notice the most obvious fact: he was in a dollhouse—a very large one to be sure—but too planned and precise to be anything else.

This town, and everything in it, was small, almost miniature. That's why he had bumped his head on the ceiling in the chapel, why the ladder going down looked so slim, and why the doors were his height. It explained why he barely fit behind the mailbox on the corner. The entire town was shrunken to only two-thirds the normal size. The streets and sidewalks were narrower. The trees were trimmed shorter. The houses and buildings, though structurally and aesthetically accurate, were made smaller. It was as if the whole town was made to fit a diminutive type of people, or, Gideon thought, more likely to fit the space inside this cavity, as big as it was.

But for what purpose?

The other interesting fact that came to light was the era in which the town was built. Judging from the architecture, layout, street signs, and lamps, this town was built sometime in the 1950s. That's why Gideon was convinced he had entered a time warp. The innocence of the place, the conformity and sameness, spoke directly to that conservative, uptight decade. From the barbershop, to the town hall, to the white picket fences, this place was lost in time.

Gideon stopped briefly to marvel at the engineering, the architecture, the technology, and the sheer will it took to pull off something like this. The scale of it was immense, yet this place's existence was virtually unknown. To keep this location a secret required a commitment and temerity he had never known the United States government to have. Public relations disasters like Area 51, also known as Groom Lake and Dreamland, simply highlighted the country's inability to keep a secret.

That thought brought him back to Harrison Gorrell and the reason for this unauthorized mission. Gideon's boss wanted information, proof that something was going on here. The only way Gideon could do that was to follow the evidence, no matter where it led him. Judging his surroundings, he was getting a pretty clear picture about just how big this situation was.

He reached the end of the next block and stopped at the intersection. He still couldn't see where the town ended. Diagonally across from him was the largest structure he'd seen thus far. The engraved sign above the white doors read LITTLETON TOWN HALL.

Gideon frowned. Very funny. Someone had a wry sense of humor.

Across from the building was a small park lined with equally small trees and hedges. In the park's center was a pond, approximately twenty feet wide and fifty feet long. The pool was shaped like a figure eight, widest at the ends and narrow—about eight feet across—in the middle. A fountain splashed noisily on the far end, and a wooden bridge spanned the narrowest part.

An ornate gazebo painted a light green, red, and yellow sat on the near side of the park. The other side held a playground and picnic area. A small grassy knoll rose and fell before ending at the next intersection. A narrow street and sidewalk ran around the entire park, which was roughly the size of a football field. Overlooking the park were a dozen homes. Most were dark, but a few had their porch or walkway lights on.

The park looked to be the center of the town, a common area; and like the spokes of a wagon wheel, all the streets—six in all—originated from this point. Where they went, and how long they were, Gideon did not know.

On the surface, this community looked peaceful and serene. Gideon could but wonder what lay beneath this facade. He crossed the road, mindful to stay between the streetlights, and entered the park. Moving low, he crossed the bridge and started toward the nearest cluster of trees. The grass under his feet was slick with evening dew.

His destination was the town hall. From the corner, he had noticed a darkened alley that ran next to the building. If he could reach it undetected, he might find a way into the building. He was only guessing, but in most towns, the town hall was where you found information. Why wouldn't that be true here as well?

Passing the swing set, he was brought up short by the sound of a little voice.

"Hello."

Gideon spun around, prepared to fire his pistol at the threat. At the last moment, he pulled the weapon up and took his finger off the trigger. He stared in stunned disbelief. Sitting on the swings, blanketed by the darkness, were two children—both girls—staring back at him with intelligent eyes that sparkled in the night.

"We've been waiting for you," one of the girls said.

A shiver ran down Gideon's spine. He dared not answer, lest his voice give him away. Instead, he nodded his head and warily moved closer.

"You don't have to be afraid," the second girl said, sounding very much like the first.

"Everything's going to be all right," the other finished. She said again, "We've been waiting for you."

"Waiting for me?" Gideon replied quietly, incredulous. His eyes darted about and scanned the nearby houses, trees, and shrubs.

"Nobody knows you're here," the first girl whispered conspiratorially.

"Just us," the other finished, her head bobbing up and down.

Gideon moved farther into the shadows to get a better look at the girls.

They were identical twins, young, maybe eight or nine years old. Both had matching purple pajamas with long sleeves. Pink fluffy slippers covered their feet. It was too dark to tell for certain, but they both appeared eerily calm, unconcerned with the unusual hour and circumstances of their meeting. Indeed, the girls behaved as if they truly were expecting him.

But that was impossible.

"What are you girls doing here?" Gideon asked gently. Inside, his heart was racing, and he had to fight to maintain control.

"We told you already," the girl on the left said with innocence.

"But how did you know I would come?"

"We wished it," the other replied, smiling proudly.

Gideon frowned skeptically. "You *wished* for me to come?"

Both girls grinned happily and nodded their heads. Two ponytails bobbed in unison.

Gideon shook his head. "What are your names?"

"My name is Emily," the girl on the right replied, "and this is my sister, Amy."

"You girls live here?"

"Uh-huh," they answered in unison.

Then Emily lowered her voice and whispered, "But this isn't a real town. It's just pretend."

Gideon smiled.

"What's your name?" Amy asked.

"John Gideon," he answered without thinking.

The girls looked at each other and giggled.

"Where are your parents?" he asked.

"Dead," the girls replied.

The girl named Amy elaborated. "They died in a car crash when we were babies." She looked over at her sibling with a pout on her face. "It was Emily's fault."

"Nuh-uh," Emily responded. "It was an accident. Uncle said so."

As the girls argued, their voices rose to a dangerous level. Gideon admonished both of them and asked them to whisper. Like they were playing a game, the girls nodded their heads enthusiastically.

"So, you live with your uncle?" Gideon asked.

"No," Emily responded. "He's dead, too."

"So are our aunt and cousin."

"What happened to them?" he asked.

"They were killed by the men."

The girls were so sure in their statements that he had to ask. "Who killed them?"

Both girls made a face, not of anger or hurt, but of childlike distaste. "Mr. DeKay did," Emily said.

Amy continued. "He's the one who brought us here."

Gideon rocked back on his heels. DeKay? He knew someone by that name. His pulse quickened. It couldn't be. Cautiously, he asked, "Do you mean Cross DeKay?"

The girls nodded.

Gideon was stunned. "Did he kill your parents, too?" he asked.

The girls shook their heads.

"I told you," Amy stubbornly replied. "That was Emily's fault."

Gideon interjected before the girls could begin arguing again. "When did this happen?"

"We were two then," Emily answered. She smiled and said, "We're almost eight now."

Gideon couldn't believe what he was hearing. DeKay had killed the girls' family and kidnapped them? Why? It had been years since he'd even heard the name DeKay. What was he doing here?

"What . . . do you do . . . in this town?" Gideon pried. The girls were his only link to the reason behind this place. He needed to get as much information as possible from them. "What is this place and why are you here? What does DeKay do?"

Before they could answer, the sound of a woman's voice reached Gideon's ears. The girls heard it, too. She was calling for them.

Emily frowned. "That's Dr. Sossoman."

"She looks after us," Amy finished. "We have to go now, or she'll get in trouble."

Gideon began to hear other sounds, doors being opened and closed, windows raised. Then he heard other voices joining in with the woman's. Men's voices. Urgent voices.

"Mr. Gideon, will you be coming back?" Amy asked, hopeful.

"If you want me to," Gideon replied.

She smiled. "You promise?"

Without hesitation, Gideon responded, "Yes."

Then he began to worry. What if the girls told DeKay about his visit? His cover would be blown. Also, how was he going to get out of here? Until now, he had given his escape very little thought. Gideon started to ask, but the girls were way ahead of him.

"You need to leave. Now!" Amy said urgently. She pointed behind Gideon. "Go that way, behind the town hall. That's the way you need to go to get out. And don't worry. We won't tell."

Amy jumped off the swing and hugged Gideon tightly around the neck.

Then she kissed him on the cheek. The girl appeared to be very happy. Emily merely smiled shyly, her head bowed low.

"Come back," Amy said. Then she pleaded, "Please, don't forget us."

Gideon didn't have time to reply as the girls turned abruptly and ran off into the darkness. He followed their progress until they exited the park and ran up a side street. The voices were getting louder, more insistent, and organized.

The girls were correct. He did'nt have much time before the search converged on the park itself.

Keeping low, he scrambled to the edge of the playground and sprinted across the narrow road to the alley beside the town hall. Once again concealed in darkness, he sat back and watched. Moments later, he observed a large group of men and women come together on the commons, meeting under the gazebo. Most were dressed casually in pajamas or sweats. A few, however, played the role of policemen.

The two girls were with them. Each held a hand of an older woman.

That must be Dr. Sossoman, Gideon thought to himself.

From the looks of it, Dr. Sossoman had been roused from her night's sleep by the girls' absence. She looked tired and anxious, but with the girls now in her care, he could see that relief was quickly replacing her apprehension.

Gideon settled in to watch the town's inhabitants, when he heard a scuffling sound behind him. Responding to instinct and training, he dropped and rolled, smoothly coming to one knee in a combat firing position. His swift actions startled the man sneaking up on him, who quickly raised his hands in the air.

"P-please, don't h-hurt me. I'm here to help you. The girls, they asked me to show you the way out." Slowly, the man lowered his arms and turned away, motioning for Gideon to follow.

Gideon didn't budge, and his pistol never left the man's head.

"Y-you don't understand," the man said urgently, though he moved slowly back to Gideon. "When the girls get out, they shut the town down. Once they get back, no one can leave. They'll look everywhere to see if anyone got in. A lot of bad people want those girls. If we stay here, they'll find you!"

Gideon's eyes narrowed as he took in the man. He had light blond hair, pale blue eyes, and fair, almost translucent, skin. His lips were not the normal red color but bordered on a light shade of pink. Dressed in blue coveralls, he walked with an awkward gait, and his head listed to one side. His voice was hesitant, almost unsure, as if speaking was something he did with great reluctance. And he was small, just over five feet tall. Not imposing at all, though Gideon had seen enough tonight that he trusted nothing.

"Put your hands behind your head."

The man did as instructed, and Gideon proceeded to search him for weapons and communications equipment.

When he finished, the man again pleaded with him to follow. Reluctantly, Gideon nodded his head. The man took off, scrambling down the alley to the back of the town hall.

Alone in this foreign environment, with no visible means of escape, Gideon had no choice but to trust his instincts. And his instincts told him this man was here for a reason. The girls had pointed him in the right direction, and this man was waiting for him. If it was a trap, all the man had to do was sound the alarm, and the town would have converged on his position. If he was an assassin, Gideon would be dead right now. In the dark alley, the man could have put a bullet behind his ear while he crouched in the shadows. Instead, the stranger fumbled awkwardly, sounding his shuffling presence in a nonthreatening way. And then he offered assistance. Providence demanded that Gideon listen to his intuition. His immediate safety was now in the hands of the stranger.

Following the small man, Gideon crossed a street and ran through the side yard of a dark house. The farther he went, the darker it got. After a hundred yards, Gideon could scarcely see the running form in front of him. The man he followed appeared and disappeared into the darkness, forcing Gideon to rely more on his senses. When the man suddenly stopped, Gideon almost ran him over.

"We're here," the man said, his breath coming in short gasps.

Gideon was hardly winded. Before he could ask where "here" was, the world lit up with a billion candles. Dark suddenly became light. Night turned into day.

He raised his forearm to shield his eyes. It took almost a full minute before he was able to see again. And when he looked, he discovered a sight that both explained the mystery of this location and confirmed that he knew nothing at all. Whatever he had suspected before was dwarfed by this discovery.

"Come," his guide said, forcing Gideon to pay attention. "We must go. Now. They'll be here any minute."

Indeed, Gideon could hear the noisy pursuit of men running in their direction. Knowing he had no choice, that he was committed to this line of action, Gideon gave himself over to the stranger. Besides, he was too numb to think for himself. He had just seen a world reborn, and it was breathtaking.

This was going to take time to absorb.

CHAPTER 13

Five Years Earlier
Redfield, Iowa

"Alpha Team is in position."

"Bravo Team is a go."

"Delta Team is ready. The home is surrounded. Everything's quiet. Alpha and Bravo, you're clear to enter the structure when ready."

"Roger that, Delta leader. Bravo Team, on my mark. Remember, by the book. In and out. No witnesses. No survivors."

"Clear on that, Alpha leader."

The occupants of the house could not hear the hushed whispers and stealthy movements of the special operations unit getting into position outside. The humming noise from the air conditioners fighting the hot and muggy night effectively drowned out any noise. Still, the soldiers moved with quietly, their rubber-soled boots scarcely heard above the men's heavy, excited breath.

In a well-rehearsed maneuver, the two teams expertly picked the locks and entered the ranch house. Alpha Team entered from the back door, Bravo from the side at the large living room window. Delta Team maintained area integrity and secured their extraction route.

Strategically placed infrared sensors showed that the occupants were where they should be. Sensitive listening devices confirmed that everyone was asleep. Two adults were in the front left quadrant, spooned together in the middle of the bed. The teenager was in the back room to the left. Acoustic sensors placed on the window further indicated she had fallen asleep with headphones on. Two more children were in the rear bedroom.

The teams were ahead of schedule.

Silently, the two four-man units converged in the home's center. The agents moved in a stacked position, their left hand on the shoulder of the man in front of them, the right clutching a weapon.

Using hand signals, the teams split up, one going to the front, and the other turning right, down a long hallway. Everyone wore military-grade night-vision goggles, enabling them to see clearly in the dark house.

At the adults' bedroom, the team leader turned the doorknob and entered the room. Quickly, two men passed, black KA-BAR combat knives in their hands. The men crept to the edge of the bed and glanced at one another. In one motion, each clasped his hand over the mouth of their victim. Aimed for the soft flesh of the neck, their razor-sharp knives carved easily through muscle, cartilage, and artery.

Death came quickly.

Down the hall, a similar scene unfolded. This time, however, the soldier opted to break the girl's neck, cleanly snapping it in two with one violent twist.

Seconds later, the two teams merged back into the hallway, stacked again in formation as they moved to the children's bedroom.

The tension and urgency was palpable.

Everything was going smoothly. Too smoothly. The ease by which the operation was proceeding heightened their senses.

Alpha leader moved silently to the last room in the hallway. Turning the knob, he cringed as the door's hinges creaked loudly. Not wasting the element of surprise, the eight men charged into the dark room . . . and stopped.

"Hello."

"We've been waiting for you."

The grown men stared in disbelief. The two children were not asleep. Both girls were sitting upright in bed, dressed, their short legs dangling over the sides, feet far from reaching the floor.

A shiver ran down Alpha leader's spine. He dared not answer; instead he nodded his head, and two men approached the girls.

"You don't have to be afraid," the first girl said.

"Everything's going to be all right," the other finished.

Without responding, the agents placed rags soaked with a sedative over the girls' mouths and noses, holding them there until they fell unconscious. The girls did not resist. From behind, two more men appeared with black nylon sacks. Inside the sacks were two small pigs. The dead pigs were laid on the bed and placed under the covers. The unconscious girls were placed inside the sacks, the zippers drawn around them.

"Right," Alpha leader said into his microphone. "Everyone out, quickly. Bravo leader, set the charges to blow five minutes after we evacuate. Delta leader, we're coming out the back."

Shaken by the encounter, Alpha leader ordered his team to exfiltrate, leaving nothing but the remains of their victims behind. His new wards were slung over the shoulders of two large men.

Moments later the teams disappeared into the night.

Present Day
Littleton

Cross DeKay exited the small house on the corner and looked out over Littleton. It had been almost six years since he led the mission to abduct the girls, and he was beginning to regret it. He didn't like surprises, especially those that came in pairs or in the middle of the night. More importantly, he hated the feeling of not knowing how the girls got out of their room, how they evaded their watchers, or how they made it to the center of Littleton undetected. It was now approaching two hours since he ordered the town locked down, and he still didn't have any answers.

How long were they gone? What did they do in that time frame? Worst of all, he hated not knowing what was going on in their minds. The two girls were devious and manipulative under the best of circumstances, but lately, their attempts at subterfuge had become bolder, blatant even. They were testing his ability to command, and that was unacceptable.

"Who had the watch?" DeKay demanded as he walked briskly toward the center of town. "How did they get out this time? Damn it, I thought we had this covered!"

"We're looking into it," one of DeKay's subordinates reported before taking off in a sprint.

DeKay stopped abruptly to square off at the woman walking next to him. Surprised by the change in momentum, the woman stumbled awkwardly before turning back to DeKay. Her clumsiness only served to anger the man even more.

"Your instructions were explicit," he charged. "Gain the girls' trust, get inside their heads, and predict their actions. You're the child psychologist here. You tell me—why can't we keep these girls under control? What's wrong with them?"

Dr. Majel Sossoman bit back a reply that would surely have earned DeKay's ire, probably an official reprimand, or perhaps even worse. She had heard stories of the man's unorthodox methods at maintaining security. Trouble employees often went missing for days and then suddenly returned with no explanation of their absence. But she knew, as a trained psychologist, that these individuals weren't the same. They were different, changed, defeated. It was in their eyes, their demeanor. They exhibited signs of acute stress and trauma. Some never returned at all, and she shivered to think about what happened to *them*. As a result, DeKay was universally feared and despised for his tactics. But he got the job done, and that's all that mattered around here.

Sossoman, on the other hand, took her feelings for DeKay one step further. She openly loathed the man and railed against everything he stood for. If it weren't for the children, she would have found a way out of here long before now.

Since discovering the twins' disappearance tonight, she had been expecting the questions DeKay asked. Still, she weighed her answers carefully before replying.

"You have to understand, psychology draws a distinction between rebelliousness as a youth and disobedience as a child. The normal seven-year-old child will disobey through carelessness, simply to reject something they dislike. At that age, actions are instinctual, visceral, and violent. But they're also short-lived. Once the emotion is released, the child moves on, focusing on the next fixation that will stimulate them emotionally or physically. These girls, despite their young age, behave like teenagers. As such, the very notion of obedience is incompatible with temporal gratification. They *choose* to disobey. They're quite advanced for their age, and their disobedience stems from the subordinate nature of their environment."

"In English, please, Doctor." Cross DeKay was not a patient man to begin with, and tonight's lapse in security tested his already low tolerance for failure and incompetence.

Sossoman eyed DeKay warily. More and more she recognized behavioral tendencies in him that bordered on schizophrenia. The man exhibited conspicuous personality traits that, while not necessarily pathological, caused serious problems with his staff. The man's behavior was often rigid, inflexible, and maladaptive. He frequently interpreted the actions of other people as deliberately threatening or demeaning. It was a classic case of untreated paranoid personality disorder. The disorder usually surfaced by early adulthood and manifested itself by an omnipresent sense of distrust and unjustified suspicion. In DeKay's case, he was unable to acknowledge his own negative feelings toward others. Most of the time, his mistrust and suspicions were baseless, leading to persistent misinterpretation of those around him. As a result, he confided in no one, even those who had proven themselves trustworthy.

Sossoman had treated many cases of paranoid personality disorder—most of them more severe and debilitating than DeKay's—during her residency at Johns Hopkins. DeKay was at least still rooted in a sense of reality; though, in her opinion, that made him even more dangerous.

All the more reason to stay on guard, be careful, and answer the man's questions, she thought.

"What it means," Sossoman replied evenly, leaving the condescension she felt for the man from her voice, "is that the girls are testing the boundaries of their environment. And I don't simply mean this *place.* They resent the authority you exert over them. They see me as an obstacle, someone to get around, to manipulate. They know where they are. They're keenly aware of their situation and take exception to the confines and rules placed upon them. Quite simply, they're rebelling in the only way they know how, as only seven-year-olds can."

"Need I remind you, Doctor, that these children will be eight shortly?"

Sossoman shuddered at the thought. It was brutal, barbaric even, to think of the fate awaiting the twins. Under the surface, their predicament burned her heart and tore her insides apart. These children deserved better. She was their teacher and mentor. She tried to nurture them, both spiritually and emotionally. She took care of their needs and provided for their safety. Sossoman acted as a buffer, trying desperately to keep the harsh demands of DeKay—and his mission—from permanently damaging their spirit. Their fire was bright—DeKay was right about that. Her mission was to see that it continued to burn, lest DeKay decide that it needed to be doused forever.

Sossoman had come to love the girls as a mother would. She could relate to them. She knew exactly what they were going through, could feel their pain and their burden. Yet history could not be discounted. If she failed them as a psychologist, then she knew DeKay would act. He would *have* to act. And there was nothing she could do to stop him.

DeKay's interrogation of Dr. Sossoman was short-lived. The two-way radio at his side chirped to life, breaking the tension.

"What is it?" he barked into the radio.

"Sir, we've discovered a set of fresh tracks in the commons. The grass was cut this afternoon, and a trail is clearly visible on the lawn. We're checking to verify whether it belongs to any of the residents."

Angry to be interrupted over trivial news, DeKay responded testily, "Update me when you know something for sure."

The security agent wasn't finished. He paused briefly before continuing. "That's not all, sir. Teams searching the north side of town report a disturbance in the chapel. A loose ventilation grate shows signs of forced entry."

DeKay was instantly alert. He knew from the schematics that that particular ventilation trunk led directly to the surface. Littleton had been breached. He raised the radio to his lips and screamed frantically into the microphone. "Shut down! I repeat, shut everything down! I want this place secure. Now!"

Everyone within earshot stopped what they were doing and turned to the director of operations.

DeKay's natural sense of paranoia overrode any semblance of calm or civility. He could not lose control of this facility. Even though he didn't know the threat, he knew one existed.

He turned to Sossoman. His eyes were on fire, focused on the immediate future and nothing else. "I need you to stay with your wards, Doctor. Make sure nothing happens to them."

DeKay grabbed Sossoman by the upper arm, turned her around, and began walking back to the house on the corner. His grip was tight, and she felt the pain of heavy pressure from his strong fingers. It was awkward for her to walk, with her left shoulder being forced higher than her right.

"I'm moving up the timetable," DeKay said to no one in particular. "Nothing will stand in my way."

God help the girls, Sossoman thought, *if they give him any more trouble tonight.*

Too frightened to speak or act, she let herself be led.

CHAPTER 14

Gideon was safely hidden from the search of Littleton. He and his newfound accomplice were neatly tucked inside a small electrical trunk, an obscure alcove dug straight into the bedrock. No more than a sliver of light penetrated the recess, and it worked only to soften the darkness.

It had been three long, nerve-wracking hours since their hasty retreat into the small space. During that time dozens of men passed by as search parties combed Littleton for the intruder. Gideon was on a constant state of high alert. At any moment he expected an inquisitive head to pop through the narrow opening and discover their hiding place. He wouldn't have been surprised to see a smoke canister come bouncing in, a safe precaution to make sure the alcove was all clear. That's what he would have done. But no one came to check inside the crevice, and after a while the traffic slowed as the searchers came up empty.

After another fifteen minutes of silence, Gideon felt it was safe to speak. "What is this place?" he whispered. "What's going on? Who are you?"

"My name is Charlie Simmons," the man replied softly. "I'm a janitor here. I work in Littleton. Amy and Emily are my friends."

"What is Littleton?"

"It's the place where I live," he replied innocently.

Gideon was not in the mood for obfuscation. He reached over and grabbed the man by his shirt and asked again. "What is Littleton? How long have you lived there? What's the town doing here?"

Charlie looked confused. He replied again, "Littleton is where I live. I've been here a long time, though. I don't know how long. The girls live here, too. We're friends. Good friends. They help me, and I help them. I helped them get out tonight, to meet with you. I'm also going to help you get out of here."

Frustrated by the lack of direct answers, Gideon couldn't decide whether the man was simply dim-witted or being intentionally evasive. Even in the darkness, he could see that the man was smiling broadly.

"Who are these girls? What are they doing here?" he asked.

Charlie shrugged his shoulders. "I can't say."

"You can't? Or won't?"

"I can't, really."

Gideon stared hard.

"Listen," Charlie said, "I know the girls don't want to be here anymore. I know that DeKay is evil. He wants to hurt the girls. He's going to hurt Littleton, too, if you don't stop him."

"What do you mean if I don't stop him?" Gideon said. "What have I got to do with this?"

"The girls said you were coming. They wished for you, just like they did for me."

That was the second time the term *wished* had been used in relation to the girls. *What the hell is going on here?* Gideon wondered. Who was this guy sitting in front of him, the one with all the answers but providing no information whatsoever?

Apparently, Charlie had had enough of the interrogation. With seeming indifference to Gideon's angry stare, the small man turned toward the opening. "That's all I can say. Come on," he beckoned. "It'll be light soon." He pointed skyward, indicating the surface up above. "You need to get out of here before they start looking up there."

Gideon knew when to give up on a lost cause. He threw up his hands in defeat. He would have to wait patiently for another opportunity to get the answers he so desperately needed. Squirming on his belly like a newborn from the mother's womb, he followed Charlie out of the alcove.

Once free of the confined space, Gideon was surprised by the intense brightness that greeted him, except unlike before, he was now outside of Littleton, looking in.

Littleton was a fake. No surprise there, but Gideon was aghast at the scale of the deception. Littleton was built like a giant snow globe inside a monstrous cavern.

Earlier, to escape the search parties, Charlie had opened a small recess panel in the outer wall of the town. In the darkness, Gideon did not stop to think that the town had limits. He simply ran, following Charlie's lead.

Then, the sudden light had blinded Gideon. It was Charlie who had pulled him through the doorway, guiding him quickly down one corridor to another, climbing long staircases and catwalks until they reached the hidden alcove. Running for his life, Gideon had scant time to review his surroundings. Now, he tried to take it all in.

Stretched out before him was a vast, complex infrastructure, the scale of which surpassed most modern skyscrapers. What he witnessed was an engineering marvel, a feat worthy of both praise and damnation. Praise, for the architectural miracles employed to achieve such magnificence. Damnation, because something so beautiful, yet secret, could come to no good.

What he saw, Gideon knew, would never be published in any architectural journal, nor would it pass the scrutiny of any government oversight or controlling body. Littleton, for all its wonder and beauty, was never meant to exist beyond the confines of its bedrock cocoon.

In his experience, this kind of place benefited only those who strove to keep it hidden from public scrutiny.

Damn, he thought. He had stumbled onto something far greater than he had first imagined. Littleton, and what it implied, was not what he had expected to discover. This was not a case of simple espionage or murder. The magnitude made him feel insignificant, a pawn dwarfed by the scale of the deception. Decades of lies, deceit, and murder had gone into keeping this place a secret from the world. Gideon knew if he was not careful, the security protocols likely in place would spell his untimely death. He now understood why Reyes was targeted for death, and why foreign countries would want to infiltrate the base. He realized with growing apprehension that if he was in charge of something like this, the only way he could ensure its secrecy would be to eliminate all threats to its existence. He could but wonder how many people had died over the years to keep this place a secret.

Gideon shook his head and looked out at Littleton. A translucent filament dome, suspended smoothly from miles and miles of interlocking aluminum tubing, covered the town. The dome itself reached to the highest point of the cavern, over 150 feet high, and curved like the roof over a football stadium. This structure was easily five times larger than any stadium he had ever seen. Further, the roof was crisscrossed with heavy cables, connecting gangplanks and catwalks, and massive support beams that affixed it securely to the cavern ceiling.

Also amazing were the millions upon millions of monofilament optical fibers covering the sphere. Each individual thread glowed brightly, pulsing with a life of its own. Like a painter's palette, the sinewy material displayed a constantly shifting array of colors. When combined and sequenced, the strands danced in a strange ballet, the colored light pulsing to project the bluest sky Gideon had ever seen. The sunshine was perfect. The clouds were soft and white. The birds were real enough to land on his shoulder. The effect was startling, even on the outside. He could only imagine the impact inside Littleton.

Yet he did know, as these were the same fibers that projected the beautiful night sky that shined hours earlier.

The fibers were spaced evenly across the dome and were actually woven into the very fabric of the enclosure. At various points, they were bound together into thick strands. These strands formed together into larger cables, and so forth and so on, until they all came together at the apex of the dome. At that point, they entered a large steel box—as big as ten semitrucks tied together—suspended from the cavern ceiling. This box was where the fibers received the light signals that were disbursed over Littleton.

Charlie had to keep Gideon moving, so he explained everything that he knew as they walked.

"They can show whatever image they want on the dome's surface. It's like a giant movie, except whatever is happening outside happens down here in Littleton, too."

Gideon wrung his hands together as he came to grips with the advanced technology deployed at Littleton. "You must have some really smart people working here," he said. "It takes a lot of brainpower to create a synchronous image from above and then project it onto the dome's surface. It's amazing."

"Uh-huh," Charlie responded. "Daytime down here is the same as on the surface. The same goes with the night. That's the easiest thing to do. Otherwise, they have to work really hard to create something new, like right now."

Stopping to admire the vast network of fiber-optic cables, Gideon said, "Combined like they are, the monofilament fibers provide enough ultraviolet rays that the environment inside Littleton actually thinks it's outdoors. These must be adapted from the latest military applications. I've heard of similar research going on to make ships at sea virtually invisible. But I always thought the research was years away."

He turned toward his guide, but Charlie merely shrugged his shoulders. For all his time down here, the little man didn't truly understand the technology or how it was applied. Gideon was coming to realize that Charlie wasn't quite normal.

"If DeKay wanted to," Charlie answered, "he could have all four seasons here. We get snow, rain, and wind—you name it. DeKay is like a god. He controls everything."

Behind Gideon, a sheer wall rose sixty feet in the air and was at least one hundred feet long. This wall was not made of rock. It was man-made, concrete. He stopped to touch it. The rough surface was covered in small stones. It was also cool to the touch, almost cold, and a slick sheen of moisture covered the surface. Black mold grew at the edges and in the recesses where light did not reach.

Partway up the wall, a long electrical conduit ran horizontally across the concrete span. Evenly spaced along the width of the pipe were ten black boxes bolted securely to the wall. The size of shoeboxes, each container was sealed with wax, making them impermeable to the condensation coating the surface.

Realizing that Gideon had stopped, Charlie turned around and returned. "That's the only thing holding the ocean back," he said, placing his hand gently against the surface.

Charlie looked up at the wall, and for the first time, Gideon saw doubt cross the man's face. Or was it fear? Clearly, he was uncomfortable standing there.

"Twenty feet of steel-reinforced concrete, poured like a dam to keep the water out."

"You mean," Gideon said, awed even further, "that this is a natural cavern? That someone had the audacity to wall off the Atlantic Ocean, pump the water out, and *then* build the town?"

It was an engineering miracle, one that Gideon never would have suspected. He did not even know that the technology existed to perform something like this. It must have cost millions, even billions, of dollars to accomplish this feat.

How many men did it take? Hundreds? Thousands? More importantly, how did they keep it a secret?

Gideon had naturally assumed that the town was built inside a cavern discovered from above. Did they discover it from the outside instead? It seemed impossible. On the other side of this wall was a sheer cliff that dropped right into the ocean. The pounding waves and jagged rocks kept even the stoutest swimmers and divers away. Ships traversing the area knew to steer clear of the dangerous rocky outcrops, keeping wide of the warning buoys strung along the unrelenting granite cliffs.

Gideon shook his head, awed by the overwhelming magnitude of Littleton. Still, he could not fathom its purpose. Why go to all this trouble? The answers would have to come later, when he was safely up on the surface. Right now, he needed to get out before he was discovered. He followed Charlie away from the concrete wall and the monster it kept at bay.

"Where is everybody?" Gideon asked, fearful that they might run into someone.

Charlie glanced at his watch. "By now," he said, "they're probably in the middle of Littleton. They don't have enough people to keep them at all the checkpoints, so they search in teams, moving in circles as they go, until they get to the center of town, at the commons."

"What about video surveillance, motion sensors, infrared detection?"

"I think they have some on the edges of town, but not inside," Charlie answered. "But, you don't have to worry. I've been here long enough to know where everything is hidden. I have to take you the long way, but we'll get around everything DeKay has put in since he's been here."

"How long has that been?" Gideon asked.

"He came here almost six years ago—when he brought the girls in."

"You've been here longer than that?"

"Uh-huh, yes, much longer."

"What about Littleton? Surely they have cameras positioned inside."

"They used to," Charlie replied. "But they don't anymore. These girls are different than the others. They won't let DeKay have video cameras inside the town, or listening devices, either."

Gideon's head spun. These girls? What the hell was going on here? And how could they alone keep DeKay from doing his job? What kind of influence did these children have?

Gideon continued to pepper Charlie with questions, but the strange little man was not forthcoming with answers. Charlie's lack of cooperation was frustrating, but short of threatening him, what more could he do?

Gideon decided on a different tack and asked, "How old are you? Why don't you know how long you've been here?"

Charlie smiled. "It's a long story, and now's not the time to tell it." He looked skeptically at Gideon. "Besides, you wouldn't believe me if I told you. The girls told me you weren't ready to learn the truth. They said it would take some time."

Gideon was exasperated.

Charlie's route out of Littleton was circuitous. Narrow corridors, some hewn into the rock, others lined with rough plaster, wound around the town in a maze that confused Gideon's sense of direction and provided enough disorientation that he could not, even if his life depended on it, repeat the pattern. The only direction he recognized was that Charlie headed primarily northwest, counterclockwise around the town.

Still, it was only a guess. It had been some time since Gideon had seen the town. Shortly after emerging from their hiding spot, the tunnels and corridors branched off in different directions, the light provided by a string of feeble bulbs. But if Gideon had to estimate, he would guess that they were on the west side of Littleton.

Coming to a wide intersection, Charlie slowed and then stopped at the corner. He motioned for Gideon to keep quiet. Charlie peered around the corner before motioning for him to follow.

Gideon moved ahead cautiously, his silenced weapon sighted in front of him.

The two men entered a long corridor cut directly into the bedrock. The poorly lit hallway led straight ahead. Narrow support columns rose at regular intervals along both sides of the corridor. Small halogen lamps provided just enough light for Gideon to see a door at the end, about a hundred feet away. He could also see the security camera watching the length of the corridor.

Shit, Gideon thought. *How are we going to get past that?*

Charlie turned back to Gideon and whispered in his ear. "I'm going to walk down that hall and through the door. I'll leave it open. Now, this is important. In two minutes, you need to follow me. Don't worry about the camera—I'm going to distract the guard watching the hall. When you get to the door. . . ." Charlie's face blushed a deep red. "Um, you need to take care of the guard."

"Take care of him?" Gideon asked.

"Well, yeah, so you can get out. He's too big for me."

Gideon nodded. "Okay, I can do that. But what if there's more than one guard?"

Charlie blanched white. "Well, um, there shouldn't be. There almost never is." His wan smile was less than reassuring. "Okay, now, straight across from the guard station is the entrance to a large tunnel. When you enter the tunnel, stay in the shadows. Cameras are positioned inside, but if you're careful and stay hidden, you won't have any problems. After a few hundred yards, you'll come to a ladder hanging from the ceiling. That'll take you to the surface. You'll still be inside the base, near the outer fence, west of the base headquarters."

"Where does the rest of the tunnel lead to?" Gideon asked.

"The tunnel is three miles long. It ends at a parking garage that's owned by the man who runs Littleton. There's a secret entrance hidden in the lower level that is used to supply the town and for people to move in and out undetected. There are other ways in, but that's the one most people here have access to."

"What about the man who owns the garage?"

Charlie shook his head. "No more questions," he said, interrupting Gideon. His face hardened. "You're too close to getting out of here. It's time to go. Now."

Gideon frowned deeply, maddened by the confusion that raged within his mind. Things were moving fast—too fast. He had questions that needed answers, and so far, Charlie was the only one who could provide them. Unfortunately, getting him to open up was proving difficult.

In any event, he had discovered part of the secret behind Kulbeda's existence. The director was not going to be happy with the news. The scale of this operation meant that a vast conspiracy had been under way for years, operating without oversight right under the noses of the Central Intelligence Agency. He still needed to find out who else knew about this and how deep the secret was buried. Most important, he needed to know what purpose Littleton served. Who benefited most from its existence? Once he answered that question, he would be in a position to act.

Unfortunately, Charlie had reached his limit. No more questions. He was ready to proceed to the next phase of his plan. Shrugging off Gideon's pleading look, he moved into the corridor, walking slowly toward the door.

Charlie's head was bowed low. Even from behind, Gideon could see that his hands were raised to his chest, like he was holding a secret close to his heart. He also walked with a pronounced limp, something Gideon had failed to recognize during their time together. No, that wasn't exactly true. Earlier, Charlie had an odd gait, but not the limp he now showed.

When Charlie reached the entrance, he did not look back. As promised, he opened the door, leaving it ajar as he passed through. He disappeared into the unknown.

Gideon watched, apprehensive of the stranger's plan. Was there an ambush waiting on the other side? Was this an elaborate trap? It was absurd; he was going to trust his life to a man he did not know. Yet what choice did he have? He was in this predicament of his own volition. He did not know where he was. He had no clue how to get out of here. If he wanted to get out alive, he had to trust the odd little man.

Charlie has gotten me this far, he thought. *Hasn't he?*

The two minutes expired quickly. Gideon sprang to the corridor, weapon raised and ready. He did not hesitate. Moving straight to the door, he peeked through, surprised by the sight that greeted him.

Charlie was having a heated, one-way conversation with the lone security guard stationed outside the door. The janitor was very animated. Spittle flew from his mouth, and his movements were awkward and pronounced. Equally odd, the security guard was unfazed by Charlie's display of erratic behavior.

Gideon moved farther into the doorway, lining up the sights of his Sig. Spotting Gideon's movement and anticipating the gunshot, Charlie flinched and turned his head away.

It was just enough movement to alert the security guard to his presence.

Hurling Charlie away, the guard dove for cover behind his desk, pulling his weapon out at the same time. Gideon aimed and fired, tracking the man as he moved. His first and second shots missed wide. The third wounded his opponent, hitting him in the right shoulder. Unfortunately, it wasn't enough to keep the fast-moving guard from disappearing behind his desk. Seconds later, Gideon could hear him yelling into his radio. He was alerting Littleton's security team and calling for backup.

Gideon needed to move fast. From here on out, every second counted.

Without hesitation, he moved from the doorway into the large room. When the guard rose suddenly and began shooting, Gideon rolled to his right, returning fire as best he could. Both missed their intended target:

Gideon because he was tumbling and firing at the same time, the guard because he had only one functioning hand to support his aim.

Moreover, the guard had a MAC-10, the wrong weapon for one-handed operation. Often mistaken for an UZI, the MAC-10 is a highly compact, recoil-operated, select-fire submachine gun. With its small size, simple design, and few moving parts, the lightweight weapon has a high rate of fire, almost eleven hundred rounds per minute. It is very powerful for its size. And it is nearly impossible to control when fired single-handedly, like the guard was now forced to do. Being such a short weapon, the long burst caused the gun to twist violently in the man's hand, until it literally jumped from his grasp.

The guard was lucky that the weapon didn't fire back at him as it tumbled to the top of his desk. He was unlucky in that Gideon had recovered from his roll and was now lining up the guard in his sights.

It was now a lopsided standoff. The wounded guard lunged for the submachine gun. Ready this time, Gideon put two rounds into the middle of his chest. The guard landed on the desk with a crash and slumped to the floor, dead before he came to rest.

Gideon approached the desk, calling out, "Charlie, are you all right?"

Visibly shaken, Charlie rose from where he was thrown and approached Gideon. "You killed him," he said.

"What did you think I was going to do?" Gideon replied sarcastically.

"I . . . don't know. I didn't think that far ahead. . . ." Charlie continued to stare at the guard, frozen in place. "I've never seen a dead man before," he said faintly.

"Charlie," Gideon said, turning him away from the body. "I need you to be okay with this. I have to get out of here."

To underscore Gideon's statement, alarms suddenly went off throughout the underground installation. It wouldn't be long now before DeKay's security response team arrived.

Fearing the worst, Gideon turned to leave until Charlie halted him. "Hold on," he cried. "I almost forgot. The computer next to the desk. It stores images from the security cameras. They get sent to the central computer every hour. You need to destroy it or else they'll have your picture. They'll find out who you are and that I helped you."

Gideon grabbed the guard's MAC-10 and rounded the desk. He kicked the computer until he could grab the edge of the case and rip it open. Then, holding the MAC-10 in both of his gloved hands, he emptied the remaining bullets into the computer, making sure the hard drive was destroyed. The damaged circuits sizzled and popped as the computer terminal died.

"That should do it," Gideon said. One last time, he asked, "Are you going to be okay?"

Charlie answered a little too quickly, but there was nothing else Gideon could do. "Yes, yes, I'll be all right," he replied. "Now go, before DeKay's men get here. There are plenty of places for me to hide until it's safe. Hurry, go."

Gideon turned on his heels, sprinted across the room, and entered the large tunnel. Once inside, he followed Charlie's instructions, moving quickly but staying to the shadows, until he came to the ladder. As promised, the ladder hung a foot below the ceiling. Gideon leapt high, his hands reaching out to grab the bottom rung. Then he pulled himself hand over hand until his feet touched the ladder.

Putting his trust again in the odd little man, Gideon began to climb the narrow vertical tube cut into the rock. Above him was blackness. Hand over hand, one rung at a time, he climbed. After what seemed an eternity, he finally reached the top.

Gideon stood still on the ladder and waited until he had caught his breath. Then he pushed open the lid. The light of morning was just beginning to add definition to the forest. Without hesitation he scrambled to the surface.

He was in a small clearing ringed by dense foliage. Charlie said he would emerge along the western perimeter, and true enough, there it was.

Gideon closed the hatch and took off into the woods. He would exit the same way he entered. Unlike earlier in the evening, this trespass would not go unnoticed. He needed to move fast and not worry about the security measures. He pulled the balaclava back over his head to disguise his appearance. Hopefully, by the time they responded to his presence, he would be far away from the place. His backpack and supplies would have to stay behind. There was nothing there to identify Gideon as the intruder, but he nonetheless hated to leave a trail of evidence.

Agent Reyes was not going believe the story he had to tell. Hell, he didn't believe it himself. First things first—the director needed to be warned. The proverbial shit was going to hit the fan. If the director had a fault, it was that he was prone to action. It would take all of Gideon's persuasiveness to keep his boss from ringing the bell. There was more at stake here besides the truth. If Gorrell acted now, two little girls would be caught in the crossfire. Gideon had never knowingly killed or intentionally endangered an innocent civilian, and he wasn't going to start now. Whatever the next step, it would require meticulous planning. More importantly, he needed to be the one doing the planning.

Damn it, he thought. *The director is definitely not going to like this.*

CHAPTER 15

The Next Day
Pyongyang, North Korea

Pak Te Hwan slammed the satellite phone down on his desk. His face shined bright red with anger. A man of considerable stature and influence, he was not accustomed to being told what to do. Worse, he did not appreciate the outright implication that he was lying. Under normal circumstances, such impudence would land the guilty party in prison, and it wouldn't end there. Oftentimes, the offender's entire family, close friends, and neighbors would join him in prison. Once incarcerated, only Pak's unique brand of generosity, combined with a sincere show of contrition, could rescind a certain and painful death. Regardless, any forgiveness or pardon on his part would not be given without a measure of reconciliation, the kind that usually left the guilty party physically and emotionally marred in some way.

Pak knew how to deal with those who failed to show him the deference and respect he deserved. It was one of the reasons he had been able to hold on to his position of power—his actions against detractors were always swift, decisive, and often brutal. Though thousands of miles away, the American was no different.

Pak's accomplice had accused him of breaking their agreement. The man believed one of Pak's men had infiltrated his facility, had tried to kidnap the twins. It was ludicrous, of course, and Pak spent more time than necessary convincing the man of that fact. His men were not even on American soil yet. They were still on the boat, having just left international waters. Besides, if Pak wanted to take those girls by force, he would have done so already. He had even considered it. In fact, there were plans designed to do just that—go in, remove the girls, and destroy all evidence of their existence. In the end he had decided it was not worth the risk. The girls were more valuable alive, and anything could happen on a mission, especially if there was shooting involved.

The fact was, he needed those girls. They were crucial to his plans for North Korea.

The American fool was a minor annoyance. It was a shame he even had to deal with this cretin. Like all Westerners, the man was an insignificant buffoon, a hand hired to keep his investment safe and protected. *Once the transaction was complete,* Pak thought, smiling to himself, *then nothing, and no one, will stop me from creating the world's next superpower.*

Calming himself for what he had to do next, Pak picked up the phone and dialed the number from memory. His unease was growing. The American was coming apart at the seams. The clues were there if you listened closely. He lacked logic, clarity of thought. It was a dangerous gambit to accuse Pak like he had, with no evidence to support him. Clearly, the man could no longer be trusted to keep his end of the agreement. Alternative arrangements needed to be made, just in case. It was time to broaden the rules of engagement, take control of the situation.

For the first time in a long while, Pak felt alive. Things were coming along very nicely. Soon, his new life would begin.

Fifteen miles off the United States Coastline

The *Loujian* was not a comfortable ship, nor was it fast. Built in 1973, the aging 420-foot freighter housed a small crew of six, including the captain and steward. It was a no-nonsense, no-frills kind of vessel that lacked the modern accoutrements afforded the newer, sleeker cargo ships. The cabins were small and dank, air-conditioning was provided by the tiny portholes, and every square foot of metal showed signs of rust and decay.

With a gross tonnage just over 9,500, the *Loujian* was small for its class. Only sixty-three feet abeam, its official cargo consisted mainly of toys and trinkets, durable goods and nonperishables, convenience items that were not needed in a hurry. The cargo's owners accepted their wares when they got them, early, late, sometimes not at all. They never once complained, even if the goods were slightly damaged.

That's because, unofficially, the *Loujian* carried a much more precious consignment. This payload was not durable, and many of these goods were damaged during transit. They were bruised, broken, bent, sometimes by accident, but more often by the cruelty of humans. This cargo was not valued by its immediate resale value but by the future return on investment. Losses during transit were acceptable, to a point.

The *Loujian* traded in human flesh.

Originating from Hong Kong, the ship was owned by a small conglomerate out of Singapore. Run by Chinese Triads, the consortium trafficked in the ten-billion-dollar illegal immigration and smuggling market.

Locked in its hold were hundreds of illegal immigrants, peasants mostly, sequestered in dark steel containers, using buckets for toilets, and a small generator for power. Their only nourishment was the stored food and the water they brought with them. Due to malnutrition, many could no longer stand. They were forced to sit and lie in their own filth. Sickness and disease was a cost of doing business. Treatment for those healthy enough would not be offered until after landfall.

There was nothing first-class about this cruise.

The Triads brokered arrangements with other gangs in the United States. They arranged for people to board ships in exchange for exorbitant fees, delivering the survivors into indentured servitude, modern slavery with no visible means of escape. Operating inside a huge network, with over twenty million Chinese waiting in line to make the journey, it was all about supply and demand, and the economics were mind-boggling.

On this particular trip, the *Loujian* had four additional passengers. These men were not stored below with the chattel. They were special, booked for passage by someone the gangs respected, even feared. These individuals rated the best cabins. They prepared their own meals and kept to their own schedule. The crew of the *Loujian* kept clear of these men, not on any orders from the captain, but from an instinct that warned of danger. These men were not to be trifled with, and the crew knew it.

Captain Choi Yong Jin led the four-man assault team. A member of North Korea's elite reconnaissance brigade, Captain Choi was responsible for leading seven raids into South Korea. Where most raids had failed, Choi's succeeded. Designing probes that penetrated deep behind the demilitarized zone—the boundary between North Korea and South Korea that is manned by American soldiers—he exposed weak points in the enemy's defenses. His accomplishments led to operation strategies and tactics that, if called upon, could disrupt the command and control infrastructure of South Korea's military establishment and threaten lines of communication and supply.

If it ever came to war, his unit's primary responsibility was to secure information, neutralize targets, and disrupt rear areas. To execute these operations, his troops were trained in the art of disguise, sabotage, espionage, and demolition. They were also desensitized, stripped of their ingrained communist training so they could easily pass for South Korean military personnel and civilians.

Today, Choi and his men were far from home, ensconced in a boat, having only recently entered American waters. Twelve weeks earlier, they had been handpicked by Pak Te Hwan, an influential Party leader, and redeployed out of the forward corps. Based out of Tasa-ri, on the west coast of North Korea, he and his men had undergone weeks of operation planning, preparing every detail and nuance specifically for this mission.

The assignment was deemed top secret, and Choi's team was isolated the entire time, communicating solely with Vice President Pak. The plans called for an insertion at night, so training was held from just after dusk to right before dawn. They were not allowed to say good-bye to loved ones, write letters should they not return, or leave any evidence behind of their existence. They were ghosts in the machine, coming and going as if they had never existed.

Now, twelve miles off the Delaware coast, Choi's mission had suddenly changed, become more complex. Pak had broadened the rules of engagement, adding a new objective, one that required a different timetable. The end result was still the same, but his superior wanted additional precautions put in place to ensure success.

Choi received his new orders without complaint. A good and obedient soldier, he was not one to question his commander. He and his men would leave within the hour, in broad daylight, risking the chance of interception by the authorities. At this distance from shore and still twenty-four hours from their destination point of New York City, it was a small risk, one the vice president felt was worth taking.

There could be no evidence of his men's infiltration into the United States. There could be no trace of their presence left behind. Choi had taken extraordinary precautions to get this far unnoticed, including the trip on this godforsaken, rat-infested ship. Choi detested the use of a pipeline that traded his comrades into slavery, but he needed a way into the country, and this was the best option available to him.

One benefit to the change of plans was that launching from sea would shave valuable time off the original schedule while providing an element of surprise he hoped to use to his advantage. The team would launch from the freighter in a small outboard skiff disguised as a fishing boat. All four men spoke flawless English and would pass easily for sport fishermen. Each man also carried forged documentation that would pass a cursory examination. The vice president had provided these documents—licenses, birth certificates, family photographs, and local receipts—before they left North Korea. Once onshore, their gear would stow easily in backpacks and they would scuttle the boat. Upon completion of their assignment, they would exfiltrate farther south to Baltimore, Maryland. The vice president himself made further arrangements to get them home from there.

Choi eyed the rising swells of the Atlantic. Salt air and spray caressed his face as wind-blown whitecaps crashed against the freighter's bow. Landfall loomed close. The dark skyline stretched for miles in both directions. His adrenaline rose with each passing minute. The familiar sensation provided comfort against what lay ahead. He had never been to the United

States of America, and he had no desire to stay any longer than necessary. The sooner his mission was complete, the sooner he could set foot back on familiar soil.

Let's get this over with, Choi thought.

He was prepared to enter the land of his greatest enemy—America. With any luck, America was not prepared for him.

CHAPTER 16

"Cross DeKay?" Reyes asked. "I've never heard of him."

Gideon was not surprised. "DeKay is someone I thought—really, hoped—I'd never see again. He was my superior, my mentor, back in the Army. It was on his recommendation that I joined the Special Forces. It was also because of him that I left the military."

Gideon and Agent Reyes were back at the hotel room they had rented a few miles from Kulbeda Station, near the cozy center of Curtis Cove. For the time being, this was their new base of operations. The walls were covered with a tapestry of printouts, charts, maps, and notes taken from the research and planning that went into Gideon's infiltration of Kulbeda. The two unmade beds were covered with paperwork hastily organized into piles of information. The floor and tables were littered with empty pizza boxes, tubs of spoiling Chinese food, and a wide assortment of cans, bottles, and cups. The only thing fresh was the pot of coffee that sat percolating next to the vanity.

Director Gorrell was not happy with the new partnership, but he had reluctantly agreed with Gideon's analysis of the situation. Reyes might indeed prove useful. She was familiar with the case and had a vested interest in its outcome; therefore, she was properly motivated. Moreover, she was currently on the outs with her employers. They wouldn't miss her for a while. As a result, this was still a company-run operation with the help, albeit covertly, of the FBI. Still, it didn't keep Gorrell from having a few stipulations to the relationship. Reyes agreed that she would not inform her supervisors of her actions until the appropriate time, as defined by the director. She also agreed that Gideon was taking the lead and that he would not show up in any official reports. His continued anonymity was not negotiable. If Gideon had his way, the FBI brass wouldn't discover what was going on until after the operation was over, at which point he would disappear back into the shadows and let Reyes spin it however she wished. He knew things would not be that simple and that Gorrell would ultimately be forced to insert his considerable influence, but that wasn't his problem.

"You say DeKay got quite a few medals in the field," Reyes said. "I can tell from the way you're speaking that whatever happened between you was personal."

"You have no idea," Gideon responded angrily. DeKay's involvement in this was a complication he didn't need. Putting his head in his hands, Gideon sighed loudly. He had no choice. He tore open the wound he thought had long since healed.

"DeKay was a brilliant commander," he began. "Yet his career, his life, was destroyed by one single, violent action."

"What did he do?" Reyes interrupted.

Gideon smirked and shook his head. "He killed a couple of innocent Iraqi children, a twelve-year-old boy and his younger sister, just outside of Al Busayyah. The girl was no more than five years old. He compromised the team and willfully disobeyed the rules of engagement, and he undermined the mission. He very nearly got us all killed."

Gideon leaned back in the chair and closed his eyes. Vivid memories flowed forth in a dizzying rush. "It was during the first war in Iraq. We were performing reconnaissance, hunkered down just outside of the small village, providing forward intelligence for the Second Infantry Division. For over a week, we had watched and waited. Nothing happened. We knew our guys had entered Kuwait and were pushing the Iraqi army our way. Soon we would be overrun with retreating forces and our exfiltration route would be compromised.

"Then, just hours before we were scheduled to pull out, four Scud missile units pull up to the town. We could tell from the markings on the fuselage that these were a variant of the Scud-B, what the Iraqis called the *Al Hussein*. A missile just like these had hit a U.S. military base in Dhahran, Saudi Arabia. Twenty-eight soldiers were killed on that one strike alone. Over one hundred more were injured. Our patience had finally paid off."

He paused for a moment and then continued. "Before we could call in the air strike, an observation post covering our right flank notices the kids approaching from behind. They were damned goat herders from the village. We'd watched them leave earlier in the day, heading north with their flock, and now they were returning, apparently having circled around us in a wide loop. We were so focused on the arrival of the Scuds, they slipped though our net. They were almost on top of us before we could react. Without discussion, DeKay waited until the boy got close enough to see us, then he shot him in the head. The sister, too."

He recalled the incident with clarity, and the image of the boy's head exploding was sharp in his mind. For years, that same image would wake him from a sleep wracked with nightmares. Familiar anger returned to his voice. "Those children were no threat to us. We were prepared to let them pass and make a quiet retreat. Killing them was not only a waste of life, it violated every rule of engagement. It needlessly exposed us to the enemy and threatened our ability to execute the mission. What's worse is that the children's mother witnessed the whole thing from the edge of town. I can still hear her screams.

"Within minutes, Iraqi soldiers began firing on our position. We were forced to call in the air strike while in full retreat, with over one hundred soldiers and incensed townsfolk on our tail. We fought the entire way, moving from one location to another until we finally got support from incoming Black Hawks. Three men were wounded in that retreat, including DeKay. One of the men, the son of a senator, didn't make it back alive." Gideon rubbed his face and eyes. "It was such a waste."

"What did DeKay have to say about the incident?" Reyes asked softly. She could see the pain in Gideon's eyes, the wound open and sore.

"He was defiant," he said angrily. "His report glossed over the facts. 'We got the job done,' he stated. 'Mission accomplished. The Scuds were destroyed. The United States Army overran the Iraqis. In the end, we saved lives.' He left out the fact that because of his actions a member of the team lost his life."

"What happened to you?" she asked.

"Me?" Sarcasm laced Gideon's laugh. "I received the Bronze Star. But that's all confidential. The entire episode was sealed from the public. Too distasteful—politically, that is. The government couldn't punish DeKay for his actions because we had saved hundreds, if not thousands, of lives. Yet they could not condone the unsanctioned killing of innocent civilians. The senator whose son died commissioned an inquiry to look into the incident. Closed-door hearings were held. Witnesses were called to testify. The senator threatened to take the information public. In the end, a compromise was reached. DeKay lost his commission in the military and forfeited his pension, but he walked away free nonetheless. I carried that bastard five miles on my shoulders. He was unconscious the entire time. How's that for justice?"

Gideon still believed that DeKay had gotten off easy. "It was a devastating blow to the man's ego. The military was DeKay's life. Before the court-martial, he was in line for a promotion to lieutenant colonel. A high-level position at the Pentagon had been waiting for him. The paperwork was complete. All he needed to do was fulfill his latest command assignment."

"When was the last time you saw DeKay?"

"Almost sixteen years ago, at his court-martial. He passed right by me on the way out of the courtroom. 'You're dead.' Those were the last words he spoke to me."

It had been a long time since Gideon last saw DeKay. The man had never acted on his threat. But now, it looked like their paths were going to cross again.

CHAPTER 17

Littleton

"How are the girls doing?" Arthur Frist asked, his voice distant and tinny, the necessary result of their secure communications.

"They're resting comfortably," DeKay replied. "After their latest insubordination, I felt they needed to be sedated. They'll be fine. More importantly, they're manageable."

"And the good doctor Sossoman?"

"She's holding up her end. Like you suspected, her past is beginning to influence the decisions she makes. She doesn't want to see the girls harmed. The doctor is trying very hard to gain their confidence. We were fortunate she agreed so willingly to be involved in this project. She understands these girls and relates to them better than anyone else we've had before."

"Believe me," Frist warned, "despite her eager participation, she had no real choice in the matter. Don't let her compliance fool you. She's quite resourceful. Dr. Sossoman is not as naïve as you think."

"Does she speak of her past?" Frist asked, curious.

"No. She's reluctant to talk about it beyond what's already in the file. I suspect there's more to her than we know."

Frist pondered this information but did not comment further. There was only so much he was going to divulge to his subordinate. "Thank you, Mr. DeKay," he responded formally, ending the conversation. "Stay on top of the situation. Find our intruder. And for your sake, keep those children under control."

"Yes, sir," DeKay responded evenly.

It didn't do any good to argue with Arthur Frist. He was a powerful man used to ordering people around and getting his way in return. The billionaire threw his influence around like a grand master chess player. He was a skilled manipulator and a meticulous planner. He knocked over opponents one by one, eliciting barely a ripple of resistance until he reached his objective. Checkmate. In most cases, enemies of Arthur Frist didn't find out they were targets until the rug was ripped out from underneath them.

If one was an employee, Frist not only demanded, but also expected, absolute obedience. From his small circle of officers, like DeKay, he expected the same ruthlessness he possessed. Failure was not acceptable.

DeKay hung up the phone and sat down behind his large mahogany desk. He didn't know when the habit began, but he always rose to attention whenever he spoke to his employer. The act was unconscious, and it bothered him that he had such a weakness. He bowed to no man.

He sighed out loud. A few more days, that was all he needed. By the end of the week, it would be done. His plan was coming along nicely. President Yi's survival was only a temporary setback.

He turned his chair around and looked out the window of his two-story Colonial. Across the street was the commons, its green grass, lush trees, and ornamental pond an anomaly underneath all this stone, metal, and technology. But that's what this whole place was, one big anomaly. The postman delivering mail, the police officers patrolling the streets, the young men and women who operated the grocery store, the butcher shop, and the bank—they were all out of place in this miniature world carved out by Mother Nature and then subjugated by man. Yet Littleton could not exist without them. It required the simple ruse of daily life and routine to promote the illusion of normalcy. The human psyche required it, whether you were seventy years old or seven, as Littleton's permanent guests were. Without Mr. Smith the schoolteacher, Reverend Halloway the minister, or Delores McKutchins the kind and gentle spinster who acted as the town's librarian, there would not be the backdrop to support the town's veneer of reality. It was all a big hoax, even the twins knew that, but in this game the pretend world helped keep everyone sane.

The ringing telephone interrupted DeKay's thoughts. He spun around and grabbed the receiver. "Hello," he answered brusquely.

On the line was one of DeKay's security men. "It's about the girls," the man reported nervously.

"What about them?" DeKay barked. A sinking feeling entered his gut.

"They're gone. We've searched everywhere, but they're nowhere to be found."

Again? DeKay thought. The onset of a painful migraine began to work its way into his temples. *This can't be happening.* He gripped the receiver tightly, his knuckles white with strain. Forcing a veneer of calm into his voice, he answered. "Find them. I don't care how, or where, just find them." He almost hung up before a thought stopped him. "Where's Dr. Sossoman?"

"She's leading the search," the man replied.

"Bring her to me," DeKay barked, all pretense at patience lost. He slammed the phone onto its cradle, nearly splitting the machine in two. His head spun round and round in a dizzying rush. He was seething with uncontrolled anger. If he could, he would have snapped the girls' little necks.

"Tell me again what we're doing here?" Reyes asked. The weary agent rearranged herself in the seat before stretching her legs, back, and arms. A number of joints and ligaments cracked and popped as she worked the kinks out of her sore, tired body. The cramped, midsize car didn't allow room for her to extend completely, but she sighed in relief nonetheless.

Gideon watched with amused admiration as she squirmed against the uncomfortable seat before gracefully settling back down. All in all, Reyes wasn't bad company. She was smart as a whip, had a good sense of humor—which was a change from most federal agents he knew—and worked tirelessly day and night, ably keeping up with Gideon, who was known to keep a brutal schedule during an operation. The fact that she was attractive didn't hurt, either.

She was more than attractive, actually. More and more, Gideon found himself stealing glances when she wasn't looking, and some even when she was. Lately, she had started wearing her blonde hair unkempt, letting it go straight from the shower with nothing but a towel-dry and a comb-through with her fingers. It was a good look for her. The stern appearance she had when they first met had softened. She now looked more approachable, vulnerable. Surprisingly enough, he discovered she didn't wear any makeup. She didn't need to, either. Her skin was perfect—smooth when she slept, and with all the right wrinkles in all the right places when she smiled or laughed. He even noticed that her short, straight nose turned slightly upright when she was deep in concentration. He noticed the little things, which happened when you spent time with another person, eating, sleeping, working, day in, day out.

Working closely like they were, it was easy for him to internalize the way she moved, her scent after a shower, the subtle ways her body displayed emotions. He was pretty sure she was sizing him up as well. Her eyes darted away when he caught her looking at him. There was the subtle hint of a blush, the awkward stammer in response to a question, the hand that lingered too long on his shoulder. It was distracting, to say the least. Yet through it all, there was a professionalism that never wavered. Gideon knew now was not the time to explore his budding feelings. Sharing the small hotel room was enough of a diversion. He didn't need to bring sex into the equation.

The mission comes first. That was Gideon's mantra. Lately, though, he found himself having to repeat it often as his mind wandered to other, more pleasurable thoughts. Once again, Gideon chastised himself for getting distracted. It was time to change the subject.

"So, tell me, Agent Reyes, why the FBI? What attracted you to law enforcement?"

She leaned her head back against the seat and exhaled loudly through her nose. "Why not?" she eventually replied. "I don't mean that in a negative way, but I've been around the law all my life. My father spent most of his adult life working for the Chicago PD and then the FBI. He put a lot of criminals away. He was a legend of a man, larger than life in all respects."

She paused and ran her fingers through her hair. "I was raised by the wife of a peace officer. We didn't have a lot of money. My father worked long hours on cases. Sometimes, when he was on difficult assignments, he wouldn't come home for days, or weeks. We'd be lucky if he took the time to call and check in on us. I stayed up with my mother on countless nights, wondering if he was going to come walking through that front door, or if we were going to get a call telling us to come to the hospital."

"It must have been a rough way to grow up."

"It took a toll on my mother. She started drinking when I was very young. First it was just when my father worked late, but then, the days became too long for her to manage. I know now that her drinking was mostly to drown out the pain of loneliness, but that's just an excuse. Toward the end you couldn't keep the bottle out of her hand." Gideon listened patiently. "Not that she was abusive. She just wasn't there, even when she was. You know what I mean?"

He nodded. "I have friends in police forces throughout the world. They're all the same, even those in the intelligence community."

"She died when I was twelve." Reyes rubbed her fists tight against her eyes. "No, that's not exactly right. She killed herself with an overdose of pills and gin." Her voice turned bitter. "There was no suicide note, no good-bye letter, but that was just like my mother. She was never one to complain or put up a fight. She just decided one day to check out. I waited after school for her to come pick me up, but she never showed. One of dad's friends from work eventually came and got me." She chuckled. "It's funny. I remember, my father was furious."

"What do you mean?" Gideon asked. "That he wasn't there for you?"

She pulled her legs up to her chest and placed her feet on the dashboard. She rested her chin in between her knees. The bitterness returned. "No, at the time, my dad had been running a deep undercover operation, working a racketeering case between the Chicago and New York City mobs. My mother's death was a terrible inconvenience to him. He had to be pulled out. It set the investigation back two years. To the day he died, he never forgave her for what she did."

"What about you, though?" Gideon asked, turning sideways so he could face her. "I would think a career in law enforcement would be the furthest thing from your mind."

"Not true," she answered. "After seeing my mother waste away, I vowed to never let that kind of weakness control me. I swore to be a stronger, better person than her, to be someone more like my father—tough, disciplined, focused. He was my dad. I craved his approval and was constantly looking for ways to be closer to him. Joining the FBI and devoting my life to the service was the best way I knew to do that."

"You know, don't you, that sometimes no matter what you do, no matter how hard you try, you can't please everyone."

"Even those you love?" Reyes asked.

"Love doesn't come with strings attached. Sometimes you just have to look after yourself. The rest will work itself out over time."

"Sounds about right." She continued to look straight ahead out the window. "Why are you interested in all this? It's not a great story."

"But it is the truth," he replied. "At least from your perspective. You're my partner now, and it helps for me to understand who you are, at least just a little."

"The truth means a lot to you, doesn't it?"

"More and more, anyway," Gideon said. "It's been a long time since the truth mattered."

"Well, to tell you the truth, I'm getting tired of just sitting here." Reyes sighed and checked her watch. "Thirty-six hours and we have nothing to show for it. How do you know this is the right place?"

Gideon flowed easily with the change in subject. The conversation had touched a raw nerve. He didn't need to probe further. "Charlie Simmons told me that Littleton had a secret exit at a parking garage on the outskirts of town," he replied. "I checked. This is the only garage with a lower level. It's the only one with sophisticated security cameras and motion sensors. Every other parking garage is on the other side of town, closer to the beaches and the parks. This has to be it."

Gideon and Reyes were parked a block away in the driveway of a vacant store. They had taken turns watching the parking lot through the night and into the day, splitting up only twice to replenish their supply of food and coffee. He knew that Reyes was right. It had been hours since they started watching the place, and there had been no activity. The place was so quiet that he, too, was beginning to wonder whether they had the right location. Gideon never liked to second-guess his decisions. It was bad for morale. His instincts were almost always right, and over the years he had come to trust them like he would any other fact.

"Who owns the place?" Reyes asked. "Surely that's a lead we can follow up on."

"I don't know," he replied. He didn't try to mask his frustration. "The company that owns it is a shell for an offshore group that I've never heard of, which in turn is owned by another unknown entity. Except for the paper they are printed on, the company officers don't exist, and the addresses are empty lots of land. The director has been quietly poking around. The paper trail leads through the Bahamas straight to Switzerland. And that's only half the problem. Even with the spirit of cooperation and the new banking laws between our two countries, getting the Swiss to open up is going to be difficult. And if we push too hard, we're likely to alert the wrong parties."

Gideon rubbed his eyes and yawned. Reyes was right about another thing. This stakeout was exhausting. He continued, "I suspect that even if we did get access to the files, the trail would continue on. Littleton has been around for decades, long enough that whoever owns it has been able to cover their tracks."

He rubbed his face again. When he opened his eyes, he had to blink twice. His eyes grew as wide as saucers. Reyes bolted upright in her seat, almost bumping her head on the roof.

Across the street, a lone woman had suddenly emerged from the side entrance of the parking garage. It was Dr. Sossoman, the bedraggled, gray-haired, older woman Gideon had seen holding the girls during his short time in Littleton. It had been a few days since he first saw her, and now she was wearing professional attire, but he recognized her instantly.

Dr. Sossoman glanced around nervously before walking quickly toward the center of town, away from where they were parked. She looked rushed, as if time was of the essence. Gideon looked over at Reyes, who also sat transfixed at the woman's sudden appearance.

"Don't just sit there!" she cried frantically. "Move, before she disappears."

A feeling of desperation overcame Gideon. This woman's presence was an ominous portent. Yes, she was a link to Littleton, but he could feel it inside, his intuition running wild. As the girls' keeper, her appearance on the surface was a warning of ill tidings. What was she doing here, so seemingly out of place in the daylight? Why wasn't she with the girls?

The car's engine purred to life. He pulled slowly into the street.

Up ahead, Sossoman stopped at a corner and hailed a passing taxi. She got into the yellow cab, provided brief directions, and took off. Gideon pulled into traffic a short distance behind.

Even three cars back, Gideon could see the doctor's face as she looked behind to see if anyone was following.

"She's awfully paranoid," Reyes observed in the passenger seat. "I don't think she gets out much."

"More likely," Gideon responded, "this little excursion is off the books. I suspect the good doctor has left the reservation without permission."

"Damn," Reyes swore out loud. "We're not prepared for this kind of surveillance. We need at least six additional agents if we want to do this properly, or at least another car. If she employs countermeasures to see if she's being tailed, we'll lose her in a second. Or even worse, she'll make us and head back to Littleton before we can learn anything useful."

Gideon was undeterred. "We'll just keep our distance and see what she does next. This isn't New York City or Los Angeles. There are only so many places she can go around here in a taxi."

"Awful confident of yourself," Reyes said.

"Let's just see what happens."

Just as Gideon finished speaking, he was forced to slam on the brakes and come to an abrupt halt. The car in front had stopped suddenly at a red light. Any chance of following Dr. Sossoman faded as the taxi pulled farther away. They were stuck. Pulling around the car and running the light was too risky. It would give them away for sure. Gideon pounded on the steering wheel in frustration.

"Keep an eye on her!" he shouted needlessly to Reyes. She was already craning her head upward, watching the yellow taxi as far as she could. It took all his patience not to lean on the horn and show his displeasure at the driver in front.

"The taxi has turned right," Reyes shouted. "Four blocks up, at the next set of lights."

Gideon's hands gripped the steering wheel. His eyes narrowed to slits. With the doctor no longer in sight, now was the time to make a move. He checked the rearview mirror. Another car had pulled in close behind him. He was boxed in. Gideon swore under his breath. It was imperative that they get back on Sossoman's tail before she reached her destination.

Every second mattered.

"Hold tight," he warned Reyes.

He put the car in reverse and braced himself for the impact to come. The driver behind him leaned heavy on the horn as Gideon plowed into the man's front grill. Metal pushed against metal. Plastic and glass cracked and splintered. Tires squealed and smoke billowed as Gideon pushed the car back. His trunk buckled under the strain, but after a few feet, he had enough room to maneuver again. He turned back around in his seat. A light wind had blown the heavy smoke right into the intersection. The screen of white was so thick it looked like a fog had rolled in off the ocean.

Gideon frowned at the sight. He had inadvertently created another obstacle. If he couldn't see the cars entering the intersection, how could he avoid them? The loud shriek of skidding tires brought a smile to his lips. Apparently, he wasn't the only one concerned with the obstacle. Though he couldn't see the ensuing commotion, the sound of horns blaring told him that traffic had momentarily stalled. Without hesitation, he put the car into drive, turned sharply to the left, and gunned the accelerator.

The car fishtailed into the oncoming lane and shot forward toward the intersection. The smoke was thickest here but he was able to make out the still shapes of one car and then another. Trusting his reflexes, he turned right and then sharply left, narrowly avoiding them both. More horns blared. Gideon ignored them, focusing only on the road ahead of him, until he was through and out the other side.

Now he had to make up for lost time. One block after another sped past as he urged the car faster. The fourth corner approached quickly as Gideon slowed just enough to make the turn. This time, he ignored the red light, passing through to the next street just behind another car. Rounding the corner, he slowed the car down and scanned ahead. There wasn't a single yellow cab in sight. They had lost her. Gideon's heart sank.

"There!" Reyes shouted suddenly, pointing with her finger.

"Where?" Gideon shouted back.

"Pull over here at the curb. Right here!"

Gideon pulled over to the curb.

"See that theater?" Reyes asked, pointing across the street. "I saw her, just before she went inside."

"Are you sure? If you're wrong, then we've lost her."

"I'm positive. I saw her go inside."

Gideon unbuckled and reached for the door handle.

"Where are you going?" Reyes asked. "Let's wait here and see where she goes next."

"I'm not going to wait outside. If she's there, I want to talk to her and find out more about Littleton. You stay here and keep an eye on things."

Reyes opened her door and stepped out onto the sidewalk. "Like hell I will," she said, a smile on her face. "I'm coming with you. We're partners, remember?"

Gideon didn't bother arguing with her. The fact was he might need her. He had no idea what he was going to find inside the theater. He was not used to operating under these conditions. Praised by his superiors for his strategic and tactical mission planning, he always had backups in place as a fail-safe against the unexpected. In Iraq, when DeKay's careless actions threatened the team, he had safeguards in place that helped ensure the team's survival.

Now he was on foreign territory, operating without a net. All advantages went to DeKay, who had the manpower and the technological resources. This was his turf.

What do I have? Gideon shook his head and peered skyward, a worried expression on his face. Overhead, the sky was gray and overcast. It looked like rain was in their future. As if someone had heard his prediction, a sharp, biting wind blew across the street. Gideon pulled his jacket close around him, the sudden drop in temperature giving him goose bumps.

If it were easy, they wouldn't call it a challenge, he thought. He just hoped this challenge wouldn't be his last.

The Clover Theater was like a blast out of time and space. Reminiscent of the roaring twenties—a decade that brought America flappers, prohibition, and Al Capone—the theater was a relic, a leftover indulgence that continued to pay homage to the golden age of filmmaking. Like many theaters of its kind, this one was struggling to stay afloat. Showing discounted movies often weeks or months after their original release, the Clover catered to a dwindling audience that considered ambience an important part of their entertainment value.

Gideon walked across the street, surprised by the cold chill that enveloped him. The approaching storm had caused the temperature to drop, and he was glad that he had his jacket. He stepped up on the curb. Reyes stood next to him.

Judging by the building's condition, the owners were behind in their maintenance. The red neon sign that rose to the heavens flashed sporadically, the bright lights no longer working in rhythm. Like the neon sign above it, the attraction board was dirty and pitted from neglect. Rimmed with theater lights, the sign glowed an ugly yellow. The black letters—many of them missing, broken, or improvised into new shapes—promoted the movies inside.

Gideon could imagine the majesty this theater must have once displayed, but now a complete restoration was in order. When he was a child, he had spent a lot of time in a theater just like this one. While the theater's name escaped him, he did remember what it was like to learn and explore inside one of these historic landmarks. The memories danced around his head like flies, thick and real enough that he could have swatted them with his hand.

When he was growing up in a small town in Nebraska, his mother was one of two cashiers who worked at the local theater. Oftentimes, he was allowed to tag along. While she sold tickets and refreshments, he had the time of his life, sometimes watching two or three movies a day. Even today, he could still picture the ushers: slender young men sporting snappy, light gray uniforms with a forest green chest and a double row of bright brass buttons running up to their padded shoulder boards. Gideon used to call them admirals for the way the gold-and-green tassels looped around their shoulders. They looked important, at least to a five-year-old.

Back then, the ushers still used flashlights to escort patrons to their seats. At each movie he saw, whether it was in the same screening room or not, he would have them show him to his seat. It was a small pleasure, but it made him feel important. Best of all, between movies they would give him piggyback rides up and down the aisles.

The theater was one of his greatest pleasures as a kid. It was in the theater that Gideon first learned to be patient, to embrace the darkness as the lights dimmed and the movie started. It was all a game to him. He learned how to be quiet, to slip in and out without making a sound, unnoticed by anyone, even the theater's manager. How well he remembered the delicious sensation of entering the cool depths of the screening room on a blistering hot summer day. Equally wonderful was the warming sensation of the setting sun on his face and arms when he emerged again, his mother holding his small hand as they walked home.

That theater was demolished years ago, destroyed by a fire when he was eight. His mother died a few months later giving birth to his brother. The baby was stillborn. Gideon didn't understand at the time. How could he? What followed were years of neglect and loneliness. Raised by a father who knew nothing of children, Gideon wished more than once that he could have retreated back into the theater. There, his life had been happy and without worry.

That was a lifetime ago.

"You okay?"

Reyes's question brought Gideon back to the task at hand. "Come on," he said, swallowing hard. "It's time we got to the bottom of this."

He escorted Reyes through the revolving door, a growing sense of purpose driving him to action.

Kulbeda Station had twenty-four security cameras located throughout the base. One of them, DeKay prayed, must have caught something. Apparently, the girls had been missing since early this morning, right after his last check on them. They were supposed to be sedated, incapable of acting on their own. The mystery simply confirmed DeKay's suspicions that someone else inside Littleton was aiding them. He was obsessed with finding out who had betrayed him.

Minutes earlier, his men found evidence that one of the lifts leading from Littleton to the surface had been broken into. Someone very clever had covered their tracks, because the security measures were overridden, including a bypass that would have alerted him of the lift's operation.

DeKay loaded security feeds for the past few hours, hoping to find signs of the twins' disappearance or anything out of the ordinary. He moved through his progressions, settling on one of two cameras that covered the base's parade grounds. Next, he accessed the computer database that stored the security images. Standard protocol required that images be stored for forty-eight hours before being either saved or destroyed. With any luck, discovering what happened to the girls might be easier than he anticipated. DeKay rewound the digital tapes, watching as the world spun backward.

After a few minutes he stopped, both excited and puzzled by what he saw. To say he was shocked would be an understatement. The black-and-white image displayed Charlie Simmons on the surface, warily exiting the motor pool. Since DeKay had been at Littleton, this was the first time he had ever seen Charlie out in the real world. Now, he watched the screen as the little janitor stopped to confirm that the coast was clear before he strolled across the parade ground, pushing a large, soiled-linen basket in front of him. Head bent low, Charlie walked like a man on a mission.

"What is he doing up there?" DeKay asked aloud. "He can't tie his own shoes without help. How did he manage this?"

DeKay followed the image closely until Charlie passed out of sight. Going to the next camera, he followed Charlie as he made his way toward a small utility shack.

"Just where do you think you're going?"

Charlie walked past the utility shed, without a glance, to a delivery truck parked next to the base's supply building. The sign on the truck's door advertised fresh uniforms and linens with next-day service. This was one of the approved contractors for the base, a mom-and-pop organization out of Curtis Cove.

Charlie disappeared behind the vehicle. Minutes passed. Finally, the truck's driver ambled into view. Clipboard in hand, the man entered the cab, started the engine, and drove out of sight. Left behind was an empty linen basket. Charlie was nowhere to be found.

Clever, Charlie, DeKay thought. *That's real clever.*

DeKay now knew the culprit behind the girls' disappearance. The truth was not pleasant. The girls were no longer on the base and his search below was fruitless. More disconcerting, it was only a matter of time before Frist discovered the tape of Charlie Simmons leaving Kulbeda. Then, all hell would break loose. DeKay figured that he had a two-hour window to find the girls before Frist got involved.

Next, DeKay scanned through additional feeds searching for his second problem. Within a few minutes he found an image of Dr. Sossoman. Unlike Charlie Simmons, he found the doctor exiting the main entrance at the parking complex.

Sossoman's failure to report in had aroused his suspicion. For the second time this week Littleton was in lockdown. The girls were nowhere to be found, and their primary warden was pointedly ignoring every attempt at contact. Now he knew why.

DeKay accessed tapes from all the video cameras that supported the parking structure. One of the feeds in particular enabled him to follow Sossoman's movements up to the point where she entered a yellow taxi at the street corner.

DeKay smiled. The taxi shouldn't be too hard to trace. This was a small town with only one cab service. A personal visit with the taxi company's manager, and he would have the information he needed. What troubled DeKay most was the series of events leading up to this moment.

He held his fury in check, letting his natural curiosity and paranoia drive his actions. Clearly, Dr. Sossoman knew where the children were, or else she wouldn't have left the premises. Now, like a mouse to cheese, he would follow her to the girls. Then he would take care of the good doctor once and for all. DeKay's smile turned to an evil grin. His keen mind quickly worked through the options available to him, settling on a few that might work to his advantage. His teeth flashed even and white. The girls' latest defiance might actually work in his favor.

CHAPTER 18

Dr. Sossoman was an unusually tall, thin woman, quite a bit taller than Gideon. He found himself looking up into her sharp, defiant blue eyes. Remnants of brilliant blonde hair were still visible at her temples, though gray was the dominant color covering her head. Gideon guessed the doctor was in her mid-sixties, and, judging from the fight she put up when he confronted her, was still physically fit.

The two were alone in a small alcove just outside the screening room for one of the Clover Theater's movies. He had caught her alone, just as she was preparing to enter the room. Reyes stood just out of sight, keeping watch and making sure he wasn't disturbed.

"Who are you?" Sossoman rasped in a voice filled with surprise and rage. "What do you want with me?"

Gideon came straight to the point. "I want to know more about Littleton. I want to know why you're holding two little girls prisoner. Most important, I want to know what Cross DeKay is up to."

Sossoman gasped in shock. Her eyes grew wide and wild. Her breath became rapid and shallow. "How do you know of Littleton?" she whispered. Then her eyes widened as she came to the first, most plausible answer. "It was you," she stammered. "You are the intruder." Her mind caught up with everything Gideon had said. "You know about the girls?"

"I do," he responded. His voice—cool, deliberate, and laced with purpose—flowed like the fog of dry ice. "We had a nice conversation before I was forced to leave. They told me all about you and Littleton. Nice girls, cute as a button. But I don't have all the answers. That's where you come in."

"I can't tell you anything," she pleaded. "DeKay will kill me. With the girls' latest disappearance, he might kill me anyway."

Gideon's surprise was genuine. "The girls are missing?" Then he looked behind him to the screening room. Now it all made sense. Sossoman didn't come here to see a movie, or to meet with someone. She came here looking for the twins. "They're in there?" he asked.

Sossoman nodded. "I received a note this morning from Amy, telling me that they had left and where they could be found. They left Littleton with someone they trust. Amy asked me to meet them here. She knew I would come alone."

"Is Charlie Simmons with them?"

Sossoman's mouth dropped open. "How. . . ?"

"It doesn't matter," Gideon said. "This is quite a coincidence. The twins are here. Charlie. You." His arms swung wide. "All of us in the same place at the same time."

"*Coincidence* is not a word we use as far as the girls are concerned," Sossoman replied. "The two have been planning this for some time. I don't know the role you will ultimately play, but believe me, you're here for a reason, too."

Gideon detected a slight accent in the woman's voice. She looked and dressed like an American, but her tone and inflection had subtle lapses. Having been abroad, he guessed she had spent considerable time in Germany or Austria, perhaps.

Sossoman deflated. The bravado she displayed in confronting Gideon left her in a rush of spent energy. Right before his eyes, the doctor wilted, looking more her age. When her eyes opened, she focused on Gideon, her gaze searching deep for answers.

A moment of silence lapsed between them. Sossoman was searching her soul for answers her mind could not grasp. A future with uncertain possibilities had been laid at her doorstep. Should she pursue or close the door shut? The decision to run and hide was easier than uncertain change, but in the long run, the results were often the same. Now this stranger had entered her life, and he presented the possibility, however slim, that she might take control of her future.

Sossoman looked at Gideon with growing excitement, like he had answers to all her questions, held the keys that would unlock the chains around her neck. "What is your name?" she asked in a strong, clear voice.

"John Gideon."

"I need your help," she pleaded. Sweat began to bead on her face. "*We* need your help."

Gideon felt a chill run up his spine. Cross DeKay, Charlie Simmons, and Dr. Sossoman, and now he and Reyes. They were all connected to the girls. Who else was involved? How could it be anything but coincidence? Now Sossoman knew of his visit to Littleton. His mind raced with the possibilities and permutations, all the things that could go wrong. The list was endless.

Gideon pulled away. His eyes narrowed with suspicion.

Sensing Gideon's growing reluctance, Sossoman pressed forward. "You must help us," she pleaded. "I promised to look after the twins, that I would let nothing happen to them as long as I was alive. If DeKay finds them, he will hurt them. Or. . . ." Sossoman's hand rose to her mouth. "Or he might do something even worse."

Gideon shook his head and sighed. Everything she said was impossible. Like Dr. Sossoman, he, too, had made the girls a promise. It was a promise he thought nothing of at the time, yet now it troubled him deeply.

Everything about his assignment at Kulbeda Station was based on lies and half-truths. He sensed that what he didn't know could fill volumes, yet he still felt compelled to act. There was something going on here, something deeper, more urgent, than Littleton. A clock was ticking, winding down to an uncertain end.

"First," Gideon demanded, "I want some information. What is Littleton? Who are these girls, and why are they important to DeKay? Believe me, I know the man. There's a long history between us. If you want to live long enough to see these girls reach their next birthday, you'd better get me up to speed. Otherwise, there are no guarantees any of you will be alive tomorrow."

Sossoman swallowed hard. Her whole life had been about secrets. Keeping them, creating them, doling them out in small parcels only when absolutely necessary. She had been in and out of Littleton many times over the past forty years, coming when needed, leaving when the work failed. In many ways she was no better than DeKay. The two shared a similar history, one that troubled her heart and threatened her soul. The only real difference between them was that she had been doing it longer. The fact that DeKay was prepared to kill the girls was a minor technicality. Her recommendations over the years had led to the death of many others. That she had never pulled the trigger was of small condolence. She was part of the same wicked agenda. Now she was looking for redemption. She wanted out of Littleton, away from the secrets and lies. Amy and Emily were her last best hope for salvation. It had been a long time since she'd had girls of their caliber, and she wasn't about to fail them.

Sossoman looked long and hard at Gideon, studying the outline of his strong chin and square cheekbones. His deep blue eyes were almost kind, decidedly honest, and deadly determined. He was ruggedly handsome, with his short-cropped hair and tanned complexion. Many women would find him attractive. *If only I were younger,* she thought. In her youth, she, too, was an attractive woman.

Sossoman sighed. How much should she tell him? What did he need to know?

As if he were reading her mind, Gideon prompted again. "Listen, I need to be familiar with everything important about Littleton. Skip the details. Give me the broad strokes. If I have any questions, I'll ask them."

Sossoman weighed the options, deciding to trust her instincts and provide the information Gideon requested. "Littleton," she began, "is part of a covert government program called Project Gemini. The project is very secret—only a few high-placed officials within the government know about it—and many people have been killed to keep it that way. Outside of those underneath Kulbeda Station, the precise location of the town is unknown to all but a select few."

"What is Project Gemini?" Gideon asked. "Start there."

Sossoman took a deep breath and let it out slowly. When she began, her voice was soft and steady. "To appreciate Project Gemini, you first have to understand the past. Throughout history, mighty leaders have risen to positions of absolute power. Cleopatra, Genghis Kahn, Napoleon Bonaparte, Adolph Hitler, each one ruled with an iron fist. These leaders started wars that killed millions. They conquered and enslaved whole nations to worship and serve them and in the process expanded their rule to encompass half the known world. What most do not realize is that these rulers had help in their rise to dominion.

"John, this is going to sound farfetched, but you must believe what I'm about to tell you." She paused briefly before continuing. "There are certain individuals who are born with a special gift, a talent so powerful that they can bring about equal measures of joy and abundance or devastation and destruction. These individuals have the unique ability to alter the future.

"You've no doubt heard about the Butterfly Effect, a theory where even the beat of a single butterfly's wing can cause a hurricane halfway around the world. In essence, the girls are like butterflies. They can set specific events in motion, small actions or crises, that cascade into one another until the end result is what was originally 'wished' for. We call them 'wellwishers.' Revered by those who control them and feared by those who only suspect their existence, these wellwishers have shaped the future of many a king and queen.

"But there's a twist to this story. Wellwishers are always girls. They are always identical twins, down to the minutest detail. They have IQs that rival history's most brilliant scientists and philosophers. And they rarely live beyond their eighth birthday. Most important, however, is that upon their death they often bring ruin to those around them."

Sossoman paused to let her story sink in. Gideon looked up to see Reyes approaching. She, too, was engaged in the story. The doctor appeared uncertain at Reyes's arrival but continued at Gideon's urging.

"Despite this knowledge, there are some whose ambitions are so powerful that they will stop at nothing to identify, acquire, and control these girls and their abilities. They believe the future is malleable and that history is only a tool, not something to be respected or feared. Project Gemini exists solely to harness this power; these people want to control and channel this power and use it to their advantage. Over the years, Littleton has held more than a dozen wellwishers. Some were more powerful than others, but none of them worked out. Until now, that is."

Gideon looked at Sossoman, doubt in his eyes. The doctor returned his stare with equal measure.

"You're telling me," he said, "that these girls are wellwishers? That they have the ability to shape the future? That's impossible."

"I'm afraid it's more than possible, John. The fact is, the United States government has known for some time about these two special children. Amy and Emily Chase were kidnapped at two years of age from a small farm in Iowa. To cover the disappearance, their entire family was brutally murdered and then destroyed in an explosion. The kidnappers transported the girls to Littleton and have spent the last five years trying to bend them to their will."

"For what purpose?" Gideon asked. The last part about the girls' kidnapping was exactly what Amy told him the other night.

Sossoman was quick to answer. "The girls are pawns in a game between the United States and any nation that opposes it. For example, what if Britain's prime minister didn't support the President's strategic arms initiatives? Could a single catastrophic event change policy? Or what if Germany's chancellor decided not to acknowledge the continuation of NATO? Would a rogue missile from a competing nation change his mind? When the President talks about the Axis of evil, what do you think drives change? Policy alone? That's too naïve, even for you."

"I don't understand," Gideon said. His mind spun wildly. "How are the girls able to do this? Why isn't this common knowledge? I mean, I've never heard anything like this before. And if it's true, what about free will, destiny, and the chaos of the universe? How can anyone control or influence their future when cause and effect creates infinite possibilities with equally infinite outcomes?"

"Project Gemini is successful because everyone who has ever posed a threat to its existence has been eliminated. Period. As for how the girls do it. . . ." Sossoman shrugged her shoulders. "The brightest scientists in the world can't explain it. No test can quantify it. There's no smoking gun to point to and say, 'That's how they do it.' Yet the fact remains—these children have extraordinary abilities. The best that we can tell, the girls need to be close to each other for their gift to work. They show no signs of wellwishing when they're apart. But together, they're able to manipulate the world around them, oftentimes with deadly consequences. I don't know how they do it. No one does. And we have no idea how their gift will evolve over time."

"If they're so powerful, then how come they've been captive for so long? Why don't they 'wish' themselves to be free?"

Sossoman laughed. "You don't understand—for all their abilities, the girls are still only seven years old. They're children. They still need to be nurtured, loved, and cared for. They have the same insecurities and instinctual cravings for safety and security that we all have. The girls react to what they experience, which, as you can imagine, is very little, given their confinement. They're told what they need to know, nothing more. Just enough so they can perform for DeKay."

"So, what's changed?" Reyes asked.

"Their intellect and instinct are getting ahead of DeKay's security protocols. These girls are extremely gifted, and he's ill-prepared to deal with them. They're far more advanced than any recorded wellwishers. To put it simply, Littleton has become too small for them."

"And when they turn eight, what happens then?" Gideon asked.

Sossoman's face clouded over. "Most wellwishers don't live past the age of two," she said. "See, these kids have the ability to shape the future, simply by wishing for something to happen. Imagine a one-year-old crying because she's hungry, or uncomfortable, or irritated because she can't reach a favorite toy. The infant's action is visceral, without any thought to the consequences. Now imagine that you're the parent, the object of the child's displeasure. We know from experience that these parents don't live very long. Nor, for that matter, do the next set of guardians, the uncles or aunts."

"They kill their parents?" Gideon asked.

"Not on purpose," she responded. "Nor can they wish for a heart attack, or cancer, or anything like that. They're far too young to associate a negative, lucid, or reasoned reaction to what's troubling them. But what they can do is react instinctively, impulsively—like any infant would—against the object of their displeasure. Next thing you know, unusually strong winds cause a tree to fall, or the car crashes in an unexpected storm. Maybe the parent slips on spilled juice and bangs their head on the kitchen counter. There are usually multiple events that occur in sequence, all of them seemingly unrelated and individually benign, but when combined, the results are what the child wanted at the time—punishment."

"This is all too much," Gideon said. His head was spinning, and she still hadn't answered his original question. Instead of pushing her, he changed the subject. "Who's the mastermind behind Project Gemini? Not DeKay.

He's not that well-connected."

"You've heard of Arthur Frist." It was not a question, though Gideon nodded his head anyway. "Frist has been involved from the very beginning. He was a rising star in business and politics when Littleton was first conceived. President Eisenhower called upon him to put Project Gemini together. The government funded the whole thing but left all the details to Frist. At the time, Frist Industries was a Department of Defense cover for the operation. Since then, the business and the man have taken on lives all their own. Most don't realize it, but he's one of the most powerful men in the United States."

"How many twins like this are there?" Gideon asked. It was too fantastic to believe, but he couldn't help but become engaged in the story.

"Amy and Emily are the third set of twins with any real abilities to occupy Littleton since the Project's inception," she said. "The first set came out of Seoul, during the Korean War. The second was smuggled out of East Germany in the late sixties. It was the height of the Cold War, and the United States could not let the Communists get those twins. There have been many others with lesser abilities, but they didn't last long.

"In terms of statistics, we estimate that the chance of having twins in the twenty-first century is one in fifty. Of those, less than two one hundredths of a percent show limited signs of wellwishing. Most of the time, the power is equated to twins thinking alike, being in tune with one another, when in fact there is a deeper connection. It's very rare when any of those children exhibit abilities even close to Amy and Emily. The last known wellwishers with this kind of power were captives of Hitler during World War II."

Gideon was struggling to absorb what he had just heard. He had met these girls, had spoken with them. They appeared normal, like any other kids he knew. Yet the entire time, there was an undercurrent of mystery. There was an air of electricity that at the time he could not place.

"They wished for me," he whispered.

"What did you say?" Sossoman asked.

"The girls," he responded. "They wished for me. That's what they said that night. They knew I would come, because they wished it. No wonder they weren't surprised by my visit."

"What else did they say?" Sossoman was insistent.

Gideon recalled the night, responding with open awe. "They said I didn't have to be afraid. That everything was going to be all right. Then, I think it was Amy, she asked me not to forget them. I . . ." Gideon paused, looking up to Sossoman's eyes. "I promised I would be back to help them."

Sossoman smiled broadly. "I knew it," she said. "I told you! It's true.

You're here for a reason."

Gideon chewed absently on his lip. How could this be? He was here for a reason? Even after what he had heard, it didn't make sense. His discovery of the vent in the woods was based on infrared satellite imagery that the director ordered, that's all. There was no invisible hand guiding him to the commons that night, to where the girls lay in wait. Try as he might, he could not connect the dots. Short of their appearance in the park, there was no visible sign that the girls had manipulated anything.

He had heard plenty about paranormal charlatans through the years. People who could communicate with the dead, or move objects with their minds, even predict the future. Rubbish. There wasn't a single independently verified example of anyone who could perform feats like those. And the reasons were obvious. It couldn't be done. For the moment, he was skeptical. It was a wonderful tale, and it was loosely supported by Littleton's very existence. Until he knew more, however, he needed to keep a distance between what the doctor knew and what he believed. Let time—and the evidence—speak for itself.

Sossoman broke the silence. "Tell me, John. Would you like to see the girls again?"

Gideon felt his head nod of its own volition, as if he had no control over the act.

"In there," she said, pointing with her chin.

Gideon turned around, a lump lodged in his throat.

Reyes refused to meet his gaze. *What were they afraid of?* she thought. *Two girls and a janitor, that's it.*

"All right," he said, a slight quiver in his voice. "Let's go."

CHAPTER 19

"Hello, Charlie."

Charlie didn't look back. Engrossed in the movie, he simply tilted his head back and said, "Hi, John. What took you so long?" His eyes never left the screen.

Two rows up, the girls sat shoulder to shoulder, their mouths agape, transfixed by the digitally remastered black-and-white classic *Gunga Din*. Gideon suspected that it was the first movie they had ever seen. What a choice. The girls were oblivious to their surroundings. The popcorn beside them was untouched, the drinks still full to the top.

The small theater was dark, lit only by the silver screen and the thin sliver of light emanating from the doors behind them. The rank smell of stale popcorn, spilled butter, and musty seat cushions combined to assail Gideon's senses.

The inside was no different than the exterior. The Clover Theater was not about creature comforts or the niceties found in large, modern multiplexes. It was all about ambience, architectural aesthetics, and the cerebral remembrances of times and theaters past. Thick carpet stretched from wall to wall, the bubble gum and candy trash decades old, embedded forever in the thread-worn tapestry. Intricate gilt archways swept patrons from one room to another. On the walls, gold-leafed sconces provided subdued lighting.

"We need to talk, Charlie."

Charlie's shoulders slumped, displaying his annoyance at being interrupted during the movie. Reluctantly, he turned around to engage Gideon.

Charlie's annoyance turned quickly to alarm. At seeing Dr. Sossoman, the man's eyes grew wide with surprise. He shrank down in his chair, his gaze darting wildly between Gideon and the doctor.

To Gideon, Charlie looked like a feral animal, trapped in a corner with nowhere to run or hide.

"What is she doing here?" Charlie screeched. "The girls said only you were coming."

The theater was mostly empty. The few patrons who heard the noise quickly turned back to the movie, but not before throwing harsh requests for them to be quiet. The girls remained oblivious to the commotion.

Charlie's eyes displayed his confusion and anger. Gideon had betrayed him, bringing with him an instrument of DeKay, the man he despised and feared most in the world. Being an object of DeKay's ire was not something he had planned on. His mind was reeling at the possible actions DeKay could take against him.

He had every reason to be afraid, but not of Gideon or Dr. Sossoman. Gideon spoke quickly and quietly, calming the man as he summarized the events leading to his discovery at the Clover Theater. After a few tense moments, as he realized the danger to him and the girls was not imminent, Charlie settled down, though not enough to make Gideon comfortable.

Charlie continued to bow his head and refused to make eye contact with Dr. Sossoman. His hands were curled into a tight ball and tucked under his chin. To Gideon, the position appeared instinctual, an unconscious reaction to stress or a supplication to authority. This behavior was unusual, and Gideon was at a loss to understand the man's reaction. Sossoman, however, had some notion of why Charlie behaved like he did.

"Charlie," Dr. Sossoman spoke firmly from behind Gideon. "Look at me."

Prior to entering the cinema, the doctor had agreed to deal with Charlie first, before confronting the girls. Gideon fully expected her to break that arrangement the minute she saw Amy and Emily, so he was surprised by the level of constraint she had shown thus far.

Charlie slowly raised his eyes to meet hers. The two stared at each other. No words were spoken between them. A full minute of tense silence passed with both individuals refusing to break eye contact. With each passing second, Charlie grew bolder, breaking out of his self-imposed shell to square off at Sossoman. After another minute went by, Gideon was surprised to hear Sossoman's sharp intake of breath.

"Dear God," she said. "How long have you been like this?" Sossoman looked at Charlie, seeing a person she didn't know.

He smiled broadly and replied, "Almost six months. Every day is better than the last."

"What about the seizures?"

"Gone," he replied.

"The stuttering, the heart palpitations, what about the—"

"All gone," he replied proudly.

Sossoman slumped into the seat next to Gideon. Meanwhile, Charlie beamed with pride.

"Will someone please fill me in?" Gideon asked. He felt like an interloper, an intruder trespassing on sacred ground. He didn't like being the last to know.

Sossoman held up her hand, admonishing Gideon to sit patiently and wait.

"The girls?" was all she asked, awe creeping into her voice.

"Yes." Charlie's eyes brimmed with tears. "They wished for me."

Sossoman gripped Gideon's hand tightly. She turned to him and said, "As an infant, Charlie was diagnosed with phenylketonuria, a rare genetic disorder that causes the amino acid phenylalanine to build up in the blood. If not treated properly, this imbalance can result in severe, and irreversible, mental retardation. In Charlie's case, he went untreated until he was almost six months old."

Gideon stared back with a blank face, the implications of the doctor's explanation unclear to him. Sossoman tried another explanation. "At birth, babies with phenylketonuria have no signs or symptoms of the disorder. The mother's body is designed to act like a filter, removing phenylalanine from her system during pregnancy. When the filter is dysfunctional, as was the case with Charlie's mother, symptoms don't appear until after the baby starts consuming protein, most notably from breast milk. Because the disorder was not diagnosed or treated properly, it caused progressively severe mental retardation and other problems to his nervous system. Whatever mental and physical abilities Charlie lost during this period should never have been regained."

"How do you explain this?" Gideon asked. Charlie sat before him, his back straight, head held high. For all appearances, he was physically healthy and mentally strong, no different than Gideon or Sossoman.

"I can't explain it," she replied. "Charlie has been in Littleton for almost twenty years. I've been treating him for the last five. As long as I've known him, he's had problems—frequent seizures and episodes of uncontrollable mania. He's never been physically violent, and most people in Littleton have come to live with his eccentricities. The most severe problem, however, has been the lack of mental development. It took Charlie twenty years to develop the mental and physical acuity of a ten-year-old. Emotionally, however, he deals with the environment around him, especially people, like a six-year-old would."

Sossoman turned to Charlie, her delicate hands caressing his face. "The girls wished for you to be normal? Is that even possible? I can't believe it. That's truly remarkable. I saw no signs of this, nothing to indicate that you were changing. All those sessions together," she admonished, "you had a secret."

"Well, you *were* busy," Charlie replied sheepishly. "Besides, the girls made me promise I wouldn't tell anyone." He saw the look of disappointment on Sossoman and continued eagerly. "No, it's okay. They've been helping me, teaching me. Every day, I got better, stronger, and smarter. Amy gets me books to read. Emily helped me learn to speak better, so I don't act afraid when I meet people. They said I needed to blend into the real world, for when we left Littleton forever. I even fooled him." He looked at Gideon, smiling wide. "Didn't I?"

Gideon ignored the question, focusing instead on the two children who were now standing beside them in the aisle.

"The movie's over," Emily said. "Can we watch it again?"

Gideon looked up in time to see the final credits disappear off the screen. Seconds later, the lights came on to illuminate the small theater. The half dozen patrons still remaining filed out, some of them staring angrily as they passed. The die-hard fans of classic cinema were annoyed at Charlie's vocal interruption during the movie.

"Pleeease," Amy begged, "just once more. We have plenty of time before the bad man gets here."

While Gideon's answer was disappointing, the girls did not argue or pout. Instead, they turned toward their guardian and said in unison, "Hello, Dr. Sossoman."

Emily broke away from her sister to give the doctor a warm hug and a kiss on the cheek. More reserved in her affection, Amy hung back, nodding politely. She offered a big smile to Gideon.

"Sorry we snuck away again," Emily said. "We're glad you're here, though."

"Wait a minute," Reyes broke in. "What was that about the bad man coming here? Where is he now?"

The girls looked at each other, smirked, and shrugged their shoulders.

"We don't know where he is, but he is coming," Emily replied with confidence.

"Did you wish for that, too?" Gideon didn't even try to keep the sarcasm from his tone.

"That's quite enough." Sossoman's tone was soft but firm. "If the girls say that DeKay is coming, then he is. That's all you need to know. The question is, what are we going to do now? We can't go back. You know too much, and I've betrayed a confidence. As for the girls, they've given him enough trouble. Who knows what he'll do to them."

"All right, let's go," Gideon ordered. "Outside. We'll figure out where once we're away from here."

He was still skeptical about everything he had learned. Girls who could shape the future with a simple wish? A mentally retarded adult gaining his senses? A well-respected billionaire funding Littleton? None of it made any sense.

The only thing he knew for certain was that Cross DeKay was trouble—with a capital T. Talk about wishes. If he had one, it would be to get as far away from there as possible.

Gideon's wish did not come true.

Reyes, who was walking ahead of them, turned sharply around at the edge of the theater lobby. Her weapon was raised in warning. Immediately following her movement, Gideon could hear the loud sound of tires screeching on the pavement outside.

"Two cars," Reyes said when she drew close. "I'm sure they're not here for the afternoon matinee."

Gideon spun on his heels, his weapon drawn. "Back inside the theater. Hurry!"

The small group ran down the hallway, back the way they had come. Frightened patrons, confused by the sudden panic, moved aside, their backs to the wall. Those too slow to get out of the way were thrust aside. The swinging screening-room doors loomed large as they raced headlong from DeKay's arriving forces.

"Something's not right," Gideon shouted to Reyes. Years of training and finely honed instincts took over. "It's like we're being corralled into a pen. That team in front arrived in a hurry. They made no pretense at stealth or subtlety. They wanted us to know they were out front."

"Why would they do that?" Reyes asked.

"Other teams must already be in place, coming through the back doors." Gideon ran his fingers through his hair. He leaned close to Reyes. "DeKay will want to capture the twins without drawing attention. To do that, he has to keep them in the theater. If this gets to the street, all those innocent bystanders become potential witnesses. That's bad for Littleton. The screeching tires were meant as a warning to drive Dr. Sossoman and the children back the way they had come, into an ambush." Gideon smiled a mischievous grin. "But I'm guessing they still don't know anything about you and me."

Without hesitating, Gideon rushed past the children, pushing Charlie aside, and exploded into the small screening room. Two men in dark suits were entering the theater from the fire exit opposite the entrance. Both men had their weapons drawn, but neither was expecting someone like Gideon to come barging into the room. Taken off guard, the men fired wildly at the new threat. The shots whipped by Gideon's head, shattering the doorframe and splintering the ornate molding. The fact that the men came close to him despite their shock was a testament to their skill as marksmen. The fact that they missed provided an opportunity for Gideon to gain control of the situation.

Gideon flinched slightly as the bullets passed, but he held his ground. Before DeKay's men could adjust, he squared his shoulders and returned fire. His weapon echoed loudly in the chamber.

His first shot hit one of the men square in the chest. The agent fell back into his partner, forcing him off-balance. Gideon fired again, but this time he missed. Already falling, the second man used his momentum to dive for cover. Gideon's next shots peppered the seat backs, sending tufts of padding and fabric into the air.

In the silence that followed, Gideon could hear the agent reporting to those outside. The element of surprise had evaporated like the mist of dawn, only faster. *Shit*, he thought. By now, DeKay's men would be rearming for the new threat. Their response would be more violent, the firepower more lethal.

Gideon had to assume that all the exits were covered. That left one option open to him, to do what he was trained to do. Adapt, improvise, think outside the box, and then push forward. Retreat was not on the menu.

Gideon motioned outside for the others to stay low and wait where they were. Then he did the unexpected. He sprinted down the center aisle, his weapon aimed at the front row. Five feet turned to ten. Ten feet flew into twenty. With only a few rows remaining and the gunman nowhere in sight, Gideon dove. His momentum carried him past the front few rows in a headlong rush. The second man from Kulbeda was caught out of position, exposed. The man had wrongly assumed that Gideon was going to retreat back into the main part of the building to protect the children and was content to wait for reinforcements to arrive. The mistake cost him.

Gideon flew into the open, past the stunned man. Time seemed to slow down. He watched the assailant's eyes grow wide at the sight. He could even see the man's pupils dilate as his body reacted to the threat. He saw the silenced weapon rise in his hands. Still in midair, Gideon fired a shot that entered under the assailant's right armpit. At such close range, the internal damage would be devastating—and fatal. Gideon didn't bother wasting a second bullet. The man was dead before he hit the ground.

Gideon rose slowly, hampered by the bruising reception the hard floor gave him when he landed.

Reyes came running down the aisle, her weapon sweeping left to right. "Are you all right?" she asked.

"Grab his weapon and spare ammunition," he instructed.

Reyes obeyed without comment. Like the others, she was still reeling at the unexpected turn of events. She was also amazed at the sheer bravery Gideon displayed. She had never seen someone act with such absolute determination and skill. Although she had seen him kill other men, each instance was different, unique. Today, he displayed a singular tactic, a feline cunning that went beyond training or experience. He acted on pure instinct. It was like Gideon was born to do this, like he possessed a sixth and seventh sense that imbued him with action and resolve, a will beyond anything she had ever seen. No one she had ever known dove into danger, quite literally, like he did.

Reyes turned back to Gideon, watching with open admiration as he patiently escorted the girls past the two dead men. The twins had their eyes closed and were hugging tight to Dr. Sossoman, but they were not crying. For her part, the doctor was not afraid to look upon death. She assessed the dead men with an analytical detachment, her emotions saved for the children. Reyes paid little attention to Charlie, who brought up the rear.

Gideon slowly approached the fire exit and carefully poked his head through the opening. He pulled it back quickly; bullets thudded into the heavy wood door as it closed shut.

"Damn it," he swore. He opened the door a crack and fired three quick shots into the alley. The men charging toward them dove for cover. *That should buy us a few seconds,* he thought.

Gideon closed the heavy bolt that locked the door, knowing all too well it would only slow them down, not stop them.

"Up the stairs!" he shouted. He pushed Reyes to the lead, watching as she hurried up the small flight of steps to the theater's stage. Gideon followed a second later.

"This way," he said calmly after catching up to Reyes. He walked behind the white screen to a narrow staircase. "This should lead to the lighting area above the theater. From there, we go to the roof. Stay close, move as fast as you can, and keep quiet."

Gideon bounded quietly up the stairs, taking them three at a time. When he reached the top, he found the door locked. He pulled a lockpick set from his pocket and began to work the mechanism. His hands were steady as he inserted a tension wrench into the keyhole and turned the cylinder plug in the same direction as he would a key. Next, he inserted a pick into the keyhole and began to lift the tumblers into the surrounding housing, all the while maintaining pressure on the tension wrench. The stairwell was silent, save for the labored breathing of those behind him. A slight click rewarded Gideon's efforts, signaling that the lock had been sprung. Relieved, he turned the lock and opened the door. The entire process took no more than a few seconds.

"Let's go," Gideon whispered.

At that moment, the theater erupted with deafening explosions and isolated gunfire. Assault teams were storming the screening room, entering after three flashbang grenades exploded with their million candelas of light and almost two hundred decibels of noise. If they had been caught below, the sheer force of those grenades would have knocked them senseless. For anyone not affected by the blast, the suppressive gunfire would have overwhelmed any kind of response.

Safely above the fray, Gideon closed the door quietly behind him, cringing as the lock clicked loudly into place. It was a reflexive action only. Given the noise below, there was little chance that anyone heard it.

Following Gideon, the harried group quickly made their way to the roof exit. There was no place to hide on this floor. All four screening rooms had stairways leading up here. Aside from the narrow, winding corridor, the entire space was lined with thick electrical cables, bulbous aluminum lights, metal trusses, miscellaneous wood crates, and all the staging needed to manage a small theater. Every alcove, closet, or room was filled with fifty years of the junk. They couldn't stay here even if they wanted to.

Gideon reached the roof exit and turned the doorknob. The heavy metal door opened only a sliver, but the bright light that entered lit up the dark space. Gideon opened the door wider. The roof looked empty—for now.

"Stay here," he instructed. "I'll be right back."

Five frightened individuals huddled in the semidarkness. Below, they could hear the search expand to other screening rooms. They listened to people scream in panic as the armed men moved from room to room. The search beneath them pulsed with activity as the theater's confused and bewildered patrons ran for safety. It wouldn't be long before DeKay's men discovered the stairways.

The sudden explosion of light from the doorway startled the huddled group. Gideon's face was shadowed by the bright light of day behind him, making it difficult to read his facial expressions. His words, however, left no doubt to the severity of the situation.

"The theater is surrounded. DeKay's men have every exit covered. The police will be here in a few minutes, and then all hell's going to break loose."

"What are we going to do?" Sossoman asked.

"We should try to hide out on the roof, maybe make a stand until the police arrive," Gideon responded. "There are a lot of witnesses. DeKay won't act with so many eyes on us."

The doctor looked hopeful, but it was clear that she did not believe him.

"What about the CIA, can't they help us?" Reyes asked.

"There's not enough time. Whatever's going down, it's going to happen very quickly—like in the next few minutes. We need to take care of this ourselves."

"We may not be as bad off as you think."

Their eyes turned to Dr. Sossoman, wondering what she meant. She was looking at the girls, a smile on her weathered face.

Amy and Emily were holding hands. Their eyes were locked tight in intense concentration. Their tiny shoulders rose and fell in time with their rapid breathing. All of a sudden, dozens, then quickly hundreds, of ladybugs began to fly around the roof opening. More and more followed, until the air and ground were thick with them. Gideon watched the infestation in amazement, wondering where all these beautiful insects had come from. The little red-and-black bugs were everywhere—in the air, on the ground, crawling all over them—but not a single one landed on the girls. It was as if they were attracted to the twins by some ethereal force but at the same time were unable to light upon them.

Dr. Sossoman looked up at Gideon. Hope filled her teary eyes. Charlie was smiling from ear to ear. Reyes could scarcely believe her eyes.

"Be prepared," Sossoman said, her tone ominous. "I don't know what, or when, or how, but be prepared for what is about to happen." She made the sign of the cross across her breast and whispered, "God bless anyone caught up in their wish. They are simply children. They don't know what they are about to cause."

Gideon turned around and stared outside, watching, anticipating what God only knew was about to transpire. His heart skipped a beat and then pounded faster in his chest. Could this truly be happening? Had the old woman been telling the truth all along? He was hard-pressed to explain the sudden swarm of ladybugs. And, clearly, the children were not acting. Maybe, just maybe, there was more to this than he thought.

Then, all hell broke loose.

CHAPTER 20

Jill Wechsler loved her dog, Roman. A large golden retriever she adopted at the local shelter, he was more than she ever hoped he would be. Obedient, thoughtful, and playful, he was a perfect companion in every way, certainly better than her last four boyfriends combined, each of whom had the attention span of a fruit fly and the consideration of a quarrelsome two-year-old. Roman wasn't like them at all. He was always there when she needed him. He was someone who listened attentively, did as he was told, and didn't leave the seat up after he went to the bathroom. In other words, he was everything she needed in a man right now.

"Beautiful dog."

"Thank you," Jill replied, looking up at the man who had offered the compliment. She had seen him here many times before, walking his Boston terrier in the park, but they had never spoken. She bent down and ruffled the hair on the terrier. "And what's your name?" she cooed to the dog.

The man reached down and scratched the dog behind the ears. "This is Duke. He's small in size, but he has the heart of a lion." The man stood up next to Jill. "My name is Michael."

"Jill," she responded with a smile and a blush. "It's nice to meet you." She was not unhappy at the sudden introduction. She had been watching Michael from afar for some time now. Not that he was handsome, or tall, or overly athletic. His hairline was receding, the glasses didn't exactly fit his face, and he could spare to lose the few extra pounds he carried around the middle. She just liked the way he treated his dog. He was kind to Duke, always had treats to reward good behavior, and never once failed to clean up after the dog did its business. She suspected that he was a man who would put the toilet seat back down, and that pleased her.

"Mind if we let them off the leash?" he asked boldly. "Duke plays nice, and he's due for a run."

Jill hesitated for a moment. She was not used to flirting. Besides, city ordinance required a leash at all times. She looked around the park. They were alone. Not another soul in sight.

"Why not," she said, her face blushing deeper than before.

She bent down and unclasped the leash. Roman looked up at her with an inquisitive look before taking off after the retreating terrier. He wasn't about to miss an opportunity at unfettered freedom. He was a dog, after all.

Minutes passed by like seconds as Jill and Michael became acquainted. The park was quiet save for the growing wind that hinted at a pending storm coming off the ocean. Realizing that maybe things were too quiet, Jill looked up, her eyes scanning the park grounds.

"Where's Roman?" she asked.

Jeff Miller was trying very hard to be patient. Between his wife's non-stop talking and his daughter's crying wails, his head was about to split open. Marcy sat next to him in the passenger seat of their new Toyota Sequoia, pointedly ignoring the gale-force tantrum in the backseat. She was rehashing the latest scandal at the law firm where she temped, something about one lawyer screwing another one and the spouses who recently found out about it.

Who cares? Couldn't have happened to a better bunch of people, Jeff thought. He stopped listening.

Meanwhile, their eighteen-month-old daughter, Jackie, was strapped into her car seat and was not happy about it. She wanted to be in her mother's arms, and nothing short of that was going to quiet her. With three blocks to go until they got home, little Jackie would soon get her wish.

"Are you listening to a word I say?"

Busted. His wife had finally caught on, and the answer was no, he wasn't paying any attention. "Honey, I've heard every word," he lied with practiced ease. It was a small lie, so he didn't feel too bad about it. "John at work—"

"Jack," she corrected.

"Right. Jack is screwing Melissa—"

"Michelle," she said with impatience.

"Whatever," Jeff said, about to give up entirely. He turned to his wife, a sharp retort on his lips.

The frightened look in Marcy's eyes brought his head spinning back to the road.

"Look out!" she screamed.

A large gray squirrel had scampered into the road right in front of the SUV. At the last second, Jeff swerved to the right to avoid the critter. No thud. No small bump. He missed it. He glanced in the side mirror, looking for the cause of his wife's fright and his near heart attack. *Damn squirrel,* he cursed to himself.

Marcy's piercing scream brought Jeff's heart to his throat. Chasing the squirrel was a black-and-white Boston terrier. The dog ran blindly into the street after its quarry. Heedless of oncoming traffic, it ran right in front of the speeding car.

Once again, Jeff took evasive action. To avoid this animal, he swerved farther right, his rear wheels skidding on the pavement. His hands worked frantically on the steering wheel to maintain control. Then Jeff's problems got even worse. Another dog, this one a large retriever, came on the heels of the terrier. Marcy screamed again. Her right hand rose instinctively to the door handles. Her left grabbed hold of Jeff's arm and yanked hard to the right, but she was too late. The SUV ran over the retriever with a sickening crash. Jeff heard the dog yelp in pain. He could feel the body bang underneath, the violent vibrations hammering his feet and ankles as the car flew over it. Now skidding out of control, the Sequoia traveled with a leap onto the sidewalk and with a jarring crash through the shrubs surrounding a small park. Bouncing uncontrollably in his seat, Jeff jammed his foot on the brake, only to discover that in all the commotion he had accidentally pressed the accelerator.

The SUV took off through the park even faster than before. It careened over a small knoll, through more bushes, and back onto the opposite street.

This time, both Jeff and Marcy screamed as the SUV ran headfirst into the back end of a Greyhound bus. Airbags throughout the vehicle deployed with violent precision as the car spun counterclockwise on two wheels. An oncoming car skidded to a halt, but not before clipping the Toyota and sending it into another dizzying circle.

Coughing and wheezing as the airbags deflated, Jeff took stock of himself and everyone else in the car. They were all dizzy and disoriented, but no one appeared hurt. He looked out the shattered window and was dismayed to see the bus on a collision course with a woman and her food-laden shopping cart.

"Oh, my God," Jeff said aloud. He turned his head, unable to watch the impending disaster. His wife's eyes were filled with tears. He turned to the backseat. The little girl had a smile on her cherubic face.

Jeff sighed, relieved that his family was spared from harm. Then it occurred to him that his daughter had stopped her crying at last.

Buster Kennedy did everything he could to maintain control of the damaged bus. He narrowly avoided the lady crossing the street, but the shopping cart was now entangled underneath. Even worse, the cart had apparently cut through his brake lines and was wreaking havoc with his steering. The bus was going to crash, and there was nothing he could do about it.

Behind him sat a group called the Geezer Brigade. The eighty-year-old-plus seniors were on their regular pilgrimage to Atlantic City. Kennedy had driven this trip at least three dozen times in the last twenty years. He knew most of the group personally and could recite many of their grandchildren's names and ages.

It was the one trip he enjoyed the most, even though it saddened him, year after year, seeing the group change like it did. For many, this would be their last outing. Others would be too infirm to travel. Still, the brigade was replenished by an ever-growing number of octogenarians. People were living longer. Medical technology was advancing at a rapid rate. Some of these folks were likely to outlive him.

Kennedy liked to joke about it. Soon, he would be old enough to join in with them on this voyage. The thought pleased him, though he knew full well his pension wouldn't even cover the bus fare, never mind the cost of the hotel where these people stayed.

He tried in vain to make the brakes work, but they had bled dry. Frantically, he reached down and pulled on the emergency brake. It took all his strength, but he was finally able to slow the bus down. He breathed a small sigh of relief.

But it was too early to celebrate. At that moment, the steering gave way completely. The bus veered awkwardly to the left, narrowly missing an oncoming car. People on the sidewalk—once stunned onlookers, now potential targets—screamed and ran for cover as the bus suddenly changed direction.

Fifty-four thousand pounds of metal and glass crashed onto the sidewalk, destroying two parked cars in the process. Crumpled by the force of the collision, the corners of the bus caved inward, crushing Kennedy's legs and pinning him to the seat. The pain was excruciating. Blood flowed from a number of deep gashes in his legs. Fighting through the blinding pain, he tried valiantly, heroically, to maintain consciousness. It was a lost cause.

The last thing Kennedy saw before the pain and shock overwhelmed his system was the sight of a large neon sign teetering above his broken front windows. He heard the snap of wires and the twisting of metal. His feeble mind grew numb to the growing commotion outside. He closed his eyes, wondering why he was so sleepy. As he drifted off, a troubling thought crossed his mind. In all his forty years of service, with his unblemished record, he had never fallen asleep at the wheel. What a damn shame.

Paramedics would later discover that Buster Kennedy had bled to death from ruptured arteries in his legs. Miraculously, all forty-three seniors survived the crash without a scratch, and all credited Buster with saving their lives.

* * *

It all happened so fast. Gideon heard the first thunderous crash a block away. The screams that followed grew closer and closer. Whatever was coming was going to be big. The rumble of a large diesel engine in trouble was followed quickly by a shattering crash that shook the building from its very foundations.

Dr. Sossoman was yelling for them to move. Gideon responded quickly by pulling them through the roof opening, starting first with Charlie and then Reyes. When he looked back down at the doctor, he saw that she wasn't moving.

"I need your help," she pleaded. She held the twins in her arms. Both girls lay completely still, and Emily had a stream of blood running from her nose.

"What's wrong with them?" he yelled through the noise outside. A moment of panic overcame him.

"It's the wellwishing," she replied. "It knocks them out afterward. They won't wake up for another couple of hours."

Panic turned to disbelief. Gideon looked to the heavens, a curse fresh on his lips. He made no effort to hide his frustration. The moment of their escape was upon them, and now they were hampered by the same power that had intervened on their behalf. Fate was a fickle mistress. He wished, just once, that she would make up her mind and decide whose side she was on.

"Give me one of them," he demanded. "Quickly, now."

Sossoman handed one of the girls up to Gideon, who promptly handed her over to Charlie. Then he reached back down and tossed the other girl across his shoulder. Precious seconds had been wasted. He prayed that their moment had not passed; another miracle was not likely forthcoming. They had better make the most out of this one.

"Follow me," Gideon said, moving to the edge of the building. He heard Reyes gasp behind him. "Keep down," he ordered. She was too eager to see what was happening on the street and was not paying attention to what they were doing up there. Gideon cautiously raised his eyes over the edge.

Below them was pure mayhem. A large bus had lost control and run into the front of the movie theater, slicing through two other vehicles in the process. The two demolished cars were upended and lying at odd angles against the building. The fierce impact had snapped most of the moorings supporting the large neon marquee. Jarred loose by the crash, the sign had fallen toward the street. One end embedded itself like a giant can opener in the middle of the Greyhound's roof; the other rested against the building.

Confusion reigned. It seemed that everyone within two blocks of the crash had converged on the scene to either render assistance or gawk at the accident. People were trying desperately to get the passengers off the bus. Meanwhile, DeKay's men searched frantically through the milling crowd for signs of the girls. The two groups were working at odds with each other, and the crowd was starting to get angry about it.

The authorities were still blocks away. If he was going to act, now was the time.

Gideon turned back to his small team. "Now, pay attention. We have to move fast. Once we start, don't slow down. Don't look around or get caught up with what's happening below. Stay close to me and keep moving. When we're spotted"—and Gideon had no doubt they would be—"no one will shoot at us. There are too many witnesses. That will buy us at least a few minutes, but after that, all bets are off." He looked around at the concerned faces. "Listen, if you follow me and do what I do," he reassured them, "we'll have a very good chance of getting out of this. I promise."

"Did you see DeKay down there?" Charlie asked nervously.

"No, I did not," he responded honestly. "That doesn't mean he's not there, just that we have to move fast. The element of surprise is on *our* side now. We have to take advantage of it while it lasts."

Gideon watched their doubt turn into determination. There were no other choices available to them. This was their one chance at escape, and they knew it.

Gideon nodded once and then stood up on the edge of the building. He tested the damaged sign and then put his full weight upon it. It held. With a little girl on his shoulder, he began walking toward the top of the bus. The metal sign made a natural bridge. It spanned the gap perfectly and was just wide enough for them to walk on. Charlie followed second, carrying the other twin. One after another they followed Gideon, ignoring the commotion below and the angry comments thrown their way. Then someone shouted Dr. Sossoman's name. Gideon thought he heard his name, but the noise was too loud for him to tell.

As Gideon predicted, no shots were fired, but they could all sense the growing excitement. They didn't need to look to see that DeKay's men were being mobilized to go after them.

In short order they were all across and standing atop the bus. Reyes felt naked up there, knowing the hostility that awaited them if they were caught. If not for the rescue effort to get everyone off the damaged bus, DeKay's men would have clamored up there by now. But she couldn't worry about that. Instead, she put her faith in Gideon and kept her eyes squarely on his shoulders. Like him, she ran to the front of the bus where it had crashed into the building. Gideon had already jumped down the short distance to the mangled car. She followed suit. Avoiding the slippery glass fragments, she walked to where the trunk normally would have been. Now it was a tangled mess of bent sheet metal with razor-sharp edges. Fortunately, Gideon was there to help her and the others to the ground.

For the first time in minutes, Reyes stopped to breathe a sigh of relief. Then she saw Gideon draw his firearm. His eyes turned dark.

"Most of DeKay's men are still inside the building or caught on the other side of the bus," he observed with tactical efficiency. "For the moment, they'll be hampered by the crowd, but that won't last long. We need more time."

He raised his weapon in the air and fired three quick shots. The effect was instantaneous. People began running in every direction. Pandemonium broke loose as the crowd turned into a disorderly mob. It was the perfect diversion and would give them a few more minutes to escape.

"Let's go!" Gideon shouted. But instead of running away from the crowd, he ran straight into it.

He started across the street at a steep angle away from the accident. Traffic had all but stopped on the busy street. He used the crowd to his advantage, weaving between frightened pedestrians, darting around cars, trying to blend in with the chaotic surroundings. Reyes, Sossoman, and Charlie followed close behind. When they reached the other side, they didn't slow down. Instead, Gideon ran faster, ducking at the last minute down a side alley. Reyes caught up a second later, followed quickly by Dr. Sossoman.

"Where's Charlie?" Gideon asked when he failed to show.

"He was right behind me," Sossoman said. Her face displayed the same worried emotion evident in her tone of voice.

Gideon handed the immobile girl to Reyes. He moved back to the corner and peered around the edge of the building.

The crowd was still mostly in disarray, but a semblance of order was starting to take hold. Gideon put himself in the shoes of the bystanders: *Maybe that wasn't gunfire. Maybe the noise came as an aftereffect of the accident. If so, then we need to get those people off the bus.* It was a logical conclusion, one that Gideon might have made if he didn't know better.

After a brief search, Gideon spotted Charlie. His heart sank. Two armed men were taking the timid little man away at gunpoint. One of them had a girl draped over his shoulder. Gideon turned back around and closed his eyes. *Shit.* It was suicide to go after them. It was only a matter of time, seconds really, before DeKay unleashed the hounds. Now that they had one girl, he would stop at nothing to get the other.

The decision was painful but easy.

"Charlie's not coming," he informed the others. "DeKay has them."

"Go after him!" Sossoman demanded. "We can't let—"

"We have no choice," Gideon replied coldly. "Our only option is to get away, to stay ahead of DeKay." He stroked the face of the unconscious child in Reyes's arms. "He has one. We have the other. The game is going to another level, and we need to be prepared. Getting killed won't help these girls."

Sossoman stared hard at Gideon. A tear fell down her cheek. She nodded sharply. Gideon was right, and she hated him for it. If they were alive, then they could fight another day. But that idea didn't keep her heart from aching.

God help me if something happens to these children, she thought. She couldn't live with the consequences.

CHAPTER 21

"Gideon!" DeKay's scream of rage was drowned out by the commotion surrounding him.

He couldn't believe his eyes. What the hell was John Gideon doing here? One minute, he had Dr. Sossoman and the girls trapped inside the shitty little theater. The next minute they were being whisked off by someone he thought was gone forever from his life. He blinked once, twice, but the image of John Gideon was seared into his brain.

This can't be happening, he thought more than once.

DeKay spoke quickly into his radio, ordering the few men remaining outside the theater into pursuit. That the girls were being carried did not escape his attention. In fact, the sight of the prone twins fueled his rage. They caused this to happen. They wished for it. His suspicions were justified at last. His right hand stroked the polymer handle of his Heckler & Koch USP pistol. At the moment, the weapon remained secure in its holster, but just barely. If not for the hundred or so witnesses, he would have whipped it out and loosed a full clip of .40-caliber bullets at the retreating miscreants.

DeKay loathed missed opportunities. He should have killed John Gideon when he had the chance. He'd had plenty of opportunities through the years. There were times when he was clinically depressed, struggling to come to grips with his failure as a military officer. It took him a long time to get past the court-martial, and there were countless nights where he could have acted in a fit of rage and killed the man who had testified against him. It was only after years of introspection, planning, and the opportunity provided by Arthur Frist that he had come to the patience he had today, which even he admitted was nothing more than a shallow pool.

Now, seeing Gideon again under these circumstances, all the pent-up emotions and past failures threatened to overwhelm him. His fingers curled into tight fists. His knuckles turned pale white. He *would* kill John Gideon for this. He would use his bare hands to do it. His face would be inches from the man he despised as he gasped his last breath. Then he would rip his heart out. His own hands would squeeze out the last beat.

And when the deed was done, he would enter his new life as planned. He would start over, truly cleansed of his past.

That thought alone brought a wicked smile to DeKay's thin lips, and for the moment he forgot all about John Gideon and the troublemaking twins. He didn't notice the nervous looks, the hurried signs of the cross, or the whispered prayers of those unfortunate rescuers milling around him, the unlucky ones who happened to see his face at that precise moment. He didn't register them shrinking away as an uneasy feeling overcame them like a chill breeze across the shoulder in the dead of night. There was malevolence in this man. They didn't need to know him to feel, intuitively, that he was evil.

"Mr. DeKay," a subordinate reported moments later, "we have one of the girls."

DeKay whirled on the man. "Only one?" He glared.

The mercenary shrank from DeKay's angry stare. "Yes, sir," he replied nervously. "But we also have the janitor, Charlie Simmons." The man hesitated slightly before continuing. "We need a few more men to go after the others. They ran down the alley across the street. If we hurry, we can catch up with them."

The request was meek, just like the soldier before him. DeKay didn't know this one, must be one of the colonel's men. Undisciplined. Unmotivated. He would remember this man, who was a liability he didn't need.

"Well, don't just stand there with your thumb up your ass," DeKay ordered. "Assemble a team and get after them." He reached out, gripped the man by the collar, and drew him close. "I want that girl brought back to me alive. Do you understand?" The man nodded sharply, his eyes wide. "I want the man who helped them escape, too. Alive. Kill the doctor, she's no longer any use to me." He let go of the man and stepped back.

"And, soldier," he said as the man turned to leave, "if you fail to complete this mission, don't bother coming back. Find a deep, dark hole and dig yourself into it, because if I find you. . . ." He let the threat linger in the air between them.

The man took off in a dead run, gathering others to follow as he went.

DeKay laughed out loud. Power. It was the one drug he let himself become addicted to. It made him euphoric, invincible. There was nothing else in the world like it, and he relished every opportunity he had to abuse it. Soon, he would exercise his power in the most absolute way. John Gideon was not a concern, merely a speed bump under his wheels. As long as he had the one child, he knew Gideon would stay close. It was the nature of the man. He was soft, weak, just like all the others. And if there was one thing DeKay knew, it was how to deal with weakness.

CHAPTER 22

"Should we follow them?"

Captain Choi Yong Jin watched the scene unfold in front of them, his brow furrowed with concern. The situation was more complex than he had anticipated. The mission planning did not account for third-party interference. Nevertheless, he was used to overcoming wrinkles far more difficult than this one. His methods were considered unorthodox within the conservative Democratic People's Republic of Korea military, but that was why Vice President Pak had chosen him for this mission. Unlike many of his brethren, he could "think outside the box," as the Americans were fond of saying.

Choi turned to the second most senior member on his team. "Sergeant Han Soo," he commanded, "you will stay here and watch DeKay and his men. Follow their movements and gather as much intelligence as possible. Find out where this hidden base is located, where they keep the children. Find a way for us to get inside undetected. We will rendezvous with you as soon as we can."

Han nodded his head sharply. As the communications officer, Han was skilled in several languages and spoke nearly flawless American English. Of everyone on the team, he looked the most Western. His father was an imperialist French soldier captured in Vietnam in the 1950s by the Communist Chinese. How he ended up in North Korea was a mystery, but someone had the foresight to match the man with a Korean woman, who bore a son. Choi hoped that pairing could now work in his favor.

Choi turned to the rest of the team. "We were very lucky to witness DeKay and his men leaving the parking garage. In their haste to get here, they failed to notice that we were watching. Now is our chance to further our advantage. The second girl will not get far. It won't be long before DeKay's men catch up to them. The net will grow tighter as the search intensifies. We will follow behind and wait for the right moment to strike."

"What about the other girl?" Jung Dak-ho asked. He was the team's demolitions expert and carried enough firepower to level a bridge.

"Once we have secured one of the children, we will look to acquire the second," he replied with confidence. "Vice President Pak has placed a great confidence in us. We will not let him down." Choi looked to his team of highly skilled warriors, making and holding eye contact with each. "We will not fail."

Such was the leadership of Captain Choi that each man nodded his head, not out of obedience or ritual, but from complete and utter confidence that he was right. They would not fail, and each man knew it.

Korean Workers' Party Headquarters

Pak Te Hwan leaned back in his opulent leather chair and inhaled deeply on his cigarette. After holding the acrid smoke a heartbeat in his lungs, he let it out in a rush toward the ceiling. Overhead, the slow-moving fan swirled the smoke around and around before dispersing it throughout the room.

Pak smiled wide. Things were coming along nicely. His men in America had made exemplary progress and were far ahead of schedule. Choi's report was naturally conservative, but Pak knew how the military operated. Professional soldiers tended to downplay progress in an effort to minimize scrutiny from their superiors. The practice was common in North Korea, as failure, or even the prospect of it, could end your career in a most unpleasant way.

Pak was not concerned. With so many variables in his favor, this mission had a high probability of success. He had good intelligence, the right team in place to execute the mission, and most important, there was a set of twins with a demonstrable gift. There was no use doubting the girls' abilities. He had asked for a test of their power, and they had delivered.

Then there was the matter of greed. Money. In this case, his partner in America was looking to cash in, to disappear with enough of it to live comfortably for the rest of his life. To Pak's knowledge, the American Cross DeKay had approached at least three other parties with the same deal. It was an even exchange, gold and diamonds for the two girls. That the North Korean wasn't the only one interested in these children was not a surprise, but his bid was the highest.

DeKay had researched his potential clients well. Each had a need for the girls' unique services. They had problems that needed to be overcome, enemies to be dealt with, and ambitions that could not be sated. As expected, all who were invited had tendered offers to acquire the wellwishers. One was a Saudi Arabian prince turned terrorist who had been exiled by his family to the mountains of Afghanistan. His enemies were hunting him like a dog. Living like an animal in rat-infested caves, his substantial assets frozen, it was no surprise that his bid had come up short. Then there was the Colombian drug lord. Mired in a turf war against competing cartels, his original bid was substantial. Unfortunately, his rivals got to him first. The bomb that blew up his car—with him inside it—ended any aspirations he had to grow his business into an international empire.

Finally, there was the South African industrialist looking to bring back apartheid. Pak considered him his greatest rival. That's where the test of the girl's abilities came in. His proposal to the American was simple: demonstrate to him that the twins were real, that their powers were great, and he would double the standing offer. DeKay jumped at the opportunity. Two weeks later, the millionaire racist died while on a hunting expedition in Kenya. He was stalking a lion in the bush when his rifle tragically jammed. The sound alerted the lion to his presence, and the animal decided to charge the now defenseless hunter. According to the local trackers, the man's screams could be heard for miles on the flat, grassy plains. Authorities never did recover the man's head. The lion had kept a trophy of its own.

In the end, Pak was left standing alone, as he knew he would be. Nothing would come between him and greatness. His plans were foolproof. Secret preparations were already under way to house and care for these children. The best scientists and psychologists were ready to begin the brutal indoctrination process required to control the girls. It would not take long. The North Koreans were experts at mind control and behavior modification. They learned from the best, the Chinese, and then took it a step further. Neuroinfluencing was part art, part science. Through the use of electromagnetic and acoustic technologies, his doctors would break the girls' will to disobey. Once broken, the real work would begin. The precise application of drugs, hypnosis, and induced trauma would reshape their young minds, molding their desires, instilling in them the overwhelming desire to please their new master. In the end, they would bow to his will. If he so desired, they would learn to call him father. Their every wish, literally, would be to further his goals.

The peninsula *would* be reunited. But that was simply the first part of his plan, a teaser of what would come afterward. His ultimate goal was to become the leader of a powerful new nation, one destined to become a superpower. Then he would control the world stage. It was all coming together. Once he had the girls, nothing, no nation on earth, would stand in his way.

CHAPTER 23

Curtis Cove, Delaware

"What do we do now?"

"We sit tight and wait," Gideon replied to Reyes. "We have no transportation, no backup, and we just left a free-for-all back at the theater. This hotel room is registered under a false identity. We're safe, for the moment."

"Everything happened so fast," Sossoman pitched in. "It will take DeKay a while to sort through the mess. He has to take care of the local law enforcement, smooth things over with the theater owner, and regroup his men. He won't be so quick to come after us this time, knowing that we have outside help." She sat back in her chair. "But he will come," she said ominously. "He's not stupid. Once he catches our scent again, he'll come after us with a vengeance, only this time he'll be prepared."

"Let him come," Gideon boasted. "Once I update the director, we'll have the resources of the Central Intelligence Agency to go after him and get Emily back."

Sossoman leaned forward. Her eyes narrowed. "Don't underestimate DeKay or the power of Arthur Frist. Littleton has been secret for over fifty years. That kind of success doesn't happen by accident. It takes determination and a willingness to do anything, kill anyone, to keep it hidden. These girls won't be the last wellwishers to walk the earth. Once they become more trouble than they're worth, he'll eliminate them, and then the search for the next ones will intensify."

"Eliminate who?" The tiny voice on the bed cut through the tension and broke the moment.

"Nobody, Amy," Gideon said softly as he sat down next to the waking child. "We were just talking, that's all."

Amy smiled up at Gideon and reached her arms around his neck, drawing him close for a hug. "You knew it was me," she said happily.

"Of course I did," Gideon replied, though he just realized it himself.

"Most people can't tell us apart," she said. "It usually takes a few weeks before they know who's who. But you knew right away, didn't you?"

"It was easy." Gideon ran his fingers across her face. "You're the one with the rosy cheeks."

Amy beamed at the attention. Then she looked around the room. Her eyes turned down. "DeKay has Emily," she said solemnly. "She's back at Littleton, isn't she?"

Dr. Sossoman rushed over as tears began to fall down Amy's cheeks. She hugged the girl close to her breast.

"Everything will be all right, sweetheart," Sossoman cooed. "We'll get Emily back." She looked over at Gideon with a pleading look in her eyes.

"The doctor is right," he said, his hand stroking Amy's blonde hair. "We will get your sister back."

Amy left the doctor and threw her arms around Gideon. Her tiny heart beat against his chest. Her tears were wet on his neck. "Do you promise," she said between sobs, "you won't let anything bad happen to her?"

"I promise," he replied honestly.

"And when it's all over," she continued, "you won't let anything bad happen to either of us?"

Gideon suddenly felt overcome by powerful emotions. But it was more than emotional—it was physical, too, a strong combination of feelings he could not explain. It started as a tingling in his fingertips, a warmth that flushed his face red. He was suddenly imbued with a sense of righteousness, clear purpose, and absolute virtue, all bound into an overwhelming urge to protect these children. It was something he had never experienced before, and it hit him hard. This was right. It felt good. The need to lie, to obfuscate, to mislead, all of it evaporated in an instant. He was in a position where he could do something good, for people who deserved it. There was no gray area.

He drew the girl close in a tight hug. "I promise," he whispered in her ear. "Whatever it takes. I will not let you down."

Director Harrison Gorrell closed his cell phone and placed it on the desk. What the hell had they gotten themselves into? Gideon's report was so fantastic, it bordered on unbelievable. If not for the man himself, he would have discounted the report as madness. But he trusted Gideon implicitly. His secret weapon had never failed or led him in the wrong direction. A man like Gideon lived by his word. It was his bond. When given to someone, he would go to the ends of the earth to see that he delivered as promised. If Gideon said the situation was dire, then it was. If he said he needed help, which was extremely rare for him, then he did. And it was up to the director to make sure Gideon got what was needed.

He was prepared to mobilize the entire agency if necessary. His number one operative was at the end of a tenuous line of rope. His troubleshooter was in trouble. This mission had gone in directions neither of them thought possible, but Gideon had done it, he had uncovered the truth behind Kulbeda Station. It was now time to bring in reinforcements.

First, he needed to brief the President.

Harrison Gorrell picked up the phone on his desk and dialed his assistant. She answered on the first ring. "Get me the White House," he said, straightening his tie with his free hand. "I need to meet with the President. It's of the utmost urgency."

Sergeant Han Soo was disappointed in the Americans. Infiltrating Kulbeda Station was easier than he thought it would be. By North Korean standards, security was lax, proving no real test to the commando soldier. In his country, the officer responsible for such a breach would be hauled in front of a firing squad. In some cases, the officer's own men might be forced to join him.

On the other hand, Sergeant Han was astounded by how advanced the Americans were compared to his poorer country. As he peered out the small window to overlook what he now knew was Littleton, the Korean soldier was amazed at what he saw. The sight took his breath away. Littleton was a marvel to behold.

He was fortunate that Kulbeda's security wasn't as sophisticated. It didn't take much effort to subdue and kill one of DeKay's men in all the mayhem back at the theater. He was of the right size and build, same hair and skin color. All Han needed to do was don the man's uniform and his dark sunglasses, then tag along and stay low until he had safely infiltrated the base. No one questioned his identity or purpose for being there. Lazy Americans. Back in his home country, every mission was greeted with a thorough identity check followed by a lengthy debriefing with the ever dangerous political officers corps. Not here. Upon arrival, most of the teams scattered for a hot meal and shower. The unlucky ones were still looking for the second twin.

Once inside, a world of opportunity opened up to him. Half the houses in Littleton, he estimated, were unoccupied. As soon as he was alone, he found himself an empty one overlooking a small park, set up his equipment, and began planning his next moves. It was still daylight outside, though he knew the cloud-covered sky overhead was artificial. Assuming they kept the same schedule as aboveground, then it would be dark soon. He would be ready by then. There was ample time to take in the marvels of this hidden American wonder. Captain Choi would not believe his eyes when he saw the miracles these Americans could perform. Han scarcely believed it himself, yet here he sat, captivated by the wonder surrounding him.

The next phase of his mission would be reconnaissance. Before his team arrived, he needed to search this place, probe for weak spots, and gather intelligence. He would wait until dark, when he could move about more easily. Of utmost importance, he needed to find a way to get a message to Choi. Nothing in their training could have prepared them for what he had discovered. The captain needed to know about this place.

Han Soo settled down for a quick rest. He pulled a rations pouch from his pack and began to eat it cold. For the briefest moment he envied the Americans. Many of them were heading for hot showers, warm meals, and comfortable beds.

Han Soo smiled. *Let them get comfortable,* he thought. The small team of North Korean soldiers was vastly outnumbered, but Han knew the Americans had no idea what they were in for.

CHAPTER 24

"What do you mean you can't help me?"

"My hands are tied. I'm sorry, but this mission has become political."

"Political?" Gideon steamed. He threw his hands up in the air. "But you're the DCI. It's your job to make sure it doesn't get political!"

"Listen up." Harrison Gorrell leaned forward, a no-bullshit look on his face. "This operation has had a severe change in custody. Oversight has been passed up the chain of command. It's been ripped from my hands, and there is nothing I can do about it. Do you understand me? The President has become involved in this—personally."

Gideon leaned back on the park bench. "Shit," he said, deflated. He ran a hand through his short hair. "Why is the President involved in this?" he asked. "I thought we were running deep black?"

"Damn it, Gideon!" Director Gorrell exclaimed. "Why do you think we're meeting out here, in the open, instead of in the bubble at Langley? The Reflecting Pool is nice, and I'm partial to the Lincoln Memorial, but I'm not sure even this place is secure enough. Don't you see? The mission is compromised.

"I screwed up. After your report to me, I decided it was time to brief the President. He needed to know what was happening. I mean, come on, *mercenaries* are running a United States military base? A secret town is buried underneath a hundred feet of granite and has been for over *five decades*? Wellwishers are influencing world history? Clearly, these are things the President should be aware of. But, guess what?" Gorrell drew closer to Gideon, a smirk on his face. "He knew already. No, let me rephrase that, he *knows* all about Littleton. More than you and I combined. And now he knows that *we* know."

Director Gorrell let the words sink in.

Gideon looked around, his heart pounding loud in his ears. Leave it to the director. This was the perfect place for a setup. His senses prickled. He found danger everywhere he looked. The Mall was crowded this morning, filled with the usual throng of tourists, politicians, staffers, protesters, and an assorted host of Washington bureaucrats. If he was in harm's way, there would be no way to know until after it happened. And by then, he would be dead. Gideon looked at the director and gave him an unhappy scowl.

Gorrell shrugged but offered no apology. Instead, he looked tired, haggard, like he had aged ten years since the last time Gideon saw him. He sounded tired, too, and his voice had a raw, raspy edge to it. Director Gorrell was the most unflappable man Gideon knew. It must have taken a big hit for the man to be shaken like this.

At the director's insistence, this meeting was an impromptu one, the time and place delivered in code so that only the two of them knew exactly where and when. The fact that the director demanded they meet in person was not so unusual, though they hadn't seen each other face-to-face in over a year. Instead, it was the circumstances behind the meeting, the urgency conveyed in the man's voice. He couldn't tell Gideon what was happening over the phone, even if the line was encrypted. It was too important. Only a face-to-face meeting would do. Even more disturbing, he had wanted to see Gideon immediately.

Gideon continued to survey the area. To his left was the Lincoln Memorial, to the right, the Washington Monument. In front was the Reflecting Pool, and beyond that, in the distance, the White House. Overhead, the sky was blanketed by thick gray clouds that cast no shadows and whose reflection looked ominous in the still waters of the pool. A storm was forecast to hit the D.C. area later that evening, bringing with it torrential rains, high winds, and lightning, which explained the reason for the unusually heavy pedestrian activity. No one wanted to be caught in the storm, and this morning offered the best opportunity to see the sights. If this storm lived up to its billing, it wouldn't leave the area for at least forty-eight hours.

"But how could he know?" Gideon asked, at last satisfied that the area was clear, or at least that anyone watching them was professional enough not to be seen. "No one does. There is no evidence of its existence anywhere. We've looked. There's nothing out there."

"Exactly, which is why I went to see him right after our discussion." Gideon straightened in his seat as Gorrell filled him in. "When I broached the subject, he immediately sent his staffers out of the room, including Andy Parr, his chief of staff." The director's eyebrows rose and fell with the news. Everyone in Washington knew that the President did nothing without the counsel of his right-hand man. Gorrell put his hand on Gideon's shoulder and squeezed slightly. "You're not going to like this."

"I don't like it already," Gideon replied, preparing to hear the worst.

"It's not what we thought. Kulbeda Station, Littleton, this thing called Project Gemini, are all part of an ultra-secret black program run by the

United States government. But it's not really run by the government, at least not in the traditional ways. In fact, it goes deeper than anything I've ever seen or heard of, and believe me, I'm privy to some pretty fantastic shit."

"What did the President say?" Gideon said. The director was leading up to something, and for the first time since Gideon had known him, the man was having a hard time coming directly to the point.

"According to the President," Gorrell continued without missing a beat, "the only politician to know of the operation's existence is the President himself. No one else in the United States government is involved. It's total deniability on a scale I've never seen before."

"This thing is run by whom? Frist Industries?" Gideon asked. "He has complete reign?"

"Absolute and unprecedented control," Gorrell replied, "with twenty-four-hour access to the President for, as he calls it, 'guidance and council' on sensitive and strategic matters of state."

"Arthur Frist. I can't believe it." Gideon was dumbfounded. Everything Dr. Sossoman had told him was true, but it went much further than even she knew.

"There's more," Gorrell continued. "Every year, you hear stories of multiples and twins organizations getting together. They meet, tell stories, play games, and romp around. Many of those get-togethers, the biggest anyway, are either organized or influenced by Project Gemini as covert opportunities for twin testing and recruiting. Even though they have viable wellwishers in Littleton, they never stop looking for the next set to come into the world."

"The organization must be huge."

"It's international," the director finished, "run by the corporate front known as Frist Industries. But it's highly compartmentalized, and many of the different organizations don't even know they're connected or, if they do, the significance of that connection."

"It's a tightly run ship," Gideon observed.

"Exactly."

"So, what do I do now?" Gideon asked. "If this thing is that big. . . ."

The director cleared his throat before continuing. "I have a request, direct from the President himself."

Gideon steeled himself for what came next.

"The President would like you to turn over the second child. He wants this operation terminated, immediately. He said that if you complied, no further action would be taken against you. If you continue—"

The director didn't need to finish the sentence. Gideon got the message, loud and clear. "Is that what you want me to do?" he asked.

"Hey," the director said with thinly veiled anger, "I took the same oath you did. We both swore to protect, uphold, and obey the Constitution of the United States. Project Gemini is a legitimate operation with government oversight. I can't go against it."

Gideon wasn't surprised by the answer. The director was covering his back. Gorrell was afraid. Terrified was more like it. Project Gemini was larger and more covert than anything he had ever seen. It could swallow him whole and continue on without missing a beat. He had children at home and in college. Grandchildren were only a few years off. His wife of over twenty years was active in the Beltway. His whole life was at risk, along with everyone in it. He had already done what Gideon was about to do—assess the options and come to a fateful decision. The director had made his. He was turning his back on this mission and was advising Gideon to do the same. This meeting was a professional courtesy, a way to try to keep things nice and orderly. The President's threat was very real. If Gideon continued on this course, he too would find himself on the short end of a very tight leash, one that would certainly choke the life out of him.

"Did the meeting take place?"

"Yes, Mr. President."

"What did they talk about? Were you able to listen in on their conversation?"

"Only bits and pieces. Director Gorrell went against your wishes. He did not meet with his operative in his office as planned. He chose someplace public, with a lot of pedestrians and background traffic noise. We caught enough to know that the director told more than we wanted him to."

The President swore softly to himself. He paced around the Oval Office and moved behind the large mahogany desk that once belonged to Thomas Jefferson. He turned his back on his visitor and looked out the bulletproof windows overlooking the Rose Garden.

"And this agent of his, were you able to follow him and find the other girl?"

"No, we lost him shortly after the meeting broke up. The director was right, this man, John Gideon, is very good at what he does. Don't worry, we'll find him. It's only a matter of time."

"So, what happens now?"

"You don't need to know the details, Mr. President."

The President's eyes shined bright with a sharp intelligence. His back was ramrod straight, the by-product of twenty-two years as a highly decorated Marine officer. His military experience had taught him when to know and when to let things slide. Director Gorrell was a good friend of his. He wanted to know.

He turned to his visitor. "Tell me," he said, leaving no room for debate.

The man stepped forward with a folded sheet of white paper. He handed the paper to the President.

"What's this?" the President asked. On the parchment was a list of ten names; he knew each personally.

"Your short list of candidates to fill the vacant role of Director, Central Intelligence Agency," the man replied calmly.

The President looked up sharply. "What do you mean by this? Since when do I need a new DCI?"

The well-tailored man raised his arm and looked at the twenty-four-karat-gold watch on his wrist. On the outside, his demeanor and posture appeared poised and controlled. Inside, he allowed himself a small smile. This president was just like the rest of them, easily manipulated and prone to moments of weakness. He would handle this president like he handled the others—calmly, but firm, politely, but insistent. Only if he absolutely had to would he resort to coercion or threats. In all his years, he had never had to stoop to that level. These were smart, sometimes brilliant, men. And they were all politically ambitious to a fault.

"Since about five minutes ago," Arthur Frist replied. This time he couldn't keep the smile off his face.

CHAPTER 25

Coven Nightclub
Trenton, New Jersey

Coven, to put it mildly, was a dump—at least on the outside—and was located at the intersection of two long alleyways, with one narrow side street running in between to lend it credibility. Barely a warehouse, the nightclub's exterior was covered with large sheets of corrugated metal. Half of the building was littered with overlapping band and party posters wallpapered to the metal structure as high as arms could reach. Each layer represented a new theme, band, pop style, or attraction. Smaller posters colored yellow, pink, and orange dotted the landscape, promoting "Help Wanted," "Lost," "Found," "Roommates Needed," the little pieces that held phone numbers and e-mail addresses long torn from the bottom.

Gideon wouldn't have been surprised to find an archaeologist on-site, peeling back the thin sheets like the rings of a tree to discover that each layer represented a contrasting culture. He would probably find it went back to the birth of the hippie movement in the sixties. Some of the older layers—the ones still visible that is—weren't weathering too well. Their edges were frayed and torn, waiting to be covered by another class of grassroots marketing professionals working their way through college.

The club's main entrance was located on the second floor, roughly twelve feet above the sidewalk. To get there, Gideon and Reyes climbed two flights of narrow metal stairs until they reached a large rectangular space made of poured concrete. Cigarettes, gum, and trash littered the landing, which was covered by a sloping tin roof held aloft by two rusted poles, one at each corner. Underneath the metal awning was a double glass door, tinted black. The left door displayed the establishment's logo, a winged gothic bat. The letters intertwined inside the creature to form a single word: *Coven*. The right door featured a different message: NO SOLICITATION.

Gideon shook his head. He hadn't been here in years, yet it looked exactly the same, except now it was a goth nightclub.

"You've got to be shitting me," Reyes said out loud.

Though Gideon was not surprised by her bias—it was not the kind of place you would see an up-and-comer from the FBI—he worried that it might affect her judgment.

"Agent Reyes," Gideon said, "the best way to get yourself killed is to assume something before you have all the facts. You end up underestimating the situation, or the enemy, because you can't see all the angles. It's the kind of habit that will get you killed." He put his hands on her shoulders. "This has been a long day. But you need to put your exhaustion aside. Think logically, be analytical, take everything in and process it. Look for anomalies, things that are out of place, like they don't belong. And above all, be prepared."

"We're the anomalies," she said. "Inside there, we're the ones out of place, the ones that don't belong."

"Natalie, let me put this to you another way. We're in a bind. We don't have the luxury to choose whom we will and will not associate with. We go where we need to. Sometimes, the people we deal with make you sick, dirty, like you want to scrub yourself clean when you're done with them. Oftentimes, they're on the bottom rung of life, people you normally wouldn't give the time of day to. Other times, they look like you and I, but, guess what, the person you just dealt with might like screwing little girls, or dealing drugs, or murdering for pleasure. This is the business, get used to it."

"Fine. Sorry. I just overreacted. Let's just get this over with."

"Put aside your unease for now. I need you to concentrate on what we're doing."

Reyes swallowed hard and nodded sharply in reply. It *had* been a long day, that's all. Soon, she hoped, they would be able to rest, at least for a little while.

Once inside Coven, a very large bouncer stopped Gideon at the door.

"Do you know what kind of place this is?" he asked in a voice that was far too high-pitched for his size. "You," he said to Reyes with a smile that alleged she was welcome anytime, "can come in and look around. I'd be happy to give you a tour, show you some of the better dens to visit."

The giant was drooling over Reyes, though Gideon suspected the saliva emanating from the corners of his mouth was actually caused by the four or five piercings that ran along his lower lip, each connected to the other by a thin silver chain. Silver lipstick, white makeup, and red eye shadow made up the rest of his face. His hair was dyed the blackest black and matched the Coven T-shirt, pants, and platform boots he wore. Here was the keeper of the keys to Gotham, and he both looked and acted the part perfectly.

Reyes responded slyly, "Sorry, we're not here for pleasure, just business."

The goth bouncer crossed his arms and widened his stance. "The sign says 'No Solicitation.' We're not looking to buy anything."

"We're here to see Jimmy Chin," Gideon informed the bouncer.

"Jimmy who?"

"Jimmy Chin. He still owns this place, right?"

"Don't know anybody by that name."

"Well," Gideon pressed on, "maybe we can speak to some of your customers, perhaps the bartender or manager. They may know the person we seek."

"Sorry, I know everyone in the building. He's not here."

Gideon wasn't getting anyplace with this meathead. "Maybe this will help," he said. He pulled out his Sig Sauer and placed the barrel under the man's chin. "We're not cops," he said menacingly. Just for good measure, he reached up and grabbed a handful of the chain that dangled from the bouncer's pierced lips.

"O-o-oh," the giant stuttered. His eyes opened wide with fright and pain. "*That* Jimmy Chin. Why don't you wait here, and I'll see if Jimmy is available to see you."

Gideon released his grip on the man and lowered his pistol. The bouncer turned toward the nightclub's entrance. His hand massaged his sore mouth. "Stay here," he mumbled, though he was much more polite than before. He spun and disappeared into the dark hallway leading into the club. The staccato of loud music rang clear when he opened the door. Both Gideon and Reyes leaned in unison to their left, trying to see inside the club. The curving corridor did its job and hid the sights within.

Ten minutes turned into twenty while the two waited. Gideon began to worry about Dr. Sossoman and Amy. They were back in the car, parked a block away. Both were sound asleep when he left.

The drive from D.C. to New Jersey had been long and disappointing. The much-needed help Gideon had promised them had vanished in a puff of smoke. He was more disappointed than the others. The man he held to a high standard had let him down. And look what good it did him. An hour after they left the city, news reports came over the radio. Director Harrison Gorrell was dead, the victim of a hit-and-run as he crossed the street after meeting with White House officials. Likely story. Gideon knew exactly how it happened. After his meeting this morning, the director was called into an obscure office in the downtown area to give a debriefing of his encounter with Gideon. The meeting was short and cordial. Gorrell left the building assured that everything was all right, that he had played his role as instructed. He probably never even saw the car that hit him.

Arthur Frist never intended to let Director Gorrell live. That meant Gideon had nothing to lose. He was marked for death as well. Not that he would have reneged on his promises to help the children, but it did make his decision that much easier.

As for Natalie Reyes, she quickly found out her status at the FBI was no better than Gideon's with the CIA. The entire Washington field office was out looking for her. An APB had been issued in Virginia and Maryland citing Reyes as a rogue agent responsible for the deaths of two agents in Lisbon, Portugal. It was all bullshit, but it showed that Frist had serious pull in virtually every sector of the government.

Her friends and coworkers were all off-limits. Each was likely to have surveillance waiting outside their home or work. Their phones were tapped, the neighbors were told to report any suspicious activity. She knew the drill, having done this many times to others, though they usually deserved it.

Now Reyes found herself in the same situation as Gideon, though she was untrained to handle it. That meant, whether he liked it or not, they were truly partners. Wherever he went, she went.

After an additional few minutes of waiting, Gideon had enough and decided to move forward into the club. He pulled the door open and stepped inside. Reyes was right behind him. The noise inside the room assaulted Gideon's eardrums. He had never heard this kind of music before. It was angry and violent and had a rhythm that beat faster than a locomotive engine. The place was also packed full of people that resembled, in one way or another, the giant bouncer.

And that's just who they ran into at the bottom of the stairs. The bouncer's great bulk blocked almost the entire stairwell. Gideon was still a step above the floor, yet he was just now able to look the man square in the eyes.

Fortunately, the bouncer wasn't there to fight. Gideon's display of aggression outside had served its purpose. He motioned for them to follow as he headed into the club's interior. Gideon and Reyes followed close behind until they came to a small, shabby office. They were motioned inside, and the door closed quietly behind them.

The office was empty. Gideon and Reyes looked at each other in mild annoyance. Where was the man they had come to see? The answer came in the form of a flushing toilet. In the corner, behind a closed narrow door, they heard the splash of running water followed by the sound of a paper towel dispenser being activated. A few seconds later, a man exited and approached them. In his hand was a pair of bifocals that he was cleaning with a paper towel.

"I'm Jimmy Chin," he announced, squinting up at the intruders. He put the glasses back on. His eyes widened with recognition. "Marty Mitchell," he said. He reached forward and grasped Gideon's hand. "How are you? It's been, what, four years since I saw you last?"

"Five," Gideon said as he pumped the man's hand.

Reyes leaned in close and whispered, "Marty Mitchell?"

Chin looked at the woman and winked. "Well, you don't think he's going to tell me his real name do you?" He smiled at Gideon, a knowing look in his eyes. "Not in his line of—" Chin threw his hands up in the air. "Not that I know anything, mind you. I don't. But I never forget a face. I told you that when we first met, didn't I?" He poked his index finger against his temple. "Especially the good customers. I never forget them."

Gideon smiled in return and introduced Agent Reyes. Then he came to the reason for the visit. "We need your help," he explained.

"Of course you do," Chin replied quickly. "Why else would you be here?"

Gideon explained in detail what he needed. Chin nodded his head, taking in the request. He asked questions only to clarify an issue. When he finished, Gideon looked at Reyes. This was a hard decision for her. She was giving up a lot by coming here. It was a step Gideon had contemplated many times in his career, but he never thought it would come this soon. Reyes, on the other hand, was confident in her future. She had a good, stable career, friends who cared for her. Unlike Gideon, she had roots. But she had never thought that someday she might be on the run, her life hanging in the balance. Reyes closed her eyes and slowly nodded her head.

"Excellent. Come, follow me," Chin beckoned. "We have much work to do."

They headed back up the stairwell into the maelstrom, Chin in the lead.

"I see you have new clientele," Gideon observed when they had reached the main floor.

Chin shrugged his shoulders. "Times change, my friend. This is a business. I have to be willing to adapt with the clientele," he explained to Reyes as they walked. "This building is an engineering miracle. The site was originally built as a warehouse, did you know that?" Reyes didn't, but she could have guessed. "It wasn't until the late seventies that it was made into a nightclub. Back then, when disco was popular, there were a variety of dance styles, moves, and music. The interior was designed to accommodate as many of them as possible. They put dance floors throughout the building, on this floor and the one below it, each with the ability to play its own music and showcase different dance styles. I bought this place in the mid-eighties when it started to fall into disrepair."

Reyes looked around. It seemed that the old warehouse hadn't recovered much.

"In the early nineties, the nightclub was heavy into the grunge scene. This place was perfect for kids who wanted to listen and hang out with peers that were into the same cultural rebellion." He must have recognized the doubt on Reyes's face, because he responded, "I know, grunge is grunge, right? But you'd be surprised how segmented they were as a group, either by the kind of music they listened to or the activities they brought with them. Just like today, with the goth scene, there are those that are hardcore into the lifestyle, living it everyday. Some are rebelling and will likely evolve from it. Others come out of the closet once a week. A few are simply curious. It's not likely that we'll see them more than once or twice."

Chin guided them to the middle of the club, where a large stairwell descended to a subterranean realm. This was where the devoted goths—those who lived the culture 24 hours a day, 365 days a year—spent their evening holding court.

The nightclub employees were doing a poor job keeping the stairwell clear, and they were forced to squeeze their way through to the bottom, working past the throng of black-and-white characters in a winding, serpentine pattern toward the building's rear. At the junction of another stairwell that went back up to the first floor, Chin stopped and turned to face a black door. The poor lighting and the absence of moldings hid the door from cursory view. He inserted a key and opened the door, ushering them into the club's storage closet. Mops, brooms, cleaning supplies, toilet paper—you name it, this closet stored it. Every shelf was neatly organized, the various supplies in their proper place on shelves or hanging from hooks on the walls.

"Over this way," he said.

They followed him to a corner of the large closet.

"Had this installed a few years ago after the fraud division of the Trenton Police Department raided the place. Scared the shit out of me. I was forced to call in a few markers, to people who know how to do these kind of things." He turned to Gideon. "I didn't have this when you were here last time."

Chin reached behind a shelf, found a specific nook or cranny, and activated a hydraulic device that raised the entire shelving unit from the floor about four feet. Gideon had thought the shelves were permanent, and most of them were, but this one opened to reveal a hidden staircase down to another level beneath the structure.

Chin started down. After two flights, with only dim light to guide the way, he announced that they had reached their destination. "Here we are," he said as he turned on a bank of very bright lights.

The room was approximately fifteen feet wide and another fifty long, but it housed some incredibly sophisticated equipment. Digital scanners, an electron microscope, a small, four-color printing press, and a digital printer made up some of the larger equipment. Along one wall was a workbench that held no less than five different workstations, each with a powerful magnifying glass of varying magnitudes. Tools of all shapes and sizes adorned the walls, hanging from pegboard or stored in small cabinets. On the far end hung a square of white fabric, a number of cameras, and strobe lights pointing at it so he could snap both digital and film headshots, depending on the customer's requirements.

Everything in the room looked like it belonged in a print shop, a photographer's studio, or an engraver's workshop. And the room was immaculately clean. The one thing that looked out of place stood next to them at the bottom of the stairwell. It was an old metal pot.

Chin was describing the layout and the equipment he used when Gideon asked, "What do you use this for?"

"That," Chin replied, "is an aluminum smelting pot. One of the things you need in my business is a variety of metal stamps, current ones, the kind used by notary publics to authenticate documents. In my case, I need the kind of stamps governments use on their passports and other official documents." He walked over to a large cabinet. "Here are stamps that I've made throughout the years. United States, Britain, France, China, Japan, even some for Iraq and Iran. I have stamps for most countries, and the ones I don't, I can make special—for a price, of course. I'm constantly making new ones as governments alter them or adopt modern, more stringent security measures that I need to emulate. The U.S. Treasury Department is finally getting into the habit of doing that as well, so most of this," he said, sweeping a hand over the section housing the U.S. stamps, "will have to be replaced."

"The smelting pot is used to make stamps from the carvings and molds you produce?" Reyes asked.

In her career in the FBI, she had been tasked with rounding up the country's top counterfeiters. Jimmy Chin wasn't even on the radarscope. That meant he must be good—real good.

"Yes, exactly," Chin replied proudly. "That's one of the reasons I'm considered the best at what I do. This smelting pot dissolves aluminum to liquid at about 660 degrees Celsius. The material I use is rated at 99.7 percent purity and flows easily into the molds I create, holding to the form in incredible detail. Now, aluminum stamps don't last as long at the steel-and-titanium ones used by the government, but I only make a few at a time, and it's relatively easy to replace them once I have a mold to pour into." Chin was very proud of his abilities and didn't mind telling them how good he was. "I look to every detail of the document in question and try to replicate as much as I can internally, to maintain quality control. Sometimes I have to go outside to a few specialists, but I'd say ninety-five percent of what is created is done here in my workshop. "

"Where do you learn stuff like this?" Reyes asked.

Chin shrugged his shoulders like it was a stupid question. "UCLA, School of the Arts, class of '78. Where else?"

Reyes was incredulous. She turned to Gideon and asked, "How much business have you done with Mr. Chin? Doesn't the organization you work for have these capabilities?"

Gideon cleared his throat and shrugged his shoulders apologetically. Chin just waved him off. No big deal.

"I have found it to my advantage to use outside resources from time to time," Gideon answered. "There were a number of years where I needed the best. Agents were getting turned or killed in part because they had poor documentation. Jimmy Chin is the best. Ask anyone."

"Yeah, right," Reyes replied. "And just who would I ask?"

"Why, anyone with enough money or connections to afford me," Chin replied easily. He reached into a drawer and pulled out a manila envelope. "Take a look at these samples," he said, handing the envelope to Reyes. "I made them as a wedding gift for a couple of friends of mine."

Reyes dumped the envelope's contents into her hand.

"Looks like any other United States passport, right?" Chin asked, watching Reyes for a response as she thumbed through the pages.

"As far as I can tell," she said, handing the passport over to Gideon.

"Even the credit cards have been hand rubbed and worn to illustrate age and use," Chin explained. He rubbed his hands together eagerly. This was his element. The nightclub upstairs was a hobby in comparison. "The photos all have a degree of wear around the edges," he continued. "Notice the dog-eared corners. I even have material stuck to the back like they'd been in the wallet for years." Chin looked on expectantly. "Well, can you see any flaws in the work?"

Gideon took the passport and thumbed through to the end, inspecting each page. He threw it back to Chin, commenting, "I'm not the expert here, you are. You tell me why your friends won't be detained if they use these."

Chin smiled broadly. "If done right, a counterfeit passport can fool even the best document experts. In fact, the only way to tell the difference between these and a real one is to take it apart." Chin opened the passport and pointed out why his were the best of the best. "You see, there are a variety of countermeasures the United States government takes to prevent passport forgery. The printing, paper, seals, fonts, sewing thread, and even the way it's cut is designed to make it extraordinarily difficult, if not impossible, to duplicate.

"A number of years ago," Chin continued, "the United States began to issue passports with the applicant's digital image printed directly on the paper, so you could no longer simply cut-and-paste a new picture onto a stolen passport. Not only that, they developed a new laminate that makes it harder to tamper with and included holograms, ultraviolet purple inks, and microline printing that are all tricky to reproduce. It took me a few years, but I was finally able to duplicate all the materials, tools, and techniques I needed. Now I can make whatever papers someone might need to travel throughout the world without worry.

"The paper quality," he said, holding it close to his face, slowly rubbing his thumb and forefinger across the surface, his eyes glued to every detail, "matches the original's caliber, brightness, opacity, and gloss. The sewing thread is interwoven with colored filament and even reflects par colors under fluorescent light. The stitching holes and patterns are an exact match, even when compared under an electron microscope. The wording in the document is identical, from the shape and size to the spacing interval, line thickness, and dot density. Finally, the official seals, embossing stamps, and the security film, which is interlaced with the United States hologram, has been reproduced down to the minutest detail." He dropped the sample passports back into the manila envelope. His face beamed with confidence. "This passport will pass inspection. So will everything else I create. I guarantee it."

"Jimmy," Gideon said when the man had finished, "why don't you give us a few minutes alone."

Chin looked back and forth at his two customers, understanding in his eyes. "Sure, yeah, okay," the forger replied, his hands raised high. He walked over to the far corner of the shop.

Gideon turned to Reyes.

"What's up?" she asked, perplexed. Gideon had suddenly turned serious.

"Are you sure you want to do this?" he asked softly. "It's not too late. You can still pull out."

"And do what?" she replied, frustrated. "My friends and coworkers are all out looking for me. I'm a marked woman. They think I've gone bad. The agency doesn't want the embarrassment, or my picture would be printed in every paper and wanted poster in America. I'm lucky my boss even gave me the heads-up. If anyone finds out, he'll lose his job for sure."

Gideon held his ground. "We can try to fight it. Not everyone you worked with believes what Frist has fabricated. Your boss didn't. The story won't hold up. You must have other supporters, or friends that can help. We can find out who they are—"

"And what then?" Reyes interrupted. "What if the story holds? I'll be killed on the way to the jailhouse, or by some other plausible 'accident' that can easily be arranged. You know how this works. Project Gemini is too big. Littleton is too secret. The girls are too important. There's too much at stake for me to worry about just myself. I mean, what's the death of one FBI agent to these people? Or more innocents if I get others involved? No, I can't take that risk."

"It means giving up everything," Gideon said finally. "Your friends, family, career, the life that you've taken for granted. Nothing will ever be the same again."

She smiled and then laughed. "Do you know how many people I've put into the witness relocation program? Lots. I've always been on the outside, watching as these people, mostly criminals beating the system, sometimes whole families, including the innocent children, say good-bye to their former lives. I never once thought that someday I might be doing the same thing." She looked Gideon straight in the eyes. "Ironic, isn't it, where life takes you? I can't say that I'm prepared for this, but I have resigned myself to it. So don't worry about me. Let's just get it done."

Satisfied that Reyes was going to be okay, Gideon called Chin back over and handed him photographs of Amy, Emily, Dr. Sossoman, and Reyes. He had taken the pictures earlier in the day on their way there. He already had his own identification and didn't need anything new.

Jimmy Chin put his pen and paper down and moved on to the next set of questions. Gideon knew exactly where he was going—money.

"Now, if we can change subjects, just for a moment," Chin began. "The documents you're asking for, with the level of quality I'm going to provide, don't come without a price. But because you're a good customer, I'm willing to give you a discount. Ten thousand."

"Dollars?" Reyes was shocked.

"Each," he added.

Reyes didn't know how much new identification should cost, but forty thousand dollars sounded absurd. She looked sideways at Gideon. Where was he going to come up with that kind of money? She definitely worked for the wrong agency.

"Fine," Gideon replied without hesitation. "But I need them ready in twenty-four hours."

"I can do that," Chin sighed, "but it will cost you an extra ten grand. And that's nonnegotiable."

"Okay, then," Gideon approved without batting an eye. "Get started."

CHAPTER 26

When Gideon and Reyes exited Coven, both were optimistic of their future. So far, Gideon's Plan B was falling neatly into place. That optimism evaporated in an instant.

"Don't move and nobody gets hurt."

The voice that came from the shadows was heavily accented. "Raise your hands and place them behind your head," the voice demanded. "Lock your fingers together tightly."

Gideon and Reyes complied. Strong, calloused hands gripped their interlocking fingers. Gideon tried to move but was discouraged by a blunt knee to the small of his back. The blow knocked the air from his lungs. He struggled to catch his breath, but the man's grip never weakened. The man gave a short command, and four armed men emerged from the darkness.

"Search them."

The men approached warily, but Gideon was in no position to defend himself. The search was thorough and professional. The men removed their weapons, identification, and cell phones.

Gideon looked over at Reyes. She looked surprised and scared but otherwise was holding up okay. She gave him a weak smile.

A large black SUV rounded the corner and pulled up to them. The back door opened. "Inside," the voice demanded. Strong hands pushed Gideon toward the vehicle.

"Where are you taking us?" he responded angrily. He started to push back.

Before Gideon could move, a blinding white light exploded in his head, followed quickly by a mind-numbing pain. He heard Reyes scream and had the sensation of falling. Then everything went black.

When Gideon awoke, he thought his head was going to split in two. The pain overrode all sensation. At first, his sight was blurred, but it soon returned to normal. As he regained his vision, he also began to hear people talking. Then he realized that his head was nestled in the lap of Dr. Sossoman.

"Shhh," she said softly. "Don't try to move."

He couldn't move even if he tried.

"Give me some of that water," she said to someone out of his line of sight.

Sossoman was handed a small glass. She slowly raised his head and let a trickle fall between his lips. It hurt even to swallow. Then Gideon realized that someone was holding his right hand. He felt small fingers encircling his thumb and forefinger. He struggled to sit upright and saw Amy smiling back at him. A worried expression was on her face, though she strove to look brave.

"Are you okay, Mr. Gideon?" she asked.

He fought through the pain and dizziness and straightened his back. All his muscles, from his shoulders to the lower back, were stiff and sore. He raised a hand to the back of his head and felt a large bump where he had been struck.

"I'll be all right," he said more out of hopefulness than any assurance that he was actually going to recover. The pain was terrible but was ever so slowly receding. He took the glass from Sossoman and finished what was left.

"Where are we?" he asked.

Reyes replied from behind. "We're being held by the Russian mob, at a place called Little Odessa. I think it's a restaurant or bar of some kind. A man named Pavel Fetisov brought us here. Does the name ring a bell?"

Gideon thought through the pain. "Yes," he groaned, less from pain and more from the recognition of their captor. "I know the name."

Pavel Fetisov had spent sixteen years in the *Glavnoye Razvedyvatel'noye Upravlenie,* or the GRU, Russia's military intelligence apparatus. He began his career during the Cold War, originally assigned to the Second Directorate, which ran counterintelligence operations in Western Europe. He rose quickly through the ranks, demonstrating an uncanny knack to blend into his surroundings, pass himself off as a local, and gather human intelligence with great efficiency. Before long, Fetisov was promoted to the rank of major and given responsibility for Berlin operations. Once there, he established an elite task force designed to turn foreign agents and recruit new ones. His success resulted in the creation of an elaborate spy ring that, while run out of Berlin, had tentacles reaching all across Europe.

Unfortunately for Fetisov, he became too good at what he did.

"He said you would remember him," Reyes said. She moved in front of Gideon. "Why does he know you?"

"In 2001, he was the target of a CIA sting. Even though the Cold War had ended, he was still too successful at the intelligence game. Consequently, he was set up for failure. Compromising photographs were taken of him in the presence of a known Mossad agent. The photographs were embarrassing, to say the least. The information was leaked in a very public way. Fetisov's career was over."

"What does any of this have to do with you?" she asked.

"I was the agent who ran the operation in Berlin. I'm the one who got him kicked out of the military."

Reyes closed her eyes and sighed. "You have a funny habit of doing that to people," she said, referring to Cross DeKay. "I hope this Fetisov has a better sense of humor."

"Agent John Gideon of the CIA," Fetisov boomed when they were brought into his presence. The big Russian approached Gideon and embraced him in a bear hug. "I thought I'd never see you again. What do you think of my Little Odessa?"

Fetisov lifted Gideon off the ground and tossed him from side to side in his arms. Then he kissed him on both cheeks before letting him go. Gideon winced in pain at the rough treatment.

Fetisov responded to Gideon's discomfort with good humor. "Ah, I told Alexi not to damage you, but he can be a little strong in his treatment of people. I do apologize for that. How is your head?"

Gideon straightened his shoulders. "No need to apologize," he replied evenly, though his head screamed in pain. "Nothing a few aspirin can't cure. What are you doing in the United States?"

"Excellent question," Fetisov boomed. "Back in Russia, I was recruited by one of the more powerful crime syndicates. I was so successful that Zavarskaya himself requested that I come to this country. He had need of my services."

"Who is Zavarskaya?" Reyes asked nervously.

Gideon responded. "Vasily Zavarskaya is the leader of one of the largest Russian crime syndicates on the East Coast."

"*The* biggest," Fetisov corrected. "Zavarskaya goes by the nickname Morozko now. He wanted me to be a *pakhan*—a boss."

Gideon knew the scenario well. When he was stationed in Russia, one crime family or another impacted just about everything he did. He couldn't get anything done, or go anywhere, without dealing with the mob. Now Fetisov was a *pakhan,* which meant he reported directly to the syndicate leader, Zavarskaya, and controlled up to four crime cells run by intermediaries called "brigadiers." The brigadiers were usually former Spetsnaz or KGB agents who were trained to establish and run spy rings, which proved to be a lucrative employment opportunity, so the switch to organized crime wasn't too far a stretch, and the money was much better.

The brigadiers ran enforcers who specialized in various types of criminal activity, such as drugs, prostitution, extortion, armed robbery, auto theft, money laundering, loan sharking, and homicide. The bottom level of the organization was made up of ex-convicts. Following the Cold War, Russia released millions of prisoners, many of them hard-core criminals, allowing them to emigrate wherever they wished. A great number ended up in the Unites States, most of them illegally. Once there, it didn't take long for them to settle back into the life they lived before their incarceration.

"This Morozko," Reyes asked with more confidence than she felt, "are we going to have to deal with him, too?"

"No," Fetisov answered patiently, almost fatherly. "Morozko is based out of New York and is responsible for three major families in Philadelphia, Atlantic City, and his home city. He acquired the nickname Morozko—which means Father Frost—back in the Ukraine. In the harsh winters, he used to murder his enemies outside, in the cold. Always outside. It was rumored that he liked to watch the hot steam exit his victims' bodies as they cooled."

"Sounds like a swell guy," she answered sarcastically.

Fetisov laughed loud. "Yes, he is. A very nice man."

"Why are we here?" Gideon asked boldly.

"I'm glad you asked," he said with a grin. "Doctor, would you like to explain?"

Gideon turned to Dr. Sossoman and saw that Fetisov was not in jest. Sossoman's face flushed red and she struggled to respond.

"It's not what you think," she began.

But Gideon had stopped listening. The pain in his head increased with his anger until he found himself falling backward. As he slipped into unconsciousness, the last thing he heard was Fetisov's booming laugh.

Gideon woke slowly to the pungent aroma of Russian cooking: roasted pork, steamed vegetables, and broiled chicken. It had been a long time since he'd had authentic Russian cuisine, and he relished the pleasant scent. Then he remembered where he was and how he had gotten there. The pain in his head throbbed with the beat of his heart. That part he didn't mind—pain meant that he was still alive.

He slowly opened his eyes and found himself looking up at a large scowling man with square shoulders and bulging arms. His face held the characteristic Slavic look: square jaw, high, prominent cheekbones, full lips, and a large forehead seamed with creases, topped by a mat of thick, curly black hair. His eyes, also dark, held no emotion. Both arms were exposed, revealing a history of tattooing. Gideon knew from experience that this man was a criminal, with many years spent in incarceration. His prison tattoos—and there were many of them—told a graphic story of his criminal activity.

"Where is Comrade Fetisov?" Gideon asked the man.

The reply came from across the room. "I see you've met Alexi."

With a little effort, Gideon was able to sit upright. He had been lying on a cushioned bench in what appeared to be a small waiting area of a restaurant, which itself was empty, save for their host, his two bodyguards, and a couple of waitresses.

"Come over here if you can," Fetisov called. "Join us for some drink."

Gideon glanced at his watch. It was just after midnight. He had been out only twenty minutes, but his head felt much better than before. He looked up at the large man. Alexi smiled slightly but didn't move an inch to help him.

Gideon stood up slowly and walked over to the Russian crime boss. Seated next to him were Natalie Reyes and Majel Sossoman. Amy sat opposite the mobster, almost as if he was keeping her at arm's length, like he would a wild animal. Alexi stood right behind his boss, arms folded across his large chest.

The table was heaped with steaming food. Gideon suddenly realized that it had been almost twenty-four hours since he had eaten last, and he was famished. Putting aside his pain—and the questions raging through his head—he sat down to eat and think.

Little Odessa was a long, narrow restaurant with a bar and mirror on the right side and tables on the left; French doors separated one part of the establishment from the other. Dim lanterns provided little light, and the air was heavy with stale cigarette smoke. The walls were adorned with an extensive collection of Russian Mezen folk art.

Historically, Mezen folk art held great importance to Russian peasants. Made from ordinary household objects—carved wooden eggs, plates and platters, rectangular and circular boxes, small chairs—each is painted a rustic brownish-red, the images tightly outlined in black. Accompanying a man from birth, the collection grew as he did. The scenes typically depict birds, horses, and deer intermingled with symmetrical shapes and designs, in patterns that represent the man's life. No two Mezen works are alike, although the paintings might be similar in style and color.

"What would you like to drink?" Fetisov asked when Gideon's plate was almost empty. "I must apologize in advance, I can only offer you vodka."

"What kind do you have?" he asked, suddenly very thirsty.

"Ah, you are a connoisseur?"

"Perhaps," Gideon replied, playing the game.

"Little Odessa has an excellent selection. We have Stolichnaya, Moskovskaya, Russkaya, Sibirskaya, Stolovaya. You name it, we have it in stock."

Gideon paused in thought before replying. "We'll have Pyatiszvezdnaya," he said, "if you have it. With a rose Shampanskoye, from Rostov, if you please."

Fetisov was unfazed by the order. "Vodka from St. Petersburg, and to accompany it, a sparkling wine from the vineyards off the Black Sea. A very good choice. A little weak to my liking, but as you're my guest. . . ." He waved his hand, and a barmaid appeared with their order.

"*Vashe zdorovie!* To your health," Gideon toasted. He downed the vodka in one gulp. He sipped the wine.

Fetisov flashed his white teeth. "*Vashe zdorovie!*" he followed and ordered another round.

Gideon turned to Sossoman. He'd had enough with the pleasantries. "Do you want to tell me what happened?" he asked.

The doctor raised a napkin to her lips and wiped them clean. She sat up straight and turned to face Gideon.

"I called Mr. Fetisov while you were in the nightclub," she began. "I knew who he was from a man that worked at Littleton. This man—Dimitri was his name—was a member of the Gorgon Medusa. He was part of the security detail. The girls and I, we befriended him. He was not like the rest. He hated DeKay and didn't like working under all that rock. I actually treated him for his claustrophobia.

"It turns out he was Fetisov's nephew. After a while of begging and pleading, he agreed to help us get out of Littleton. That's where Mr. Fetisov comes in. Dimitri went to him for help." Sossoman covered Gideon's hands with hers. "I knew you wouldn't approve," she pleaded, "but I thought he could help us. I'm sorry for not telling you earlier."

"What happened to your nephew?" Gideon asked.

"He is dead," Fetisov replied. "He was found decapitated in the trunk of a car, like a common criminal."

Gideon sat upright. "That was your nephew?" he asked, thinking back on the grisly clue that had started this investigation. "That's why they decapitated him and shaved off his tattoos. DeKay knew you would identify him and come asking questions."

"I found out anyway," Fetisov replied angrily. "And I've been trying to get into that base so I can ask him those questions myself. It has become personal between DeKay and me."

"But why was he killed?" Gideon asked.

"He was killed," Sossoman answered, "for trying to help me get the twins out of Littleton."

Fetisov let out a short bark that Gideon assumed was a laugh. "Not quite," he said. His face turned to stone. "Dimitri was butchered because he was trying to smuggle the girls out to me so I could have them for my very own."

Sossoman sat still in her chair, too stunned to move or speak. Her face paled.

It was Amy who responded. "But Dimitri said he would get us away from DeKay. We were going to start a new life, one without someone controlling us."

"He lied," Fetisov replied coldly. "You and your sister will be mine, so I can become boss and run my own syndicate." He turned to Gideon. "Now I have one of them. I will soon have the other. All the time and money I've put into this, trying to buy information, sending my soldiers into Kulbeda, and here you are, coming straight to me." He flashed a toothy grin, but there was no warmth in it.

"Then I'm glad he's dead," Amy spat back.

Sossoman's rebuke was swift. "That's not a nice thing to say."

Amy crossed her arms and looked away.

"That was your man in Lisbon?" Reyes asked. "He killed my partners."

"And I'm very glad that he didn't kill you, too," Fetisov replied callously. "Else you might not have been here to see this."

Gideon glared at the calculating Russian. The remnants of a long thin scar ran down the left side of Fetisov's face, from his temple all the way down to his jaw, in the sloping shape of a crescent. His nose had the look of being broken several times but only set right on a few occasions. His smile was full of straight, bright, white teeth, the work of American dentists in the last few years, something he could never have gotten in Russia. His hands were folded on the table. Gideon noticed that his fingers were oddly misshapen, not that they weren't functional, but still not quite right, like they, too, had been broken and reset too hastily . . . or too late. The life of a Russian soldier or mobster was not always a pleasant one.

Pavel Fetisov was much taller than Gideon and was at least fifty pounds heavier. Not that he was paunchy or showed his weight—it was just his frame, which was wide at the shoulders. Any extra weight he did carry settled evenly on him, distributed over the years and added to by his rich Russian diet. Still, underneath it all Gideon could see the vestiges of his youth and how he must have looked as a trim and fit soldier of the Soviet Union.

"What is it that you want, Fetisov?" Gideon asked. "Revenge for the embarrassment I caused you? The death of Cross DeKay for murdering your nephew?"

Fetisov waved his hand and the room filled with four heavily armed men. When he spoke, his words were clear and deliberate. "I grew up in the Chita region of Russia, along the border with China and Mongolia. My father, brothers, and uncles all raised sheep and horses or worked in the forests. It was a hard life on the frontier, but a proud one. I was first in my family to attend university, to move away from the land. Life was simple at home. Life was simple in the army. We had strong backs and legs, good rifles, and the approval of our comrades. We knew what we were supposed to do. Today, things are more complicated." He paused, thinking. "Now I have a duty to my new family, to see them grow and prosper. I grow first, of course. These girls can help me do that."

"What about your duty to the boss?" Gideon asked. "How can you turn your back on the loyalties you once held dear?"

Fetisov leaned forward toward Gideon. "Loyalties change," he replied. "But you should not worry about that now. Your time will come, I promise."

Fetisov's eyes were cold and dark. They bored through Gideon with an intense cruelty, seeing him only as a thing, not a human being worth caring for. Gideon returned the stare with equal measure. What he saw diminished any hope that reason might prevail. There was nothing there to reason with, just a bottomless pit, a black hole that swallowed up and destroyed anything in its path. The waitress came and handed Gideon another full glass of vodka.

"Did you know," Fetisov said, changing the subject, "that the tales of Russian drinking are all absolutely true? A long time ago, many Russian czars, including Ivan the Terrible, tried to outlaw the consumption of alcohol. Every attempt backfired and in many cases actually promoted excessive drinking. So the czars decreed that alcohol could only be sold on 'special weekdays' or only during significant church holidays. That led to a new Russian tradition—to drink excessively whenever we were allowed."

Fetisov raised his glass high in the air. "Come, my friend. One more toast before you die. *Vashe zdorovie!*"

The drink never reached Fetisov's lips. The sound of breaking glass was immediately followed by the sudden appearance of a neat hole in the middle of the mobster's forehead. Everyone in the room stared in stunned silence as the Russian fell face-first onto the table.

CHAPTER 27

Little Odessa erupted in a hail of gunfire.

The restaurant's windows imploded. Gideon watched as the body of Alexi was nearly cut in two. Another Russian danced and twitched as bullets slammed into him unmercifully.

Gideon reacted fast, pulling Amy and Dr. Sossoman to the floor under the table and shielding them with his body. Reyes crawled over to him a second later.

"Who's shooting at us?" she screamed.

"They're not shooting at us," Gideon shouted back.

It was a well-coordinated strike. The detached part of his mind was impressed with the attackers' proficiency. Each Russian target was hit at almost the same instant, which indicated a team of at least six was outside. He also noted that Reyes, Sossoman, and Amy were unharmed, which also meant they were in no immediate danger. If they were on the hit list, they would already be dead.

Unfortunately, the fact that they were alive meant that DeKay had found them. Gideon shook his head. They hadn't lasted much more than a day on the run.

Damn, he thought as the bullets whipped by overhead. *Where did I go wrong?*

More Russian mobsters emerged from the back of the restaurant, their guns blazing white flames. After the death of Fetisov, anyone still alive was fair game. These men were indiscriminate in their fire. If it moved, they shredded it to pieces. No one was safe, and that included the waitress who had served Gideon moments before. A hail of bullets slammed into her as she ran for cover.

From Gideon's vantage point, he was able to watch the particulars of the melee unfold with little more than detached curiosity. What the bodyguards failed to realize was that the threat was outside the restaurant, not inside. Even worse, they were standing inside a confined space under the restaurant's bright lights. Lit up under a spotlight, the Russians had made a fatal tactical mistake, misjudging the impact of raw firepower over that of superior position. For those outside, it was like shooting fish in a barrel.

In quick succession the Russian mobsters fell. Finally realizing their mistake, the last two men alive turned around and ran straight into two men who had come in through the rear entrance. In seconds the gunfight was over. DeKay's men now had control of the restaurant.

A small team of men moved into the room. Their heavy black combat boots ground the broken glass on the floor into small pieces. Each man wore black combat gear, balaclavas, and goggles. A communications device was barely visible in the left ear of each man. The weapons they carried varied: the H&K MP5, the Colt M4 carbine, or the Glock 18 pistol, which included a selector switch on the left rear of the slide that allowed fully automatic fire.

Gideon stood up and brushed debris and food off his now filthy coat. As he suspected, this was a well-trained, experienced combat unit.

"Are you John Gideon?" the man in the lead asked.

"I am," he replied.

The man motioned with the tip of his pistol. "Move away from the table."

Gideon moved to his right a few steps, stepping over Alexi's body. A member of the team kept his assault rifle aimed at the center of Gideon's chest.

"How did you find us?" Gideon asked.

The team leader smiled. His teeth were bright white against the balaclava. He reached to the side and pulled out a small electronics device no bigger than a video game controller.

"Your old friend, Director Gorrell," he said with an air of superiority. "He planted a tracking device underneath your coat collar. It made our job a lot easier. We simply waited for the right time to make our move, and here we are." The irritating smile returned.

Gideon thought back to his meeting with the director. He remembered that Gorrell had placed his hand on his shoulder. That's when he must have planted the bug. Frustrated, Gideon reached up to his coat's collar and searched with his fingers until he found the nickel-sized device.

"Satellite tracking," the man said smugly. "The latest and greatest the United States intelligence community has to offer. And if I'm not mistaken, that model there was developed by your guys." The man laughed at his own joke.

Gideon didn't think it was a bit funny. *That bastard,* he swore to himself. He felt betrayed.

All the time he thought the director was there to help him, to provide information, direction, and advice. Now it turned out the meeting was staged, a setup meant to spook Gideon, to send him running. The team followed close behind so they could take them down far away from the capital when no one was looking.

What bothered him most was that he had fallen for it. He had trusted Harrison Gorrell. He should have known better, should never have lowered his guard. He was the professional, the one responsible. His carelessness had put everyone in jeopardy.

When things went wrong, Gideon was hardest on himself.

Two men walked over to the table and lifted Amy and Dr. Sossoman off the floor. Reyes remained on her hands and knees. Neither put up a fight, and Amy held her head high. Her eyes locked on Gideon as she was marched to the front of the restaurant. Four men, including the team leader, remained in the restaurant.

"You won't get away with this," Amy said to the man holding her. She turned back to Gideon, her body silhouetted by the night. "Gideon," she said.

"Yes, Amy," he replied.

"Everything is going to be all right. But you're going to have to hurry. Littleton won't be around much longer, and I don't want to die there."

Chills ran up Gideon's spine. Amy's voice was pure and innocent. Despite her troubled past, the death and destruction she and her sister had wrought, and the captivity they were forced to endure, she still made a point to try to soothe Gideon's deep sense of failure. It was just another reminder that, when you boiled it all down, she was, after all, just a child.

"What did you do, Amy?" he asked kindly with no accusation or fear in his voice. "Tell me what's going to happen." He no longer doubted the girls' abilities. They were very special children.

She smiled wide and innocent, like only a child of seven can. "You'll see," she sang in a cheerful tone. "It's a surprise."

The team leader motioned for the men to move outside. When he turned back, his pistol was aimed at Gideon's head.

"Oh, I almost forgot," Amy's voice was clear, but farther away. "Don't forget to close your eyes real tight."

Gideon frowned in confusion. The team leader raised his pistol.

"DeKay originally wanted you taken alive," the man taunted, "so he could kill you himself." A smile spread across his face. "That changed once he had a chance to cool off. Now, he just wants you dead, and doesn't care how it happens."

Gideon ignored the threat, asking instead, "What do you think she meant, the wellwisher? 'Don't forget to close your eyes.'"

"I think she knows that I'm going to shoot you in the head."

"Really?" Gideon murmured. "Because, you know who she is, what she's capable of. Don't you think it might mean something else?"

"You're just stalling for time," he replied, though doubt was evident.

"Maybe she wished for something?" Gideon relaxed the muscles in his legs and lower back.

The team leader looked uncertain. "The other sister isn't here," he said. "That's not how things work."

"Is that a statement, or a question?" Gideon asked conversationally. He shifted his weight to the balls of his feet. "How could you possibly know for certain?"

The team leader was at a loss for words. He didn't know for certain, and that was the problem. If his time at Littleton had taught him anything, it was that anything was possible. The girls were unpredictable at best. At their worst, they were known to deeply resent their captors.

Gideon surveyed the remaining men in the restaurant. Uncertainty, if not fear, had gripped them as well.

Suddenly, the streetlights just outside the restaurant popped and went dark. The shattered glass rained down on the pavement.

The team leader's eyes grew wide. The gun aimed at Gideon's head wavered. Then, in the distance, Gideon heard Amy shriek. The two men shared a look of confusion.

As if things couldn't become more strained, the lights inside the restaurant blinked once and abruptly went out. Someone had cut the power, and the guy standing in front of Gideon wasn't the one who ordered it. Darkness enveloped the restaurant.

Gideon didn't hesitate. His strong legs coiled like a torsion spring, storing valuable force that when released would propel his body forward. He dove low, narrowly avoiding the three-shot burst meant to take his life. His arms reached out, searching in the darkness. If he could only tackle and subdue the team leader, then he and Reyes might stand a chance.

That's how he hoped it would work . . . but it didn't. The man was swifter than Gideon expected. Like him, at the first sign of trouble he had instantly shifted his position, firing at the same time to keep Gideon distracted, hoping that his shot made contact.

Gideon landed with a heavy thud, his momentum carrying him across the floor. The team leader fired from his new position, aiming at the space Gideon once occupied. The bullets narrowly missed Gideon as he slid past and came to a halt.

The restaurant was suddenly cloaked in silence. No one moved. No one dared breathe, lest they give away their position. The other gunmen in the room held their fire, not knowing where Gideon was or if he was alive or dead. None wanted to kill their leader by mistake. A tenuous stalemate settled on the room.

Gideon knew the situation would change once their eyes adjusted to the darkness. He needed to act before the balance shifted again.

Just then, a heavy object bounced across the tiled floor, shattering the silence. The men fired blindly toward the sound.

Realization dawned on Gideon as the child's prescient warning suddenly made sense. An image of the object flashed before his eyes. He knew instantly what the sound was and what was going to happen next. With no time to spare, he pressed his hands against his ears and curled into a compact ball. He shut his eyes tight against the darkness.

One . . . two . . . three, he counted inside his head.

The explosion of light and sound was debilitating. In an instant, one million candelas and one hundred and eighty decibels combined to temporarily blind, deafen, and disorient the unprepared mercenaries. Past the ringing in his ears, Gideon could hear moaning and cursing from within the restaurant. The lead attacker stumbled over Gideon and fell with a crash next to him. The man moaned loudly in pain. Gideon could picture his hands clutching feebly at his eyes and ears.

Slowly Gideon's limited night vision returned. Peering through the darkness, he could see two other men writhing on the floor in pain, each clutching their head with both hands, their weapons discarded and forgotten. Another lay motionless near the counter where the grenade had exploded. He took the brunt of the detonation and appeared to be unconscious. Reyes was farther back in the darkness. Gideon could not see her and did not know how she had fared.

Gideon started to move, when a faint silhouette at the broken front windows stopped him cold. Entering the restaurant was a single man, small and wiry, walking softly on the broken shards of glass. In his hand was the slender outline of a pistol, the long-barreled silencer giving it a surreal look in the darkness.

The unknown assailant walked up to the first mercenary writhing in pain. *Phewt!* A spit of yellow-orange fire flared from the gun's muzzle as he put a bullet through the man's skull. He then calmly walked over and put two shots into the still form by the counter.

No assumptions about who was alive or dead. This man was a professional. Everyone was going to get the same treatment. The dark assailant continued his death walk, killing each mercenary he came to, until he finally reached the team leader.

Gideon knew instinctually that he was next if he didn't take action.

Very slowly, he ran his hand along the leg of the man who had fallen over him. The stranger took another step forward. He raised the silenced pistol and aimed it at the mercenary's head. Gideon's hand closed around a hard leather handle. He slowly rotated his head until he was looking up at the new assailant.

The weapon went off. The muzzle flared bright for an instant. The man next to him jerked once and then lay still.

In that moment, bathed in the glow of muzzle fire, Gideon found himself looking straight into the executioner's eyes. He saw the pupils dilate in the bright flash. He witnessed the eyes widen in shock when the killer realized Gideon was unharmed, and worse, armed with a deadly weapon.

Gideon pulled the seven-inch KA-BAR combat knife from the dead mercenary's calf sheath and swung it up in a short arc. The sharp knife pierced flesh, embedding deep into the man's thigh. The assailant let out a bloodcurdling scream as he doubled over in searing pain. The sound was unholy in Gideon's ears as it pierced the darkness.

But Gideon wasn't done. Moving with blinding speed, he reached up with his free hand and grabbed hold of the man's combat vest. Then he pulled the screaming man toward the floor. At the same time, he jerked the blade free, spun the knife on its perfectly balanced handle, and thrust upward. The matte black blade sliced through the soft flesh of the neck, severing arteries, muscles, and the man's windpipe before deflecting sideways off the spinal column.

Gideon fell with the man and used the momentum to tumble forward onto the balls of his feet. He found and retrieved the dead assassin's gun. He left the knife embedded in the man's throat.

The sound of a door slamming closed brought Gideon running to the front of the restaurant and straight through the large broken window. He landed on the sidewalk and kept going, for as soon as he exited, gunfire erupted from the corner a block away. He dove to the ground and rolled right behind a parked car. The spray of bullets pinged harmlessly off metal and concrete.

Rising to a firing stance, he fired four quick shots at the shooter. The man was over fifty yards away, and the shots were wide to the left but still close enough that the man dove into the car. The driver revved the engine and took off, the tires squealing down the street.

Gideon considered emptying the entire clip into the fleeing vehicle, but he didn't know where Amy was, and if the past few minutes were any indication, she was very likely in that car.

CHAPTER 28

Captain Choi Yong Jin was more than a little upset. His fist slammed into the steering wheel. He cursed aloud in his native tongue.

He looked into the rearview mirror at the reason for his anger and switched to English. "Do not speak a word," he cautioned the little girl in the backseat.

At first, the child did not respond. She just sat there, watching his every move, her clear, unblinking blue eyes hinting at intelligence far beyond her years. She had already told him twice that he was going to pay for what he was doing. And if not for his threat of bodily pain, it was likely that she would have kept on telling him.

"Your friend didn't have to die," she said a moment later, ignoring his command to be silent. "You don't have to either, if you do as I say."

Choi rolled his eyes and tried hard to suppress his anger. He found it hard to believe that this girl and her identical sister were of such value to the vice president. In his culture, no girl was worth the death of one man. For that matter, no girl was equal to that of a boy, period. They could not wage war or work the fields with equal results. It was a fact that girls were not as productive as boys and cost more to bring up. Most fathers he knew would feel cursed if forced to carry the burden of twin girls. In North Korea, some didn't even bother. Though illegal, it was not uncommon for desperate fathers, especially those living in poor rural areas, to abandon newborn girls at birth. And those were the fortunate ones. Every once in a while he would hear stories of babies buried alive or thrown into a river inside a sack filled with stones. He was not *that* callous, but enough was enough.

Choi turned around to the man also in the backseat. "Bind her hands and cover her mouth," he ordered in English so the child would understand what her impertinence had wrought. "I've heard enough from this one."

The child didn't resist as the man beside her placed foul-tasting tape across her mouth. She even held up her hands, wrists together, so he could easily bind them with hard plastic ties.

Choi continued to watch the girl from the front seat. He shook his head in wonder, begrudgingly amazed at her poise and composure. She seemed to have an endless patience, as if she was used to being right and that it was only a matter of time before he realized it, too.

The more he thought about it, however, she *was* right about one thing. He hated to admit it, but it was true—it was his fault that one of his men was dead. His carelessness had caused the death of a good man. He should have considered that not everyone was incapacitated inside the Russian restaurant. It was foolish to send Corporal Ch'eon P'ung-cho in there alone. He should have been there as a backup. Instead, he let his conceited overconfidence get the better of him.

Now he was down to three men, though one of them was presumably inside Kulbeda Station. Even though he had not heard from Sergeant Han since they split up, Choi had to assume, at least for the moment, that he had made it safely inside. It would then be up to Han to get a message to him. The man had proven himself resourceful over the years, and Choi was confident that he would hear from him.

The captain glanced in the rearview mirror again, this time looking past the little girl to the traffic behind him. Somewhere back there was the man who had killed Corporal Ch'eon. The corporal was a skilled soldier, as experienced as anyone else on the team. His killer must have been very lucky to have been unaffected by the stun grenade and then take out the armed man. As much as he tried, however, Choi couldn't shake the odd feeling that crept into his subconscious. Maybe it wasn't luck after all. What if Ch'eon was killed by someone more skilled than he was? A chill ran down his spine. What if that same man was coming after them?

The sound of heavy raindrops hitting the windshield brought Choi's attention back to the road. He turned on the windshield wipers and gripped the steering wheel tighter. The storm previously forecast on the radio had finally hit land.

Choi shook his head in frustration. The rain would slow him down. A sudden gust of wind shook the car. He was not a superstitious man by nature, but this was a bad omen. The chill returned, but this time he turned up the car's heater.

Let it rain, he dared. *Let the heavens release their worst.*

A crack of lightning answered him in the distance.

Choi's brow furrowed in concern. A bad omen indeed.

CHAPTER 29

"Where are they?" Reyes asked as she recovered from the grenade blast. Her face was smeared with soot, dirt, and small spatters of blood. Her coat was torn at the shoulders and had a few buttons missing. Other than that, she looked to be in one piece. "Are they all right?"

"I think so," Gideon replied as he helped the agent to her feet. "Whoever killed DeKay's men got away. I think Amy and Sossoman are with them."

Gideon looked around at what remained of the restaurant. Weak light filtered in from the remaining streetlights outside, but it was enough to help him see. The inside was in shambles. It was nothing more than a dark shell of its former self. The walls were riddled with bullet holes, the floor was slick with blood. The bodies were strewn about like marionettes with their strings cut. He covered his nose with his hand. The smell of spent cordite, rusted iron, and human waste was overpowering in the confined space. The restaurant closely resembled the aftermath of a brutal terrorist attack, which, in some ways, he surmised it was.

Whoever attacked them didn't represent the United States government. Those men were dead, just like the Russians. It had to be a foreign power, but who could it be? Who was ruthless enough, ambitious enough, and bold enough to plan and execute an attack against heavily armed mercenaries and vengeful mobsters? More importantly, who was good enough to pull it off?

The sound of movement off to the side caught Gideon's attention. He raised his pistol and approached the source. A shocked and disoriented waitress rose slowly from behind the bar. She looked to Gideon and Reyes and then burst into tears.

Gideon moved closer and spoke softly to the woman in Russian. The waitress wiped her eyes and calmed down. She nodded her head a few times and then responded. Reyes watched from the darkness, unable to comprehend what was being said as the conversation stretched into a second minute. Then the woman reached behind the counter and pulled out a small flashlight.

"*Spasibo*. Thank you," he said, taking the flashlight from her shaking hands.

"*Ne za shto,*" she replied.

Gideon turned around and walked back over to Reyes.

"What did she say?"

He looked back at the Russian and smiled. He turned to Reyes and said, "Well, first off, we don't have to worry about the police showing up. This is a bad area of town. The Russians run it with an iron fist, and they don't take kindly to American intervention." He tilted his head at the bartender. "She says the police won't show up until it's light outside."

"That makes sense," Reyes replied. "The Bureau has been trying to get someone inside the Russian mob for years, but each time we try, the agent ends up dead or missing. It's gotten to the point where they've stopped trying."

"The second thing she said is good news for us." Gideon turned on the flashlight and shined it on the ground until he found what he was looking for. He walked over to Alexi's body and pulled a set of keys from the dead man's jacket. "She says the black SUV outside belonged to Fetisov. She says it's built like a tank, bulletproof windows and doors, blast-proof undercarriage. If it's the same one that brought us here, then all our gear should be in the back."

"Then what are we waiting for?" Reyes asked. "Let's get going. It's a sure thing that whoever attacked us is heading back to Kulbeda Station. They didn't go to all this trouble to get just one of the twins."

She turned and sprinted toward the front of the restaurant. Gideon moved more slowly, stopping to shine his light on the man he had killed. Lifeless eyes in the shape of almonds stared back at him.

"And who are you?" he asked no one in particular. The man could have been from a dozen countries bold enough to act against the United States—China and North Korea at the top of the list.

But Gideon didn't have time to ponder the man's identity. Reyes's urgent call from outside brought him running. When he got outside, he spotted her kneeling over a still form. His heart sank.

"I found her off to the side," Reyes offered by way of explanation. "She's hurt real bad."

Gideon looked down and saw the feeble smile of Dr. Sossoman looking back up at him. Her eyes were still bright, but he could tell she was in trouble. Her breathing was labored, and her skin was colored a pasty white. A red blotch of blood covered her midsection. The woman was propped up at an odd angle against the building, in between two trash cans.

Reyes grasped Sossoman's frail shoulders and gently lowered her to the ground. She rested the doctor's head between her thighs. Gideon knelt down next to her.

"How do you feel?" he asked softly.

"I've felt better," Sossoman responded weakly.

"We need to get her to a hospital," Reyes interjected. "If we can stop the bleeding—"

Dr. Sossoman raised her right hand and placed it on the agent's shoulder. "No," she said. "It's too late for me." Reyes started to object but was cut off. "Listen to me," the dying woman muttered. "I don't have much time left, and there are some things you need to know."

Dr. Sossoman took in a ragged breath. The end was near. Judging her condition, Gideon suspected she had a collapsed lung and ruptured organs. He had seen wounds like hers many times before in the field. Even with immediate medical attention, her chances for survival were slim.

Her eyes fixed hard on Gideon. "I tried to save her," she said. "But they didn't want me. Only the girl. They just shot me and threw me aside."

"It's all right," Gideon assured her. "You did everything you could."

"Not everything," she said.

"Who were they?" Reyes asked. "The ones who attacked us."

"North Koreans." Sossoman continued between fits of coughing, "On DeKay's orders, the twins have been trying to use their gift to kill President Yi Sang Gojong. So far, every attempt has failed. But there's more—I think DeKay has a side deal with the Korean Workers' Party vice president. He's trying to sell the girls to him, while they still have value. The girls will be eight soon. After that. . . ." Sossoman left the sentence unfinished. Her eyes began to close.

Gideon shook her gently. "Dr. Sossoman," he pleaded. "Wake up."

The doctor's eyes fluttered open. She smiled warmly up at him.

"Did you know," she asked, "that I had a sister?"

Gideon and Reyes glanced at each other.

"No," he responded. He reached his hand to her face and brushed a lock of hair away from her eyes. "I didn't."

Sossoman looked beyond Gideon as the past came back to life. "Adalia," she said, smiling. "We grew up in a small town in Austria. Those were such happy times. Adalia was a beautiful child, so carefree and friendly. Not as strong as I was. I looked out for her. People would take advantage of her kindness. Aah," she sighed, remembering. "Sweet Adalia, full of life and energy. Such innocence. She would never hurt a soul." Tears welled in her eyes. Her face turned dark. "Adalia was my twin sister."

Reyes gasped in shock. Dr. Majel Sossoman was a wellwisher.

"It was wartime, and the Third Reich had control of Austria. My aunt tried very hard to protect us, but he found us." She spoke haltingly between spasms of pain. "Hitler searched and searched. He found us right in his own backyard." Sossoman grimaced as memories gripped her.

"You helped Adolph Hitler?" Reyes asked, horrified.

Sossoman nodded. "We were so young then, so naïve. At first, we thought Hitler was a visionary. What does a child know about evil?" She sighed deeply. "No excuses. Adalia and I were held for much of the war. So much of the Third Reich's success came as a result of what we wished for. All the death and destruction—how many millions did we kill in our efforts to please? How many more could we have saved? Poor Adalia . . . the strain . . . it broke her spirit. By 1945, the light inside of her had gone out. That was the year we turned eight years old, when we came to realize all that we had done."

Sossoman broke into another fit.

"In February 1945, we were moved to the Führerbunker, Hitler's fortified retreat. By then, Adalia and I were using all our strength to wish against the war effort. Slowly, things began to change. Hitler began to behave erratically. We could tell that the strain was getting to him, that he was losing his grip on reality.

"I remember the date, April 30th, like it was yesterday. When the Führer was away, we would often play hide-and-seek in his study. There was always confusion, officers coming and going. By then it was easy to get away from our watchers. We were hiding in the study when Hitler ordered the room emptied. Eva was the first to go. She took a glass pill filled with cyanide. Her death was slow and horrible to watch. Then Hitler, too cowardly to die like his wife, shot himself in the head."

"What happened to Adalia?" Gideon asked.

Through fits and coughs Sossoman related the untimely death of her sister. Shortly after Hitler's demise, the Allies freed the twins. The Americans found Hitler's personal notes, explaining who they were and what they could do. The United States didn't have experts in the paranormal, but they soon became convinced. The evidence Hitler had collected was overwhelming. The girls were handed over to the OSS, the precursor to the CIA.

Adalia was tired of wellwishing, more so than Sossoman ever thought. One morning, she woke to find Adalia curled into a tight ball beside her. Her skin was cold and had the color of ripe cherries. Doctors rushed her to the infirmary, but it was too late. Her sister was gone forever. She later found out that Adalia died of acute cyanide poisoning. She must have taken the death pill meant for Hitler.

Gideon and Reyes sat in silence, stunned. What could they say? Nothing could have prepared them for the story Sossoman had just revealed.

Strong hands gripped Gideon's wrist. "These girls must be saved," Sossoman pleaded. "I've spent my entire life hiding from the past, from Adalia's death. No more. My guilt has caught up with me. Don't you see, I understand these children, what they're going through. I wanted to make a difference in their lives."

Her steel blue eyes bore into Gideon, daring him to challenge her. But he could not. He had already given himself over to fate.

Sossoman's grip weakened. "Save them," she gasped. "Let them live a normal life."

With that, Dr. Sossoman's body began to convulse. Gideon tried to hold her still, but death was coming for her. In a last heroic effort of strength, she reached out her arms, searching until her hands grasped hold of the large purse lying next to her. She raised her head one last time and pushed the bag into Gideon's hands. Then she fell back, a long, ragged breath leaving her body.

Reyes sat still as Dr. Sossoman passed on. She watched Gideon mouth a silent prayer and then stand. He offered his hand to her. She looked up into his strong, caring eyes, watching as he buried the newly formed emotions behind clenched teeth.

Just then, a heavy raindrop fell on Reyes's cheek. More followed until her face and hair were drenched with water. She didn't mind the rain at all. *Let it fall,* she thought. It was just what she needed right then, for the rain masked the tears streaming down her face.

CHAPTER 30

An hour later Gideon and Reyes were driving down I-95, approaching Dover, Delaware. At this time of night the roads were mostly empty, and Gideon made good time. They rode back to Kulbeda Station in silence. The urgency to save the children was still there, but the shock of Dr. Sossoman's revelation and her death left a pall between them. Shooting the doctor was needless and cruel. The North Korean soldiers acted without mercy or compunction. They were single-minded in their mission, and the absence of human compassion was something Gideon could not forgive.

But first he had to catch up with them.

Across the horizon a spark of lightning lit up the night sky. A peal of thunder followed, the loud rumbling an ominous portent of the tempest heading their way. The storm was fast approaching, driven by an unseen force from some distant point over the Atlantic.

Another brilliant flash of blue and white arched overhead.

Gideon was resolute, his focus on the road ahead. The storm raged against the SUV. The wind howled from the east, driving the heavy rain against the car. Every minute, the downpour seemed to fall harder, pelting the car like a fist with every gust. He ignored it as he would background noise.

"This is amazing," Reyes said, finally breaking the silence.

In her lap was a small notebook computer she had recovered from the back of the Suburban. The screen's blue light bathed the agent in an eerie glow. She was currently reviewing a compact disc Gideon had recovered from Sossoman's bag.

"Dr. Sossoman has what looks like over thirty years of research on this disc," Reyes said. "All her key findings, statistics, observations . . . it's all here. It also includes excerpts from her diary, notes on tests that were run, as well as theories of child development related specifically to wellwishers."

"Any advice on how to get into Littleton undetected?" he asked, hopeful.

"Sorry," Reyes replied. "It's full of psychological evaluations on the twins and clinical diagnoses of other wellwishers in the past, but that's it. There's actually quite a bit here about Amy and Emily."

"Does it say anything in there about what happens after the girls turn eight?" he asked.

"Yes," Reyes replied. "Dr. Sossoman has quite a bit of data on that, though most of her conclusions are based on speculation and supposition. It seems there aren't any hard facts."

"That's because most of these girls are eliminated by the time they turn eight," Gideon replied. "What does she say about that?"

"According to Dr. Sossoman," Reyes answered a few minutes later, "the short answer is sibling rivalry."

Gideon looked sideways at her, prompting for more.

Reyes continued. "I'm paraphrasing, but it says here that, under normal conditions, sibling rivalry is just the hostility between brothers or sisters. This antagonism manifests itself in manageable circumstances such as fighting or personal enmity. The typical family can handle this in a number of ways, all of them usually resulting in normal behavioral changes.

"But with wellwishers, the problem of sibling rivalry goes much deeper. Because of their higher-than-average intelligence and the demands placed upon them to use their gifts, the need for individuality and independence is heightened. The drive to be a unique person becomes almost instinctual, and at a much earlier age than most children. Like in nature, the problem is basically one of competition for limited or scarce resources. Whereas in the wild, the focus is usually for food or shelter, with wellwishers, there are two strong individuals who consume their habitat, all for the sake of dominance. It comes down to survival of the fittest. Sossoman theorizes that eventually they will fight each other, overtly or via the subconscious, until one of them manages to kill or drive the other out."

"That still doesn't explain the fear or the need to kill the girls around this age," Gideon shot back.

Reyes continued reading in silence and then responded. "Dr. Sossoman calls this age, somewhere between seven and nine years old, the Age of Enlightenment. Right around this time, self-awareness, or the ability to perceive one's own unique existence, begins to take form. It's the start, from an epistemological sense, where self-awareness becomes the very core of one's own identity. In layman's terms, the girls want to lead their own lives. Their emotional well-being hinges on the fulfillment of this need. It affects their personality traits, self-worth, motivation, and, most importantly, their sense of security. Where most children or teenagers fantasize of rebellion, their ability to change their environment is limited by what they can do physically and emotionally. But with wellwishers, once they start visualizing a future without sibling restraints, without barriers or adult interference, their image of self-realization can be acted upon. Except, as we've learned this past week, nothing with these children is small. No wish is simple, and they cannot control the impact of their gift. Ultimately, the girls end up bringing ruin to those around them and, unintentionally, to themselves as well."

"Which is why," Gideon said, "once they enter this Age of Enlightenment, it is only a matter of time before they wish for something bad to happen to their sibling." It all became clear to him. "Whereas earlier in life, the laws of nature would keep the girls from harming themselves, once they have self-realization, their gift works differently. They're almost able to act independently, and without realizing it, against each other."

"That's right," Reyes replied, excited. "And because the girls are always kept together, the destruction that ensues usually kills both of them and all those around them." She whistled. "No wonder they've always had to eliminate the children before they grew too old. Littleton would never have lasted this long if they didn't." She thought for a moment in silence, then asked, "But why don't they just separate them? Keep them apart when they reach a certain age?"

"I have a theory for that," he replied. "Dr. Sossoman had been working with wellwishers for over thirty years. They're constantly on the lookout for replacements, but it's not like there are hundreds of these children running around. These girls are the most powerful they've ever had, maybe will ever get. And Arthur Frist is getting old. His better years at Littleton are behind him. My guess is this: I don't think there was enough data to make any concrete decisions, at least not enough that someone like Frist would accept. Add to that the allure of power. These children provided life to Littleton. It gave the place a sense of purpose. My guess is he was willing to risk keeping them alive for as long as possible, ignoring the evidence, just to maintain what he has."

"And once he realizes the mistake?" Reyes asked.

"Littleton wasn't made to house the girls in separate quarters," he replied. "It's not big enough. DeKay doesn't have the same feeling toward Littleton that Frist has. He would have killed them eventually."

"Or sold them to the highest bidder," Reyes answered. "Just as Dr. Sossoman suspected."

"All the more reason to get back to Littleton," Gideon countered. "I can't tell if the North Koreans are operating with DeKay's knowledge or trying to double-cross him. Either way, the deal is going to go down soon, probably tonight. And once possession of the girls changes hands, we'll never see them again."

CHAPTER 31

Skaarsgard *Containership*
Twenty Miles off the Delaware Coast

Captain Martti Hyssälä looked out over his ship to the flared bow as it pounded through the waves. The bow rose and fell before him, disappearing with a shudder into the ocean as the deck was immersed with swirling green water.

This storm didn't make any sense. The ship was heading across forty-foot seas that seemed to get bigger by the minute. Yet according to the ship's instruments and his thirty years' experience sailing the world's oceans, the waves should be only half what they were right now.

The small Finnish sailor stared out the windows of the bridge, his steel-gray eyes angry and bewildered at what they saw. At just under five and a half feet tall, Hyssälä was not an imposing man by any physical standard. He was shorter than every other member of the crew. At fifty-four, he was the oldest on board. And he was by far the quietest, most introspective person within a hundred miles of the ship. Thirty years of sun and salt had turned his skin into tanned leather that wrinkled around the eyes and mouth. His hair was a mass of wild blond curls that encircled his head like a wreath before blending seamlessly into a beard shrouding most of his face.

For those who didn't know the captain, nothing about the man contradicted the first impression that he cared not how he looked, which was absolutely true. In fact, he cared little for what others thought of him. That impression, however, was different from those who knew or worked with him. For if you looked closely, you couldn't miss the strong, calloused hands that could squeeze tighter than a vice. The thick, heavily tattooed forearms, built up from years as a merchant marine, could outmuscle men twice his size. One could see his bowed legs standing wide to effortlessly absorb the roll of the ship. His ramrod-straight back was the result of standing endless watches in pilothouses and bridges on more than a hundred vessels. To those who knew him, Hyssälä showed two kinds of looks:

old and wizened when he tried to smile, which was often, and downright demonic when he was angry or upset, which was seldom.

Yet what made Captain Hyssälä tower over his crew was his vast experience and knowledge of the sea. In his years of sailing, the captain had seen and done it all. He'd survived typhoons off the coast of Japan in nothing but a schooner, fought off bitter winter storms in the Bering Strait as captain of a fishing vessel, rounded Cape Horn in a tug boat, and repelled pirates throughout the Caribbean in his sixty-four-foot catamaran sailboat. A brilliant strategist, renowned navigator, and the model for seafaring efficiency, Hyssälä had become a legend in the tight-knit sailing community.

Yet, Captain Hyssälä had never seen anything like this before. Long ago he learned that every storm had a unique personality, a mind of its own. And that personality changed depending on where you were in the world.

Hurricanes, typhoons, cyclones—he had sailed through them all. But this storm wasn't like any of them. It certainly wasn't a hurricane, the name given to storms formed in the Atlantic. This one did not originate off the coast of West Africa. There were no swirling cloud formations creating an unmistakable eye, the fingerprint of every hurricane. And it did not bob and weave in an erratic, unpredictable pattern. Instead, it moved in a straight line, as if it had a specific destination.

Captain Hyssälä was puzzled. This storm behaved as if it had a will of its own, like it was spawned by the devil himself. Outrunning it was impossible. The storm appeared and then grew with such speed and ferocity that he and the other vessels in the area were caught completely off guard. And it was fast, traveling across the water at speeds approaching thirty knots.

Not that he was really worried. The *Skaarsgard* was a big ship. In fact, she was bigger than most. Classified as an A1 container carrier, the vessel was just over 713 feet long with a beam of 105 feet. She wasn't quite the size of the newer post-Panamax containerships—which ranged beyond one thousand feet in length—but with a top speed of twenty-four knots, she could keep pace with the best of them. Besides, he knew this ship well and trusted its capabilities. It was a workhorse, still well within its prime with many years of service left in it.

"What is the wind bearing and speed?" Hyssälä called out.

Benjamin Nguyen, his Singapore-born first officer, responded immediately. "Winds are south-southeast, standing steady at sixty-three knots, Captain." Just over seventy-two miles per hour. "I've recorded gusts over one hundred knots."

"The lashings won't hold at our current heading," Hyssälä announced. "Turn course forty degrees to starboard. We'll head straight into the storm. Increase speed to twenty knots."

"Aye, aye, Captain," Nguyen acknowledged, relaying the order for course and speed correction to the ship's navigator. The captain's orders were then typed via keyboard onto a liquid-crystal display built into the bridge console. That was about the only manual activity that needed to be performed.

As this was a modern vessel, the helmsman did not alter course with a large steering wheel like they did in the days of yore. Now everything was electronically programmed, controlled from a central location by the ship's powerful onboard computer. The automated control system, also called "the Beastie" by the ship's captain, was fed a constant stream of data, including wind speed and direction, wave conditions, currents, and a host of other readings from the meteorological array located above the superstructure. The computer's brain then measured and anticipated the ever-changing ocean landscape—even judging time and location of wave crests—and then automatically adjusted to the course and speed that would enable the ship to safely plow through the maelstrom.

At times like this all the captain had to do was strap into his raised leather chair, which Hyssälä seldom used, and let the control system take over. Yet his eyes never rested. He constantly scanned the horizon, looking for treacherous rogue waves that might bury the ship under millions of gallons of frothy seawater. He checked and rechecked every instrument, gauge, and reading, verifying what his eyes and experience told him. Though he trusted the automated control system implicitly, he never knew when conditions might conspire to outwit even the most powerful of computer programs; hence, he was prepared to intervene at a moment's notice and take command.

But Captain Hyssälä wasn't worried about the navigation system. What worried him was far more sinister.

The *Skaarsgard* was powered by a state-of-the-art B&W 8180MC diesel engine with a single screw that could produce over thirty-three thousand horsepower. Under normal conditions, the ship had more than enough thrust to get through this storm. But the *Skaarsgard* was also fully loaded. Stored below deck and lashed topside were just over nineteen hundred twenty-foot cargo containers, as much as she could carry on the trip from Hamburg, Germany, to New York City. Piled five high and twelve wide on the deck, the containers resembled a patchwork quilt of multicolored metal. They were anchored down with quarter-inch cables, and the storm was working the lashings to their extreme limits. Hyssälä had already heard the loud ping of wires snapping close to the deckhouse, and the crew reported more, closer to the bow, where the storm hit with greater fury. If the lashings failed to hold, the weight distribution on the deck might shift.

And if that happened, she would become unbalanced and flounder worse than a pig in a pool of mud.

Overhead, lightning split the dark, cloud-filled sky, showing the storm's roiling underbelly, and lit up the deck. The immediate crash of thunder rattled the windows.

Hyssälä turned to his first officer. The captain's voice was measured and steady. "Contact the Coast Guard and check our readings against their satellite imagery," he ordered. "Also, advise them that we're heading back out to sea until the storm subsides. Send the same message back to Helsinki. There's no way harbor control at New York is ready for us. Let them know we're going to be late."

First Officer Nguyen never got to respond. At that moment, the *Skaarsgard* was hit by a series of brilliant lightning strikes that caused both men to stare out the bridge windows in wide-eyed shock.

The lightning came fast and furious, one hit after the other, reminding Hyssälä of the press cameras at a Hollywood movie premier. From his vantage point—eight stories above the deck—the ship appeared to be enveloped in an electrostatic bubble. The darkness came alive. The air danced and sizzled with sound and light.

Starting at the bow, white lightning hit the vessel in a near continuous stream of electricity until Hyssälä could no longer keep count of the strikes. The sound of the supercharged metal being sprayed by the cool Atlantic was horrendous, like a million banshees had been released from the underworld.

Slowly, methodically, the lightning worked its way aft, until it struck the antenna array above the deckhouse with a tremendous surge of energy. Ordinarily, the ship would have harmlessly absorbed and displaced the electric current, but not this time. The 1,000-watt, 500-kHz transmitter sizzled and popped as the excess current ran through it. Two windows on the port side imploded, spraying glass and driving rain into the bridge. On the other side of the deck, sparks flew into the air, burning anything or anyone they touched. The state-of-the-art electronics equipment housed underneath the console caught fire. Flames poked through the smooth walnut counter. The heavy lacquer finish started to burn and sizzle.

Officer Nguyen was the first to act. Undaunted by the fireworks, he grabbed a nearby fire extinguisher and sprayed down the burning console. A second bridge hand quickly joined him. In minutes, the fire was extinguished, but the smell of burnt wood, plastic, rubber, and metal remained.

No one was seriously injured, though everyone was shaken by the experience. Outside, the sky was turning a dark charcoal gray as morning approached. The lightning, once pulsing with life and energy, disappeared as quickly as it had come, leaving nothing but horrific images forever seared into the retinas of the men who witnessed it.

Visibility was back to a few feet, and every minute or so, bright streaks of lightning would light up the surrounding ocean.

His hands trembling, Nguyen tried the radio. It was dead. He looked to Hyssälä and shook his head.

"All right," the captain said more calmly than he felt. "Fire up the Immarsat satellite communications network and send word of our situation. Then get a technician up here to fix that radio." In all his years of sailing, he had never experienced an event like this. Hyssälä was not an overly superstitious man, but this phenomenon defied logical explanation. He hoped to never see another like it.

Nguyen walked quickly over to another console. He picked up the satellite phone and turned it on. It, too, was dead.

"Captain," he said, slowly regaining his composure, "there must be too much interference. I can't get a connection to any of the satellites."

Hyssälä lowered his head and sighed. "Fine," he said. "Get on the teletype. See if that works." The captain was not one to lose his patience, but at that moment, he turned to his first officer, his tone short and angry, and said, "Get that technician up here, immediately."

Nguyen hurried from the bridge. The other officers knew to keep their mouths shut.

Hyssälä turned back to the storm outside. "What have you got in store for me?" the Finnish captain asked.

The skirmish between him and the tempest had become personal. He didn't like losing, but he loved a good challenge. These ships had the ability to sail themselves, and rarely did they present a problem he couldn't easily overcome. More often than not he was forced to play the role of nursemaid, pushing buttons and turning dials. The home office in Helsinki had taken much of the fun of sailing out of the ship, leaving technology to do most of the work.

Maybe today will be different, Hyssälä mused. The captain glanced up at the clock on the bridge wall. The minute and hour hands split the clock face in two. It was precisely six o'clock in the morning. *Yes,* he thought with a wry grin, *the day has already started more different than any other day in my life. And I have little doubt it won't continue that way.*

Coast Guard Station, Group Operations Center
Cape May, New Jersey

"I have a message coming off the teletype," Operations Specialist Paula O'Brien announced. "It's from the *Skaarsgard.*" She moved to another console and pulled up the ship's record off the registry. "She's a containership out of Helsinki, Finland. Captain is Martti Hyssälä. They have a load of dry goods bound for trains to the West Coast."

"Are they sending a distress?" the watch commander asked. He leaned forward in his chair.

"No, they just want us to know that they're going to ride the storm out before heading into port. They've provided their last position and bearing, just in case. The first officer says they've lost both radio transmitter and satellite communications, but otherwise all systems are normal."

"Thank you, Paula," the commander replied. This was a very busy night for the Coast Guard station. Both of their HH-60 Jayhawk helicopters were grounded until the winds died down, and the only cutter capable of handling the storm's fury was responding to a distress call farther up the coast. "Confirm to the *Skaarsgard* that we've received their message and then log it in the system."

"Yes, sir," O'Brien replied.

The commander turned back to his own computer terminal. On his monitor was a satellite image of the storm system moving inward off the coast of New Jersey. It was a huge event, stretching from Boston all the way to Baltimore, with the strongest part reserved for the Garden State. In the storm's center was a very large section, almost as big as the state itself, colored red and yellow. Still roughly fifty miles offshore, this area highlighted isolated cells of extreme weather within the storm. Sustained winds in this region exceeded one hundred miles per hour, with gusts approaching 150 miles per hour. Gale-force winds that extreme were found only in hurricanes, but the data didn't lie. This was a hundred-year event, a once-in-a-lifetime storm. This was one for the history books. "That captain must know what he's doing," he said. "The *Skaarsgard* is heading right into the worst of the storm."

O'Brien came over to stand next to her supervisor. Her eyes widened. "They've got a rough time ahead of them," she said, thankful to be on dry land. As was her habit, she said a silent prayer for the crew of the *Skaarsgard* and then went back to her workstation. This night was a busy one for all Coast Guard stations in the mid-Atlantic corridor, and she didn't have time to worry about a containership the size of the *Skaarsgard*.

Within minutes, she was on to another set of problems. For the moment, the *Skaarsgard* was forgotten.

CHAPTER 32

At the same moment that O'Brien returned to her work, DeKay was dealing with his own set of problems in Littleton.

Frist was crawling all over him, demanding that the second twin be found and recovered and those helping her eliminated. The man's anger over the girl's disappearance was rising with each passing hour. He was close to the boiling point, furious with DeKay, with his handling of the wellwishers and the lack of results thus far.

DeKay closed his eyes and recalled Frist's heated accusations. "I handed you this John Gideon on a platter," he had said more than once, rubbing the wound raw. "My influence over the President persuaded Director Gorrell to plant the tracking device. I'm the one who arranged for his death afterward. All you had to do was follow Gideon, kill the adults, and bring that little brat back here unharmed. How hard could that be?" The last barbed indictment stung the hardest. "You should have handled this yourself, personally!"

On that point alone, DeKay agreed with his powerful employer. He should have been the one out there. It was his ultimate responsibility. He alone was charged with keeping the girls inside Littleton and any interested parties out. Security was his number one priority, and he had failed. He didn't need Frist's angry reminder to know that he had fallen short. The results of the past week spoke for themselves. First, there was the intrusion. He now realized that John Gideon must have somehow found out about Littleton and then gotten inside. How was still a mystery, though he likely had the help of Dr. Sossoman all along, despite her outward surprise on that fateful night. She was a fine actress, but he should have seen through it. Then he had allowed the janitor to smuggle the twins out of Littleton. Of all the people, that half-wit had managed to bypass every security protocol and just waltz right out. Someone was going to pay for that. And the botched raid on the Clover Theater? He didn't even want to think about it. Yes, they did recover one of the girls and a conspirator, but the cover-up was going to cost millions in bribes and probably cause a few more deaths. The bus accident alone made national headlines, bringing the scrutiny of millions dangerously close to Littleton. All in all, it was a colossal train wreck.

DeKay's thoughts wandered back to the angry Arthur Frist. *Tough shit,* he thought more than once. He was doing everything he could to find Amy Chase, and no amount of cajoling, meddling, or intimidation was going to change the outcome. He would have both girls here soon enough. Until then, Frist would have to wait, just like everyone else.

Unfortunately, Frist was not a man accustomed to waiting. He expected results and was used to getting them. But he was only part of the problem this morning.

DeKay picked up his radio. "Any luck getting through to the advance team?" he asked.

"No, sir," one of his men responded. "We've been modulating frequencies for the past hour, but there's been no response since the last update."

DeKay cursed aloud. It had been almost three hours since the last report. At the time, the runaways were being held at gunpoint by the Russian mob, and whatever was happening inside the restaurant didn't look good. DeKay ordered his men to take it down at the first signs of trouble. It was a risk, but he could not afford to have Amy killed or kidnapped.

On the positive side, he now knew who had tried to storm the cliffs the other night. It all made sense. The Russian man he beheaded months ago was somehow linked to the mob. He had been passing information to outsiders interested in the twins. Now this third party was involved.

All the more reason to get the girls out of here, before they disappear for good, he thought.

DeKay raised the radio to his lips. "Any chance this storm might be interfering with the radios?" he asked. If their radios were inoperable, he might not hear from the team until they got closer, which in this storm might take a while.

"Not a chance," the man replied. "We're picking up traffic from all over the state on different frequencies. The team just hasn't responded yet. Unless their radios are—"

The radio went dead.

DeKay bent his ear to the speaker, listening. He heard nothing but static. He toggled the radio switch. "Hello? Say again. Report." Nothing but dead air.

Just then, the floor under DeKay's feet began to vibrate and shake.

"What the hell?" he said, reaching a hand out to steady himself.

Then he heard an explosion in the distance. His head snapped up. It was a small explosion, but the shockwaves were powerful enough to reach the center of Littleton. The lights flickered overhead and then went out.

"Now what's happening?" he muttered angrily.

DeKay walked across the room, avoiding his large desk by feel and memory, and looked out his window. Littleton was cast in absolute darkness. For the first time since the girls were captured, the filament dome overhead was black. It was so dark, he couldn't see his own hand in front of his face. He reached out with his fingers until he touched smooth glass. If not for his sense of touch, he wouldn't even know he was standing at a window. He heard confusion outside as others fumbled about.

He counted: one . . . two . . . three. . . . He held his breath. The emergency lights flickered on, illuminating different parts of the town in stark white light. Anywhere the light didn't reach remained pitch black. The dome overhead looked like a blank canvas waiting to be painted upon.

People outside began mingling in small groups under the lights, worried expressions on their faces. Someone broke out a case of flashlights. DeKay looked out across the small park. At the town hall, the door opened to reveal a confused Arthur Frist. DeKay watched the man walk down the marble steps and cross the street to the park. He was heading straight to DeKay's office, ostensibly to blame him for the blackout.

No matter what happened, it was always his fault.

Suddenly, Littleton lit up like the Fourth of July. DeKay watched in shock as the town hall erupted in a ball of yellow flame, the mushroom cloud of smoke and fire rising high into the air. The explosion was big enough to burn straight through the filament dome overhead.

Frist was no longer walking—he was running as fast as his legs could carry him. So, too, was everyone else. All hell had broken loose.

It was now apparent that Littleton was under siege. DeKay's heart sank. This, he realized with anger, just might be his fault.

Choi's men easily overpowered the guards. They pushed aside the men's black jeep and drove into the dark tunnel entrance that would lead them to Littleton. As Choi drove, Littleton's emergency lights began to flicker on, one after another, enabling him to turn off his own headlights. It was still too dark for him to drive recklessly, so he took it slow. With three miles to go until he reached Littleton, it was going to take a few minutes to get there.

That's where Sergeant Han came in. His job was to keep the defenders inside Littleton confused while they approached. Once inside, they would regroup and plan their next moves. It was imperative they find and capture the second twin before base security was able to mount an adequate counterattack. The North Korean soldiers were sorely outnumbered and needed to maintain the element of surprise for as long as possible. He hoped Sergeant Han would be able to stay ahead of the enemy.

Coordinating with the sergeant had been easier than expected. The ever-resourceful soldier had recorded a brief message for Choi on a small Chinese-made communications device. He then hid the transmitter on a vehicle that was leaving the base. Once outside, the device initiated a burst transmission to one of the dozen Chinese military satellites circling the globe. The message was then sent back to Choi on a prearranged frequency. All he had to do was decode the message and be in position as Han instructed. The timing of the assault was a bit of a gamble, but there was no way around it. Until they were inside, there was no way to communicate with the sergeant.

After two miles of driving, Choi began to pass small pockets of people struggling to escape Littleton. These individuals were unarmed and paid little attention to the oncoming vehicle or its occupants. They were too busy trying to get out from under the crushing rock cavern, fleeing whatever terror Sergeant Han had rigged up.

Seeing the confused and frightened Americans brought a smile to Choi's face. As long as they were heading in the opposite direction, the element of surprise was still his. So far, he was encouraged by what he saw. He pressed against the accelerator, and the car shot forward down the dark tunnel. Those on foot were forced to flatten against the tunnel's walls as he sped past.

This is working out better than planned, Choi thought. *With any luck, we will have the second girl in custody and be gone before Littleton's defenders know what hit them.*

Charlie Simmons felt the explosion before he heard it. At first he didn't know what was happening, but he bolted upright in his bed as the sound rattled off the windows. He looked over at Emily, who was just waking up on the bed next to his. Her eyes were wide in shock.

"Was that thunder?' she asked groggily.

"No, sweetheart," he replied. "It sounded like an explosion over by the power station."

"Oh," the girl replied with a yawn.

"Did you wish for that to happen?" Charlie asked.

"No. I can only wish for things when my sister is near. You know that."

Charlie smiled. "I know," he said kindly. "I was just hoping it was you."

Then the lights flickered off, and the room was cast in darkness.

"What's happening?" Emily asked. Her voice was laced with fear.

"I don't know," Charlie responded with more calm than he felt. "But whatever it is, we should try to get out of here before the lights come back on."

Charlie reached out his hand, groping in the pitch black until he touched Emily. Her small hand found his and clasped tight. Together, they reached for the doorway, fumbling around in the dark until they found it. The door had no lock, so getting through it would be no problem. The men in the other room would be.

Charlie could hear panicked and erratic movement outside the room as their guards stumbled around. He heard them curse and moan as they bumped painfully into furniture, walls, and each other. Then he heard something strange. He pressed his ear to the door.

"What do you want?" one of the guards said.

Charlie listened closely. He heard a small cough. One of the guards moaned and then fell to the floor. The thump was unmistakable. He heard the second guard plead, "No, no, please, don't!" The door absorbed most of the sound, but he could hear the second guard struggling, fighting, or trying to get out of the way. He heard the crash of furniture, then nothing. Seconds passed in silence. The door handle started to turn.

"What's going on?" Emily whispered in his ear.

"Shush," he whispered back. "Be very quiet."

Charlie was almost hit by the door, managing to just avoid it as it rushed open. He and Emily flattened against the wall.

The glow of a red light entered the room.

"Don't move and you won't get hurt," the man said from the threshold. "There's no need to be afraid. Stay where you are until I find you."

The voice had a slight accent to it, one that he couldn't place. He didn't know this man, but he knew enough to stay hidden. One foot crossed the threshold. Then the other followed. The beam of red light began to sweep the room. He could now see the flashlight in one of the man's hands. In the other was a pistol with a silencer attached to the barrel.

He didn't wait for the beam of light to find him. As the man took his next step, he stuck out his foot. The man stumbled over it, but he didn't fall. It took a hard shove from Charlie to send him crashing loudly onto the floor. The flashlight fell from the man's grasp, skittered across the floor, and rolled under one of the beds. The light flickered once and then went out. The room was sent back into darkness.

He ignored the man's angry curse. Lifting Emily into his arms, he slipped out of the room and began working his way along the walls. Somewhere nearby he heard the soft moan of a dying man. Charlie prayed he wouldn't trip over one of the guards. Fortunately, he came to the front door without further incident.

Then he heard heavy footsteps on the floor above him.

That must be DeKay, he thought. Ever since they were captured, he and

Emily were kept in the small room below his office. After the fiasco at the theater, DeKay wanted to keep them close and under twenty-four-hour guard. They couldn't even use the bathroom without someone watching their every move.

A lot of good that did, Charlie thought. Now both guards were dead and some maniac was trying to get them. The urge to run was overwhelming.

He turned the knob and pulled open the door. At that moment, the emergency lights flickered on outside.

"Don't move." The unknown assailant stood at the door to their bedroom prison, a wicked-looking knife in his hand.

He must have lost the gun, too, Charlie surmised.

The man looked very angry. Charlie didn't hesitate. Carrying Emily, he bounded down the front steps to the sidewalk. He stopped briefly, looking right and left, trying to decide which way to go. There were many people out on the street, but none of them paid him any attention. He looked back to see the stranger exit the house. He was dressed like the men who guarded Littleton, but he wasn't one of them. Charlie knew everyone here by name and face. This man wasn't here to protect them. Right now, he looked like he was going to tear Charlie in two.

As if things couldn't get any worse, the town hall suddenly exploded in a tremendous fireball. Charlie could see the explosion reflected off the man's eyes. He didn't need to turn around to know it was horrific. He could feel the wave of heat on his back and neck as it expanded outward.

The man at the doorway paused, transfixed by the sight. It wasn't surprise that Charlie saw in his eyes, it was more akin to pride, like he was witnessing the birth of a child. For the briefest moment, Charlie and Emily were forgotten.

Without looking back, Charlie ran down the street as fast as his legs would carry him. He didn't look to see if he was being followed, he just assumed he was. All he needed was a head start. No one knew Littleton like he did. This was his world, his playground.

In seconds, Charlie was gone. His pursuer was quickly left behind in a maze of rights and lefts, hidden doorways, dark alleys, and long-forgotten pathways. After minutes of running, Charlie found himself outside the city limits. He had come to the twisting, turning maze of catacomb-like tunnels encircling the town. These were the tunnels first excavated to assist in the town's construction. Most were unused, but he knew them all. He ran into them without pausing to think, taking a number of paths that he knew better than the back of his hand. Once he was deeply into them, he finally came to a panting stop at the intersection of two narrow tunnels. A dim bulb glowed overhead.

He set Emily down beside him. His breathing was shallow, and his legs were trembling from the physical exertion. The muscles in his arms and shoulders burned. He wasn't that much bigger than Emily, yet without thought, he had carried her during their flight.

Suddenly, Emily's hand covered Charlie's mouth. "Shhh," she whispered urgently. "Be quiet. I think I hear someone coming."

Charlie and Emily shrank back into the shadows and waited. She was right. Someone *was* coming. Seconds later, the shadowy figure of a small man emerged from the same tunnel they had just come from. He stepped into the light and stopped.

It was the stranger.

Charlie was aghast. How could this man have followed them this far without getting lost? Most people didn't like being in the rock-hewn tunnels. It was too confining, the narrow walls and low ceilings claustrophobic to all but the hardiest. Yet this man looked completely at ease. He shrank farther back into the tunnel, too afraid to run lest the slightest sound give away their position.

The stranger looked down the two tunnels, trying to decide which one to take. With Charlie and Emily hidden in the darkness, the man's eyes looked right at—and past—Charlie without any recognition. The man's face turned angry. He pulled out a small notebook and held it up to the light. He thumbed through the pages until he found the one he was looking for. Then he turned to the wall, where Charlie saw a small chalk mark. The man turned back to his notebook, studying it.

So that's how he did it, Charlie observed. *This man has been here before. He must have scoped out this area and marked different reference points along the way. That's how he was able to follow us. How long has he been here? And how many more are there?*

Charlie could see from the glow of the light that this man was different. He looked American, but there was something in his eyes and the shape of his face that wasn't right. The man checked his watch and then pulled a radio from his vest pocket. He keyed the radio twice and seemed surprised when there was a corresponding answer. He spoke urgently into the radio.

By simply listening to the man, Charlie knew without doubt that the situation was dire. Fear gripped the janitor's heart. The stranger was speaking a foreign language that Charlie, in his limited exposure to the outside world, had never heard before. But it wasn't just the language—it was the way the man spoke, the crisp dialogue and the detached demeanor. He didn't need to understand a word of it to know he was planning something bad.

The stranger turned the radio off and swung the backpack off his shoulders. Next, he laid the bag down on the ground and settled onto one knee.

He began to pull a variety of metal objects out of the satchel, placing each one carefully on the ground. In no time, he had a dozen pieces laid out before him. One by one, he began to pick them up. With practiced ease, he pieced the separate parts together, locking each in place with a snap or a screw until he had created a long sniper rifle. The stranger then tested all the moving parts, looking for any sign that it was not functioning properly.

Satisfied with his inspection, the man produced four cartridges of ammunition from a large pouch on the side of the bag. Three cartridges went into his two breast pockets. One went into the rifle.

Then the man stood and without hesitation took off down the right-hand tunnel. Charlie relaxed and exhaled, not realizing that he had been holding his breath. He waited until the man was a fair distance away, then he stood up and set off in the opposite direction.

Emily, however, had other plans. She tugged urgently on his hand.

"No," she whispered. "We have to go this way, back the way we came."

Charlie cocked his head to the side, confused. It wasn't the right decision, he was sure of it. That tunnel headed back toward the center of town. That's where DeKay was.

"You have to trust me," Emily said. She pointed down the tunnel in the direction they had just come from. "Amy's that way. We have to save my sister."

Charlie smiled down at the little girl. Amy and Emily had saved his life, opening up a world of possibilities that hadn't existed before they arrived. He owed them everything. It went against his better judgment, but he couldn't let the child down.

"Okay," he said. He reached out his hand, and Emily placed hers in his. "Let's go save your sister."

The two walked hand in hand into the heart of darkness.

CHAPTER 33

Skaarsgard Containership

"This is not working," Captain Hyssälä said to his first officer. The two men were huddled on the far side of the bridge, discussing their options. "During that last wave, the ship heeled thirty-two degrees to starboard. Another roll like that and she'll turn completely over."

The two men looked out over the bow. Eighty feet below them the deck was a total disaster. Half of the topside containers had been lost to the raging seas. The steel cable lashings could no longer hold out under the constant onslaught of wind and water. God only knew what kept the remaining containers on board. Certainly, those lashings were at their end as well.

The two men watched the turbulent seas in awe. One wave crest after another topped the gunwales only to be blown away by hurricane-force winds. Like mischievous sprites dancing in the moonlight, the swirls of foaming spray separated from the swell, pirouetted in midair, and then disappeared instantly into the driving rain.

Neither man had ever experienced a storm of this magnitude and fury before. Even hurricanes were predictable to a point, but this storm seemed to be single-minded in its brutality. It acted like a heavyweight prizefighter, throwing all its weight and muscle against the ship in an effort to bring it to the mat. Too many times, the *Skaarsgard* had been punched, kicked, and whipped around. The storm was never-ending and seemed only to get angrier as time wore on. It was awesome and horrific all at once.

Captain Hyssälä envied the crew housed below deck. They didn't have to witness the storm's brutality, they didn't have to watch as the waves battered the ship and wonder if this was going to be the one that put an end to the *Skaarsgard*.

One look at the immense seas would have brought lesser men to their knees, but not Captain Hyssälä. He held firm as a gigantic wave—eighty feet tall, a thousand feet in length, and driven by 120-mile-per-hour winds—rushed the *Skaarsgard*. It was one of many such waves to hit them in the last half hour. The spectacular height and ferocity of the swell defied rational explanation. The men on the bridge could only stand and watch as millions of gallons of foamy green seawater engulfed the ship. The *Skaarsgard* shuddered as it plowed into the monstrous wave until the bridge was also buried underwater. The hastily repaired windows gave in under the strain, and the bridge was flooded once again. Captain Hyssälä stood his ground, but just barely. Others were not so lucky. The raging water swept men aside and threw them in a jumble across the bridge. In seconds, over a foot of water had filled the cabin. The release ports, not built for such volume, were slow to drain the deluge.

Captain Hyssälä stood helpless at his post.

Meanwhile, underneath the ship, the twenty-seven-foot, fixed-pitch, nickel-bronze-aluminum propeller bit hard into the swirling ocean, relentlessly driving the *Skaarsgard* forward. Agonizing seconds passed as the ship struggled to break free of the ocean's grasp. The cabin filled with even more water. The captain began to wonder if this was finally the end.

Then, he felt the bow ever so slowly rise up on the wave. Driven forward by the mighty propeller, the *Skaarsgard* suddenly broke free and bobbed to the surface. Fresh air, driven by the howling wind, replaced the torrent of water.

"That's quite enough!" Hyssälä shouted angrily at the storm. This was madness, trying to fight the devil head on. Throughout the vessel, the crew of twenty-one reported hearing the groan and shriek of tortured metal as the ship's framework was stretched and twisted by the waves.

"First Officer, its time to heave to," Hyssälä ordered. "We won't last heading into it. Let's see if we can't ride with it for a spell and let it pass over us."

A dripping-wet Nguyen smiled in relief. "Yes, sir," he responded eagerly.

Anything was better than the pounding they were forced to take at their current heading. It was a fine gambit, heading into the maelstrom, but the storm was proving to be too much for the *Skaarsgard*. She was a worthy vessel, but the sea knew no bounds. Sooner or later, if they continued to slug it out head on, the ocean was going to win.

"Turn us around, Mr. Nguyen. Hard to port and deploy the bow thrusters. Use the wind and waves to our advantage. Once we're on course, reduce speed to ten knots."

As Nguyen turned to relay the orders, a gigantic rogue wave rose up and hit the ship broadside. The ship rolled well past thirty-two degrees. The wave was so tremendous that the *Skaarsgard* was physically thrown to port. The entire ship rose above the ocean like a piece of balsa wood floating in the tide and was then thrown down like a discarded toy into the trough. The force of the landing shook the ship from bow to stern. Not a single joint, seam, or rivet escaped the jarring impact. The remaining windows on the bridge imploded, exposing the occupants to the storm's full fury.

This time, Mother Nature drew blood as the remaining deck containers broke free of their lashings and tumbled overboard. Like a child playing with blocks, the ocean picked up the containers and swept them away. The rectangular shaped blocks were tossed about with such ease and recklessness that Hyssälä could only stare and marvel at the ocean's might.

Throughout the ship, the crew began to report the damage. Toward the bow, a wayward container had ripped a large gash in the hull. Seawater was pouring in, forcing Hyssälä to order the compartment evacuated and then sealed shut. Elsewhere, faulty pipes broke apart. Small cracks became large ones. Worn electrical wires short-circuited in their conduits. Pumps were turned on full power to try to fight the flow of seawater as the crew hurried to repair the leaks.

Then the worst news of all reached the bridge.

"Captain," Nguyen reported, his face ashen, "engineering says that we've run afoul of a number of overboard containers. The propeller is bent or broken, he can't tell which, and we've lost full swing in the rudder."

Captain Hyssälä grabbed the phone from his first officer. "Tell it to me straight, Joshua. What's going on down there?"

The engineering officer was brutally honest. "Captain, the propeller is almost useless. That last crash destroyed the blades. You should have heard it. It sounded like someone put silverware in a blender and turned it on high. It was awful. She'll go no more than ten knots at full power. Also, we've lost rudder motion for hard to port and starboard maneuvering. It'll move a little, but not much." The panicked engineer fell silent. Hyssälä could hear a deep intake of breath. When the man continued, the strain in his voice was evident. "But that's not the worst of it," he said. "The propeller shaft wasn't meant to torque like it did on that last roll. It's got a bend in it somewhere. My guys are lubricating it as we speak, but eventually it's going to overheat and bind in its mounts. If we don't want to lose the engine, I'll have to shut it down before that happens. After that, we'll be dead in the water."

"How much longer will we have propulsion?"

"Another ten, maybe fifteen, minutes before she overheats," the engineer replied.

"All right," Hyssälä spoke gravely into the phone. "Give me all the power you can, for as long as you can. Shut down the engines at the last possible moment, but don't overload them. We don't need to be fighting fires as well as the storm."

"Aye, aye, Captain." Engineering sounded off.

Captain Hyssälä hung up the phone and turned to the bridge crew. He relayed the news without emotion. The faces were long and etched with fatigue. A few of them showed signs of seasickness, yet no one complained.

At that moment, the captain had never been more proud of a crew than the one that stood before him. These were brave, proud men. They had taken the best the storm had to offer and gave back with equal measure. Like him, they were men born to the sea. It was their calling. Seawater surged through their veins, and rope and tackle made up their muscle. They were battle tested, bloodied, and whipped, but survivors all. Their fear of the storm had passed to weary acceptance and even anger. Everyone knew they were in the midst of a terrific battle whose outcome was not yet etched in stone.

Hyssälä looked each man square in the eye. He had the utmost confidence in every one of them and knew he could count on them to do whatever he asked. "Listen up," he bellowed. "I won't lie to you. We're knee-deep into it. The sea's thrown her best at us and we're still here. But if you want to see tomorrow, you'll do exactly as I say."

The men drew closer.

Captain Hyssälä's face split into a wicked smile. These were good men. With their help, and a little luck, they would get through this.

CHAPTER 34

"Where is everyone going?" Reyes asked.

"I don't know, but whatever DeKay and the Koreans have planned has already started."

"It must be pretty big if everyone's bugging out like this," Reyes observed.

"We'll find out soon enough," Gideon said, glancing over at her. "You better make sure you're ready. Once we hit Littleton we have to be prepared for anything."

Reyes set about checking her equipment.

Gideon drove the SUV through the tunnel without slowing down. They were already well behind schedule, having been delayed by the storm raging outside. He could only pray they weren't too late.

After a mile, they stopped running into people trying to get out.

"Whoever is left inside Littleton must have the job of defending the town," Gideon observed. "It looks like all the nonessential personnel have gotten out. Anyone still here is being paid to stay behind."

"Unless they're hiding," Reyes said. "From the way you described it, there's no shortage of places to hole up in."

Gideon wrinkled his brow at the thought of just how difficult it might be to find the twins. After all, Littleton was a small town, with dozens of houses, buildings, and who knew what else. He sure could use a map of the place, but Dr. Sossoman had neglected to provide one. Whether he liked it or not, Gideon was forced to concede that locating the girls might just be the toughest part of getting them out.

"What's that up ahead?" Reyes asked.

Gideon turned on his headlights. A hundred yards ahead of them was the end of the tunnel. Blocking it was a small dark car. "I know that car," he said excitedly. "That's the car I saw outside of Fetisov's place, the one the Koreans drove away in."

"Ram it," Reyes pushed. "It's blocking the way. Drive right through it and head into Littleton." Reyes braced herself with her arms.

Gideon was tempted to plow through the car, but a nagging doubt forced him to pull behind it and stop instead.

"We don't have time for this!" Reyes shouted, frustrated. "Every minute we waste puts the girls farther away from us."

Gideon knew she was right, but he felt compelled to investigate the automobile. Maybe there were clues left behind by the kidnappers. He pulled out his Sig and opened the door.

"Stay here," he said. "I'll only be a minute."

Gideon closed the door and walked over to the abandoned car. He checked the front and back seats. Both were empty. The keys were missing from the ignition.

Maybe Reyes was right, he thought.

He started back to the SUV, when he heard a small banging noise coming from the trunk of the car. He moved closer. The noise grew louder. He rapped his knuckles on the trunk lid. Whatever, or whoever, was inside pounded back. Gideon's heart leapt to his throat. He rushed to the driver's door and reached inside. He pulled back the lever that opened the trunk.

When he returned to the back, he was elated to see Amy struggling to climb out of the confined space.

"Amy!" Gideon yelled. He rushed over to her, pulled out his knife, and sliced through the bonds that held her hands and feet. Then he removed the tape covering her mouth. He lifted the child high into the air and twirled her round and round. Reyes ran from the SUV and threw her arms around both of them.

Amy hugged Gideon tight around the neck. "John," she exclaimed, "you found me! I so hoped you would."

"Why were you in the trunk?" Reyes asked. Tears of joy filled her eyes.

"The North Korean man put me in there," Amy replied, angry at the ill treatment. "They didn't have enough men to have someone watching me while they looked for Emily. And I was being too much of a nuisance for them to take me with them. So they tied my hands and feet together and put me in the trunk."

Gideon and Reyes couldn't believe their luck.

"The men were very angry. They thought Emily and I were always together. They didn't plan on having to get us one at a time. It really messed up their plans. The leader didn't have a choice but to hide me in the trunk."

"How many are there?" Gideon asked.

"Three," she said. "There were four, but you killed one back at the restaurant. The leader was very mad about that, by the way. That leaves three, but I only saw two of them. The third man has been inside Littleton since yesterday, that's why they couldn't take me with them. All three of them are going after Emily. They're going to steal her away from Mr. DeKay. On the way here, they called a man named Pak. He must have been very important, because he gave them lots of orders."

Gideon's eyes grew wide. Could Amy be referring to North Korean Vice President Pak Te Hwan, second in line to President Yi?

"How do you know all this?" Reyes asked with a laugh. The little girl was full of surprises.

"I'm a good listener," Amy said shyly. "Besides, I speak pretty good Chinese, and I understood them."

Gideon and Reyes looked at each other. To say they were surprised would have been an understatement.

Amy continued, "They spoke English whenever they wanted to talk to me, but then they would switch languages when they had something important to say."

"How many languages do you speak?" Gideon asked, curious.

"Five fluently," she replied. She counted with her fingers. "Chinese, German, Spanish, Portuguese, and English, of course."

"Is that information on Dr. Sossoman's disc?" Gideon asked Reyes.

"Not that I could see."

"I'm also learning Russian and French," Amy volunteered like a child trying to show off a precious skill. "Emily is the one that's good at math and science. She's learning high school stuff now. The doctor says I have an ear for languages." Amy looked into the car, her eyes searching. She turned back to Gideon. "Dr. Sossoman isn't coming, is she?"

"No, honey, she isn't," Gideon said. "But she loved you a great deal. She told us so."

"I know she did," Amy said. The girl turned sad. Her eyes stared into the distance, recalling a memory. "She was going to buy a house for us to live in, one with a swing in the backyard. We were going to have real grass, and trees that grew taller than the house, and a sky that went on forever and ever." A single tear fell down her cheek. "We were going to be a family together, without all the bad men. I'm going to miss her."

Gideon didn't know what to say. He simply held her tight to his chest and whispered, "Well, I'm very happy that you're with us now. And we're not going to leave you behind. You're coming with us, away from here."

Amy hugged him back. "After we get Emily," she said matter-of-factly.

"Right," Gideon replied.

Gideon carried the small child to the SUV and buckled her into the backseat while Reyes got in beside her. He got into the driver's seat, shut the door, and gunned the engine. "Hold on tight," he said. The large SUV surged forward, ramming into the smaller car. Amy let out a squeal of surprise. It didn't take much effort for Gideon to push the car aside, boxing it into a tight spot between two rock formations.

"That's not going anywhere," Reyes said as he drove past. "I hope the Koreans have another way to get out of here."

Gideon turned around to look at Amy. "There's another reason I'm glad you're here," he said. "You know this place better than anyone. I need you to show us around. Are you okay with that?"

Amy nodded her head enthusiastically.

"Good," he said. "Let's get going."

They drove straight into Littleton.

Skaarsgard *Containership*

Getting the *Skaarsgard* turned around was harder than Captain Hyssälä thought it would be, but they did it. Maneuvering a ship in heavy seas was tricky enough under normal conditions, but doing it at quarter speed in a storm this ferocious was almost impossible.

He almost lost the ship twice during the move. The first came as they attempted the 180-degree port-side turn. Under calm seas and without tug support, the ship would need at least two miles to execute the maneuver safely. But as soon as they presented their starboard bow, one wave after another began to pummel the floundering vessel. Seawater poured over the gunwales until Hyssälä could no longer see the deck.

Literally being pushed by the waves, the *Skaarsgard* turned at a sharp angle, almost as if she were on a coaster, until her entire beam was exposed to the elements. The ship started a death roll, listing past thirty-five degrees. Hyssälä could almost reach out and touch the ocean. It took all the power the ship had, using full port bow thrusters, to keep the waves from rolling the ship farther as it fell into the trough of a gigantic wave.

Ultimately, the sea that was trying to destroy the *Skaarsgard* also saved her. While in the trough, a rogue wave almost ninety feet high hit the ship from behind, slamming violently into the eight-story deckhouse. The wave's impact both righted the ship and turned her forty-five degrees until she was facing almost inland. Seizing the moment, Captain Hyssälä ordered engineering to give it all she had. The damaged screw bit into the ocean. All power in the bow thrusters was shifted to starboard. Ever so slowly, the *Skaarsgard* came out of the trough, turning as she did until they were pointing due west.

Captain Hyssälä then ordered the engines cut before they exploded. Meanwhile, the crew cheered loudly as the waves were now pounding into the stern.

The danger didn't end there. The *Skaarsgard* was now running without propeller in following and stern-quartering seas. Parametric rolling, an unstable phenomenon resulting from large roll angles and significant pitching, threatened to tear the ship asunder.

Having lost the topside containers was at first a blessing as it reduced the ship's weight. Now it posed a problem as the hull rode higher in the water and was more exposed to both pitch and roll. To compensate, Captain Hyssälä ordered the bow compartments flooded, hoping the added ballast would make the ship more stable.

"What's our heading?" he shouted out. The driving wind and rain howled through the smashed windows, making normal conversation impossible.

"Still westward at twenty-six knots," Nguyen reported with a smile. "The superstructure is acting like a giant sail. The wind is actually pushing us forward."

"Thank God for small miracles," Hyssälä said.

First Officer Nguyen was amazed at the captain's ability to keep the ship on course. Any other man would have folded under the pressure by now. The *Skaarsgard* had no propulsion, limited steerage from the damaged rudder, and overworked bow thrusters, but it held true.

Captain Hyssälä walked into the navigation room. Nguyen followed. A series of nautical maps covered the center table. Hyssälä went immediately to the ones showing the waters around New Jersey and Delaware.

"Where are we due to make landfall?" Hyssälä asked, looking at the sea topography.

Nguyen picked up a grease pen. "Our current position is here," he said, marking a point less than twenty miles offshore. He drew a line across the chart. "Given the wind and wave direction, and factoring currents. . . ." He calculated in his head. "We should end up right about here."

Captain Hyssälä looked at the mark on the map.

"That's if we don't hit shallow water," Nguyen corrected.

"There's no fear of that happening," Hyssälä replied. "Delaware Bay is dredged regularly for deepwater vessels. By the look of it, we're going to miss the beaches by a good two miles. No, I think your calculations are accurate." He placed his finger on the map and bent down close. "Curtis Cove it is, then. Better get back on the teletype and warn the Coast Guard."

He looked over to where his technician was trying desperately to fix the radio. It was a lost cause. Seawater had flooded the circuitry, causing more shorts throughout the system. He commended the electrical engineer for not giving up, but there was no way it would be fixed in time.

"Twenty knots in following seas," Hyssälä mumbled to himself. He looked again at the mark on the map. The miracle he had alluded to earlier might be the same thing that killed them. "God help us all."

Ten minutes later, Coast Guard Operations Specialist Paula O'Brien tore the sheet off the teletype and read the message. If she'd had any emotions left, her heart would have sunk with the news. Instead, she was spent. The storm was now a natural disaster, causing death and mayhem up and down the coast.

She put the latest report down on her supervisor's desk.

"The *Skaarsgard* is sending a distress call," she said robotically. "The skipper says they're dead in the water. They've lost all their topside cargo and they have no propulsion and limited rudder control. They're asking for help getting the crew to safety before they run aground."

"Tell them to get in line," the supervisor replied coldly. "We've already lost contact with the containership farther north of them. Three other commercial vessels have stopped responding to our radio signals, including the LNG container en route to New York City. And Lord knows how many fishing vessels are lost out there."

O'Brien didn't budge. "What do you want me to tell them, sir?"

The supervisor let out a deep breath and rubbed his eyes. This storm was a nightmare, taxing resources all along the East Coast. Leaders in Washington were likely to mobilize the United States Navy in response to the maritime disaster.

"Tell them," he said more patiently this time, "that until the winds die down, we cannot launch an air rescue. That, until the waves die down, there's no way we can launch a cutter. In these seas, rescue crews would be in as much danger as the containership. They're going to have to ride it out for a little while longer."

It was on days like this that O'Brien hated her job, but her supervisor was right. In this storm there was little they could do. She walked over to the teletype and composed her message to the captain of the *Skaarsgard*. When she was finished, she couldn't help but think it sounded ominously close to a death warrant.

CHAPTER 35

Littleton

Even though they couldn't see the combatants, they could hear sporadic gunfire in the distance.

Gideon drove slowly through the outskirts of Littleton with the lights off, trying to attract as little attention as possible to their entrance into the fray. So far they hadn't seen a soul, but the large black Suburban stuck out like a sore thumb. It was hard to miss no matter where you looked.

Gideon was stunned by the change in Littleton. The town looked so much different than he remembered. Cast in dark shadows, the place resembled an old movie filmed in grainy black and white. Bereft of color, the town's patterns, shapes, and lines showed clean and crisp in the subdued emergency lighting. There was no gray to confuse or befuddle the imagination. It was an honest image, pure, without the fantastic colors that made it look like it belonged in a snow globe. Even still, from the deepest, darkest, blackest corners to the bright white spotlights that cast even longer shadows, the sight of Littleton held his attention, luring him, daring him to look beneath the surface.

Gideon followed Amy's directions until they came as close to the center of town as he dared. Then he backed into a narrow driveway and killed the engine. He twisted in his seat to face the woman and child.

"You know what you have to do?" he asked Reyes.

"Yes," she replied. "But I don't like it. Why can't I come with you?"

"You have to stay here with Amy," he said. "Keep her safe. This is what I was trained to do. It's what I'm good at. I can move faster if I'm by myself. And, besides, things are likely to get messy. Amy doesn't need to be involved in that."

"But I want to go with you," Amy whined.

Gideon was gentle but firm. "Let me find Emily and bring her back here. You two stay low and out of sight. That's the kind of help I really need, so I don't have to worry about you. Okay?"

Amy slowly nodded her head.

"Great." He pulled a balaclava over his head and turned off the car's interior light before opening the door and stepping outside. Reyes met him at the front of the SUV. She handed him a black satchel, which he slung over his shoulder.

"Be careful," she said. Then she did something completely out of character. Without thinking, she lifted the black hood, leaned in, and kissed Gideon full on the lips. His breath was warm and moist, his mouth soft and receptive. And that's what surprised her most—he was kissing her back.

Gideon broke contact at precisely the right moment. He didn't smile. He didn't say a word. He simply turned around and disappeared into the shadows. Reyes got back into the SUV only to find Amy smiling broadly at her.

"Don't say a word," Reyes said before Amy could respond. "Not one word."

"The man has left the SUV. He crossed the street and disappeared into the second ring of buildings surrounding the park."

"Were you able to identify him?"

"No, sir. It's too dark. But there's at least one other person in the car. A woman. How would you like me to proceed?"

"Tell your man to stay where he is," DeKay instructed Colonel Allbright. "If my hunch is right, John Gideon has come back to Littleton."

"That means the woman is probably Agent Reyes from the FBI," the colonel surmised.

"Yes," DeKay sneered. "They've come for the second child."

"Are they the ones behind the explosions and the dead men downstairs?" Frist asked. "Did they take Emily?"

"I intend to answer that question very shortly."

"Just remember," Frist reminded DeKay, "finding the twins is your number one priority. Emily is here somewhere, we just need to track her down. If John Gideon is now in Littleton, as you suspect, then Amy might be here as well. Get them back. After that, you can do whatever you want with the intruders."

DeKay assembled a small team of men and exited through the back door of the house. At the moment, he could not use the front door because an unknown sniper was roaming the aluminum framework overlooking the town's center. The gunman had a clear, 360-degree angle of fire and was taking potshots at DeKay's men. The sniper was an excellent marksman and the death toll was rising.

There were also disturbing reports of two heavily armed men roaming around town. Small skirmishes had erupted, but no one had been able to identify them as of yet. Whenever DeKay's men responded in force, the men seemed to vanish into the darkness. The hit-and-run tactics were very much like the probing attacks he had used during the Gulf War. This small team was testing their defenses and response times, looking for weaknesses. And if they and the sniper were working together, which he strongly suspected was the case, then he was up against some real pros.

Until his men found and killed these perpetrators, no one was safe.

As for Gideon . . . DeKay would take care of his old friend personally.

What a mess, Gideon thought to himself.

Across the park was the demolished pile of scorched rubble, splintered wood, and twisted metal that used to be the town hall. There was nothing left of the building save its wrecked aftermath. Flames still flickered with life within the rubble. Embers still piping hot slowly cooled on the periphery. Overhead was a gaping hole in the filament dome where the fire had surged through it. Higher overhead he could hear the loud hum of an emergency exhaust vent as it sucked the smoke out of the cavern. He assumed that the back-up ventilation system, like the emergency lights, must run on battery power or a gas generator hidden somewhere in the town.

Gideon looked around the square. Without power there was no way to tell which houses were occupied and which ones weren't. There were dozens of buildings to choose from. Emily could be in any of them, or none. She could be back on the surface somewhere. Maybe Frist whisked her off at the first signs of trouble. Maybe he had killed her.

The futility of not knowing drove him mad. He felt like screaming in rage. Then it hit him. Why not? Throwing caution aside, Gideon reared back and yelled at the top of his lungs.

"Emily!" he shouted. His voice echoed loudly in the cavern. "Can you hear me?" He paused to listen. He called again. "Emily Chase, this is John Gideon! I've come to find you!"

The cavern was suddenly filled with silence. Nothing stirred save the crackle of burning wood across the street. The sporadic gunfire had all but stopped. It was as if a hush had fallen over Littleton, as its remaining inhabitants waited with equal anticipation to see if Gideon's call would be answered.

"So much for the element of surprise," he said aloud.

Minutes passed like hours. He listened for the slightest noise. Nothing. He was about to try again when he heard a reply that made his heart soar. A child's voice called out his name. At first the voice was faint, but then it grew stronger, louder, closer.

"John!" Emily yelled. "We're over here! Charlie and I, we're all right."

Gideon saw a small child emerge from between two houses across the park. "Stay there," he yelled. "I'll come and get you."

The battle-hardened CIA agent risked it all. Running as fast as he could, he crossed the street and entered the park. His action broke the spell that gripped all of Littleton. No sooner had his boots hit grass than the sod began to fly all around him. He glanced right and left to assess the threat. A group of men had entered the square to the right, but they weren't firing yet. No one else was in sight. Whoever was shooting at him must be firing from one of the houses that ringed the commons, or from the exposed dome infrastructure overhead. Judging the trajectory and impact of the bullets, he guessed it was the latter.

Gideon raised his pistol and fired blindly at the cavern roof. The rain of bullets continued unabated. He needed to find cover quickly before one of them found him.

He feinted right and dove left toward the small stand of trees in the park's center, making it safely to the leafy canopy in three large strides. The shooting immediately stopped. He was safe for the moment, but the news was not all good, for now he was trapped and Emily was still in danger.

DeKay and his men closed in on the Suburban. The black tinted windows prohibited him from seeing who was inside, but he knew they were there. His heart raced with anticipation. Then he heard a noise that made his hair stand on end.

John Gideon. He was calling for Emily.

DeKay thought his head was going to explode. The mere sound of the man's voice brought a flood of memories, not one of them pleasant. He chastised himself again for not killing him when he'd had the chance. He would not miss this opportunity.

Just then the driver's-side door opened. A female emerged from the car, facing toward the center of town. She, too, had heard Gideon's call.

By now, DeKay had reached the back of the car undetected. Quieter than a mouse, he snuck up behind the unsuspecting female. Other men were positioned on the other side of the vehicle.

DeKay smiled. He could tell right away it was Agent Reyes. The blonde hair, long neck, slender figure, the pistol dangling from her right hand—even in darkness she cut quite a figure. Too bad she was caught up in all of this. She was in the deep ocean now. Treading water with the likes of John Gideon was bound to get you in all kinds of trouble. He should know. Gideon had almost ruined his life, the self-righteous son-of-a-bitch. Now he had corrupted this woman. The meddlesome FBI agent didn't know when to quit. It was a shame, too, having to kill a woman as beautiful as her. He wouldn't get the same thrill out of taking her life like he would with Gideon. This was business. The other was personal.

Then DeKay heard a sound that made everything all right. It was like a ray of sunlight had penetrated the heavy rock above. Amy Chase screamed at Reyes from the front seat, but her warning came too late. DeKay was at the agent before she could turn around. He drove his gun into the small of her back. Then he pressed himself tightly against her.

"Just give me a reason, Agent Reyes," DeKay cooed menacingly into her ear. "Not that I need one after all the trouble you've caused me."

Amy was pulled from the front seat by one of his men and brought around to face him.

"Well, hello there, you little brat," he said, sneering with pleasure. "Enjoy your time outdoors. I can assure you, it will be the last time you ever see the light of day."

Amy stood stoically, refusing to comment on DeKay's threat.

"Don't you dare hurt her," Reyes warned.

"Why, the thought never crossed my mind." He patted Amy on the top of her head. "And it's not me she needs to worry about. This little girl is worth a fortune. No, it's her new owners that she'll have to please." Turning to Amy, he said, "You'll meet them as soon as we get your sister."

"I've already met them," Amy said with disdain.

"What do you mean?" DeKay asked. He knew from experience these girls never did or said anything that didn't have a larger meaning. He grabbed Amy's jaw tightly in his strong right hand. "Tell me," he demanded.

"The North Koreans," she cried in pain. "They're here to steal us away from you."

"You're a liar," DeKay said without conviction. *Would Pak screw me over?*

"No, she's not," Reyes interjected. "They're the ones who killed your men last night. They killed Dr. Sossoman, too. We've been chasing them ever since. They had Amy in their custody up until a few minutes ago."

DeKay thought long and hard. It sounded true. He would not put it past Vice President Pak to try to double-cross him. It was the way the North Koreans operated in general. Why would this situation be any different? Besides, there was no way Gideon could have caused all this destruction by himself in such a short period of time. And the tactics came right out of the Communist handbook for guerilla warfare.

"Tell me what you know," he said to Amy.

The sound of gunfire brought the reunion to an abrupt end. At first, the noise came from a single source, but soon after, others joined in until the battle had reached a fevered pitch.

DeKay grabbed Amy and lifted her into his arms. "Tell me as we walk," he said to the girl. "And don't try to trick me, or I'll kill everyone you hold dear, starting with Agent Reyes."

Leaving nothing out, Amy began to tell the story of how they had escaped from Littleton . . . and then ended up right back there again.

Gideon opened fire on the approaching men, killing one and scattering the rest across the park. The return fire was heavy, forcing him to find cover behind a dense copse of trees. Once there, he peered through the foliage and took stock of the situation. He didn't like what he saw. First, he was badly outnumbered and outgunned. He counted at least six men approaching from the far end of the park. They were real pros, too, creating a staggered line of constant fire, each man leapfrogging past the other as they moved methodically forward. It was a sound strategy, meant to keep him pinned down while they approached. If he allowed them to succeed, they would be able to move dangerously close to his position.

Second, the sniper overhead kept him from retreating through the back of the park. If he was right about the man's probable location, then he would be dead before he got ten feet past the tree line. The only positive was that it also kept DeKay's men from trying to come in from behind. They were equally vulnerable to attack.

Third, he had not spotted the other two North Korean soldiers. They were out there, he was sure of it. For now, they elected to sit back and watch the show. *With any luck*, he thought bitterly, *they will all shoot themselves and make my job easier.*

And finally, Emily and Charlie, stranded on the other side of the street that circled the park, were exposed to anyone roaming that side of Littleton. For the moment he had to assume the Koreans were on the opposite side, or else they would have easily snatched them up by now. DeKay's men would not make the same mistake. Surely, they had dispatched men to work their way around the park and come up behind them.

It was a bad situation any way he looked at it.

And then, just when he thought things were at their worst, a tiny bit of hope emerged. Perched high above, the sniper started judiciously picking off DeKay's advancing men. Gideon knew immediately what was happening, and why. In the theater of battle some tactics don't change, no matter what nation or ideology you fight for. That's especially true in guerilla warfare, in which small, highly motivated groups of combatants attempt to use mobility and surprise tactics to defeat a foe or effect a military or political outcome against an oftentimes larger and better-equipped adversary. Typically, and this was the case at Littleton, the vastly outnumbered guerrilla unit tries to draw its opponents into terrain where it can conduct surprise attacks at vulnerable targets. In this instance, the sniper was taking advantage of his superior position to eliminate targets of opportunity.

In their pursuit of Gideon, Littleton's security force had forgotten about the sniper threat and had allowed itself to be drawn into the open. It was an easy decision for the sniper. Except for the remaining North Koreans, anyone on the ground was a threat and therefore open to engagement.

Gideon was not one to complain at good fortune, no matter where it came from. For the moment, he was content to watch as the sniper picked DeKay's men apart.

Three men fell in quick succession. Another was wounded in the shoulder and lay exposed out in the open. The staggered line came to a jarring halt as men scattered for whatever cover they could find. The wounded man got up to run and was promptly shot in the leg. He fell with a scream that split the air. No one moved to help him. Their blood-soaked comrade served as a constant reminder of what would happen if they tried to move. The sniper had achieved his objective: stall the mercenaries until his comrades got to Emily.

Gideon couldn't let the Koreans succeed. At the moment, Emily was their primary objective, and the mission was everything to these men. They needed her to complete the set and acquire both girls.

Moving to the edge of the tree line, he called over to Charlie, instructing him to pick up Emily and hold her close. It was a gamble, but he did not believe the sniper would fire on Charlie at the risk of hitting the little wellwisher. Gideon then asked Charlie to put his faith in him and instructed him to quickly cross the street.

Gideon held his breath as Charlie, carrying Emily in his arms, dared fate and charged forward. Charlie looked neither right nor left. His eyes never left the ground a few feet in front of him for fear of what he might see. He just ran and entered the park without incident. In seconds he was standing beside Gideon.

"That was very brave of you," Gideon said to Charlie as he hurried to catch his breath.

Charlie smiled broadly and put the girl down. As soon as her feet hit the ground she ran over and wrapped her arms around Gideon's waist.

"Can we go now?" she asked.

There was a familiar urgency in Emily's request. Her sister also displayed the same heightened sense of time. They were like two mice in a cage, so close to getting out but unable to work the latch.

"I'm working on it, honey," he replied.

"We don't have much time," she said shyly.

"I know." The words sounded patronizing even to his own ears, but at the moment he had bigger fish to fry. If they couldn't get out of this park, then there was no chance they would leave Littleton at all.

Gideon turned to Charlie. "Help me out here, Charlie."

Charlie smiled with a twinkle in his eye. "Come over here."

Gideon followed him through the small stand of trees to a depression in the center.

"It's right here," the janitor said. "Our way out of the park."

Charlie crouched down on his knees and ran his hands through the grass. At first, Gideon thought the little man had gone mad, but after a few seconds and a little effort he lifted a small metal grate off the ground.

Charlie beamed with pride. "It's a drainage pipe that runs from here to behind that house over there." He pointed to a damaged house to the left of the shattered town hall. "We can crawl through the pipe and come out at the storm drain that's behind it."

Gideon squinted into the darkness and then over at the smiling Charlie. "There's only one problem," Gideon frowned. "I won't fit into that pipe."

Charlie's smile disappeared. He scratched his head. An unpleasant thought entered his mind, one that could have disastrous consequences.

Gideon could see that he was too afraid to bring it up, so he did instead. "It's still a good idea, Charlie. You and Emily should go." He then filled them in on where the others were hiding. "Go and get some help. Tell Agent Reyes I've gotten myself pinned down in the park. She'll know what to do. You can stay behind and protect the twins until we get back, okay?"

Charlie's smile came back in a flash. "I can do that," he said.

Gideon reached down and moved the grate out of the way. He patted Charlie on the back and offered a few words of encouragement. Then, the diminutive janitor got down on his belly and crawled into the hole. His feet quickly disappeared into the pipe.

Gideon looked at Emily. She was next.

"I'm not going," she said.

"It's going to be all right," Gideon comforted her. "You don't need to be afraid. Just follow Charlie's feet."

Emily backed up a step and shook her head.

He tried a different approach. "You know what helps me when I have to go through small spaces? I pretend that I'm crawling through the forest. Close your eyes if you have to and try that. It won't take but a minute or two, and then you'll be over to the other side, safe and sound. Charlie will help you out once you get there."

She stood her ground. "I'm not afraid," she said. "And I don't need to close my eyes to pretend. I want to be here when my sister comes."

"But she's back in the car."

"No, she's not," Emily asserted. "Amy and Agent Reyes are on their way here. DeKay has them."

Gideon's eyes narrowed. "How do you know this?" he asked.

"I don't know," she replied. "I just do."

"They're on their way here?" he asked.

Emily nodded her head.

Gideon walked to the edge of the trees and looked around. All was quiet again. Everyone was waiting for someone else to make the next move. Emily walked up behind him and tugged on his sleeve. She beckoned him to come closer. He bent down on one knee and looked her in the eyes.

"They're here," she whispered.

CHAPTER 36

***Skaarsgard* Containership**

"First Officer," Captain Hyssälä announced calmly, "sound the alarm to abandon ship."

Nguyen paused briefly to stare at the captain. Even in defeat, the man's gray eyes never wavered. They displayed the same confidence and determination as before, though now the safety of the crew took precedence over that of the ship. It was a comforting moment for the first officer. He knew, without a shadow of a doubt, that the same effort the captain gave to the *Skaarsgard* would now be given to ensuring the survival of the crew. To hell with the cargo, insurance would cover the loss. The same couldn't be said for the loss of human life. So far, the captain had steered the ship and its crew through the storm. Minor injuries were reported throughout the ship, bruises mostly, a few broken bones, but no one had died.

It was a solemn moment for the crew of the *Skaarsgard*. Of the twenty-one crew members, no one had ever abandoned ship before. They had run the drills as required, maintained standard operating procedures as defined by corporate headquarters in Helsinki, but never did they have to actually perform the procedure in an emergency. It was unthinkable, giving up and running away like this. It went against the very nature of what it meant to be a sailor. But it had to be done. The ship was lost.

Minutes later, First Officer Nguyen and the crew assembled at one of the aft lifeboat stations. The men looked scared. They watched the raging seas with wide-eyed anticipation. The only saving grace was that the waves had diminished somewhat. Instead of being terrifying in their height and ferocity, they were now merely frightening. The larger waves still topped twenty feet, but this close to shore, they had lost much of their potency. The wind also had diminished, though gusts were still recorded in excess of sixty knots per hour. It wasn't much, but Nguyen was willing to accentuate the positive in any situation.

Of the six lifeboats, only two remained strapped to their berths. Three had been swept away by the containers. One succumbed to the pounding waves and ferocious winds. Nguyen considered them lucky that any had survived at all.

Under the first officer's watchful eye, the men quickly and efficiently prepared the boats for launch. Fresh fuel was added to the powerful outboard motors. The men tested the engines, confirming that each one worked as it was supposed to. They inspected the hulls for cracks or other signs of visible damage. The last thing anyone wanted was to get out to sea only to find a leak that could spell disaster.

Once both boats were deemed fit, the injured crewmembers were loaded aboard. At thirty-two feet in length, each craft could hold twenty-four crewmen comfortably. But in these seas, Nguyen ordered the men to split up into two teams. That way, the boats would remain more buoyant and, he hoped, easier to manage in the rough chop. It would also increase the chances that someone might survive the storm.

Nguyen looked up at the pilothouse eighty feet above the deck. He could just make out the lone figure of the captain high above, his image silhouetted in the broken windows. Reaching into his pocket, Nguyen pulled out a waterproof flashlight and signaled twice that the first boat was ready to depart. The captain signaled once in reply. On the next flash, Nguyen would order the boat lowered.

"Remember," he shouted to the boat's pilot over the roar of the wind and sea, "as soon as you hit the water, blow the couplings, gun the engine, and steer clear of the ship. The captain is going to give you the best chance possible when there are no rogue waves in sight. Once you're clear, head inland as fast as you can go on a course southeast of here. That will take you to the public beaches, where the water becomes shallow. The Coast Guard promises they'll have a team in place to help you ashore and take care of the wounded."

"What about you?" the man shouted back.

"As soon as you're safely away, the captain is going to come down and shove off with us."

Just then, Nguyen spotted the bright signal of the captain's flashlight. It was time. The lifeboat was lowered quickly into the ocean. Just as it touched water, the cables parted and the boat turned sharply away from the containership. The timing was just right. In seconds, the small craft was traveling at top speed over the crest of a small wave. For a moment it disappeared into the trough, only to reappear farther away over the top of another wave.

The remaining crew celebrated by raising their fists and shouting after the receding boat.

The first officer turned back to the superstructure. The captain continued to watch the small craft through his powerful binoculars. After a long minute, he gave the all-clear sign. The first boat had made it. Nguyen breathed a sigh of relief. The crew cheered again.

After another signal, Nguyen got into the boat. He saved a seat at the helm for the captain.

Then, without warning, the skiff started to lower to the sea. Fearing a malfunction, Nguyen grabbed the manual controls and stopped the boat's descent. Panicking, he looked up to find the captain still perched on the bridge. He had not moved.

"What is the captain doing?" the man next to him asked. "He has to hurry if we're going to have a chance."

The captain gave the signal to lower the boat. Nguyen's puzzled expression quickly shifted to understanding and then anguish. Captain Hyssälä wasn't coming with them. He was staying behind to make sure the crew got safely away from the ill-fated vessel. From his vantage point high above the ocean, he could see what Nguyen could not. He could read the wave patterns, judge the distance between crests, and lower them into the sea with the same chance of survival as the other boat.

The captain waved farewell to the men in the skiff. Many didn't understand the gesture. Those who did turned and saluted their captain, faces resolute, their eyes foreshadowing a mixture of pain and gratitude that would stay with them forever.

Captain Hyssälä was a man true to his word. He would see that his men were taken care of.

Reluctantly, Nguyen let go of the controls and took his place at the helm. The captain disappeared over the gunwales as the boat lowered into the sea.

Captain Hyssälä watched quietly as the second lifeboat sped away into the distance. His was an easy decision to make. The men of the *Skaarsgard* were his responsibility. They were his family away from home. The connection he felt for the crew was as strong as the one for his own wife and children.

He glanced down at the bridge controls and shook his head in wonder. Even without power, and with minimal bow steerage, the ship was traveling at close to fourteen knots. The hand of God couldn't have pushed them any faster, or with more determination, than the winds and waves created by this storm.

The devil himself had a hand in this, he was sure of it.

Through the shattered windows, Hyssälä could hear the crash of waves on a distant shore. The thundering sound grew louder by the minute, though he could not see where the ship would land.

The unexpected sound of a small alarm alerted the captain to an incoming message on the teletype. He walked over to the communications center and tore the paper off the printer. He laughed out loud as he read the message.

The Coast Guard was finally sending one of their HH-60 Jayhawk recovery helicopters to aid in the rescue effort. It appeared that the wind had diminished enough for them to take the chance. He crumpled up the paper in his fist and threw it out the window. The ball of white disappeared immediately as the wind clutched hold of it.

The note said they would be there in fifteen minutes. He knew from the sound of the ocean as it threw itself against the rocks that they would be too late.

Littleton

Gideon strained his ears, listening for any sound that DeKay had arrived as Emily had predicted. His heart raced in his chest. Emily's small hand tightened in his.

"John Gideon," DeKay's voice boomed through the silence, "I know you can hear me."

"What do you want?" Gideon responded from behind the tree line.

"A truce," the man replied. "It's been a long time—too long, as a matter of fact. It's time for you and me to clear the air. Straighten things out. There's a lot left unsaid between us."

"I've got nothing to say to you," Gideon called back. "What's done is done. It's ancient history as far as I'm concerned."

Once again, the silence stretched on for a few minutes.

"I'm glad to hear that," DeKay said finally. "I feel the same way. We were soldiers once. What happened on the battlefield stays there."

Gideon wasn't fooled for a second. "Sorry if I don't believe you right now." His eyes tried to pierce the night, to see where DeKay was stationed, but the man was too well hidden. "Why don't you come out and show yourself? Lay down your weapons."

"Great idea," DeKay yelled loud enough for everyone to hear. "What do you say we invite our North Korean friends to the table? I think they'd be interested in what I have to say."

The answer surprised Gideon. *What is DeKay up to?* he wondered.

The next voice to call over answered his question. "John," Reyes yelled, "DeKay has me and Amy. He says he's serious about us getting together."

"Of course I'm serious," DeKay answered. Then he shouted, "Captain Choi, can you hear me?"

Gideon counted the heartbeats, surprised again when a strange voice entered the bizarre conversation.

"I hear you, Mr. DeKay."

DeKay was in complete control of the situation, and he knew it. Gideon could almost see him smile.

DeKay's confident voice echoed in the chamber. "What orders do you have from Vice President Pak in case your mission is unsuccessful?" Silence followed. "Come, now. Surely you had contingency plans in place."

"If we could not apprehend both children," Choi replied from the darkness, "our orders were to continue negotiations."

"And if negotiations failed?" DeKay asked.

Choi fell silent, pondering his next move. He ultimately decided to tell the truth. "My orders were to kill at least one of the girls."

"Come, now, Gideon," DeKay challenged with a laugh. "We can't let that happen."

Gideon decided to play along with the madman. "What do you propose?" he asked.

"Right now we have a stalemate, what we used to call a Mexican standoff. At this rate no one's going to come out of this a winner. I suggest we send our men into opposite corners. My men will head west, to the end of the commons. Choi, you send yours, including the sniper up above, over to where the town hall used to be. Your men can admire their handiwork," DeKay said with sarcasm. "Meanwhile, Gideon, you stay where you are. Choi and I will come to you unarmed. How does that sound?"

"That's fine by me," Gideon responded. "But I want you to bring Agent Reyes and Amy with you."

"It's a deal," DeKay answered quickly. "Captain Choi?"

Choi answered with a few swift commands in his native tongue. Overhead, Gideon heard someone rappelling expertly down a rope. DeKay's men warily retreated to the end of the commons, taking their wounded along with them. Once they were in place, two North Korean men emerged from the shadows between two houses. One proceeded to the town hall to join his comrade. The second, Captain Choi, walked toward the cluster of trees. His empty hands were raised above his head. Next to follow was DeKay, though his hands weren't empty. He had Agent Reyes and Amy clutched tightly in each one. And though he appeared unarmed, Gideon was certain that he was not.

"Stop where you are," Gideon said as they drew close. "Release them."

DeKay complied, and the two captives rushed over to Gideon. Amy and Emily clutched each other tightly. They were both smiling and giggling like normal children. Reyes moved to stand behind him.

"What's to keep me from killing both of you right now?" Gideon asked.

"Kill me," DeKay responded evenly, "and my men will open fire."

"As will mine," Choi said in perfect English. "They have their orders and will not stop until you and the children are dead."

"Fair enough," Gideon conceded. He lowered the barrel of his weapon a fraction of an inch. It was all the invitation DeKay and Choi needed to enter the stand of trees.

"Well, gentleman," DeKay said when they were all together. "Where should we start?"

Just then, the voice of an angry man called through the darkness. "Hold on!" the man cried. "Wait just one second!"

DeKay's eyes rolled back in his head.

"It seems we have another party coming to negotiate." Captain Choi didn't try to hide the humor from his voice.

"Quite right," DeKay acknowledged through gritted teeth.

Gideon watched the scene unfold and smiled. Maybe DeKay wasn't in the driver's seat after all.

CHAPTER 37

Charlie Simmons sat forward in the driver's seat, trying desperately to think of his next move. The SUV was already running with the keys dangling from the ignition, so he didn't need to worry about that. He closed his eyes and thought hard about what to do next. How did they do this in the movies? They made it look so easy. It had been such a long time, years in fact, since he had been in the front seat of an automobile. And he certainly had never driven one before; his condition would never have allowed it. He should have paid more attention to things like this.

Think, damn it.

The funny-looking stick to the right of the steering wheel had to be it. He tried moving it up and down, but it wouldn't budge. Fear gripped him. What if he couldn't figure it out in time? Once he had exited the drainpipe and realized that Emily wasn't behind him, he considered going back after her. Then DeKay called out, and he said that Agent Reyes and Amy were with him. He knew then that nothing good was going to come of it. Paralyzing fear almost overwhelmed him, when he suddenly remembered Gideon's instructions and where the SUV was hidden.

And then a thought entered his head. Maybe he *could* do something to help, something that no one, not even Cross DeKay, would expect.

The rest was a blur. He made it safely to the SUV. Now if he could just figure out how to get it going.

Running out of things to try, Charlie reached down as far as he could and stepped with both feet on the brake. The car was so big he felt dwarfed by it. To his complete amazement, the funny-looking stick now moved in his hand. He moved the stick past reverse and neutral and stopped at drive. The rest was easy. Even though he could barely see over the steering wheel and had to reach with his right foot to press the accelerator, Charlie eased the large SUV onto the narrow street and turned right.

"This isn't so hard," he said aloud.

Ignoring the fact that he had only two wheels on the road and the others up on the sidewalk, Charlie began to work his way toward the commons. *Dr. Sossoman would be very proud of me,* he thought.

He didn't know what he was going to do once he got to the commons, but at least he was making progress. His only wish was that he wasn't too late.

Captain Hyssälä now knew where the *Skaarsgard* was heading. The steep cliffs overlooking the mouth of the Delaware Bay loomed in the distance. Fed by unnaturally high tides and driven by the storm, large waves pounded high on the slope. He watched the black water turn frothy white as the full force of Mother Nature hit the rock wall. Soon, something much harder and more terrible was going to make contact with the cliff. Twenty-five thousand tons of reinforced steel left a hell of a dent, especially when it impacted at fourteen knots.

He didn't need to look at the bow to know what part was going to strike first. Like most modern containerships, the *Skaarsgard* was outfitted with a large bulbous protrusion extending beyond the bow just below the waterline. This bulbous distortion looked much like the nose of a dolphin and was instrumental in adding stability and lowering fuel consumption as it cut a clean swath through the open seas. Now it was going to act like a battering ram, hitting the cliff first before crumpling in on itself. Then it was only a matter of time before the ship broke apart. Only a few more minutes, a drop of time compared to his lifelong love affair with the ocean, were left before the *Skaarsgard* became nothing more than scrap metal.

The captain stood firm on the bridge, his hand lightly gripping the polished brass rail that ran along the instrument panel. He was surprised at how calm he felt and decided it was best to look on the bright side of the situation. Of all the places he could have been right now, he had the best seat in town to watch the show.

Inside Littleton, an angry Arthur Frist joined the men inside the stand of trees. He looked like he had just run a marathon to come join them. The old man was huffing and puffing, trying to regain his breath and composure. Meanwhile, his eyes bulged with rage, and his face flushed the deepest red Gideon had ever seen. Even in the shadows, he could see the blush extend well below his neckline to the shoulders.

Frist ignored Gideon and Choi and turned on DeKay. "Just what in the hell do you think you're doing?" he demanded. Each word was punctuated by short jabs of his index finger. Frist wasn't foolish enough to make contact with DeKay, but he made no bones about who was, or should be, in command.

DeKay's reply was quick and sharp. "You of all people should know the value of object lessons. I'm merely following your example and teaching my new North Korean friends all about the capitalist system."

"But they're Communists!" Frist yelled up at DeKay as if the North Korean wasn't there. He lowered his voice a notch and tried to gain a measure of control. "What do you think we've been working toward this past year? We're trying to bring regime change to these godless heathens. Shine the light of Truth and Christianity on their damned souls. Bring peace and democracy to a part of the world that desperately needs it. We're so close. Everything we've worked for. Everything we've wanted. Why screw it up now?"

It was a rousing lecture, but DeKay had stopped listening. He had his own greedy agenda, and the billionaire was not going to get in the way.

"Everything *you* wanted," DeKay replied testily. "I want more. The Communist system in Asia is going to fail, just like it did in Russia. We simply need to give it time, and it will collapse under its own weight. It doesn't need our help. As for the high-and-mighty, self-righteous, God-fearing bullshit about peace and love—save the speech for the ladies' auxiliary club. I've spent my entire career watching the politicians and pundits in Washington fight over petty policy decisions that most Americans couldn't give a shit about." He leaned down and thrust his face up against Frist's. "You've made your billions, handed to you on a silver platter by the United States government. I want mine."

DeKay turned to address Gideon, a laugh in his voice. "You know, this place was found accidentally during WW II. It wasn't even discovered by Americans. A German U-boat found it while hiding from our homeland patrols. We were just lucky enough to catch them trying to escape. And what does our government do? They prop up this . . . *fool,* make him one of the most successful and influential businessmen in the world, just so he can secretly build and operate this place. Talk about hitting the mother lode." He laughed out loud in a high-pitched whine that pierced the darkness.

"You're crazy," Frist said.

"Certifiable," DeKay shot back. "But I *will* get mine. I've got a buyer with money to burn. They want the twins, and it just so happens I have a pair ready to ship over to them."

"I'm very sorry to hear you say that," Frist said softly. "Of course, you know I cannot let that happen. You of all people should know that Project Gemini will continue long after my death. And yours, for that matter. We're inconsequential, merely stewards safeguarding a secret the rest of the world can't handle. Our job—ensuring that the United States is the sole beneficiary of the wellwishers' gifts—is not just a game that we play against other countries or regimes. It's a matter of utmost national security. Our survival as a superpower, our way of life as a democracy, depends upon this. There's nothing you can do to bring the program down. And if you try, there's nowhere on earth you can hide. You'll never get away with it."

DeKay threw his arms in the air. "How are you going to stop me? I have all the leverage. The mercenaries, the twins, the buyer—all mine. Do you think John Gideon is going to stop me? No offense, John," DeKay said confidently, "but you'll be dead in a minute. And what are you going to do, *Mr. Frist*?" He spat the man's name like an indictment. "Littleton is dead. Project Gemini is *dead*."

DeKay turned to the North Korean. "Captain Choi, what is your standing offer for the twins?"

Choi stepped forward. "Forty million dollars in gold bullion and untraceable diamonds, as agreed upon," he said with a slight bow of the head.

DeKay wagged his finger back and forth.

"Plus," Choi followed up, "another ten for any trouble this little . . . *misunderstanding* may have caused you."

"You see," DeKay said, spreading his arms wide, "capitalism at its finest. Our founding fathers would be proud."

"You seem to be forgetting something," Gideon said, "I'm the one with a gun here."

"Oh," DeKay said absentmindedly, "that's right."

Before Gideon could react, DeKay's right arm shot outward with blinding speed. Gideon's left shoulder exploded with pain. His arm went numb, and the muzzle of his gun dropped. He had just enough time to register the hilt of a small throwing knife sticking out of his shoulder before DeKay was upon him. The major was as swift and ruthless as he remembered him. In mere seconds Gideon was unarmed, on the ground with a heavy knee on his chest. The knife was no longer in his shoulder but was now at his throat.

"I've been waiting a long time for this, John," DeKay said, staring straight into his eyes.

Gideon could feel the knife tip break the skin. A small rivulet of blood flowed down the side of his neck. Gideon took a ragged breath.

"That's quite enough, Cross."

Gideon looked up to see the muzzle of his discarded submachine gun embedded in the soft flesh of DeKay's neck. The first to recover from DeKay's bold move and the closest to the action, Frist had grabbed the weapon off the ground, kept Choi at bay, and now held the madman at gunpoint.

DeKay snarled once and dropped the knife. He removed his knee from Gideon's chest and stood up. Reyes and the girls were immediately at Gideon's side.

"Are you all right?" Reyes asked, concern flooding her eyes.

Gideon nodded and stood up. His pride hurt more than his shoulder. The three-ring circus that was DeKay, Frist, and Choi, combined with the shifting darkness, provided enough distraction for DeKay's gambit to work. Still, he should have been prepared for any move, no matter how desperate. He would not make the same mistake twice.

Amy tugged on Gideon's fingers to get his attention. He bent down to the little girl.

"What is it, Amy?" he asked.

"We have to go. *Now.*" Her eyes were wide with fright.

Gideon was about to discount her agitation given recent events, but intuition warned him to pay closer attention.

"Did you wish for something?"

Amy and Emily nodded.

"What was it?" he asked. "How come you're not passed out like before?"

"We wished for it a long time ago," Amy replied.

"We've been wishing real hard for it," Emily finished. She, too, was scared.

"We wished to leave here," Amy continued. "And now it's time." She pulled hard on Gideon's hand. "We have to leave now, before it's too late."

"What's going to happen?" he asked.

"I don't know."

Both girls erupted into tears. Whatever was going to happen, Gideon had no doubt it was going to be catastrophic. He stood up and looked around. Everything appeared normal. Under the circumstances, that is.

"What's wrong with them?" Frist asked.

"Nothing," Gideon replied, stalling. "They're just upset with all the activity going on around here. It's too much for them."

Frist snorted loudly and got back to business. "Like I was saying," he said, "you're finished here, DeKay."

DeKay wasn't buying it. "Shoot me, and my men will kill you."

Frist smiled. "I don't think so," he said. "You see, Colonel Allbright is looking to get promoted. He wants your job. He's currently renegotiating the contract you have with the Gorgon Medusa. I'd say he's sweetening the pot enough that they'll accept the deal. You know how mercenaries are."

DeKay looked past the old man and saw Allbright walking among his men.

"Bastard," he said. "I should never have trusted him."

"The fact is," Frist said, "you don't trust anyone. And that's the problem. You're schizophrenic. Dr. Sossoman predicted long ago that something like this would eventually happen, and she was right."

"The doctor's dead," DeKay shot back.

Frist ignored the remark. Sossoman's death was inconsequential to his plans. He would find another child psychologist, someone he could manage better. Project Gemini wouldn't miss a beat.

"It's over," Frist repeated.

DeKay scowled and reached into his breast pocket. He pulled out a small black box no bigger than a cigarette lighter. He pressed a switch on the side, activating the device. His thumb hovered over a large white button in the center.

"This device controls the explosives rigged to the retaining wall," DeKay threatened. "If I press this button, Littleton will disappear forever. It will be buried under fifty feet of seawater."

Gideon thought back to his first visit to Littleton. He remembered the shoebox-sized containers bolted to the wall and that Charlie Simmons was very uncomfortable standing close to them. So this was DeKay's final gambit. If he couldn't have the girls and his payday, everyone down here would die. The man was just demented enough to do it, too.

Frist looked at DeKay like a grandfather might look upon an insolent child—with kindness and patience. "Go ahead," he said calmly. "Once I realized you were heading down the slippery slope toward insanity, I had the detonators cut by someone I trust. The explosives are inactive. As I said before, you cannot win. Kill me, slay the twins, destroy Littleton—the simple fact remains, contingency plans for the future of this program will ensure its survival, even prosperity."

In a fit of fury, DeKay pressed the white button. He pressed it again, over and over. Nothing happened.

"Allbright," DeKay said simply.

Frist answered with a smile.

DeKay threw the arming device onto the ground. Suddenly, the entire cavern lurched with a giant shake and a tremendous rumble that broke every windowpane in Littleton. Fighting for balance, Gideon feared the explosives had gone off, despite Frist's comments to the contrary. Then, a second groundbreaking rumble followed the first one. Whatever was causing the ground to shake, it was not happening from within.

The sound of trickling water reached the small party.

All eyes turned toward the giant wall separating Littleton from the Atlantic.

"Oh, my God!" Frist exclaimed. His eyes shot toward the twins. "What did you do?"

The girls stared innocently back. The trickling water now sounded like a small stream.

"We wished to leave here," Amy replied.

"And we always get what we wish for," Emily finished.

CHAPTER 38

Ignoring the stunned onlookers, Gideon picked up the children and ran. Reyes was right behind him.

At that moment, he saw the black SUV round the corner at the top of the commons and come barreling toward them. At first, Gideon thought the car was somehow driving itself, but then he saw the top of a small head bobbing up and down behind the steering wheel.

Gideon gritted his teeth and surged toward the oncoming car. Behind him, another thunderous crash shook the retaining wall. The ground beneath him buckled, and he was almost thrown to his knees. The sound of rushing water increased tenfold until it rivaled that of a raging river. The retaining wall wasn't going to hold out much longer. It could collapse at any second.

The black SUV looked like a ghost as it sped toward them. At the last moment, the brakes engaged and the car spun around until it was facing the way it had come.

Even with the impending disaster, small arms fire began to pepper the vehicle as both the North Koreans and the mercenaries tried to halt their escape. Gideon threw open the rear doors and tossed the girls into the car. Reyes jumped in next to them and shut the door just ahead of a barrage of bullets.

Gideon dove to the ground as the spray of gunfire passed within inches of his head. To his left, he could see Arthur Frist lying on the open ground, a gaping wound across his neck. He scanned the immediate area, but DeKay was nowhere in sight.

Return fire from the mercenaries on the other side of the commons momentarily shifted the North Koreans' attention away from the SUV. Gideon took the opening and lurched for the driver's-side door. He reached it safely and threw himself into the Suburban. He came face-to-face with a smiling Charlie Simmons, who had jumped over to the passenger seat.

"How'd I do?" he said with a shout.

"Pretty good, Charlie, but if we don't get going, we'll have to swim out."

"But I can't swim," Charlie said innocently.

"Then buckle up," Gideon shouted. "It's gonna get bumpy."

Charlie settled into the passenger seat as Gideon put the SUV in gear. Just then, the passenger door opened. Before Gideon could react, DeKay was standing on the car's running board. He had Charlie by the scruff of the neck, and his bloody knife was at his throat.

"Going somewhere?" DeKay snarled. "Hello, Charlie. I missed you."

Charlie looked around wildly, pleading for help, until his eyes rested on the twins in the backseat. A visible calm overcame the small janitor. His eyes filled with tears. Gideon sat helpless in the driver's seat, watching as Charlie came to a conclusion inside his own head.

His eyes strayed to Gideon and then back to the twins. "Thank you," he said softly, a small smile on his lips.

Charlie lunged back into DeKay, driving his small legs with such force that the larger man was taken completely by surprise. This was how he chose to repay the wellwishers for their friendship, kindness, and the gift of normalcy, however fleeting, that they provided him. Propelled by his driving force, the two men fell out of the car and onto the pavement that ringed the commons. They were immediately swallowed by a three-foot wave of black seawater.

The girls screamed in shock and sorrow at Charlie's sacrifice. Reyes held them tight as they cried.

Meanwhile, the ocean poured unabated into the dark cavern. Before Gideon could press the accelerator, the wave of water threw the SUV across the park toward Frist's mercenaries. Most of the men were running away in panic, but a few stood their ground and took shots at the car. The windshield soon looked like the surface of the moon, pockmarked with numerous impacts.

The Russian mobster's bulletproof windows held.

Gideon gunned the engine, hoping that the large tires would take hold of anything solid and move them ahead of the raging water. His wish was granted. Ever so slowly, he was able to coax the Suburban to higher speeds until he found himself racing against the ocean itself. Turning on two wheels, the SUV rocketed away from the commons and down a side street. Water was everywhere now and getting deeper.

In the distance, he heard the unmistakable sound of the retaining wall giving way completely. Even inside the car, the reverberation of tumbling concrete and twisting metal was drowned out by the unbridled power and destruction being unleashed upon Littleton. To Gideon, it sounded like they were at the base of Niagara Falls.

The girls were screaming in the backseat, yelling directions at him. He looked to the right only once—a mistake. A wall of water thirty feet high was raging toward them. Whole houses were being swept away. Trees were ripped out of the ground. The metal infrastructure that made up Littleton's dome caved in on itself.

All these things combined in a churning wall of devastation that bore down on them like a speeding locomotive.

Gideon floored the accelerator, heartened as the large diesel engine responded under his foot. Up ahead was the three-mile tunnel that led out to the sleepy town of Curtis Cove.

If they could just make that tunnel.

Fist-sized pieces of stone and metal began to pelt the SUV from overhead as the cavern continued to give way. Sitting under the weakest point of the steel-reinforced vehicle, Gideon ducked his head, flinching as each impact threatened to punch through the metal roof. Then, as if Littleton was taking its very last breath, the last of the emergency lights flickered out for good. Running blind, Gideon hurried to flip the headlights on high, instantly regretting the decision.

The headlights cast a brighter and broader beam than did the dim emergency lights, and what Gideon now saw horrified him. Ahead of them was the little chapel—the same one he had first entered through days before—tumbling inexorably toward them. Ripped from its foundation, the house of worship was floating on the apex of the tidal surge, being pushed with tremendous energy toward the tunnel opening. If it got there before them, the exit would be blocked. They would die inside this cold, flooded tomb.

Gideon urged the SUV forward and adjusted course to avoid colliding with the chapel. It was going to be close. His hands gripped the steering wheel tighter as the tunnel opening, the church, and the SUV converged.

The SUV entered the tunnel traveling sixty miles an hour, mere feet ahead of the chapel. Behind them, the building plugged the hole shut, and the SUV rode again on dry land.

The silence and calm that followed was eerie, and more dangerously, fleeting. The unrelenting weight of water quickly tore through the building with an unholy screech of twisting and tortured debris. In seconds the torrent of water and wreckage was again hot on their heels.

Gideon watched as the speedometer rose to sixty-five, then seventy miles per hour. Still, the water gained on them. His heart sank with the realization—they weren't going to be able to outrun it. The ocean would overtake the SUV long before they reached the parking garage.

"Hold on!" he yelled.

His dire prediction quickly came true as the back of the car began to shake and buck. The water, like a bullet being shot out of a rifle bore, was accelerating rapidly as the cold Atlantic filled the cavern and pressed outward. Tremendous pressure was being exerted on this one vent, squeezing the water like toothpaste through a tube.

Gideon lost control of the vehicle almost one mile into the tunnel. He now held on to the steering wheel out of fright and to keep himself from being thrown about. The car pushed forward with increasing velocity. After another mile, the force of water lifted the Suburban off its wheels and banged it against the sides of the tunnel like a child's toy.

And still it accelerated.

The walls of the tunnel flew past at dizzying speeds. Gideon gripped the useless steering wheel and held on for dear life. Water enveloped the SUV, spraying into the cabin from numerous holes and fissures. Debris continued to bang and crash against the windows, allowing more water into the car. Gideon was thrown violently from side to side, held in place only by the seatbelt that cut painfully into his thighs, stomach, and chest. Reyes and the twins, who huddled together on the floor between the seats, were also being thrown about mercilessly.

Unable to take his eyes off the water, Gideon was at first confused, and then heartened, to see a small point of white light penetrate the green wall of seawater. The light slowly grew brighter. He knew then that they were either ascending to the pearly gates of Heaven, or the tunnel entrance was fast approaching. The pain in his arm and chest confirmed that he was still alive. That left only one option—St. Peter would have to wait another day.

Gideon had no idea how fast the car was moving, but as it approached the garage entrance it had to be in excess of one hundred miles per hour. He finally closed his eyes and prayed.

Gideon heard himself scream as the black Suburban—scraped, dented and pitted almost beyond recognition—shot out of the tunnel entrance like a cannonball. The wheels were three feet from the pavement and didn't hit concrete for another forty feet. When it did land, it touched down with such a jarring impact that he at first thought all four tires had blown and the suspension had crumpled. It wasn't until the car began fishtailing wildly out of control that he realized they hadn't.

Fighting the SUV's dangerous momentum, he turned the wheels hard to the right, spinning the car completely around, at least four revolutions, before it smashed to a stop against the garage's front wall. All six airbags—front, rear, and sides—deployed at once. For the briefest moment, he thought he had been in a boxing match. Every bone in his body, every muscle and joint, screamed in protest as the air was driven from his lungs.

Outside, water raged against the side of the Suburban, covering it completely as it surged over, around, and beyond the parking garage and into the street. For what seemed an eternity, the SUV rocked back and forth, pinned against the concrete wall by the water. Then, slowly, the ocean began to recede until the water's edge lapped just outside of the tunnel opening.

Gideon's breath came back to him in raging gulps of air. "Is . . . everyone . . . okay?" he asked when he could finally speak.

Reyes and the twins looked up from the floor, their heads nodding. They weren't ready to speak just yet but appeared to be none the worse for their part of the ordeal.

Gideon turned back around and pushed the airbags out of the way. His hands were shaking almost beyond control. He tried to start the engine. It had stalled. On the third try, the motor purred to life and he said a silent prayer of thanks.

Nobody in Curtis Cove noticed the dilapidated sports utility vehicle as it exited the parking garage, passed the outskirts of town, and merged onto I-95. In minutes, it had disappeared into the heart of America, its occupants never to be seen again.

Curtis Cove, Delaware

Most residents out and about were witnessing the wreck of the *Skaarsgard* containership. The ship had run aground against the cliffs overlooking the Delaware Bay. The impact was so tremendous that the eight-story superstructure collapsed onto the deck and fell into the sea. Rescue and salvage ships were already on the way, but the damage was done. By the time they arrived, nothing but scraps would ever be found.

Oddly enough, news outlets across the country wondered why a United States battleship and two rescue cutters were soon parked at the harbor mouth, keeping boating traffic away from the accident. Speculation would run wild for weeks as the nation wondered what the *Skaarsgard* was carrying to warrant such attention. Only a few individuals in high places would ever know the truth.

Korean Workers' Party Headquarters

Vice President Pak Te Hwan sat behind his large mahogany desk, contemplating his future. His mission to capture the twins was an abject failure. He hadn't heard from his men at any of the appointed meeting times and had to assume they were dead. America's ruse to cover up the destruction of Littleton might have fooled the naïve public, but not him. He knew the secret behind the subterfuge.

Now he was forced to alter his plans. His timetable to take control of North Korea would have to be delayed.

The sudden knock on his door brought Pak back to the moment. His secretary entered with a shy bow.

"What is it, Ko Mi Byun?" he said testily.

"My apologies, comrade Vice President," she replied. "But you have . . . visitors."

"Send them away," he snarled. "I wish to be alone."

Pak jumped as the doors banged open.

"Surely you have time to see me?" President Yi Sang Gojong asked from the doorway.

The president entered the room in a wide arch. He was not alone. Flanking him were two large bodyguards. Following was a man dressed entirely in black.

Pak drew his breath in with a loud sucking sound. *Storm troopers,* he thought, shuddering.

"Do you know why I'm here?" President Yi asked.

"N-n-no," Pak stammered.

"It seems one of my most trusted parliamentary members has been plotting against me," the president informed him. "I just received word of his betrayal this morning, and from all places, the United States of America. It would appear that someone over there wants to cast doubt on your loyalty. Unfortunately, whoever sent the information did so anonymously, but the evidence is very compelling." The president stepped closer. In his hands was a silver compact disc. "Do you have any idea who would slander you in such a way?"

"No, Mr. President."

"I see," President Yi said, doubtful.

Pak lowered his head and closed his eyes. He could not make eye contact with the supreme leader. Instead, he saw his world crashing in around him. Rough hands bound his arms behind his back. He envisioned the small, sterile room with no window, bed, or toilet. The small round hole in the floor would not help him escape. The bright light overhead would never go out.

"We shall see where the truth lies." The president said before he turned on his heels and marched out the door.

Pak was led from his office by the same man who would later become his executioner, but not before weeks, months, maybe even years, of torture.

EPILOGUE

One Year Later
Lisbon, Portugal

The phone rang at the appointed hour. Gideon answered it on the first ring. "Hello," he said into the receiver.

The voice on the other end sounded crisp and clear, though the person speaking was over three thousand miles away.

"How are you, John?" Natalie Reyes asked.

He covered the receiver and sighed heavily. He had been waiting anxiously for this call, counting the minutes, hours, and days as they slowly ticked by.

"We're adjusting," he replied. "Amy is a natural with languages. She's already picked up most of the local Portuguese dialects and can blend in as good as any local. With her blonde hair and blue eyes, she passes for a girl from the north fairly easily."

"Is she making friends yet?"

"A few here and there. It's tough. She misses her sister a great deal. How about you and Emily?"

"Yeah, we're coping," she answered. "I had no idea how lonely life would be without my friends . . . or you."

"I know it's rough," Gideon said. "But you know being apart from one another is the only way the girls can survive. That's what Dr. Sossoman predicted in her notes, and she was right. Until they get a handle on their emotions and their gift, they can't be together. It's for the best." Gideon listened to the silence on the other end. "You're not having second thoughts, are you?"

"No, I'm just complaining. I miss you and Amy. Talking only once a month is really hard. I can't wait for the day when we can be together again, maybe be a family. Until then, I guess I'll keep living under the identity you provided. I got a new job as an administrative assistant for a law firm downtown. It's just not the same . . . that's all."

"Boston's not a bad place to live," Gideon said, trying to cheer her up.

"It's a great place. I just worry about being this close to Washington D.C. and where Littleton used to be."

"You don't have to worry. As long as you keep a low profile and avoid the things you used to do, you'll be fine. Project Gemini, which I'm sure still exists, will be looking for a new set of twins. As far as they're concerned, Amy and Emily are dead, and us along with them." Gideon decided to change the subject. "Guess what we picked up today?"

"What?"

"A new puppy," he said cheerfully.

Reyes gasped audibly on the other end.

"What is it?" he asked.

"We got a new puppy yesterday, too. Emily named him Charlie."

Gideon had a sinking feeling in the pit of his stomach. Amy named her dog Charlie as well. Maybe they didn't move far enough away from each other. What if their plan didn't work? He walked over to Amy's room and peeked through the doorway, pushing the creaky door open just a little. The eight-year-old was sitting on her bed, looking out the window at the boats in the harbor. The dog lay obediently by her side as she stroked its head.

She turned at the noise and flashed Gideon with a bright, cheery smile.

"We got a Boston terrier," Reyes informed him. "How appropriate is that?"

He let out a sigh of relief. He smiled back at Amy, shut the door, and walked back into the kitchen. "We have a new German shepherd," he said. *It's just a coincidence, that's all.*

Reyes and Gideon went on to more pleasant topics. Meanwhile, back in her room, Amy closed her eyes and let her mind wander.

Emily: "Is he gone?"

Amy: "Yes."

Emily: "Maybe we shouldn't have gotten the puppies at the same time. It made them suspicious."

Amy: "No, it's all right. We got different ones, so they won't think anything is up."

Emily: "I don't like lying like this. I don't want to hurt either John or Natalie."

Amy: "It's not lying. This is our little secret. We're sisters. There's nothing we can't do if we stick together. And nothing is going to happen to either of them."

Emily: "I miss you. It's been a whole year, Amy. When will we be together again?"

Amy: "As soon as we can. I like the idea of us being a family. I think John would make a great dad. And you like Natalie, don't you?"

Emily: "Yeah. I want someone I can call Mom."

Amy: "Be patient. Soon we'll start wishing again. Only this time, we'll wish for the right things."

Emily: "Okay. I love you."

Amy: "I love you, too."

Amy opened her eyes and broke the ethereal connection with her twin sister. As long as they could communicate with each other whenever and wherever they wanted, they would never truly be apart. And unlike her sister, she believed no one needed to know about this ability.

A big smile spread across her lips. She got up from the bed and walked to the door. Gideon was in the process of making their dinner—spaghetti and meatballs, her favorite.

"Hi, sweetie," he said from the stove. "Are you enjoying your new puppy?"

"Yes, I am," she replied. Amy approached him slowly. "I have a question."

"Sure," he answered, turning toward her. "What is it?"

"Would it be okay if I started calling you Dad?" she asked shyly. "John is too formal, and it just doesn't seem right."

Gideon's smile matched hers in size and brightness. He reached out and hugged her tightly to his chest.

"Of course you can," he replied, beaming with pride.

Amy hugged her new dad as tight as she could. She was happy, truly happy, for the first time in her life. Nothing, she vowed, would ever happen to her new father.

And she began to wish for just that.